Praise for the Novels of Jennie Shortridge

Love and Biology at the Center of the Universe

"Smart, funny, and endearing, *Love and Biology at the Center of the Universe* is also deceptively wise. When Mira's world explodes in every possible direction, she embarks on a desperate search for what is real and what is simply a mirage, ultimately discovering that the Center of the Universe is not a place but a state of mind. Deeply drawn characters with their seams and raw edges exposed, clever dialogue, and a snappy pace make this one terrific read!"
　　　　　　　　—Garth Stein, author of *The Art of Racing in the Rain*

"This is one terrific book. A moving look at the wrongheaded ways we're taught to love, and the redemptive power of wising up and getting it right."
　　　　　　　　—Carolyn Jourdan, author of *Heart in the Right Place*

"Like a Northwest Fannie Flagg, Jennie Shortridge gives us a wry and funny portrait of Mrs. Perfect, Mira Serafino. We all know where perfection can lead, and in *Love and Biology at the Center of the Universe*, life becomes anything but *Family* freaking *Circle*. Steam a tall batch of half-caf mocha lattes for the club, throw on your slutty elf shoes, and discuss this delicious, sexy adventure of a mother at midlife."
　　　　　　　　—Diana Loevy, author of *The Book Club Companion*

"This is an honest and endearing look into the imperfect life of wife and mother Mira Serafino, a middle-aged woman of unpredictable hormones and a heart as warm and rich as the espresso shots she delivers to her coffeehouse customers. Bruised but not beaten, the indomitable Mira escapes her not-so-perfect life in search of a new beginning and instead rediscovers the woman she was always meant to be. The true-to-life characters, rain-saturated Seattle setting, and flawless storytelling make this a book to remember."
　　　　　　　　—Karen White, author of *The Memory of Water*

continued....

Written by today's freshest new talents and selected by New American Library, NAL Accent novels touch on subjects close to a woman's heart, from friendship to family to finding our place in the world. The Conversation Guides included in each book are intended to enrich the individual read-ing experience, as well as encourage us to explore these topics together because books, and life, are meant for sharing.

Eating Heaven

"*Eating Heaven* is exactly the kind of book I most love to read—rich, funny, sad, sensual, and hopeful. I devoured every single word and wanted to lick the bowl at the end. Jennie Shortridge is a wise woman, and her books are a tonic to the heart."

—Barbara Samuel, author of *Madame Mirabou's School of Love*

"Powerful and provocative, Jennie Shortridge's *Eating Heaven* is a novel you don't soon forget—and it'll give you a craving for pineapple upside-down cake, too." —Valerie Frankel, author of *I Take This Man*

"In *Eating Heaven,* Jennie Shortridge has created a delightful, charming heroine plagued with an appetite smaller than only her good and gracious heart. I loved the book!" —Ayelet Waldman, author of *Bye-Bye, Black Sheep*

"Smooth writing, a cast of nicely developed characters, and a winning portrait of Portland, Oregon, add up to one good read."

—Nancy Pearl, author of *Book Lust*

"*Eating Heaven* is about the meaning of family, about the great richness of small moments, about the tender struggle and complicated joy of the truest relationships of our lives. Jennie Shortridge's lovingly drawn characters will inhabit your soul and win your heart."

—Lisa Tucker, author of *Once Upon a Day*

"*Eating Heaven* stole my heart. It's rich and sweet, with a dash of humor, a dollop of heartbreak, and a healthy serving of love."

—Caren Lissner, author of *Starting at Square Two*

"Shortridge serves up a tasty meal with a perfect balance of sweet, sour, salty, and savory. A delightful offering, *Eating Heaven* will leave you feeling deliciously full." — Jackie Moyer Fischer, author of *An Egg on Three Sticks*

"An immensely wise and readable book that will provoke amusement, tears, and thoughtful reflection." —*Rocky Mountain News*

"[A] meat-and-potatoes story . . . that will stick to your ribs . . ."
—*The Olympian*

"Find nourishment through *Eating Heaven*. . . . An accomplished and superior novelist [with an] ability to make language flow with musical precision . . . a unique voice and a penetrating wit." —*Statesman Journal* (Salem, OR)

"A tasty novel." —*The Oregonian*

"A remarkably affecting book." —*The Denver Post*

"Funny, sweet, and, most importantly, original." —*Seattle Magazine*

"A food-obsessed read in the tradition of *Like Water for Chocolate*." —*Willamette Week* (Portland, OR)

Riding with the Queen

"Shortridge does a fine job of molding her heroine into a sympathetic, even admirable character. . . . Hits all the right notes." —*The Miami Herald*

"An absorbing novel of a family with hard edges but an unbreakable bond. . . . Shortridge's finely crafted sentences often use a single telling detail to suggest the larger picture. It's a notable debut." —*Rocky Mountain News*

"Imagine a blend of Margaret Atwood and Dolly Parton—Shortridge sneaks up on you. . . . Funny, sexy, smart. . . . Shortridge has done something few writers accomplish. Her first novel is a delight, a tightly woven tale of a nearly-on-her-last-legs country singer who finds that while you can go home again, there may be reasons not to like it. That is, until life makes you look at yourself and your relationships more honestly." —*Statesman Journal* (Salem, OR)

"A promising debut." —*Seattle Post-Intelligencer*

OTHER NAL ACCENT NOVELS BY JENNIE SHORTRIDGE

Eating Heaven
Riding with the Queen

LOVE AND BIOLOGY

at

the Center of the Universe

JENNIE SHORTRIDGE

NAL
ACCENT

NAL Accent
Published by New American Library, a division of
Penguin Group (USA) Inc., 375 Hudson Street,
New York, New York 10014, USA
Penguin Group (Canada), 90 Eglinton Avenue East, Suite 700, Toronto,
Ontario M4P 2Y3, Canada (a division of Pearson Penguin Canada Inc.)
Penguin Books Ltd., 80 Strand, London WC2R 0RL, England
Penguin Ireland, 25 St. Stephen's Green, Dublin 2,
Ireland (a division of Penguin Books Ltd.)
Penguin Group (Australia), 250 Camberwell Road, Camberwell, Victoria 3124,
Australia (a division of Pearson Australia Group Pty. Ltd.)
Penguin Books India Pvt. Ltd., 11 Community Centre, Panchsheel Park,
New Delhi - 110 017, India
Penguin Group (NZ), 67 Apollo Drive, Rosedale, North Shore 0632,
New Zealand (a division of Pearson New Zealand Ltd.)
Penguin Books (South Africa) (Pty.) Ltd., 24 Sturdee Avenue,
Rosebank, Johannesburg 2196, South Africa

Penguin Books Ltd., Registered Offices:
80 Strand, London WC2R 0RL, England

First published by New American Library,
a division of Penguin Group (USA) Inc.

First Printing, May 2008
1   3   5   7   9   10   8   6   4   2

 REGISTERED TRADEMARK—MARCA REGISTRADA

LIBRARY OF CONGRESS CATALOGING-IN-PUBLICATION DATA
Shortridge, Jennie.
Love and biology at the center of the universe / Jennie Shortridge.
p. cm.
ISBN: 978-0-451-22388-3
1. Married women—Fiction. 2. Middle aged women—Fiction. 3. Italian American women—Fiction.
4. Adultery—Fiction. 5. Coffee shops—Fiction. 6. Italian American families—Fiction. 7. Domestic fiction.
I. Title.
PS3619.H676L68 2008
813'.6—dc22   2007049722

Set in Bembo
Designed by Ginger Legato

Printed in the United States of America

For Matt, true companion on this strange and lovely ride

ACKNOWLEDGMENTS

Love and thanks are in order to so many: To Jody Rein and Claire Zion for loving the story and helping me make it better. To early readers Sherry Brown for always sticking with me, Carol Hickman and Pam Vallone for their honesty, Ellen Johnson for enthusiasm, Heidi Yorkshire for making me go all the way, Garth Stein and Stan Matthews for much-needed male points of view, and Nancy Boutin, Anne Mendel, Jeri Pushkin, Alison Galinsky, Lynne Kinghorn, and Cindy Grainger for reading on a moment's notice and answering questions. To the lovely Alice Acheson for her fervent support. To my large extended family, from my dad to my sisters and brothers-in-law and nieces and nephews and cousins and aunts and uncles, all of whom inspire me to write about family and the wonders of it. To the people of the Oregon coast and Fremont, for not getting too upset with the liberties I've taken with their wonderful communities. To my treasured readers, who keep asking for more. And most especially, of course, to Matt Gani, who makes all things possible with his love.

*"To be truly happy and contented,
one must let go of what it means to be happy or content."*

—CHINESE PROVERB

LOVE AND BIOLOGY

at

the Center of the Universe

Prologue

Her father looked like the man on television, the handsome Italian they watched sing on Saturday nights, drink in one hand, cigarette in the other. He stood shaving at the sink in his undershirt, thick black hair combed back in waves, suspenders dangling from uniform pants.

Four-year-old Mira sat on the edge of the tub watching him scrape lather from his cheeks, marveling at his movie-star good looks, then at the fog forming on the mirror. Did he create it with the largeness of his breath, the way she could make circles on the window when she peered out into the rain? Yes, she guessed. Alfonso Serafino Sr. could probably do anything.

Mira had already learned to depend more on her father than her mother, who was quiet and always tired, even more so now that she'd had the baby. Alfonso Junior cried too much, her mother slept too much, and it was only Al Senior who brought any joy into the house. Now, for instance, he was singing along with the radio, blaming it on the bossa nova, the dance of love, and waggling his behind. When Mira laughed, he stopped shaving and smiled in the mirror.

"You're Daddy's good girl, aren't you, Mirabella?" The name he usually called her mother.

Warmth flushed through her, and she nodded and stood, began to dance as Al Senior continued to sing.

That afternoon in the quiet house, Mira grew lonely. She dragged the stool she used to brush her teeth to the bathroom sink, soaped her face, and picked up her father's razor. It was heavier than she'd expected, the metal cool and smooth in her hand. She waggled her behind and scraped the razor down her left cheek, surprised when a thin red line appeared there and began to drip with blood. She ran to her parents' room and stood crying at the foot of the bed where Mrs. Mira Serafino lay sleeping with baby Fonso.

Her mother startled awake, eyes widening as she disentangled from the baby. She scrambled across the bed and took Mira into her arms. "Oh, *cara*, I just needed you to be good for a little while. What have you done?"

"I didn't do it," Mira wailed as her mother carried her to the bathroom. The razor lay in the bottom of the sink next to two tiny droplets of blood.

"Well, then, who did it, young lady?" her mother said, angry now, but even this effort seemed to exhaust her. She gripped the sink edge to steady herself. From the other room, the baby began to whimper, and the woman's face, already pale, drained of any remaining color.

"The other Mira," the girl cried, "Mirabella," picturing another four-year-old in a blue dress instead of brown, shiny black hair crackling with excitement. That Mira had taken her leave, a sly look upon her face.

She reached for her mother's embrace. "I'm good Mira," she insisted, knowing from that moment on she would do anything to make it so.

PART ONE

PART ONE

One

———•———

ON THE FRIDAY MORNING BEFORE CHRISTMAS BREAK, TWISTING south on Highway 101 and engrossed in the soaring voice of k.d. lang singing perhaps the saddest love song Leonard Cohen ever wrote, Mira Serafino found herself thinking about the ropy hip muscles of a young man she'd slept with in college, shuddering in a way she hadn't in years.

Jesus, she thought, *where did that come from?*

A burst of sunlight slashed through the forest and into her eyes. She lowered the visor, but the sun was lower. Fumbling for sunglasses in the Subaru's console, she took her eyes from the road for what seemed a second. Beneath her, the tires vibrated over the asphalt's raised lane markings as k.d. sang *hallelujah, hallelujah,* and Mira sensed rather than saw the thicket of blackberry brambles flattening as the passenger side slammed to a halt against a towering Western red cedar.

Her first thought was *Thea!* although it had been years since her daughter rode with her to school in the mornings. Her left hand gripped the wheel and her right arm barricaded the empty passenger seat. An acidic taste filled her mouth, tin and bile. *Adrenaline,* she thought, noting her rapid heartbeat, the tingling in her hands and feet. Her body had involuntarily reacted by inducing the fight or flight response, something that always amazed her, even after so many years explaining it to students.

The car was still running—how could that be?—and k.d. moved on to a waltz, equally as sad. "Oh god," Mira said, "oh god, oh god," bringing her cold hands to her face as if to check that her head was still there. Out of habit, she traced the thin scar down her cheek with her forefinger, feeling where the tiny ridge bumped out from a bad stitch, then receded and disappeared.

Slowly, she twisted her head from side to side, wondering if there was such a thing as side whiplash. "Holy Jesus," she said, though not in prayer. How had she let this happen? But she knew the answer. In the past year or so her mind had become foggier than the Oregon coast in December and no matter how many ginkgo and fish oil and black cohosh pills she swallowed, no matter how many crossword puzzles she completed, no matter how sternly she berated herself, she could no longer summon sharpness or clarity or speed when she needed to. Where once she'd had control, chaos now reigned. She was moody and unpredictable. How her husband, her co-workers tolerated her she had no idea. Her hormones were deserting her. It was either that or a brain tumor, and she could never decide which would be worse—losing your mind or losing your sex.

The sun disappeared as quickly as it had emerged, which meant it would soon resume raining. Mira switched off the car and the world fell silent. She pushed the door open and stepped to the forest floor to inspect the damage. Squeezing through damp brush to get to the other side, moisture seeped into her chinos and the Christmas tree socks inside her chunky red clogs.

There'd been no sound. How was that possible? The smashed side mirror dangled from its moorings, useless now. From front fender to rear passenger door, long metallic grooves striped the hunter green paint right up to and no doubt behind the girth of the tree. Exhaust fumes hovered in the mist over flattened flora and the mossy rock outcroppings she'd miraculously avoided. Mira's legs quivered and she decided to get back inside the car.

Fumbling the buttons on the phone keypad, she had to hit speed dial three times before getting the sequence right. Her husband didn't answer his cell phone or the landline at his coffee shop, Cyber Buzz.

She considered calling her father, then pictured him telling the story to all the other Elks, Moose, and Sons of Italy in Tillamook County, and so, their spouses, children, friends, and co-workers, until everyone knew, including her grandmother, aunts and uncles and countless cousins who spread and multiplied up and down the Oregon coast and inland, propagating the Serafino seed like dandelions. She winced at the grandeur with which Big Al would tell it; his recent retirement from the sheriff's department had left him with fewer stories to embellish, fewer chances to beat his chest and play silverback in their small community. There was no way she was going to be the butt of that joke every time she went to work, to the market, to the gynecologist, for Christ's sake. Life in Pacifica was lovely until you slipped up and gave people a reason to look at you differently, to wonder and gossip and speculate, especially dangerous for a schoolteacher in charge of shaping so many young minds.

Mira tried to think of someone else she could call: Which uncle wouldn't be too busy? What cousin? She shook her head. She was forty-five years old. She'd taken shop in eighth grade instead of home ec. She had a Triple-A card. Surely she could handle this herself.

After buckling back in, she tried the key and the engine purred to life. Mira crossed herself (a habit she thought she'd put behind her) and eased the car into reverse. The brambles tugged momentarily at the car's underworkings, then released with a snap, and this time she heard the ugly grating of metal against wood. She checked for traffic, then backed over the white painted bumps that delineated the road from, well, obviously from what had happened—from the unexpected danger and damage that lurk just outside the safety zone. Mira had crossed it and was still shaking from the experience. It wasn't that the car would be expensive to fix, or that Parker would be angry (he wouldn't), or even that she might have hit the tree head-on and been seriously hurt.

It was that she'd taken her eyes from the road in the first place.

At Pacifica K–12, Mira parked in her teacher-of-the-year spot to the side of the handicap spaces and shouldered a book bag heavy with graded papers. Her pants and socks clung to her legs, never her best feature and now showcased in the equivalent of wet T-shirt bravado.

As she walked toward the building, she turned and grimaced at the damaged car. Inside her purse, her phone played "You Light Up My Life," the joke ringtone Parker had programmed so she'd know when he was calling.

"Sorry I couldn't get the phone earlier," he said. "Everybody's late this morning, as usual. What's up?"

She relaxed at the sound of his voice. Her husband never worried, never expected anything bad to happen. Even lying together all those late nights when Thea was a teenager and out beyond her curfew, Parker hadn't shared her grim anxieties about carloads of kids veering off cliffs, juvenile delinquents influencing their daughter to try Ecstasy or crack, or whatever the drug of choice was in those days. At times Mira wondered if she'd manifested Thea's rebellious behavior by worrying so much, but then again there was her bloodline: Fonso. He'd been far worse than Thea at that age.

"I had an accident on the way to school this morning. Parker, I . . . I hit a tree. The car's pretty messed up."

"But you're okay?"

"Yeah, I'm fine. A little freaked out. I can't believe I just drove right off the road like that."

"You drove off the road?"

"No. I mean . . . I don't know, really. The sun blinded me, and I was about to put on my sunglasses, then all of a sudden I was smashed up against this huge freaking tree." She paused—would she have crashed if she hadn't been distracted by the mental image of a young man's privates? She sighed. "It scraped all down the right side, honey. It's going to be expensive."

"But you're okay."

"I'm fine."

"Where are you? Do you need someone to come get you?"

She felt a rush of something—gratitude, relief—until she realized that he probably meant one of the computer techs from his consulting business, or baristas from the coffee shop, should they ever show up. Young people who made coffee for a living seemed to be the most unreliable people on the planet.

"No, I'm at school already. The car's drivable. I'll just see you at home tonight."

"Not till late. Town council tonight. Then Lester and I are going for a beer. Talk about SPED." He'd been trying for months to get the mayor-elect on board with Pacifica's Strategic Plan for Economic Development—the latest in a long line of failed plans to save the former fishing town from extinction.

"Yeah, the rest of the town sees you more than I do."

"If you want me to come home, Mira, I will. I have to go to the council meeting, but—"

"No, no, I'm okay. It's no big deal."

"It's just that Lester is so hard to pin down. I've been trying for—"

"It's fine, Parker."

"Sure?"

"I'm about to go into the school, so I'll just see you whenever

I see you." She climbed the four concrete steps, stopped in front of the glass doors, considering as she gazed at her soggy reflection that maybe those five extra pounds did show. "Are you sure *you're* all right?"

"Me?" He laughed. "What do you mean?"

"I don't know. You just sound . . . different." She forced a smile at her reflection. If people asked about the car, she'd say it had been sideswiped on the beach road.

"You did just have an accident, Mira."

"God. I still can't believe I did that." Mira shifted the bag of papers to her other shoulder. "Well, I'm late. I'd better go. Love you."

"I know," he said, and she smiled. Their old game. The signal that all was okay.

"Butthead." She clicked off the phone and headed into the smell of musty books and damp child, and a frenetic day that would clear her mind of anything else.

Two

———— • ————

Mira's cousin Gina was the only kid in Pacifica who owned both a pink Sting-Ray bike with a flowered banana seat and real roller skates with boots and outdoor wheels, not just the clamp-on kind everyone else had. She acquired both items on her twelfth birthday.

"You're spoiling her," Nonna said at the party, not only in front of Mira, who knew better than to whine at her older cousin's good fortune, but in front of everyone sitting around the table consuming pink frosted cake and punch. Even at eleven, Mira knew her grandmother's intention: to let outsiders know this was not the Serafino way.

"Mama," Aunt Sofia said, eyes pleading. "She's been working so hard this year. All As on her report card, and she's started babysitting. She deserves a little something nice."

For her part, Gina looked oblivious to the discussion, flirting with danger and her third cousin Jeffrey, a studious but handsome fifteen-year-old. Mira coveted Gina's dress, bright yellow with baby-doll capped sleeves and a smocked top that showed where her breasts were beginning to bud. Jeffrey seemed to admire the dress, too, staring at the smocked top in much the same way Mira did.

From behind her, Mira felt something wet and warm on her ear and scrunched her shoulders, shrieking, "Uncle Tommy!" This was her favorite uncle's favorite trick, biting little girls' ears when they weren't expecting it.

Aunt Sofia looked sharply at her husband, then away.

Nonna slapped at the portly man, now retreating. "Thomas, leave the girl alone." Then, leaning toward her daughter, she murmured, "Can't you keep him from drinking?"

Aunt Sofia's dark eyes moistened. She left the table, claiming that more ice cream was needed, even though the melting carton on the table was half full.

Mira watched Gina carefully, but the girl never reacted, other than to laugh with her mouth full of cake, teeth pink with icing. Mira would be mortified if her grandmother castigated her father like that in front of everyone, but she never did. He was her only living son, and the baby of the family. Not that he'd ever do anything deserving of Nonna's ire. Mira's was the quiet family, the special family everyone was careful with, kind to.

Fonso could be a handful, but he was only seven. "All boy," Al Senior liked to say, but that was because he was usually on patrol or at the county offices in Tillamook, and didn't have to put up with many of his son's loud outbursts, his violent tantrums. Nonna took care of Mira and Fonso after school, and she'd smack the side of Fonso's dark head when he got too wild. Mira always comforted him away from the eyes of their grandmother, rocking him as they sat together in the back corner of his closet where he went to hide. He wasn't bad, Mira knew that. He just missed their mother as much as she did.

Mira knew something else that she wished she didn't. Nonna did think Fonso was bad, that something was wrong with him, although she never said anything directly to Mira about it. This was one of many topics only adults were supposed to be privy to. Her suspicions were gleaned from eavesdropping on conversations, from watching the grown-ups exchange glances and rueful expressions, from hearing their dramatic sighs.

Mira also knew, but was not supposed to, that Uncle Tommy and Aunt Sofia had "problems," caused partly by his drinking, but mostly by the fact that Aunt Sofia had failed to marry an Italian. "Blood doesn't mix," Nonna said whenever the topic of mixed marriage was raised. Mira often wondered if this had something to do with the fact that her sainted mother was dead. She'd been only half Italian, on her father's side. Mira realized this meant she and Fonso were also impure. So far, Nonna hadn't seemed to notice and Mira did everything in her power to make sure she never had reason to.

Mira rushed to her classroom, wet socks slippery inside her clogs. She passed the inevitable stragglers in the hallway—young couples making out between lockers, sloppy shuffling kids smelling of marijuana smoke—and sighed at how different high school had become in the twenty-seven years since she'd graduated from this very place. She'd been an honor roll student, a member of the debate team, class secretary in both her junior and senior years. Sure, some kids had smoked pot, some girls had fooled around with boys, but not in her small world. Her grandmother would not have tolerated it.

"You're a good girl, *cara*," Nonna would say, "just like your dear, departed mother," and Mira accepted this mission to be perfect in every way. That something else was possible—desirable, even—did not occur to her until she left home to attend college in Portland.

As she and her new roommate had finished unpacking and organizing their dorm room the first day, Mira felt fizzy with excitement. She was free. Those words kept rolling through her, but free from what? She didn't know exactly, but she felt lighter than she ever had.

They sat on their respective beds and looked at each other, giggling.

"What do you want to do now?" her roommate asked.

Mira shrugged. She had no idea what the options were.

Her roommate jumped up, pulled off her sweatshirt and rifled through their small closet. She pulled out first one garment, then another, and threw it at Mira. "Here, put this on. It will look great with your coloring."

Mira didn't realize she had coloring, but she picked up the silky red halter-top. "I can't wear this," she said, feeling the embarrassment warm her face.

"Sure you can," the other girl said, removing her bra and tying a large bandanna around her neck and waist.

"Isn't it too cold out?" Mira peered out the window into beautiful blue sky. Indian summer had its hold on Portland, a town far warmer than any on the cool Oregon coast.

"Just try it on," the girl said, grabbing her makeup bag. "Then meet me in the bathroom. I'm going to give you a makeover."

Once out in the sunshine and party atmosphere of the campus green, the two girls followed a group of cute boys who looked to be upper classmen, boys who kept throwing looks over their square shoulders, egging them on. Every time Mira held back, her roommate looked at her in exasperation, shaking her head. "Come on. What's wrong with you? Don't you like boys?"

"Of course I like boys," Mira said, pulling her top together in the middle. It exposed more skin than she'd ever let show, even at the pool. Of course she liked boys, but it had never been put to the test before. She was the sheriff's daughter. She was the straight A honor roll student. She was the one who held her small but needy family together after Nonna went home in the evenings. She didn't have time for boys, other than in her bedtime fantasies. But now . . . She swallowed against the nervous excitement in her stomach. Now she was free. And there was no one in Portland who knew her, her family, or her past.

"Are you following us?" one of the boys finally said, turning and stopping on the sidewalk in front of them.

"What if we are?" the roommate said, flipping her lemon juice–streaked hair away from her face. "Where are you going?"

"Kegger off campus," he said. "Wanna come?"

The other boys had stopped now, too. "What are your names?" a second boy asked.

"Karen," said the roommate, shifting her weight from one long leg to the other, watching the boys watch her. "What's yours?"

"How about you?" another boy asked Mira. He was the tallest, and his shoulders looked like the top of a capital T on his slim body.

She felt shy, wishing suddenly that her name were Karen, too, or Susan, or Lisa. Johnson would be a good last name, she thought. She wrapped her arms around her small chest, suddenly aware of Karen's more ample one. "Mira," she said, clearing her throat. "Mira Serafino."

"What kind of name is that?" he asked.

"Italian."

"Oh." He turned back to blond Karen, who was busy bewitching the other boys in a way that Mira could only admire. Why hadn't she made up a name?

That she was saddled with this name confirmed her different-ness, just as her Roman nose and olive skin and dark eyes were opposite of the features of the mostly Nordic inhabitants of the Pacific Northwest. Mira was not unattractive, she knew that, but she'd never be what Oregon boys considered beautiful. Standing on that sidewalk, the first day on her own, amid the maelstrom of hormones and pheromones competing and pinging off each other like pinballs off bumpers, Mira wanted a boy to look at her the way they were looking at Karen. A familiar gaping feeling opened up inside her, between ribs and stomach, a raw hunger that could

not be fed, only diverted with schoolwork or chores or busyness
of some kind. Looking at the tall boy, it worsened, and she wanted
more than anything for him to take her in his arms, hold her, kiss
her tenderly.

Mira let her arms drop to her sides, red fabric falling into
place, just skimming either side of her A-cup breasts. She'd have
to be something besides blond and bosomy. She was small and
dark, "cute," her kinder friends called her, with a frame built for
making babies, according to Nonna: hips the bottom end of a
compact triangle, a wide-legged stance that seemed to suggest the
possibility of many offspring in her future. In fact, only one would
pass through her womb, although two would rest there.

Mira walked over to the tall boy with the wide shoulders, the
sun warm on her exposed skin. She felt naked. It was unnerving.
It was thrilling.

"Take me to the party?" she asked, looking up through lashes
she knew were thick and dark, standing just a little too close to
him.

He looked down at her, reconsidering. "Sure," he said, shrugging, clearing his throat. "Uh, what's your name again?"

Mira: light of the world. Serafino: a Latin derivation of the
Hebrew word for angel. Her mother had willed her to be good
from the start—christening her in her own saintly honor—without
leaving open the possibility for anything more.

Like all daughters, though, good Mira found a way to become
as different from her mother as possible.

On the way home from work that evening, well past the five
o'clock quitting time she'd been shooting for, Mira stopped at
Lannie's Yarn and Guitar Shop to pick up her Christmas present
for Thea.

Inside, from the back room, Lannie yelled, "I'm closing in five
minutes."

"It's just me. Sorry I'm late." Mira pushed back her damp

hood. "The Weatherly twins don't need a tutor—they need a freaking referee."

"God, I'd hate your job." Lannie walked from the back room with a pristine black Gibson case. "At least I can kick kids out of here any time I want to." At six feet and nearly two hundred pounds, Lannie Langston was imposing and garbed in the way of old rock and rollers—dark Elizabeth Taylor hair, a few too many silver rings and bracelets, eyes perpetually lined in black. She didn't so much convey Ann Wilson, though, as Meat Loaf.

She laid the guitar case on the counter and lifted the cover. "Isn't she gorgeous? I wouldn't mind having this little beauty myself."

Lannie had been Thea's guitar teacher all through school, and had special-ordered the acoustic guitar with "T-H-E-A" inlaid in mother-of-pearl on the fret board. The gleaming rosewood body curved in like a cartoon vixen; the ivory tuning pegs shone white against the black velvet of the case.

"Thea's going to love it," Mira said. "You don't suppose I'm just encouraging her, do you?"

Lannie looked at her, head tilted. "Why not encourage her? She's got talent, ambition."

Mira felt herself flush. She'd hurt Lannie's feelings. "I'm just saying it's harder now to make it. You say so yourself all the time." She avoided her friend's eyes while digging for her checkbook to make the final payment.

Lannie waved her off. "Let's make that my little contribution. I, for one, would like to encourage her."

"No, you can't possibly, not after the discount."

"Sure I can. I just did."

"Lannie, I insist."

"I don't care. You don't always get to win, Miss Control Freak. Just let me."

Mira shook her head, but put her checkbook away. She was certain Lannie had lost money on the deal. She'd find another way to pay her back. "Anyway, cross your fingers this one doesn't get stolen. I wish they'd lock their doors at night."

"Nobody locks nothing up in Woden." Lannie snorted. "Reminds me of my commune days, all those punks and weirdos living in that decrepit old schoolhouse. Why doesn't she get a place in town?"

Mira sighed. "She's got a mind of her own, you know that."

"Yes, ma'am, I do." Lannie tossed a handful of guitar picks into the compartment beneath the neck of the guitar, then closed the case. "And what's with her new hairdo?"

The last time Mira had seen her daughter, her hair had looked relatively normal, for Thea. "You've seen her?"

Lannie nodded, shrugged. "She came in the other day with a couple of funny-looking kids to ogle guitars. She made a beeline for one just like this. Don't worry, I wore my poker face."

Why this made Mira crazy, she didn't know. Of course Thea would come see Lannie. Lannie was like a goddess to her, a musical role model. Mira was just a mom. She pursed her lips and lifted the guitar case, heavier than Lannie had made it look. "Well, at least she's been in touch with someone," she said. "She did promise to come for Christmas Eve."

"Speaking of lost souls returning to the fold, did you hear back from your brother?"

Mira wrinkled her nose, shook her head. "I'm not even sure he's still at that address." Presumably, he lived in Vancouver, BC. He wasn't good about sending out change-of-address notices, which he would have to do pretty often with his vagabond lifestyle. Mira didn't like talking about him because that led to thinking about him, wondering if he was all right. Worrying that he wasn't.

"Oh, hey, I need some yarn, too," she said, happy to change the subject. "Whatever you have that's cheap. I'm knitting scarves for Rainbow Town and I've run out of everything, even scraps."

Lannie tsked. "Talk about your errant communistic lifestyles," she said, squatting behind the display case to retrieve hanks of multicolored yarn from beside guitar strings and *Play Like a Pro* handbooks. "Why you take on every lost cause in the county is beyond me."

This from the woman who hosted a stitch-and-bitch for the local ferals the first of every month—those who preferred to live among the trees rather than in the tent community of Rainbow Town just outside Pacifica. "At least I let 'em knit their own damn sweaters," Lannie had argued many times, but still, she always supplied the yarn and knitting needles, instruction, coffee, and the occasional jam session.

"So," Mira said, "six o'clock for Christmas Eve next week, and don't bring anything."

"Like you ever let anyone bring anything." Lannie stuffed as much yarn into a bag as she could and jammed it beneath Mira's arm. "Go away now. I'm closing. Tell your gorgeous perfect husband hello for me."

Arms full, Mira backed through the door into the rain to load the car. She hated that the house would be dark and no one else home when she got there. She was tempted to go back into the store, ask Lannie if she wanted to grab a bite somewhere, but she'd done that on short notice too many times in the past few months. She should really drop by Nonna's apartment and check in on her. Then there were presents to wrap and cards to address, a party to plan. *Busy, busy,* she thought. She'd be fine.

Three

SINCE CHILDHOOD, CHRISTMAS EVE HAD BEEN MIRA'S FAVORITE
holiday. The Serafinos always gathered the night before Christmas, and in the days when Nonna still cooked, she'd made enormous vats of Italian fisherman's stew loaded with seafood fresh
from the trawlers of uncles and cousins and distant relations. No
presents required, no expectations other than to eat and drink
and laugh. Spouses, siblings, cousins, and children were bright and
cheery, happy to be tiny puzzle pieces in the big family picture.

Mira became especially enamored of the holiday when she
was eight, the year her mother died. That year it seemed truly a
blessed night, as Nonna proclaimed—not so much in the Jesus-
in-a-manger way, but in a candlelit, full-bellied, surrounded-by-
family way. It was one of the reasons Mira hadn't changed her
name when she married; she couldn't bear not to be a Serafino at
moments like this.

After they'd moved Nonna to her small apartment in town,
Mira became the hostess, and it was the only occasion to which

she invited everyone: the family, of course, but also her fellow teachers, neighbors, Parker's employees and fishing buddies, Thea's friends. Everyone came ostensibly for the fisherman's stew and rain-or-moonshine beach bonfire, but there was something about being part of this Italian clan, even if only for one night, that Mira knew was part of the draw.

Tonight, on this Christmas Eve, the house smelled of garlic and tomatoes, bay shrimp, clams, and crab. The tree took up half the living room with piles of gifts spilling from under it, mostly for Parker and Thea, but Mira had spotted a few unfamiliar packages. Strings of lights twinkled from every window; Thea's old paper chains and handmade ornaments flocked the mantle.

At five thirty, Mira walked through the house, lighting candles, throwing cats off couches and shooing three recently rescued dogs into the mudroom. One she would be keeping, she knew, but she'd yet to tell Parker. He'd agreed to her fostering them after Thea went to college, but they had a strict one-month-then-out policy. Little Patsy Cline, unfortunately, had stolen her heart. A skinny, spotted, and shaggy mess, she crooned along with Marvin Gaye and Dido on the CD player, Lyle Lovett and Yo-Yo Ma. One brown eye peered from under unruly bangs, and the pink spot on her nose looked like a dab of lipstick on a small unkempt girl. Soaking wet she weighed eleven pounds—Mira had weighed her after her first bath—and she loved Mira like no other dog ever had (no other person, really, except Thea in her preadolescent days). She never left her side unless pried from it.

"Parker, could you stir the pots?" Mira yelled, picking cat hair from the back of the sofa. There was no reply. "Honey?" she called again, walking from the living room through the dining room and into their freshly renovated kitchen, her new favorite room in the house and the grand finale to their twenty-year remodeling project. Three stockpots bubbled and hissed, splattering droplets of red across the white stove. "Parker?" She peered into the dark of the new great room beyond the breakfast counter. "Are you in there?"

"Mm hmm," she heard, then saw the silhouette of Parker's head leaned back against his recliner in front of the picture window. Beyond it lay the milky dark of sand and the teepee-size pile of logs for the fire, and farther, the ink of sea.

"What are you doing sitting in the dark?" She didn't say, *when so much needs to be done?*

He sniffed, shook his head, and she wondered if he was crying. It wasn't unusual for Parker to cry—at graduations and weddings, in darkened theaters or when someone he loved died—but not just sitting there. The saliva in her mouth turned sour. "Honey, what's wrong?"

She hurried to him and tried to hug him, but he sat limp and unmoving.

"I don't know," he said.

"Are you okay?" she asked.

He didn't answer.

She kneeled in front of him, rubbing his hands. They felt cold and stiff. Had he had a heart attack? A stroke? "Parker, are you okay?" she asked again, panic rising in her chest.

"Are you happy?" His voice was murky, his tone unreadable.

"Oh, honey, of course I am," she said, reaching up to hug him. "You make me very happy. Are you worried that I'm not?" Had she spoken too sharply to him? Been too grumpy lately? She'd been avoiding hormone replacement therapy but maybe she should look into it.

He didn't hug her back. "Why?" he asked. "I mean, how exactly do I make you happy?"

Mira swallowed, sat back. "Well, I don't know. You're my husband. I love you."

He nodded, sighed.

She resisted the urge to turn on the lights, to plump the pillows and light the candles and stir the stew. People would be arriving in less than twenty minutes, thirty-six people, to be exact, who would be expecting laughter and food and holiday cheer. She wanted to say, and did not: *Do we have to do this now?*

He'd been quiet all day. Was he sliding away from her again? He'd had three depressive episodes that she knew of: one as a teenager; one in their second year of marriage when she'd stupidly admitted an infatuation with someone else; and then again eight years ago, when his father had a stroke and, after five too-long months, died in a nursing home. But there were reasons for those; what could it possibly be now? Everything was fine.

Better than fine. Everything they'd been working toward their entire marriage had come to fruition: not just the house, but his dream business, Thea doing better, the rest of their lives together as they grew old, traveling, maybe, or . . . who knew? To her, the possibilities seemed endless. Didn't he see it, too?

"Aren't you hap—"

"Forget it, I'm okay." He stood and rubbed the back of his neck. "I'll go get cleaned up, and, uh . . . what do you need me to do? Bring up a case of Chianti?"

"Yes, please." Mira hugged him, and this time he hugged her back. "We'll talk later, okay, sweetie?" She cupped his jaw in her hand and he nodded, then walked away. She heard him climb the stairs, close the bathroom door. When the water started running, she exhaled a long breath and went to stir the stew.

In her sophomore year, Mira wandered into the No Nukes concert on the South Park Blocks on campus after studying at the library. She clutched her books to her chest, standing shoulder to shoulder with five thousand protesters in the afternoon drizzle of a November afternoon. Jackson Browne and Bonnie Raitt were on stage singing lyrics about morning light streaming in, getting up and doing it again. "The Pretender." She loved that song. She could smell wet hair, exhaust fumes, marijuana smoke, patchouli oil. The city buildings enveloped the crowd, traffic coursed by. She fell into the rhythmic sway of body against body, the excitement of being part of something larger than just herself, just this school, just this place.

A boy next to her held an umbrella and wore a serious expression. An out-of-state student—Oregonians wouldn't be caught dead with umbrellas. He was fair skinned, fair haired, and bright swaths of pink rode high in his cheeks from the cold. As the sky darkened toward evening, she began to shiver, and he adjusted his stance to hold the umbrella over both of them.

"Thanks." She smiled, then looked back at the performers, embarrassed at how much she wanted to look at him. A tarp had been rigged above the stage and the band played on, oblivious to the weather.

"Want to go get warm?" the boy yelled into her ear. He smelled musky and sweet.

"Yes," she said, imagining that like most boys he meant in his room, or hers, but he led her a few blocks away to a smoky coffeehouse in the basement of an old theater, holding the umbrella over her and carrying her books as they walked. He opened the door for her, a formality she wasn't used to, and held a chair for her to sit in.

This was what Nonna must have meant when she'd said to make sure she only went out with boys who treated her like a lady. Maybe she'd be able to tell her about this one, she thought.

Wanting to seem sophisticated, Mira ordered an espresso, not quite sure what it was, and the boy grimaced with her when she took her first taste.

"Sugar," he said, and handed her two slim white packets. "I can't handle that stuff; it's too strong for me. Cappuccinos are pretty good, though. Want some of mine?"

She'd thought his eyes were blue, but as she got up the nerve to really look at him, she realized they were an unusual gray, like the sky before it rains, the ocean in winter. She'd never seen eyes that color.

They talked for hours, more than she'd ever talked with a boy before, about music and books, about his life back in Kansas, hers in Pacifica—the two weren't that different.

They saw each other every day after that, but they didn't share more than a quick hug hello or awkward kiss goodbye, even though Mira was dying to lie naked with him. She suspected she'd scare him off if he knew that about her, and she liked Parker Cullen. A lot. He was different. A little nerdy, but to her surprise, she found this attractive. After the way she'd been treated by other boys, Parker seemed so . . . good. So safe.

On their third Friday night together, they sat alone in his apartment after his roommates left for a party in the West Hills. The roommates couldn't understand why Mira and Parker didn't want to go with them, and though the two hadn't discussed it, Mira hoped Parker was thinking the same thing she was: For the first time they had the place to themselves.

Mira sat on the couch watching Parker in the small galley kitchen. He bent over the fridge, extracting cans of Olympia beer, straightening as the doorbell rang, paying the pizza delivery girl. It was all so grown-up. Mira had a vision of them repeating this evening ritual from that moment on—sharing their meals, their lives. That there might be someone who would love her the rest of her life suddenly seemed possible.

She stood and walked over to him. "I can't believe you're waiting on me like this. I mean, I like it. I could get used to it."

"You could?" Parker pulled open both ring tabs and handed her a can. His hand shook. He turned to take plates from the cabinet.

"Well, that's not the only thing I like about you," she said, trying not to touch his shoulders, his back. *Jesus,* she thought, *let him make the first move.*

Parker turned with plates in hand, looked at her and blinked. Setting the plates beside the pizza, he rubbed his nose, then made a clumsy move toward her, taking her in his arms. He kissed her forehead first, then her cheek, before finally placing his mouth on hers in a way that made her want to cry at its tenderness.

They spent the rest of the weekend in his lumpy twin bed under a red wool Kansas City Chiefs blanket, skipping homework, jobs, and meals, save for an occasional foray through the apartment living room where roommates lounged, into the kitchen for cold pizza or coffee or beer. He was not as sure of himself in bed as the other boys Mira had encountered. He seemed not to know about certain parts of her anatomy until she'd press his hand into them and make a sound of pleasure. When she moved her head from the pillow to climb on top of him, to slide down his lean body, kissing every part of him until her mouth hovered near his erection, she worried that he might think she was too experienced. Too slutty.

"Oh god," he moaned in such ecstasy that she smiled and continued, and just before he climaxed, she slid back up along his body until they were fully connected. He looked at her with such passion, such gratitude, that she wanted to do this, with him, for the rest of her life.

On Sunday afternoon, she and Parker knew they'd pushed their luck far enough. There were classes to prepare for, papers to write, and lives to get on with. "I wish we didn't have to say goodbye," Parker said, taking her face into his hands and rubbing his forehead on hers. He traced the scar on her left cheek with his thumb, then kissed it.

"Why do you like me?" she asked, suddenly afraid she'd never see him again. Afraid that like the other boys, he'd only call or come over late at night, a little drunk, maybe, kissing her with a need she knew went beyond her own particular appeal.

Parker laughed at first, then, seeing she was serious, pressed his lips together and looked into her eyes for a long while, arms around her waist.

"Can't think of anything, huh?" She tried to joke, wanting to pull away.

"No," he said, "I just want to get this right because it's impor-tant."

"Oh." She felt her eyes flit left, then right. Her breathing had gone light and shallow; she wondered if he noticed.

"I like you because I've never known anyone like you before," Parker said. "I don't know how to explain it, exactly. You don't play all those girl games, you know? You're easy to talk to, and you're smart." He cleared his throat, nervous, she could tell now, and she realized she loved him. "And you're beautiful," he continued, tightening his hold around her waist. "You look like an Indian princess, like Pocahontas or something."

Mira laughed. "Please! I'm Italian, not Indian."

Parker leaned down to kiss her. "Then you're my Italian princess," he said. "So, princess, what are you doing next weekend?"

Her eyes welled. He liked her. He wanted to see her again. He didn't think she was a slut. Maybe in time she could tell him about the other boys, the pregnancy she'd ended.

Maybe he would love her no matter what.

Mira sensed that Parker Cullen from Kansas would bring out only the good in her, and she in him, and she knew something had been decided between them.

Once the doorbell started ringing and the house began to fill with people, Mira relaxed. Parker seemed himself as he took coats and offered drinks, shook hands, hugged the aunts and frail old Nonna in her Madonna-and-child Christmas sweater. "Big Al!" he said when her father arrived.

Al didn't so much hug people as consume them. Mira watched Parker disappear into his embrace, then smiled as her father turned to her.

"Hi, Dad," she said, letting herself be swept into the bulk of him, his too-small tweed blazer scratching her face and smelling of mothballs. *"Buon Natale."*

He held her a few moments longer than usual, and she knew he was thinking of the other Mira. "Merry Christmas, little girl," he said and pulled away. Sure enough, his eyes were damp. "Where's the hootch?"

She noticed Parker watching them; he smiled at her. He wasn't just okay, she decided. He was happy, especially once Thea got there, only ten minutes late and not accompanied by any dread-locked or pierced young men.

"Miss Polliwog," he said, twirling their daughter like a balle-rina in army boots. She rolled her eyes but acquiesced, and Mira was glad. Parker loved this ritual.

"Hey," Thea said, pecking Mira on the cheek as if they'd seen each other recently. It had been a month. Mira had barely con-vinced her to come home for Thanksgiving.

Out of habit, Mira breathed in, checking for intoxicants, then stopped herself. Her daughter smelled only of lotion and lip-gloss, and the slightly funky odor of living with too many other people who ate seaweed and miso, rutabagas and cabbage.

"Hi, honey. You look great."

And she did, even in the threadbare 1940s wool coat she insisted was warm enough, even with her hair twisted into multi-colored pigtails. Mira smiled; she liked the new style. Her daugh-ter had an ethereal glow, always had, and a grin that made people stop whatever they were doing to look at her.

"I'm fat," Thea said, removing her coat and setting her over-night bag in the corner. "All we eat out there is rice, rice, and more rice. I can't wait to have some real food." She did appear to have put on a few pounds, but she'd been almost obscenely voluptuous since age twelve, with a little tummy that, for the past several years, poked out of everything she wore. Mira knew better than to suggest eating protein or wearing longer shirts.

Parker and Mira worked the crowd, guiding the party along its usual course, steering guests toward the kitchen and great room for pre-dinner snacks and drinks, then back into coats for the bonfire outside under what turned out to be a starry sky. Somewhere in the dark, the constant tumult of waves roared and rumbled, a sound Mira was so used to she barely remembered to listen for it.

"God, it's freezing out here," Thea said, shivering. They stood as close to the fire as they could without being in it. Mira wrapped her arm around her and squeezed, saying nothing about the coat. Her daughter was letting her put her arm around her, even if it was out of pure physical need for warmth.

"Isn't it beautiful, though?" Mira scanned the sky for the Jewel Box, the Seven Sisters inside, so she could point out the constellation to Thea, then stopped herself. She'd probably done this every time they'd been under a starry sky together. By now, Thea knew what it looked like. If she cared, she'd look for it herself. It was a sad fact that Mira had nothing new to offer her daughter, and hadn't in a long time.

"Are you wearing enough layers, *cara*?" Nonna asked Thea from Mira's other side. "The best way to stay warm is to wear an undershirt—over your B-R-A, of course—a regular shirt or blouse, a sweater . . ." The old woman ticked off the items on her bent fingers, her voice shakier than when Mira was a girl, but the tone and cadence still as strong and sure. No wonder Mira had listened to and obeyed everything her grandmother said.

Nonna was the steel rod that ran through the family, and as much as Mira had sometimes hated her for it, she knew they would have been adrift without her. Mira slid her other arm around Nonna's tiny shoulders, felt her grandmother's arm wrap around her waist. The old woman shrank more each year and Mira feared the day would come too soon when Nonna disappeared altogether.

Parker and Big Al poked at the fire with long sticks, rearranging it for maximum flame, maximum heat. They could be cavemen in better clothes, Mira thought. Men had changed so little in the millions of years they'd inhabited Earth. Parker was different, of course. A new age guy, in touch with his feelings, but still. There was definitely something primitive about him in the firelight, the slope of his brow, the seriousness with which he took the task of tending the flames.

Mira's three aunts huddled together next to Parker and Al, gossiping about one thing or another. The two husbands left between them—Uncle Tommy had long since passed away from liver failure—faded in the dark somewhere behind, mumbling of their old fishing days when there was still a cannery in Pacifica. In their good Sunday coats and low heels, the aunts must have had trouble negotiating the sand—they were in their late sixties now, after all—but they insisted they were fine. Serafinos loved their bonfires. Kids laughed and ran in circles around the outer edges, and Lannie told jokes to Mira's cousin Gina and her family, taking a swig off what appeared to be Parker's bottle of good single malt before passing it on. Ed Pedersen, Pacifica K–12's other secondary level science teacher, stood chatting with the rest of the faculty members, a group unto themselves; it was the same with Parker's baristas and computer techs. *Everyone stays inside their comfort zone,* Mira pondered, *even me, tucked between my daughter and my grandmother.*

At a quarter till eight, Mira said, "Okay, everybody, give me twelve minutes, then it's time to eat."

Amid whoops and murmurs, she traversed the dunes back to the house, shook the sand from her clogs, and looked back at the fire. *How perfect everything is,* she thought.

Inside, she arranged dishes on the breakfast bar and began to slice the bread she'd baked earlier in the day. "Oh shoot, where's the ladle?" she said aloud, trying to picture the contents of the various utensil and junk drawers that had somehow morphed from her perfectly organized drawers over the past year or so. How on earth could she not know something as basic as where the ladle was?

"Need some help?" Lannie stood at the sliding door, rubbing gloved hands over her leather coat sleeves. "Damn, it's cold out there." Her wild hair ringed her face and her cheeks and nose glowed from the cold.

"You look like an angel," Mira said. "A dark angel, maybe, but still."

Lannie snorted and hung her coat on a peg by the door. "So, what's up with you and Parker?"

"Excuse me?"

"You two have barely looked at each other all night." Lannie sidled over and snatched a piece of bread. "It's unnatural. Don't tell me El Wando has come between you."

"Yeah, right." Mira smiled, shook her head. Lannie loved to tease her about the purchase she'd made at her cousin Teresa's GoodVibrations party years ago, even though Lannie herself had purchased an enormous purple dildo called the Porn Star 12. Mira had become quite attached to El Wando for a few years, but lost interest somewhere along the way. Maybe when Thea became a teenager and all Mira could think about was how to keep her from having sex. Maybe she had shut herself down, too. Or maybe her fleeing hormones had done it.

"Parker's just kind of sad tonight," Mira said. "I guess it's the holidays, or . . . I don't know." Napkins, she'd forgotten to buy napkins. "Damn. Do you think people will mind using paper towels?" She hoped she had more than the half roll sitting by the sink. She never used to forget to buy napkins for a party. "Can you look through the drawers over there for the ladle?"

"I bet he's missing his dad." Lannie finished the piece of bread, pressing her fingers to the counter where she'd dropped crumbs, then licking them. "Why didn't his mom come out this year?"

"She's doing Christmas in Vail with the other kids."

The door slid again, and Thea navigated Nonna over the threshold, then helped her out of her coat. Mira smiled at her from across the room and Thea shrugged. "Want to sit where it's warm, Nonna?" she asked, guiding her great-grandmother to an armchair by the fireplace.

And then everyone was coming in, laughing, pouring more wine. Lannie presented Mira with not just one ladle but two.

The children wrestled, the uncles joked with Al, and Mira's three female cousins helped dish up the meal. Parker tended to the fire outside, banking the now-smoldering logs for marshmallow roasting after dinner.

"So, Mirabella, what's this about you driving into a tree?" her father boomed across the room, and Mira closed her eyes. Everyone, save her grandmother who was hard of hearing, laughed.

"Who told?" she asked, but she didn't have to. Everyone knew everything in this family, in this town, and that was all there was to it.

Her cousins cast her sympathetic smiles. Gina hugged her and said, "Like no one else ever had a little fender bender. Everybody knows you're a good driver, sweetie."

"Everybody knows you're the queen of perfect, Mom," Thea chided her from across the room.

It stung, but Mira wouldn't let on. "Right. If only."

The door scraped open one more time and Parker stood rosy-faced between outdoors and in. His fair hair was thinning as he moved into his late forties, but he was the same good-looking, sweet-smelling boy she'd stood next to in the rain all those years ago.

"Hey, you," she called as he came inside. "You suck at keeping secrets."

In the briefest of nanoseconds, the expression on his face turned to panic, then back to normal as he sensed the jovial mood in the room. "I don't know what you're talking about." He smiled a tight smile, his eyes shifted, then he bent over to take off his shoes.

"You do, too," Thea said. "Mr. Innocent."

The others laughed, but Mira had stopped breathing. Parker walked across the room and sat with his employees. They all laughed at something he said, and she let out the breath she'd been holding. Then she poured another glass of wine and took a long drink.

"Aren't you eating?" Thea asked, sitting on a stool at the counter.

Mira shook her head. "Maybe later. I've been tasting it all day." The wine burned like vinegar in her mouth.

"Aunt Mira!" a young voice called from the back of the house, and then three dogs ran into the room, nosing people's crotches and upsetting bowls of stew, growling and tumbling together as they realized they were the center of attention.

"Stop it!" Mira yelled, then realized the entire room of people had stopped whatever they'd been doing to stare at her.

"Sorry," she said, suddenly too hot. "I meant the dogs. They're not trained, and I had them locked away, and I know they're—"

"Mom," Thea interrupted her. "It's okay. People know about dogs."

"Yeah, well, help me, okay, honey? Here, Patsy, here, Ralph." If it got any hotter, Mira thought, she might explode. Sweat trickled from beneath her bra; her hair stuck to the back of her damp neck.

Patsy Cline rushed to Mira's side, pressing herself into her leg. Ralph Cramden, the Saint Bernard mix, and Twiggy, the retired greyhound, continued to roll on the floor until Thea broke them up, giving each of them a whiff of the shrimp she held in her fingers.

"Come on, puppies," she said. "It's time to go back into the dungeon."

Four

———— • ————

THE DAY MIRA FOUND OUT SHE WAS PREGNANT WITH THEA, SHE cried as though grieving the dead. She told Parker and Al and Nonna that they were tears of happiness. She was happy, of course, but the tears were from relief, relief that the small spirit she'd said no to just a few years before had found its way back into her womb. She'd been forgiven.

From that day, Mira knew her baby was a girl. She knew she'd have curly hair and soul-window eyes. She'd felt a sense of her daughter in her first, short-lived pregnancy, and had felt her spirit hovering when she and Parker made love without birth control for the first time after they married. *Yes,* she'd said out loud to Parker in her desire; *yes,* she'd whispered to her waiting child.

Mira and young Thea were the kind of mother and daughter strangers smiled at and felt at ease talking to. "What a beautiful little girl, and she looks so much like you," they'd exclaim. At this, Thea might stand and do a little dance or, just as likely, make a face or stick out her tongue. The strangers would laugh, saying, "She's precocious, isn't she?"

Thea was scary-smart and unfettered by little-girl convention, but she loved her mother with a religious fervor Mira had never experienced. No one had ever loved her so vehemently, so selfishly, not even Parker.

It was addictive, this kind of love. It filled the gaping hole that had opened when her mother died, and Mira fed on it. She took sustenance from the way her daughter's face illuminated when she'd arrive to collect her from day care. Thea's hand was always in hers, her little body pressed against her whenever they sat for meals, or to read, or to rest. Mira drank in the adoration in Thea's eyes from the time she nursed through the gradually decreasing occurrences as she entered school, made friends, became an adolescent, and then, woefully, a surly teenager.

"You aren't really going to wear those jeans, are you?" Thea would say from the couch as Mira was on her way somewhere. "What decade did you buy them in?"

"Do you have to stand so close to me?" Thea would say at school when Mira found her in the hall between classes and wanted to chat. Or, "Mom, couldn't you, like, just sit with the other teachers for lunch?" That had been when she was in seventh grade, and Mira spent the next six years feeling shunned every time she found a place to sit in the cafeteria, as far from Thea as she could.

The worst was when Thea's ideals strayed from Mira's, a possibility she'd never considered. Thea had always loved collecting canned goods for the food bank, marching through the center of town for peace during the first Gulf War. She'd handed out composting leaflets at the farmer's market and register-to-vote leaflets at town meetings, worn Clinton buttons and a blue and red "Pro-Child, Pro-Choice" T-shirt until it wore thin enough to see through.

When news broke of Bill Clinton's extramarital dalliances in the White House, Thea was nearly fifteen and had undergone the first of what would be many radical transformations, this one from pretty young teenager to death-mask ugly in heavy makeup, black clothing, and a new, shudder-inducing piercing in her left eyebrow.

"I can't believe Bill's such an asshole," she said at the dinner table one night. They'd already been arguing over something or other, and Thea was in the darkest of her dark moods.

"I don't know if I'd say asshole so much as pretty horrible decision maker," Parker said, winking at his daughter. He'd been able to talk to her in a way she listened to throughout her early teen years, a skill Mira envied.

"I think they should fire him, and arrest him," Thea said, and Mira gasped. Thea turned her black-lined eyes toward her mother. "Maybe they should just castrate him, too, like they do in the Middle East."

"Thea!" Mira couldn't help raising her voice. "That's horrible! How can you say that, after all the good he's done? Who puts these ideas in your head? Didn't we raise you to—"

"Mira—" Parker began, and she could hear his exasperation. He thought she was too preachy with Thea.

"*I* put these ideas in my head, Mother," Thea yelled. "I'm not you. I don't go around living in some stupid pretend world where we're all saving the fucking whales and everything's fine all the time, because it fucking isn't!"

"Thea—" Parker began, but she stood and stalked from the table. "Geez," he said, sighing. "It's like World War Three around here. Where'd that come from?"

Mira shrugged, feeling the tears rise as they did too often now after one of Thea's outbursts. "She hates me," she said, a fact made worse by knowing she didn't also hate her father, at least not as much. Her daughter's sweet addictive love was no more, and Mira could never quite figure out how to win it back, or how to replace it.

* * *

The heating vents ticked; the wind off the ocean battered the clapboard siding, whistled through the windows. Mira couldn't sleep. Knowing how groggy she'd feel in the morning, Christmas morning, for Christ's sake, just made it worse, but she couldn't stop thinking about Parker in the doorway, that look on his face, just for a moment. Parker in the chair earlier in the evening, the questions he'd asked. Yet he'd acted normally throughout the party. He'd been the perfect host. No one, except Lannie, had noticed anything amiss, and she had probably just been teasing. And why had Mira had to go and scream like that, just because the stupid dogs got loose? Everyone, save Mira, had been perfectly happy.

She rolled toward Parker and draped an arm around his middle. His snoring stopped, but then he scooted back against her and it resumed. She breathed in the smell of his neck, laid her hand against the slight rise of his T-shirted belly. She'd hated his snoring for years, had done everything she could think of to avoid it: earplugs, Tylenol PM, and even, for a while, separate rooms, but she couldn't stand sleeping away from him. Somewhere along the way she'd realized she couldn't sleep anymore without first hearing him snore. They were pair-bonded for life, exchanging the necessary pheromones and hormones while they slept to keep them mated far beyond the time it took to raise offspring, a kink in nature's divine plan. Mira breathed in, imagining Parker's vasopressin entering her pores, then breathed out, releasing oxytocin, she hoped, into his every cell.

How could something be wrong between them? Nothing had changed. She scrolled back and back through the past few months, searching for clues.

He'd lost a major computer consulting client in November, and the walk-in traffic at the Internet coffeehouse was all but nonexistent this time of year, but their mortgage was over twenty years old and cheap by today's standards, and they had so few bills anymore surely they could weather a slow month or two. There'd been rumors of eventual downsizing at Pacifica K–12, but nothing substantial enough to worry about.

Mira wondered if his mood had anything to do with his mother not coming for Christmas, then remembered the relief in Parker's voice when he'd told her. For once, no road trip to Portland through lousy weather to pick her up from the airport, no watching his language for a whole week straight, no increasing barrage of passive-aggressive nagging and criticism as the week wore on.

She didn't think Thea's situation would be the culprit—it was better now than it had been in years. After two attempts at attending two different colleges, interspersed with road trips and short-lived menial jobs, their daughter had moved to Woden eight months earlier to live in the woods among other alleged musicians and artists. When she didn't die from malnutrition or hepatitis C in the first few months, they'd relaxed. Thea raved about the old schoolhouse, but Mira shuddered at the thought of the conditions—too few rooms, a strict vegan policy, and a disturbing lack of sanitation. On the plus side, Thea had apparently stopped seeing the almost-certain drug addict who'd influenced her to hate them for a time. She seemed content to be spending Christmas with them, helpful even. Mira smiled in the dark, thinking about Thea asleep in her old room, imagining the next morning, when Christmas wrappings and ribbons would be everywhere. The cats pouncing on them, the dogs chewing new rawhide bones, and Thea safe and happy at home. She'd be all hers, and Parker's of course, for the day.

The car. Maybe it was the car. Mira felt a surge of heat in her torso. No, it couldn't be that. There was no way Parker Cullen would be depressed about something as stupid as a dented car. Had he intuited the lascivious thought that caused her to crash? She often wondered about Parker's psychic ability, especially when his darker moods coincided with her occasional thoughts of other lovers, past or imagined. Parker seemed never to be troubled by his own thoughts. Monogamy came easily for him.

They had sex almost every Saturday morning in the hazy and forgiving dark before they opened the curtains. It was more efficient now than passionate; they knew each other's bodies so well that it took only a fraction of the time to achieve what used to take hours. Parker was a creature of habit in all things. She knew when each of them would achieve orgasm on these Saturday mornings as well as when to expect to hear the coffee grinder, and the toilet, and the shower.

Sometimes she missed romance and spontaneity, abandoned even before Thea woke at ungodly hours and climbed into bed with them. That Thea was long out of the house and they hadn't returned to a less economical way of making love hadn't occurred before to Mira. Maybe she should try a little something different this weekend. Still, she knew they were lucky; not many of their friends were even still together, let alone having sex, but it had always been important to Mira that they stay connected. Even when she hadn't felt like it, she told herself she didn't want there to be a reason for Parker to go looking anywhere else. The thing she didn't let herself think about was closer to the truth: She'd never wanted to give in to temptation herself.

The heat in Mira's chest and neck subsided, leaving behind a damp film. She blotted it with the sheet, rubbed her forehead against Parker's shoulder. His skin smelled sweet and soapy, and she kissed his neck. She pressed her hand more firmly against his belly, then slid it under his T-shirt. He murmured as she stroked his skin, her hand creeping to the waistband of his briefs, slipping inside. Palming his penis like a soft little bird, Mira felt her pulse quicken, her pelvis begin to rock, ever so slightly, against him. Her hand detected a stirring, and she began to stroke him there, growing more excited as he did.

It would be a new beginning for them. Empty nesters, ha! They would end up sexy senior citizens, barely able to keep their hands off each other in the kitchen, or watching television at night. Maybe they wouldn't even watch television anymore, at least not as much. They'd take cruises, walk distant sandy beaches, explore cathedrals and palaces in Italy, then rush breathlessly back to their tiny but quaint hotel rooms to fall into bed and make love.

Parker was awake now, she could tell by his breathing, but he wasn't moving. He wasn't responding, other than the involuntary hardening of his penis.

"Honey?" she whispered.

He didn't answer.

Mira quit moving her hips, stilled her hand. A lump rose in her throat, and she considered saying more, but he began to snore again. As he went soft she let go of him altogether, rolled over, and rearranged the covers, punching the pillow to create more support for her neck. Tomorrow was Christmas. She had a turkey to roast, pies to bake. Nonna and her father would be there by four in the afternoon for dinner. She really had to get some sleep.

Christmas morning was perfect, exactly the way Mira had envisioned it. It was as if each of the three of them knew everything was changing and it soon wouldn't be just them, their little unit, as it had always been. Thea would move on with her own life, move even farther away, maybe, and someday have her own family. Mira and Parker might spend holidays away, or with friends. Who knew?

Parker gave Mira a CD of Mozart piano sonatas, the new Andrea Barrett book of short stories, delicate earrings made of sea glass, and the softest sweater she'd ever touched.

"How do you always know just what to get me?" she'd asked, sitting amid wrappings and cats, dogs piled at her feet.

Parker shrugged, and she leaned over to kiss him.

"It's not like he's known you forever or anything," Thea said. The sarcasm didn't even sting the way it usually did. She sat cross-legged on the floor in front of them in the pink footy pajamas Mira had found online. The Gibson lay across her lap and she strummed it absently, pigtails undone, rainbow strands falling into her face. "Hey, Dad, you still have one left."

Parker unwrapped his last present. It was a framed photo from a Saturday the previous summer when they'd coerced Thea into joining them for the kite festival up in Long Beach. Mira had been about to take a photo of Parker and Thea in front of the dense tangle of kites when a German woman offered to take one of the three of them. Mira watched Parker study it. She hoped he saw what she saw: how happy they looked together, how naturally their arms wrapped around each other, how even Thea smiled without reservation, without that little fake smile she'd developed at thirteen.

"It's good, don't you think?" Mira asked. "I thought you might want it in your office at the Buzz."

He looked up at her and nodded, his mouth a funny shape. Tears filled his eyes.

"Oh, honey," Mira said, pushing the wrappings to the floor to scoot over and put her arms around him.

"What a softy," Thea said. "No wonder I'm a hopeless romantic." She put the guitar aside and crawled over on her knees. Mira opened her arms to include her in the embrace. Parker gripped the two of them, and Mira marveled at her husband, Mr. Sensitive. He could still surprise her, even after nearly twenty-five years.

Five

"So, what'd santa bring you?" Lannie asked, heaving a stick of driftwood toward the dense foam of the Pacific. It rotated like an ungainly satellite, arcing on a sure trajectory until it curved back to earth, splashing into murky water.

"My daughter for a whole day." Mira pulled the collar of her fleece jacket up against her chin. "And my husband, of course. My family." The only sounds other than their voices were the sluicing of waves and the occasional ping of a gull.

"You know, they say your priorities are supposed to switch back the other way when you're an empty nester." Lannie picked up another stick. "You're supposed to say 'my husband,' first, then 'my daughter.'"

"What have you been reading? *Family* freaking *Circle*? The 1950 Woman's Guide to Pleasing Her Husband?"

Lannie stepped back on her heel and flung the wood into the air. "I'm just saying."

"I know. I appreciate your concern." Why hadn't she said

Parker first? He was almost as missing in her life as Thea was. Poor guy. He was always so tired from trying to run two businesses rolled into one. She would make him a special dinner that night, something he loved that they normally avoided for fear of clogging too many arteries: prime rib, or lasagna. Maybe they would open the expensive Pinot her cousin had given them for Christmas. She could tell Lannie about Parker, about how freaked out she'd gotten on Christmas Eve, but no. Nothing was wrong. Mira was just a neurotic heap of hormones.

"Thea loved her guitar, by the way." Mira stepped around a pile of kelp buzzing with sand fleas. "I told her it was from you, too."

"All I did was make the final—"

"Lannie, I know how much of a discount you gave me. Thank you."

The larger woman shrugged, shoved her hands into her pockets.

"So, what did Santa bring you?" Mira asked.

"Oh, you know. The usual. A ten-pound stick of summer sausage from my sister, a twenty-five-dollar check from my mom. Oh, and a card from Trev. They've got a regular gig in Austin now."

Mira wondered how Lannie did it, how she let her baby-faced son traipse the country without ever seeming to worry. In fact, Lannie worried more about Thea.

"Is he coming home anytime soon?"

"Nah. Their kind of music goes over better in those shit-kicker states."

"What's their name again?"

"The Twang Gods."

"Right, right. Punk country, or something."

"Alt country. Alternative. Very big in Texas."

"He has such a sweet-sounding voice. Does he still do those pretty songs?"

Lannie stopped but didn't bend down to pick up another stick. Mira looked back at her through the mist. "Sweetie?"

"I don't know," Lannie said, staring out to sea. "I hope so."

When Thea was three years old, she'd gotten into Mira's mother's jewelry box, tucked away so long in the back of Mira's closet she had forgotten about it. Thea became enamored of the string of silver-gray pearls lying in the bottom of the box, beneath the gaudy rhinestone pins Mira and Fonso had given their mother each Christmas, and the tortoise shell bangles she never wore.

At first Mira had taken the pearls away from the toddler, trying to interest her instead in child-safe plastic toy jewelry, but Thea would have none of it. She cried and shook her head, dark ringlets bouncing when she stamped her feet in frustration. Parker joked that their daughter was born with Cadillac tastes to Volkswagen parents, but Mira knew it wasn't that the pearls were valuable. It was the smooth weight of them around Thea's neck, the way they rolled against her skin when she rubbed them. From infancy, Thea had been sensitive to rough fabrics, stiff elastic against her baby skin. She loved clothes loose and soft, or satiny, or fluffy. And she could be the most stubborn child on the planet. Mira relented and let Thea wear the pearls, just until naptime. She would keep a close eye on her.

What with folding laundry and calling area schools about possible substitute jobs, Mira put Thea down for her nap without thinking about where the pearls had gotten to. Her daughter had never been a good sleeper, so Mira didn't worry when she heard her bustling around in her room, making this or that noise. Thea often drew at her small easel or sang to her stuffed animals during naptime.

Mira had just sat down to fold the last load of towels when she heard an unusual sound in Thea's room, a sound she'd never heard her daughter make before, garbled and panicky.

"Thea!" she cried, running to her daughter's room, pushing

open the door. Thea sat on the floor in her pink ballerina underwear, chubby arms thrashing, her face a sickening gray. Half a
strand of pearls hung from her lips like a piece of spaghetti. She
was choking, not even able to cough.

Mira scrambled to the floor, pulled Thea to her and yanked
the pearls out of her mouth, each one clanking against Thea's
baby teeth at its exit. How far down had they gone? Mira wondered, horrified at the length of the strand that had been inside
her daughter. Thea coughed and sputtered, fat tears springing
from her eyes and running down her cheeks, which were already
turning pink. The string of pearls swung from Mira's hand, and it
was then she noticed the frayed end. Thea must have been chewing on it and broken it.

She was a horrible mother.

"Baby, hurry, open your mouth," Mira said to the crying child.
She rolled her finger around Thea's gums and teeth, her soft pal-
ate, beneath her tongue, making her cry harder and push at Mira
to get away.

"Did you swallow any pearls, honey?" Mira tried not to sound
panicked, but she realized she was now clenching Thea by the
arms. "Did anything go into your tummy?"

Thea screamed and wrenched away. Mira looked at the pearls
again, warm and wet from Thea's saliva. She held them up around
her own neck. How long had the strand been? Why couldn't she
remember something as simple as that?

Mira carried a wailing Thea to the living room, cooing to her,
wrapped her in one of the warm towels she'd been folding, then
hurried her out to the car. By the time they arrived at the hospital
in Tillamook, the little girl had grown calm and sleepy in the car
seat in back. *Should I have called an ambulance?* Mira wondered,
but her daughter seemed fine now. Was it even a problem to have
pearls in your stomach? Would she just find them in the toilet the
next time Thea yelled "Wipe!" from the bathroom? Or would she
be able to pass them? Mira tried not to think about the possibility

of pulling the string of pea-size pearls from her daughter's tiny bottom.

Inside the emergency room, Thea began again to scream and squirm against Mira. As Mira tried to explain what had transpired to the hard-of-hearing, lavender-haired receptionist, she felt a large presence behind her, and turned to look straight into the face of a neon-pink on blue Iggy Pop upon a large bosom.

"Need a hand there?" said a gravelly female voice, and Mira looked up into the black-rimmed eyes of one of the tallest women she'd ever seen. The woman was about her own age but dressed like a punk rocker, dark hair spiked on top and hanging down in purple and black ribbons around her shoulders.

"My boy's right over there," she said, nodding toward a stroller with a towheaded infant in it, asleep. "We're just waiting on a friend who's getting some stitches. I'm happy to look after her while you get signed in."

"Thanks, but she won't let anybody hold her but me."

"Hey, what's your name, kid?" The woman stooped to look Thea in the eye.

Thea stopped crying and crammed her middle three fingers into her mouth. The woman held out her hands and Thea lifted her elbows, allowing herself to be lifted. The towel fell to the floor.

"Well, okay," Mira said, bending to retrieve the towel. Part of the woman's height could be attributed to the four-inch platform boots she wore. Between them and the hair, she had to have been well over Parker's six foot two. Mira stood back up. "Thank you, I'll just be a sec. Don't worry, honey," she said to Thea. "I'll be right here."

Thea was already engrossed in playing with the rows of silver chains around the woman's neck as they danced their way back to the chairs.

Mira turned to the elderly receptionist and asked in a low voice, "Who is that?" Even though Tillamook was a big town compared to Pacifica, locals still knew the majority of its residents.

"Lannie Langston, she says. She's just passing through," whispered the woman. "Came in here with a fella that looks even weirder than she does, and they got no address. 'Just the bus,' they tell me. Ha!" At this the woman realized her volume had risen and lowered it again. "Who ever heard of living on a bus? I don't care if you are a musician. You still gotta have an address."

"I suppose," Mira murmured. She'd wanted to ask the receptionist—who she'd wrongly assumed to be a kindly grandmother type—if she even thought a doctor needed to see Thea, but she changed her mind. She'd ask the other woman, the one cradling her daughter now and singing to her funny little grin, imparting the message that love stinks. "Yeah, yeah," Mira sang along under her breath, watching the two of them. She'd never seen Thea take to anyone so quickly.

Six

THEA COULDN'T BELIEVE HER PARENTS GOT HER A FUCKING GUITAR for fucking Christmas. They were probably just trying to bribe her into coming home more often, but hey. It was a fucking guitar, a Gibson J-185 at that, rosewood, exactly the one she'd always wanted. Thank god for Lannie—she was the one who knew what guitar Thea wanted, not her parents. Standing on the beach road waiting for Zoe to pick her up, Thea wondered, *Why couldn't I have come from that uterus?* She'd fantasized about being Lannie's daughter her whole life. Of course, that would mean Trevor Langston would be her brother, and they were already a little too close to being like siblings as it was.

It wasn't that she didn't love her mother. It was just that Mira drove her crazy. Thea pulled her coat tighter against the wind. She'd been afraid her parents would get her something practical and totally wrong for her, like a sensible coat. Her mother disapproved of Thea's vintage coat, an almost exact replica of one Patsy Cline wore in an old *Photoplay* magazine at St. Mary's

Thrift & Collectible. Thea could remind her mother that she'd inspired her little dog's name, but it wouldn't matter. Mira was always right about everything. Maybe the coat wasn't that warm, but it was fucking Patsy Cline's coat, or just like it anyway. That was better than warm.

She heard the toy engine chatter of Zoe's old beige bug before she saw it turn off 101. Pulling her hands from warm pockets, she picked up her bag and guitar case. The weight of it, the smooth plastic handle pressing into her palm, was sweet. *I cannot wait till Colby sees this,* she thought, watching Zoe navigate the drifts of sand across the road.

The car came to a dropped-clutch halt in front of her. "Hey," Thea said, pushing the passenger seat forward enough to jam her stuff in the back. "Look what the parentals gave me."

"Spoiled little rich girl." Zoe swept her long dreads over one shoulder, exposing the African-style stretched loop of earlobe that always turned Thea's stomach. Zoe sucked a long drag off her American Spirit and Thea coughed, hoping she would finish her cigarette before the long drive back to Woden.

"I am so not spoiled," Thea said, climbing in and buckling her seat belt. "And we are so not rich. My mother's a teacher, remember?"

"Okay. You keep telling yourself that." Zoe flicked the live cherry from the cigarette out the window, then inserted the butt into a half-empty pack. Thea wondered if it was the smoking or Zoe's age that caused the little lines around her mouth. "Like that's not the nicest house in town."

"Well, now it is." Thea heard the irritation in her own voice. Why was she defending her parents? "I mean, it didn't start out that way. It was a mess when they first got it. And it wasn't like they paid to fix it up, either. They worked their asses off."

Zoe grunted and re-started the car.

It freaked Thea out to think that her parents had been her age when they bought the house, and married already. Maybe pregnant even. If she'd paid more attention, she'd know exactly when conception had occurred, implantation, the development of her nervous system, sexual organs. Her mother was crazy about details like that, and about making sure Thea knew them, ingested them. Mira was a mother bird, regurgitating what she deemed nourishing down her baby's throat, never asking if the baby wanted it or not. Thea felt like the most mothered person on the planet sometimes, but Lannie said that was just her inner drama queen coming out for a stroll.

"Your mom never even got to have a mother, not really, so think about that when you're throwing a pity party for yourself," Lannie said once, and though it hurt Thea's feelings at first, she knew that was what made her love Lannie. She was just so fucking real.

Even without Zoe smoking, the car smelled like the inside of the Driftwood Tavern on a Saturday night. Thea cracked her window. When she'd first gotten to Woden, she'd launched a campaign to help her newfound friend quit, but Zoe was not the kind of person who wanted help with anything. Thea sighed and turned her face to the fresh wind coming through the two-inch space. She couldn't fathom herself doing any of the supposedly responsible things her parents had done in their early twenties, just as she couldn't fathom her parents ever being that young.

"So what did I miss?" she asked. Most Wodenites did not spend holidays with their parents. It was a community of orphans, whether by circumstance or choice, but Thea wasn't quite able to say no when Mira asked her to come home for special days. She seemed so . . . hopeful. And the food was good. Really good. And her old bed was soft.

"Oh, same old same old," Zoe said, sticking her hand out the window to signal a left turn onto the highway. "Ryan got all pissed off at Colby because he thinks he's a poser, which maybe he is, but so is Ryan, only he thinks he's so Zen."

"Yeah." Thea laughed. "It's like he's got a Buddha complex

without the compassion. Shit. Colby's the realest person I know. What did he do?"

"He played this song he wrote, and Damien had some righteous beats for it. Everybody was all, 'that's so hot, dude,' and Ryan got jealous."

Thea smiled. "Yeah, I think I've heard him play that song. It's tight." She drummed the beats on her thighs. "Um, did Alex come by?"

Zoe shook her head. "Oh no, uh-uh. You gotta get over that mofo, girl."

Zoe had been totally down on Alex even before they broke up. Of course, most of the other Wodenites didn't like him much, either, and there were plenty of reasons for it. Thea tried to remind herself of them every day.

"I know. I was just . . . you know. Curious."

"You're tripping, sister. Like he's not your kryptonite. Move on." Zoe fumbled for the cigarette pack, then poked her finger inside to find the half-smoked butt.

"Got a joint?" Thea asked, both to change the subject and to keep her from smoking tobacco.

"No, but there might be a roach or two in the ashtray." Zoe withdrew her fingers from the pack.

Amid the ashes Thea found a roach and dusted it off. She put it to her lips, took matches from Zoe, lit it and breathed in. Fuck Alex. Colby had finally played everyone the song they wrote together, and they'd liked it. The sear of smoke felt good in her throat. A good song, a sweet little guitar. Maybe the stars were finally aligning in her favor.

Seven

ON THE MORNING OF NEW YEAR'S EVE, MIRA ALLOWED HERSELF TO sleep in, knowing she had only three more days of such luxury before the new semester began. When she woke it was dark gray outside. The weather had returned. The house was silent except for the snoring of dogs—two on the floor and one who'd sneaked into bed. Parker had long since gone to work.

She shoved Patsy Cline out of the way and rolled to Parker's side of the bed to look at the clock, the sheets cold. It was after nine. Grumpy, Mira pulled herself into a sitting position at the edge of the bed, then realized why she felt so lousy. The telltale twinge in her uterus, the sense that she was weighted by water balloons; Mira guessed she'd be bleeding by noon.

She moaned, wishing the damn thing would just quit, already. This whole biological life cycle thing was such a pain in the neck. She had no need for the last pitiful eggs that insisted on cycling through her each month, only to be wasted yet again in a painful bloody mess. With all their advances, why couldn't humans control their own biological workings? Why on earth couldn't you just turn the whole thing off? she wondered, then remembered her mother's ill-fated hysterectomy and shuddered.

In the kitchen she found the coffeepot half full and poured a cup to warm in the microwave. Piles of paper greeted her on the breakfast bar—junk mail and bills to sort, paperwork to be filed, newspapers to be recycled. She'd promised Gina she'd bring cannoli to the party at the Sons of Italy Hall that night and she'd yet to think about what to wear. Her hair had gotten too long and shapeless and there was no way she'd get an appointment now, and the five pounds had turned into eight over the holidays. The uterine twinge became cramps in her abdomen and back, and a dull ache formed in her skull. The warmed-over coffee puckered her mouth with its bitterness.

This was no way to begin a new year.

"Happy thoughts," Mira said to Patsy Cline at her feet. Patsy wagged her tail. "Do you need to go out? Here, Ralphie, here, Twiggy."

Mira followed the tumble of dogs down the hall and through the mudroom, watching them shoot out the door like a cyclone, yelping and snapping at the rain.

After downing three ibuprofen tablets, Mira made fresh coffee and sat thumbing through the mail. Credit card offers and end-of-year donation requests got thrown to the floor with Wal-Mart circulars and "Have you seen me?" postcards. She piled late Christmas cards to her right to enjoy after going through the bills, then got up to make toast. As she buttered it, the phone rang.

"Hey," Parker said. "I didn't wake you up, did I?"

"No, I dragged myself out of bed about fifteen minutes ago." Mira yawned. "I feel like crap. My period's starting." She took a sip of coffee. "How's your morning going?"

"Oh, it's pretty slow here," he said. "I might close early. What time's the party?"

"Not till seven. I just have to make a few million cannoli, but maybe we could watch a movie this afternoon, or, I don't know. Just be lazy together." The ibuprofen started to kick in. The day was definitely getting better.

"Oh," Parker said. "Okay."

"No? What did you have in mind?"

"Well, I was thinking I might get ahead with some of my paperwork before the New Year. I'm pretty behind."

"You're always behind, my dear. Why should this year be any different? Come home and hang out with your wife."

He sighed. "I've taken a lot of time off over the holidays, Mira. I need to pay attention to the business—"

"Fine." The same old tug-of-war. It didn't matter that she knew he was right. Mira stared through the kitchen window, watching the dogs run from the yard to shoreline, chasing gulls.

"I'll try to make it home by five, okay?"

"Do what you have to do." She couldn't keep the ire from her voice any more than she could shut down the blood she now felt moving through her cervix. It was all part of the package. "See you later."

"Love you," Parker said.

"I know." Mira clicked off the phone and headed for the bathroom.

Parker's projects, she'd always called them. Running for town council. Getting involved with SPED. The bottomless time-pit that was Cyber Buzz. It seemed there was always something pulling him away from her. Other husbands had jobs they went to for eight hours each day and then came home to be with their families. Even while she and Parker were still in college, he'd had a seat on the student government and volunteered as a student advisor for the Sierra Club. In his senior year, he helped launch KPSU, the college radio station, working long nights to get and keep the equipment up and running. Their dates often took place on the flat roof of the Marshall Building, where Parker had erected the radio antenna. He'd tinker with wiring and tighten bolts and she'd drink in the view of the Willamette River and Mounts Hood and Saint Helens, waiting until he came back over to sit with her and share whatever cheap wine they'd picked up. It was romantic back then.

Oftentimes Mira had no idea he'd even taken on a project until he was well into it. Early one December, when she was pregnant with Thea, Parker seemed suddenly to lose interest in her, coming home late night after night. When she'd ask him where he'd been, he'd say only, "Working late," but she knew the water treatment plant wasn't paying him any overtime.

Mira enlisted her cousin Gina to help her follow him after work one day, to see where he was going. Gina worried they'd find him with another woman, but Mira didn't think so. That wasn't the way Parker was wired.

Driving Gina's boyfriend's sister's old Corolla, a car Parker wouldn't recognize, they drove to Tillamook as the dusky sky darkened to evening, and parked at the edge of the plant's employee lot. At ten past five, they watched Parker walk to his car and get in, and pulled out after him as he turned onto the street.

"Where, oh where, are you going, Parker Cullen?" Mira murmured from the passenger seat, holding the shoulder belt off of her pregnant belly. He was keeping something secret from her, and though she wouldn't let on to Gina, it frightened her.

Just outside of Tillamook, Parker turned right at his buddy Dave's property.

"Should I turn?" Gina asked, panicked.

"No, he'll see us. Pull over past that tree." Mira wondered if this was where he always went. "Do you think they're just having beers or something after work?"

"Every day?" Gina drove just past a large Douglas fir and

parked. "You think they like each other that much?" She giggled. "Oh god, Mira. Maybe it isn't another woman at all."

Mira looked at her and shook her head. "Yeah, right. You stay here. I'm going to go take a look."

"You? He'll see you and that belly coming a mile away. I'll go."

Mira sighed. She was right. "Be careful. Don't let him see you. I think he parked near the barn."

Mira twisted in her seat to watch Gina walk back along the road. She disappeared inside a stand of conifers, but Mira kept watching until her back could no longer take it, her eyes straining to see in the dark.

Finally, Gina reemerged on the road, trotting back to the car, smiling.

"What?" Mira asked as Gina slid into the driver's seat.

"I'm not telling." She started the engine and drove out onto the road, heading for home.

"Did he see you? Why were you gone so long? Gina, you can't not tell me."

"He didn't see me and I wasn't gone that long. Just long enough to know that you have nothing to worry about."

Even though Mira had wanted to believe he'd never betray her, relief flooded her, and she bit her lip, trying not to let Gina see the tears in her eyes. She sniffed loudly and Gina reached over and grabbed her hand. "He's just making a Christmas present, honey. For you and the baby. You'll see."

Mira nodded, sniffing again. "I knew it was something good," she said.

"There you go," Gina said. "You know your husband best, after all."

"It's just my hormones making me cry," Mira said, palming her eyes. "I really didn't think he'd do anything bad."

After toweling off twelve sandy paws and pouring kibble into bowls, Mira returned to the stack of bills on the counter, slitting each one with a fingernail. The heating oil bill, the credit card bill, higher even than she'd anticipated. The cable bill, the house payment, the cell phone bill.

"Huh?" She took a second look at the high balance on the cell bill. Thea was no longer part of the family plan, so the bills had stabilized over the past few months. This month, however, the balance was almost twice as high as usual.

Mira scanned the calls listed from her phone and saw nothing unusual. A couple of long conversations with friends while she'd driven to Portland to Christmas shop earlier in the month, but nothing outrageous. She scanned Parker's calls. There were the usual numbers: home, her cell, her classroom, his mother and siblings in Kansas, various local numbers that were undoubtedly fishing buddies. He tried to use his business phone for anything work related.

One unfamiliar number popped up often, she noticed, and the call times ranged from a couple of minutes to nearly an hour. She looked closer and noticed that the number had been called several times each day, in fact. The longer calls all seemed to occur around four thirty in the afternoon, and were probably the culprit for the increased billing. *How odd,* she thought. The timing and length of the calls were so regular that she wondered if there'd been some kind of glitch in the phone company's billing system.

Scanning the bill for a customer service number, Mira picked up the phone. She started to call the 800 number, then changed her mind and dialed the suspect number instead. It was probably a consulting client and Parker could write it off. She'd have to remind him again to use his business phone. Or maybe it was town council business. Lester. That had to be it.

"Hello?" A woman's voice. Lester was a widower.

What had she been thinking? She had no idea who she'd just called and now she had to say something. She couldn't just hang up—her number was no doubt prominently displayed on this person's phone. On this woman's phone.

"Oh, hi. I'm sorry to bother you, but my name is Mira Sera-fino and I noticed that your number appears a bunch of times on my cell phone bill." Mira paused, unsure how to proceed. "So I'm just . . . you know. Checking to see if there's been a mistake." How do you say *Who the hell are you and why are you talking to my husband every day?*

The woman at the other end laughed. "That's odd. I don't think I know you, either. Are you from Tillamook?"

"Close," Mira said. "Pacifica."

"Well, I'm in Pacifica quite a bit. I'm a paper rep. You know, office supplies, printer paper. Do you buy paper from me, maybe?"

Mira closed her eyes, swallowed back too much saliva. "What's your name?"

"Jackie Anderson. West Coast Paper Supply. Ring a bell?"

"Yes, that explains it. So sorry to have bothered you." Some-how, Mira knew this woman was blond, fair skinned, like Parker.

The woman laughed. "Hey, not a problem. You're smart to check it out. Where do you work? The real estate office? The copy center?"

"At the school." Mira couldn't draw a proper breath, couldn't think, couldn't decide whether she should scream or cry or call Parker at work, or Lannie at the shop.

"Oh, that's funny. I don't handle educational accounts," the woman said. "That's Bill Whi—"

"Sorry to have bothered you," Mira said again and quickly hung up. She hoped the woman, Jackie, would not call her back.

She stared at the phone for a long while. The sky grew darker; rain began to pelt the skylight, the awning over the sliding door. Mira felt her hands and feet go cold. Even with the ibuprofen in her system, her head resumed throbbing. The two big dogs shifted on their cedar pillows in the family room, resettling for another nap. Patsy Cline sat at Mira's feet, looking at her expectantly. In the other room, a cat jumped from somewhere high to the floor and padded its way to the bathroom, where she could hear it lapping at the toilet bowl.

Nothing had changed. Everything had changed. She didn't know how she knew it, but Mira had never been more certain of anything.

Eight

PARKER PULLED INTO THE DRIVEWAY AT FIVE THIRTY-FIVE THAT evening. Mira wondered if it was the daily phone call that kept him away later than he'd promised. Or a rendezvous. Jesus. Her heart lurched, stopping for a moment; then when she thought it would never start again, it began to bang like a pile driver.

"I'm home," Parker called from the mudroom. She heard him hanging up his coat, taking off his shoes, then talking to the dogs who'd run to greet him. "Hi, guys. You need to go out? Mira, do these dogs need to go out?"

She didn't answer.

"Mira?" Parker walked into the kitchen, ruffling his wet hair so that it stood on end. He looked happier than he had in some time, handsome and rosy-cheeked. "Do you want me to let the dogs out?"

"I have a question to ask you," Mira said, the line she'd been rehearsing since that morning, the entire time she'd been rolling out dough and deep-frying cannoli shells to fill, showering and sorting through her seriously neglected wardrobe. Ignoring the rapid staccato of her heart—if she died now, it would be such sweet justice—she picked up the cell phone bill, where she'd used a hot pink highlighter to mark every call to and from Jackie Anderson.

Parker took the piece of paper, stared at it for a long time, his expression blank. Mira didn't need to see it in his face. She knew him too well. His body slumped almost imperceptibly; he swallowed every few seconds. Her body was thrumming, the electrical fizz of panic the only thing keeping her alive, she was certain, because she could barely breathe.

"Whose number is that?" she finally asked, hoping he wouldn't lie to her. Then she could never forgive him.

He lowered the paper, laid it neatly upon the stack of bills on the counter. His face had gone dim, and Mira felt a surge of pity. It was the kind of look that had made her put her arms around him so many times over the twenty-five years she'd known him. It was a look that always made her want only one thing—for him to be happy.

"Parker." She'd never noticed what an odd name that was before. It sounded wrong said out loud, like another man's name. Parker, a parker. To be parked. Unmoving.

"It's not . . . god. It's not what you think."

"What is it, then?"

"This isn't going to sound good. I don't think you'll believe me."

"Give it a whirl." The fizz had worked into a simmer.

"It's a supplier, actually. I think I told you about her—the paper lady?"

"Jackie Anderson," Mira said, and Parker's eyes widened. "She sounds nice."

"You called her?" Now he was angry, too, and they stared across the space between them as if seeing each other for the first time.

"I think the real point here is that you did," Mira said. "Many, many times."

Parker looked at her with eyes so flat, so unlike him, that she wished she could take everything back. She wished she could start the day again. She'd get up early, go for a walk on the beach, make pancakes. She'd leave the bills for after the holidays. She'd get all dressed up for the party and Parker would tell her how great she looked and . . . oh, god. Her sinuses prickled; her eyes burned.

"Why do you talk to Jackie Anderson every day for almost an hour?"

"I don't know."

"You don't know?"

"God, Mira, give me a minute to think! You're always so—" He stopped and raked his hand through his hair. "I have to figure out how to talk about this to you."

"You have to figure out—"

"I . . . shit. I can't do this now. I'm going for a walk." Parker turned and left.

Mira sat immobile at the breakfast bar long after she heard the back door close, tracing the length of the scar on her cheek up and down, over and over. Patsy Cline leaned into her calf, trembling, then lay down and licked Mira's toes.

"Oh god, oh god, oh god." The rhythm of it in Mira's head felt relentless, a ball-peen hammer at her temples. She tried not to let herself imagine her husband with someone else—she had far too much imagination to go down that road without at least hearing Parker out—but already Jackie Anderson had become a blond presence between them—someone younger, prettier, and no doubt bustier. Maybe that's why Parker seemed a little distant on Saturday mornings, getting the job done quickly and getting on with his day. Christ almighty, he and Jackie were probably doing it like jackrabbits. Cramps gripped Mira's abdomen. "Please," she prayed, "don't let them have done it here." She could only let herself imagine the couch, not their bedroom. Not their bed.

She shook her head to clear it. That failing, she slapped a hand on the countertop. "Stop it!" she said aloud, and Patsy Cline jumped.

The numbers on the stove clock continued to change with infuriating regularity. Where was he? At six o'clock, Mira wondered if she should shower, if she should get dressed for the party. She had no idea, in fact, what she should do in a situation like this. She continued to sit doing nothing.

Eighteen minutes later, the back door finally opened and closed, and she heard the rustle of Parker's blue Gore-Tex being hung on its hook. The dogs remained uncannily subdued. Mira released a long sigh. At least he came back.

She heard him walk toward the living room, not the kitchen. Was this a standoff? She—they—had no experience in matters this awful. Their fights were just another routine in their lives: she'd complain, he'd simmer, then blow. They'd talk it out at some point, and even if it took days, they knew an amicable ending would be reached after each had made their point. This was all too quiet. Too irrevocable.

Mira sighed again and stood. Her left foot had fallen asleep under Patsy's weight. "Parker?" she called, limping down the hall to the living room, trying to shake the pins and needles from her foot. From her entire being.

Parker stood at the front window, his back turned.

"Honey?" she said, wondering if she should still use that word.

"Just try to listen," he said, as if she never listened to him, as if she were somehow trying to manipulate the situation to create the outcome she most dreaded. He turned and his face looked as gray as hers felt, and she couldn't stop marveling at how much she wanted to comfort him when her other instinct was to hit him as hard as she could, preferably with something large and heavy.

"I'm listening," she said, keeping her voice even, and sat on the couch in her usual spot. Scenes from Christmas Day flooded her, though, and she got up and moved to a chair on the opposite side of the room, the one only the cats used, knowing her clothes would now be carpeted in fur.

Parker didn't move from the window. He stared at the coffee table, chewing his lip, then looked at her. "Jackie and I—"

She winced and he stopped.

"Come on, Mira. How am I supposed to do this?"

She closed her eyes. Tears pushed through. "I don't know," she whispered. "Just do it."

"We're friends, Mira. Really, really good friends."

She opened her eyes, sniffed back a rush of mucus. "How good?"

"Probably too good, I realize that now. We started talking about a lot of stuff in our lives a few months ago and it . . . it just kind of became a habit. I don't know. We just get each other, and she's funny, and she thinks I'm . . ." He stopped, blew a breath. "Shit. This really doesn't sound good. It just seemed okay at first, helpful, because she was going through this messy divorce, and her husband's a complete asshole, and . . ." He trailed off, swallowed.

"And what? What are you going through, Parker? Why couldn't you talk to me?" She was horrified at how the end of her question turned into a sob, at how much she sounded like a bad actress in a Lifetime TV movie.

"God, Mira. When we talk, it's always the same. Thea. Work. The damn dogs. The house. Everything's a problem, all the time. And nothing ever changes. I get tired of it, don't you?"

Mira cleared her throat, chin trembling. Why hadn't he ever said these things before? Or had he, and she hadn't listened? "She thinks you're what?"

"Don't." He shook his head.

They were silent. The rain started again, tapping the window behind Mira's head.

Finally, she cleared her throat. "I thought we were happy."

"I know."

"Everything's finally the way we always wanted it," she said. "The house is finished. We might even have money now to do stuff we've always wanted to. We've worked so hard."

His eyes filled with tears. "I know. I want to be happy. It's just that . . . I don't know. Is this it, for the rest of our lives?"

God. He was just depressed again. At least she hadn't caused it this time. "So, you're not happy?"

He pinched the bridge of his nose, then cleared his throat. "No."

"Why didn't you tell me?"

"How do you tell someone that?"

"You say, 'Honey, I'm depressed.' We've been through this before. We can go to counseling. We can work this out. Whatever it is that's making you sad."

Parker's face colored; he bit his lip, sniffed back mucus. "That's the problem. *This* is what's making me sad."

"This? You mean . . ."

"Us. You. Me. This."

That is not my husband, Mira decided. *This is not happening. I'm dreaming, or hallucinating, or stuck in some parallel universe with our evil twins. This is not what it looks like: the worst thing that could ever happen.*

"Are you fucking her?" Why did women need to know that? she wondered even as she said it, but she needed to know that detail more than anything else.

Parker sighed and finally sat down on the couch in his usual spot.

"No," he said. She couldn't tell if he was lying.

"Are you going to?"

"This is exactly the kind of—"

"Have you kissed her?"

He squirmed in his seat. "I knew you wouldn't listen."

"I'm listening, Parker. Believe me." Her voice was steel. "I think it's reasonable for me to want to know how far this relationship has gone."

He swallowed and nodded, folded his hands together, then pulled them apart and crossed his arms.

"I kissed her. Once."

"Fuck you," Mira said, and went to get dressed.

Nine

———•———

Mira drove north along the coast road, late for the party, twisting through the dark tree tunnel toward town. She slowed when she saw the lights of the IGA Market. Two large pans of cannoli sat next to her in the passenger seat in lieu of her husband, and two more were wedged with dog blankets against the back of the rear seat so they wouldn't slide to the floor should she have to hit the brakes too hard.

She tapped them now at the 35 MPH sign, determined that at least her cannoli would arrive intact. Her makeup was another story, most of it on the tissue clenched in her hand, and her hair looked like she'd styled it with the dogs' brush. The heavy mist in the air contributed a fine layer of frizz on top. Beneath her good coat, the navy silk dress that had hung unworn in her closet all year felt more like sausage wrapping than the slinky elegance she'd always felt before, made worse by menstrual bloating. The only heels she owned looked decidedly more ancient than she remembered from last year, and had begun to curl up at the toes, giving the overall effect of slutty elf shoes—painful slutty elf shoes, at that.

Despite the large quantities of ibuprofen she'd been eating all day, Mira's temples pounded, and she couldn't shake the feeling that somehow she'd brought all this on herself. She'd spent a lifetime trying to get everything right, make everything perfect, yet somehow she'd missed the most important detail—how to keep her husband in love with her. Had she become too complacent, let herself go? Her ass was flabby, that was for certain, her hair a little out of control. Well, more than a little. Jackie Anderson probably had one of those smooth blond hairstyles. Mira couldn't let herself think about Jackie Anderson's ass. God. Had she paid too little attention to him when she was overwhelmed with school or family or all the stupid do-gooder things she ended up doing because she couldn't say no? Should she have talked less? Made him talk more?

"Jesus!" she said. "Just stop it." *Happy thoughts,* she'd told Patsy just hours before, believing that if she just tried hard enough, if she just thought the right way, everything would be okay.

She snorted at her foolishness.

Driving through town, the cedar-shingled storefronts were dark—Pacifica's merchants had all closed early for New Year's Eve. Had Parker really done paperwork today? She turned her head away as she passed Cyber Buzz, and noticed that the antiques store on the opposite side of the road had gone out of business. Brown paper lined the windows and the sign was gone. She'd have to call Mary Ellen and offer her condolences. That was the third business in the past four months. Everything in Pacifica was dying.

It took less than a minute to pass through the town proper, and at the northern edge she sped back up to fifty miles per hour. The Sons of Italy Hall was halfway between Pacifica and Rockaway Beach, five or so miles, and Mira tried to focus her worry on the perils her friends and relatives would face driving this road after midnight, when all the drunks had stumbled from bars and parties to their cars. "One-ton weapons," she'd told Thea in the old days: cars in the hands of drunk or otherwise drugged drivers. She wouldn't have to worry about her own drive home. She'd be leaving the party shortly after she made her appearance and dropped off the cannoli. She'd already figured out her ruse—Parker at home in bed with the flu and Mira just starting to feel feverish. Flu season was in full swing; they'd be happy to see Typhoid Mira go.

A sensation familiar and nauseating had its grip on her, a gaping hole forming between her ribs and stomach, a gnawing angst, an emptiness that was impossible to fill. It had been sated for such a long time with Parker, with Thea, with work, with busyness. With all that went into building a life.

Earlier, when she'd put the last tray of cannoli into the car, Parker had stopped her in the garage and tried to put his arms around her. "I didn't say I don't love you. It's not about that."

"Don't you dare make me cry now," she'd said, wrenching away. "I finally got some makeup to stay on."

He let go, arms falling to his sides like a quadriplegic's. His cheeks and nose turned pink; tears spilled from his eyes.

Mira had to look away, squeeze her own eyes closed. "Goddamn it." She fumbled in her coat pocket for a tissue.

"Mira, you don't have to go to the party."

She wiped her nose angrily. "Of course I do. I have the fucking cannoli. You're supposed to be there, too. Everyone loves it when we're there. We have the happy marriage everyone wants, the American fucking dream—"

"Mira," he said, softly.

"Goddamn it," she said. "My fucking makeup."

"I'm sorry, Mira. I thought if I waited until after the holidays to tell you—"

"Don't, okay? Please, just let me pull myself together and do this." Mira drew a shaky breath, then another. Parker touched her arm again and she let him this time. Even though he'd been touching someone else.

"This is not how I thought I'd be starting the New Year," she said. She hoped he'd either feel horribly guilty or come to his senses, preferably both, but he turned angry.

"You think I want this to be happening?" he said, dropping his hand. "You think I want to feel this way? I can't stand it. I can't stand knowing that I've hurt you. For the past few months I feel like I've been standing in the doorway, halfway in and halfway out."

Her heart stopped. Her stomach clenched. She tried to sound casual when she asked, "So, which is it? Which way are you going to go?"

He shook his head, tears rolling down his face, but said nothing.

"Why? What did I do?"

"God, don't, Mira." He sobbed, and Mira felt the concrete give way beneath her feet. If she didn't move, she'd fall.

She walked past him into the house and up to the bedroom. She pulled her mother's old brown suitcase from beneath the bed and packed enough clothes for a few days, her toiletries. After snapping the suitcase latches closed, a surge of terror swept through her, leaving a salty residue in her throat and mouth. Her knees buckled and she sat on the soft beige carpet, thinking as she always did when walking barefoot in their bedroom how glad she was that they'd sprung for the extra thick foam padding beneath it. Tears rose again to the surface and she leaned back on the heels of her hands and tried to calm herself by focusing on her favorite piece of artwork in the house—a small blue-hued batik of a murky female figure dressed in 1930s evening wear, the gown hugging breast and nipple, belly and hip, dipping in between her thighs in a triangle, then flowing earthward in sensuous folds. Parker bought it from a sidewalk artist in Seattle's public market on her thirtieth birthday, said it reminded him of her, and she'd felt lucky that her husband saw her as so beautiful. She stood and removed it from the wall, running a finger along the top of the frame and erasing the thick layer of dust that had settled there. She opened her suitcase, wrapped the batik in a sweater, placed the bundle inside and then re-snapped the latches.

As she lugged the suitcase to the car, Parker didn't move, didn't breathe, it seemed; he just stood watching. Even when she lingered for a moment before getting into the car, he didn't say a word, just stood there, looking shell-shocked. She waited a full fifteen seconds (she counted), then shook her head and got in. She decided not to look at him again.

After backing out and just before pulling away, Mira let herself have one last glimpse of what had been.

He'd turned to go back inside the house.

At the turnoff to the hall, Mira downshifted, rocking slowly over uneven paving and down the gravel drive. Gina's white Suburban sat parked amid the fifty or so cars, and Lannie's old pickup, but surprisingly not Al's prized Buick Regal. Mira exhaled in relief. Her father had radar for her unhappiness. She hoped he wouldn't arrive until the party was in full swing and she'd made her excuses and disappeared, so he wouldn't think too hard about why Mira had come alone. Thank god Nonna had quit going to New Year's parties about the time she moved into her apartment, leaving it to the "young crowd" to greet the years of the new millennium. The last thing Mira could take was her grandmother's piercing stare or knowing jut of chin.

She parked as close as she could to the side entrance near the kitchen, turned off the car, and checked her cell phone to see if she'd missed a call. Maybe Parker had changed his mind, and she hadn't heard the phone ring. There were no messages.

Reapplying lipstick, Mira panicked at the thought of all the townspeople who would be in this building. Who might have had coffee at the Buzz today, observing a perfectly healthy Parker? Or worse, who might have seen Parker with a woman who wasn't his wife? He'd said something about a few months. How many people were avoiding her just so they didn't have to wonder whether or not they should tell her? Nothing, absolutely nothing, was a secret in Pacifica.

"Why the hell do I have to make the cannoli?" Mira threw open her door. "You'd think someone else in this damn family could make it every once in a while."

She got out and opened the rear passenger door of the car, reaching in for the dessert. One of the dog blankets had worked its way up under the plastic wrap, pushing until it covered a quarter of one of the pans, a few inches of the other.

"No," Mira said, reaching to turn on the dome light overhead. She pulled back the canine odor–infused blanket and confirmed her fear: the cannoli beneath had a fine layer of fur stuck to the cream filling at each end, and no doubt coating the shells. "No," she said again. "Goddamn it, no." She hadn't cursed so much in one day since she'd started teaching school twenty years earlier.

"Hey, hey, what's the matter?" Lannie's voice came out of the dark behind her, followed by cigarette smoke. Lannie quit smoking every New Year's Day, puffing her lungs out every New Year's Eve.

"This stupid fucking blanket ruined my stupid fucking cannoli," Mira said, unaware until that moment that she was crying. She turned away and covered her face with one hand, wrapped the other arm around her middle.

She felt Lannie come up behind her and pull her back into her cushiony and sequined bosom. "Hang on, hang on. What's the matter? What's going on?"

Mira took a deep breath and relaxed against her, waiting a moment to speak.

"I have to find a place to spend the night," she finally said, voice shaky. She felt Lannie sigh, then nod.

"No problem. You can have Trev's room. Long as you need it."

"Thank you. I can't believe this is happening." She wiped her nose on her coat sleeve. "Parker's seeing someone else."

Lannie stiffened, turned her around. "And you're the one moving out?"

Mira wiped the dampness from her face. "I know, I don't know. I just had to . . . I just had to get out of there. Our perfect fucking house. I don't think I could stand to live there anymore."

"Oh god." Lannie sighed.

"Can you help me carry in this stupid cannoli? Half of it's ruined."

Lannie studied her face, then licked a thumb and wiped beneath Mira's left eye. She said, "I'll bet we can salvage it."

Ten

────────◆────────

THE SONS OF ITALY HALL WAS LITTLE MORE THAN A WHITEWASHED cinder-block building on a windy dune in the middle of nowhere, but it had been erected with much fanfare and pride in the mid-1960s by Tillamook County's handful of Italian immigrants and their offspring, including Mira's grandfather, uncles, second cousins, and Big Al. Mira had celebrated as many rites of passage here as in St. Mary's by the Sea in Rockaway Beach—including her wedding reception. She'd forgotten that until she stepped inside.

In the green fluorescence of the catering kitchen, she and Lannie wiped the damaged cannoli clean with wet paper towels, ruining her painstaking piping detail but otherwise keeping the entire mess a secret from Gina and her party-planning cohorts, the busiest bodies in the county.

"See?" Lannie said, holding up the last pastry for inspection. "As good as new." She started to lay it on top of the other cannoli, now artfully arranged on glass platters, then bit off half of it instead. She shrugged and offered a bulging close-mouthed grin to Mira, who had yet to take off her coat. Maybe she'd just leave it on so no one would see how horrid she looked. Maybe she'd just leave.

Lannie wiped daintily at her mouth before consuming the second half, press-on nails shimmering with silver polish to match her rings and bracelets. Lannie always looked like a rock-and-roll queen on New Year's Eve, decked out in one of her old stage outfits. Tonight she'd chosen a sequined tube top and black lace shawl, tight satin black pants that put the L in Lycra, in luscious. *In lustful*, Mira thought, wondering what Parker was doing at the moment. Would he have called Jackie Anderson? Said, "Good news! My wife moved out. We can finally have a night to ourselves." If it were true that they'd yet to sleep together, which Mira doubted, maybe they'd just never had the opportunity. Maybe she'd been a little hasty packing that suitcase.

"Yoo-hoo." Lannie snapped her fingers in front of Mira's face. "Damn, I knocked one off." She stooped to retrieve a silver fingernail from the terrazzo floor.

"I think I'm just going to leave," Mira said.

The door from the ballroom swung open, her cousin Gina appearing with an empty lasagna pan and letting in loud disco music and strobes of light from the dance floor, the sparkle of family and friends done up in their gaudiest evening wear. It was the only occasion everyone dressed up for, and Mira had always loved this night.

"You're here!" Gina squealed over the music, then let her voice resume normal volume as the door swung closed. "I was starting to worry. Is everything all right?" She ticktocked her stilettos across the tile to the sink, red jersey knit hugging her stair stepper—sculpted behind—a behind Mira had always coveted.

"Is Parker somewhere in there already? I lost David about a half hour ago. I think he's in the corner with the cigar smokers, which he knows I hate. We're already out of lasagna, so you guys will have to eat rigatoni, but it's not too bad this year. Mom let

Aunt Rosa make it." Without a pause, Gina turned and exclaimed, "Oh, the cannoli look fabulous! You always do such a perfect job with them." She picked up the largest tray and carried it back out into the party.

Still kneeling, Lannie looked up, then put her hands on her thighs and pushed herself back into standing position. She squeezed Mira's hand. "If you're going to go, why don't we have a drink together first, okay? A little toast to better days. It might do you some good."

Mira swallowed and nodded. Maybe she should just get good and drunk. Lannie would drive her home. She let her friend lead her out into the ballroom.

Out in the noisy hubbub, everyone was shouting to be heard above the music, or dancing, or searching bright-eyed around the room, waiting for someone to notice them, or looking for someone to gossip with, the right group to align with for the night so that they wouldn't be stuck with the boring second cousins, the neighbors with halitosis.

Mira stood near the back wall, waiting for Lannie to return with their drinks. She smiled and nodded at people who noticed her, hoping no one was talking behind her back, pitying her. That would be too much. No one made a move to come over, though, until Gina's little sister Teresa shot toward her like an arrow. Mira braced herself.

"Honey! I was wondering where you were. Happy New Year!"

Mira squeezed a stiff smile onto her face and received her younger cousin's hug. "Just running a little late. Parker's got the flu."

"That's too bad," Teresa murmured, eyes searching the crowd.

Mira relaxed. If her family didn't know yet, then maybe no one else did.

Teresa snapped her gum. "I suppose Thea's at that pagan ritual in Woden."

Mira nodded. Maybe she should have gone to Woden's bac-
chanal instead and spent the evening with her daughter. She
imagined herself masked and swirling in an old gypsy skirt in
front of a bonfire, hypnotic foreign music pouring from crackling
speakers, the smell of marijuana smoke encircling her. "It seems
kind of fun, actually," she said.

Teresa grimaced at her, then perked up again. "Guess who's
supposed to be here tonight? Kenny Ballinger!"

The bad boy from their high school days. Mira vaguely
remembered long greasy hair, a brown leather jacket, chewing
tobacco–flecked braces. Despite all that, she'd had a crush on him
in her junior year. "Did he move back?" she asked, and Teresa
shrugged.

"I don't know. I think maybe he's just visiting his mom."

"God, I wonder what he'd look like now." Mira scanned the
sea of people. Lannie was making her way toward them with two
large red plastic cups.

"Here," she said, handing Mira a cup filled with ice and blue
liquid.

Mira sniffed the drink. "Good god, Lannie, what is it?" It
smelled like artificially sweetened turpentine.

"Just a little tonic for the soul." Lannie winked and raised her
cup to Mira. "To a brand-new year—may it kick the ass of the
old one."

Mira sighed and nodded. "I'll drink to that." She lifted the
cup to her lips, letting the sear of too many kinds of liquor dull
her senses.

Halfway through the drink, Mira's face had gone numb. She
wiggled her jaw and realized that her entire head was tingling.
She made herself think about Parker and all she felt was angry,
and even that was in an academic way. Not terrified or sad or
hurt. This was good. She took another sip and labored to tune
back into the conversation between Teresa, Lannie, and now, Chet
Moser, a road construction supervisor living in a trailer in the

woods and Lannie's latest crush. They were discussing the low Dungeness crab yield, yet another stake in Pacifica's ailing heart.

Then Mira realized others had wandered into the group: Teresa's husband and their ten-year-old, Olivia; Allan Winter and his wife, Donna, both school board members; Missy Baker, the town's only cosmetologist, and what appeared to be her date, a conservatively dressed middle-aged man who kept glancing at Mira. She switched her cup to her left hand, wedding ring out so that he wouldn't embarrass himself. Or her.

"Oh my god," Teresa said suddenly, halting the conversation. "Mira, who's that with your dad?"

Mira turned to look toward the door. Big Al was dressed in his one-and-only suit, and bore on his arm an elegantly dressed redhead. The look on her father's face told her this was no mere acquaintance.

Their eyes met and Mira tried to smile, but his weak shrug made her mouth go sour. Her father must have had a lady friend or two in the thirty-plus years since her mother died, but she assumed he'd never found someone he liked enough to couple with. He'd never flaunted any relationship in front of the entire town, and he'd never done anything this big without telling her first. And on this of all nights.

"Okay," Mira said, "it's time for me to go." She drained her drink, then noticed the group's eyes on her. "Oh, no, it has nothing to do with that," she explained, wagging her head toward Al. "I'm not feeling well. I was just having one drink. Right, Lannie?"

"I'm not sure you should be driving, honey," Teresa said. "Can Parker come get you?"

"No." Mira shook her head a little too hard and had to take a small step to steady herself. Perhaps she should have eaten something. "He's got the flu. I have to go home." She had to be very careful. If she appeared to be the teensiest bit tipsy in front of the Winters, they'd probably make sure old Ed got the one secondary

level science-teaching slot that would eventually be left in Pacifica. "Parker's really, really sick," she explained to Donna Winter.
Best to work the female half of the equation.

"It's okay, I'll take her," Lannie said, even though Mira knew her
friend wanted more than anything to stay here, flirting with Chet
who was actively flirting back. It wasn't often that fresh blood came
to town, and Lannie had long ago burned her way through any
other appropriate love interests in Tillamook County.

"Seriously, I'm fine," Mira insisted, and heard the slight slur
in her speech. She looked for Allan and Donna's reaction, but
they'd turned away and were talking to another couple. *Oh god,*
Mira thought, *is that Buck Headley, the freaking superintendent, and
his witch of a wife?*

"I'll take her," said the man Mira didn't know. She looked at
Missy, but the cosmetologist didn't seem to mind that her date
was offering to take another woman home. Missy's indifference
suggested that perhaps he was not her date after all.

"And you are?" Mira asked the man.

"Ken Ballinger. We went to school together. I gotta go check
on my mother anyway. I don't mind."

"Kenny?" Teresa said. "You're Kenny Ballinger?" He nodded, and Teresa exclaimed, "Well, why didn't you say so! Look at
you, all spiffed up. It's me, Teresa Anderson. Well, Teresa Antonelli
is how you might remember me. I was two years behind you,
remember?"

"I'm taking Mira home," said Lannie, puffing up like a hen.

Kenny—Ken—turned to Mira. "You wanna go or not?"

Did she? She had no idea, but she knew she needed to do
something, soon. The room had gone off-kilter and would soon
begin to spin.

Mira drew a deep breath, hugged Teresa and her husband, little
Olivia, and then whispered to Lannie. "I have to get out of here,
now. You should really stay." She tilted her head toward Chet,
who was scuffing a boot toe on the floor.

"You can't leave here with him," Lannie said between gritted teeth. "Everyone will see. You don't even know this guy."

"Of course I do. It's just Kenny freaking Ballinger, for god's sake, from high school." She laughed, then stifled herself with her fist, leaning in to whisper, "The worst that could happen is he'll try to sell me LSD."

Lannie shook her large head of hair, but said, "The key's where it always is. There's clean sheets on Trevor's bed."

"Thank you, sweetie, for everything." Mira reached to hug her and lost her balance. Lannie righted her and Mira murmured, "You're the one who got me drunk, you know."

"Do not let him touch you," Lannie said, then released her. "You take care of her," she barked to Ken.

Mira had never considered that he might want to touch her. That this was a possibility dizzied her even more than the booze.

"Ready?" he said.

"Sure," Mira said, although she had never been less ready for anything.

Eleven

———— ·•·•·•· ————

OUTSIDE, THE COLD NIGHT AIR CLEARED SOME OF THE FOG FROM Mira's head and the roiling from her stomach. "So, Kenny Ballinger," she said. "Or I guess it's Ken now."

"Yep." He pointed a remote at a large sedan, making it beep. The music and noise from the party faded behind them. He did not take her arm as she wobbled gracelessly in her heels over the gravel.

"Do you remember me?" Mira asked, surprised that there was something she wanted from him. Maybe just to remember her.

"Yep," he said again, opening the passenger's door. "You're Mira Serafino, unless you've changed your name."

"No, I'm still me." She looked at him up close for a moment, but found it difficult to focus. He had a reasonably good-looking face that was distantly familiar, straight teeth from the braces. He looked like he might own a car dealership, or a chain of steak houses.

"The smartest girl in school," he said. "And the best-looking chick in the class of 1980."

"Really?" So there had been a spark between them once; it hadn't been just her. "Are you still a bad boy, Kenny?" she asked, then giggled as she sat inside the car. She was having difficulty maneuvering her long coat through the door. Ken knelt to pick it up off the wet ground and tuck it beneath her legs. He let one hand rest on her ankle, just above a now soggy slutty elf shoe.

She swallowed.

"Are you still a good girl?" he asked, waiting for a moment before standing and closing her door.

They drove in silence. True to form, Kenny pulled a joint from the car's ashtray and lit it, drew in a long noisy toke before offering it to Mira.

"Clearly you don't remember me very well," she said. "I don't do drugs."

"Lighten up," he said, not moving his hand. "It's just pot."

Even though she'd smoked very little marijuana in her life, and only while in college, Mira had always secretly loved the smell of it. She reached up and took the burning joint, touching Ken's hand briefly. The skinny tip he had sucked from was warm and moist with spit. She put it to her lips, sucking, trying not to let it into her lungs—the last thing she needed was to get stoned. Instead, she held the dark tang inside her mouth as long as she could, then let it trickle out in a curling blue mist.

Ken coughed. "You live in that first big house on the beach, south of town, right?"

"Well, yes." How did he know? "But I'm staying at Lannie's tonight. Do you know where she lives?" She sat up now, unsure how far they'd come back along 101. "The turn's a half mile before town, just past the Yukwachuck Beach road."

"Okeydoke," he said, reaching for the joint. This time his fingers made full contact with hers, intertwining for a moment before letting go.

Mira pulled her hands into her lap and leaned against the

window, but the strobe effect of passing trees made her carsick. She closed her eyes.

Maybe Lannie was right. What was she thinking? Kenny Ballinger had been a hoodlum in high school; why would he be any different now? What was actually in the cigarette they were sharing? She remembered rumors of joints laced with dangerous drugs back in the old days. Angel dust or elephant tranquilizers. Something like that. And there was that date rape drug now that she'd always warned Thea about. Was Ken Ballinger going to rape her?

Mira squirmed in her seat, horrified at the tingle between her legs. How would he do it—would he force himself on her while she was still in the car, sitting in Lannie's driveway? Would he follow her up the walk, see where the key was hidden and break in on her later, or push himself against her as she opened the front door and keep pushing until they were on the couch, or the floor? Would he kiss her, or just tear off her clothes and thrust himself inside her? She could just see Parker's face when he found out, the torment, the guilt.

"You're not getting sick, are you?" Ken asked, and she opened her eyes. He'd lowered her window. He was worried she was going to puke on his nice leather seats, certainly not a good indicator that he was going to try to have his way with her.

Somehow, they were sitting in front of Lannie's house. She hadn't even felt the car turn, or the bump of the potholes in Lannie's driveway.

"How'd we get here?" she asked, sitting up.

"You gonna be okay getting inside?" He'd lit a cigarette, waiting for her to get out of the car.

"Yes, yes, I'm fine. Thank you so much, um, Ken, for the ride. I do appreciate it." What must he think of her, drunk and passed out in his car? Who would he tell?

"No problem." He tapped the ashes from his cigarette outside his window.

"Okay, then. Let's see, do I have everything?" Mira looked around, shouldered her purse. She'd left all of her things in her car. She'd have to sleep in one of Lannie's T-shirts. "Thanks again." She looked at Ken, who nodded and flashed a tight-lipped polite smile. She pushed the door open, got out, trying not to stumble on the uneven ground. She leaned down and said through the open window, "Please say hello to your mother for me."

He flicked his cigarette across Lannie's driveway. "You want me to come in?"

"Oh! Well . . ."

"Something tells me old Lannie might have some good booze in there," he said, whirring up the windows before getting out and slamming his door.

One drink. She'd let him stay for one drink. She wouldn't mind hearing how pretty she'd been in school again. Maybe he still thought she was pretty.

He walked behind her up the drive and the faded gray wooden steps to the front door. What would Parker think if he saw her now, having a nightcap with another man?

She reached behind the tall planter to the left of the door, fumbling for the small hook that held the key, both relieved and oddly disappointed when he made no move to push against her as she opened the door. Instead he walked past her through the living room into the kitchen, flipping on the light, opening cabinets until he hit pay dirt above the refrigerator.

"Bourbon?" he asked, holding up the bottle.

"I . . . I don't know." She hobbled to the kitchen table to sit. She really didn't feel very well, and her feet were killing her. "What does the label say?" She struggled out of her coat and wondered if it would be too suggestive to take off her shoes. She didn't mind having a drink with Kenny Ballinger, but that was where it would have to end.

"I mean do you want one?" He sounded on the edge of annoyance.

"Okay," she said, trying to sound fun and lighthearted, but the thought of drinking more sickened her. She'd just hold the glass, swirl it around and pretend to take sips.

She watched Ken as he opened more cabinets looking for glasses. He wore navy slacks and a leather coat, a nice one from the looks of it. His hair was going gray, short and neat, a far cry from the long greasy look she remembered, but of course that had been, what, twenty-seven, twenty-eight years ago? He'd thickened since his teenage years, although he wasn't exactly heavy. Just not as lean as Parker. "Jesus," she said, then realized it was aloud. Why did she have to keep thinking about Parker?

"What?" Ken said, carrying two glasses of whiskey to the table and pulling out a chair for himself.

"Nothing, I . . . Well, I left my husband tonight."

"Marriage is highly overrated. Three times was enough for me." He emptied his glass.

"Wow, really?" She picked up her drink, swirled the liquor, and took a sniff. The smell overwhelmed her and she set the glass back down. "Anyone I know?"

"Nah. I moved away right after high school." He sat looking at her, her glass. "You gonna drink that?"

"Well, I'm not sure I really need it. I guess I've already had a little too much." She forced a laugh. She wasn't at all sure she liked this man. He had the social graces of an orangutan.

"Mind?" He reached for her glass. "Shouldn't let it go to waste." Another long drink, and both their whiskeys were gone. "So, now what?"

"Excuse me?"

"You wanna sleep together, or what?"

"Oh! God, Kenny, Ken. I'm sorry if I led you on. I mean it's so nice of you to bring me home and everything, but—"

"No problem," he said, standing. "Thanks for the drink."

"You're leaving?"

"You just said—"

"Well, do you want to?" Why did she need to know that? Why didn't she just let this pig of a man leave?

"Hey, I'm a guy, remember? I always want to." He snapped out a laugh, and Mira realized he wore dentures. After all that money on braces. The thought of his hard wet gums on her nipples evoked a curious mixture of disgust and excitement, which quickly turned to nausea.

"I think I better go lie down," she said.

Neither of them made a move to turn on the light in Trevor's room. Mira sat on the edge of the bed, heart banging, trying to breathe deeply to quell the nausea. How had she let it go this far? Why had she let him follow her back here? Did she want to do this at some level? Was she trying to get back at Parker? But he said he'd only kissed Jackie Anderson. There was no way this little encounter would stop at a kiss.

Ken was out of his shoes and pants in seconds, leaving on his shirt and socks. It was cold after all, Mira reasoned. She tried to see if he had an erection, but his shirttail hung in the way, and it was dark in the room. The tingle she'd felt in the car had vanished. She had no desire for this man, or any man. Ever again.

As he advanced toward her, Mira suddenly remembered something, something for which she knew she'd be forever grateful: she was on her period. And not any light period, like in the old days. Hormonal changes had made her flow thick and vigorous, with clots and odors and leakage, all sorts of disgusting side effects, especially to the uninitiated, the unmarried. Parker wouldn't have cared.

"Oh, for criminy's sake. You're crying," Ken said, standing in front of her now, the sound of annoyance back in his voice. His penis was pointing straight at her chest through the tails of his shirt, a half-master she and Parker would have called it, and it slowly wilted toward the floor. "Ah, just forget it," he said and dressed as quickly as he'd undressed, then left.

Mira sat on the bed listening as his car backed down the drive. Why hadn't she said no right when he dropped her off? How on earth could anyone in her right mind think that bare gums were a turn-on? Something in her had snapped when Parker made his little confession.

In the distance she heard an explosion, then another. She didn't have to look out the window to know what it was. She lay back on Trevor's bed, hands on her face, and imagined the reds and yellows and greens of fireworks lighting the night, heralding a new year and the return of her darker side—Mirabella in a blue dress. The Mira who drank too much, who smoked pot. The Mira who had sex with strangers.

"Bad Mira," she whispered. A reprimand? A greeting? She breathed in, out, trying to fight the latest round of nausea. It wasn't just that everything had changed. It was that nothing had, not really, and wouldn't, no matter how hard she tried.

Twelve

HER HIGH SCHOOL FRIENDS HAD THOUGHT MIRA CRAZY FOR choosing Portland State over the U of O or Oregon State, even the out-of-state schools that had accepted her, but she'd known when she first stepped onto the pretty downtown campus that this was where she must go. It was less like a school for newly emancipated children and more like a place where all kinds of people decided to get together to learn things. She yearned for the exotic mix of school and city life, academia and real world, which she imagined to be far more exciting than her previous small-town life. She didn't want the grand pastoral grounds and old brick buildings her friends did, or the stuffy new East Coast friends or Colorado skiing buddies. She wanted experiences she'd never had before, but not so far from home that she couldn't hop in her car and visit on the occasional weekend.

Nor, to her high school English teacher's disappointment, did she want anything other than a basic liberal arts degree. That she ended up a science teacher always confounded Mira, but teachers in small towns couldn't afford to be choosy, and her beloved Mrs. Davies was still teaching English at Pacifica K–12 when Mira was ready to return to the workforce after Thea was in day care. Mr. Lassiter, the science teacher, however, was about to retire, so Mira boned up on biology and chemistry and won the job, gratefully leaving physics and earth sciences to her new partner, Ed Pedersen. She was surprised to find she was a natural, especially when it came time for the school board elders to break down and add the euphemistically titled Health Sciences to the curriculum. Ed refused to participate, but Mira loved teaching sex ed best of all, and not for any reasons she could explain to anyone, not even Parker. No one knew her entire history.

Before the No Nukes concert in the rain, before the boy with the umbrella who changed everything, there had been many other boys whose sweet musty smell drove Mira to distraction. She hungered for broad shoulders, angular jaws, and slim hips. When it had been too long since someone had held her or cried out in his passion for her, she'd flirt with a boy who had hard muscles, who wore ripped jeans and gelled his hair into spikes, or a shaggy-haired boy who tasted of marijuana and cigarette smoke and used the word "fuck" as often as possible. These kinds of boys made love to her with an open urgency that made her want to weep with gratitude. For the first time in her life, she could actually free herself, for hours at a time, of the feeling that she was not quite good enough to be loved so completely.

The most torrid of her trysts was with her sociology teacher, an older man in his late twenties. He ran laps around campus every morning, rain or no, in short shorts and a tank top, exposing long muscular legs, smooth pectoral muscles, firm biceps and shoulders. And he had a way of looking at Mira during class with such open desire that she wished she carried a change of underwear.

Mira loved the expensive cologne smell of his skin. She loved touching his smooth hard chest, his knotted hip muscles. He, in turn, loved touching Mira. Any female student, probably. Mira suspected she wasn't the only girl in his bed, but she knew she was special to him.

One morning she woke up and realized it had been too long since she'd had a period. Most of the boys she'd known were happy to forego intercourse for oral or manual sex, or carried condoms, but not the teacher. He had an affinity for "completion" and said it was a woman's responsibility to take care of such things. Consequently, Mira always made him pull out at the last minute. He didn't like it, but he did enjoy her appreciation of him, and almost always withdrew in time.

At the university clinic, a young intern placed one gloved hand inside Mira and one on top, pushing, twisting, manipulating her uterus with such fervor that Mira broke into a sweat and thought she might throw up. *Maybe I just miscounted,* she thought, fingers gripping the papered sides of the examination table. *Maybe it's just the stress of exams.*

"I'd say ten, eleven weeks?" The intern withdrew his hands, peeled off his gloves.

"Until what?" Mira asked, immediately pulling her legs together. It amazed her how doctors could talk to a person's face when her you-know-what was staring them in the eye.

"Twelve weeks is the cutoff." He tossed the gloves in the trash can and opened the door. Mira reached to pull the drape back over her knees. "I'll send in a counselor," he said, then as an afterthought, "You're pregnant."

Mira began to cry.

The counselor, Rosie, was nicer, putting a hand on Mira's draped knee as she explained the options to her, which didn't sound like very good options at all. Any of them. To Mira's surprise, Rosie didn't act at all judgmental. Swamped by a guilt dank and nauseating, Mira knew that if the tables were turned, she might not be so charitable.

After dressing, Mira walked to the front desk and made an

appointment for the following week. "Bring a hundred and fifty dollars in cash with you," the serious black woman said to the appointment book, then looked up at her. "Do you have someone to be with you?"

"That day?" Mira's head swam.

"For all of it. Any of it."

Mira shrugged. "I don't know. Yet."

The woman drew her lips hard against her teeth, sighed. "You let us know when you come in if you don't have someone with you. We've got volunteers around here, most of the time."

Mira wanted only to escape. "Thank you," she said, and pushed back through the doors onto the busy campus, down the winding walk of the north end and toward a low-rise brick building. Inside, she climbed the terrazzo steps to the sociology department. The teacher was in his office at the dead end of a side hallway. He looked up and smiled when he saw her.

It was the last time he would.

Outside, a light breeze had turned mean, blowing papers and knit hats and hamburger wrappers across the spongy green lawn. Mira headed for her dorm. She couldn't tell her father, or Nonna, or any of the aunts. Not even Gina, or any of the girl cousins. They were all so good. They stuck to the Serafino code.

Mira pulled open the dormitory's front door, climbed the steps. She couldn't tell a priest, or God, because she now realized such a thing could not exist. If there were a God, why would he make the one thing she wanted—no, needed—so bad?

In her room, she lay down as carefully as she could. There was someone else inside her now.

"Hello down there," she said, and started to cry again. "I am really, really sorry." She held her hands over her heart, afraid to touch her abdomen. She didn't want to get too close.

Mira never did end up telling Parker about the pregnancy, and only very little about the other boys she'd been with. She trimmed her list from double digits to single, paring out the teacher and one-night stands and sex-only canoodlings, leaving a handful of boys she'd actually dated. She'd wanted to be honest, but his own history had been so meager, his family so staid. When his parents found out Parker and Mira were expecting, Mira could almost hear them doing the arithmetic over the phone, then gushing with excitement when they ascertained that, indeed, this baby had been conceived after matrimonial proceedings.

As a sex ed teacher, what Mira loved most was telling her students the things she wished someone had told her. That there were real, physical, cellular reasons behind their pounding hearts and wild attractions to rounded breasts or wide shoulders. That thousands upon thousands of years of humanity's drive to keep the species alive influenced their hormonal minds in every desire and decision. Best of all, pregnancy could be avoided, and easily. If she'd been allowed to, she'd have handed out condoms, but she doled out information and assurances instead: it's normal, it's natural, it's the biology of love.

But, for god's sake, be careful.

Somewhere in the night, Mira cried herself sober. The thought that she'd almost done it with Kenny Ballinger unnerved her, but she took comfort in the fact that even though drunk, stoned, and in shock over her husband's confession of adulterous behavior (if not exactly adultery itself), she'd somehow held on to her sanity and refused him. Well, technically, he'd refused her, but she'd been about to tell him to forget it. That had to count for something.

She wanted to go home. Why had she gotten drunk and left her car at the hall, with her cell phone inside? Maybe Parker had called and was waiting for her to call him back. If she had her car, she could get up right now, drive home, wake him up and tell him she didn't care what he'd done, just as long as he would stay and try again. She'd be whatever he needed her to be, and they'd talk until the sky began to lighten, like they used to, work it all out, then lie down together in their bed, molded to the spooning of their bodies, his hand on her hip or hers on his.

Mira swallowed, blinking quickly to clear her eyes. She sat up and waited until the dizziness subsided. She'd left her slip on but the house was cold. Shivering, she went to rummage through Trevor's closet for a robe, a shirt, anything. She felt something soft and pulled it off its hanger, slid her arms into its sleeves and wrapped it around her as she made her way down the hall and into the kitchen. Without turning on the light, she found the phone on the wall next to the refrigerator, dialed home. *Home,* she thought, feeling as if she'd been away for months.

One ring. Even if he had Jackie there now, she could forgive him. She could certainly understand that he thought she'd left him. Two rings. After all, she'd practically done it with someone else herself tonight. Who was she to judge? Three rings, then four. The call went to voice mail; she heard her own voice say, far too cheerfully, "Hi, you've reached Mira, Parker, and Thea. Leave us a message!" She pushed the OFF button with her thumb and sank to her knees on Lannie's crumb-specked linoleum, cradling the phone against her abdomen. How could there be any liquid left in her tear ducts, she wondered, in her sinus cavities? How could she keep sobbing this way, this heaving animal way, without pulling muscles or tearing ligaments, or going completely insane?

Why hadn't she left a message? She should have left a message. What if he'd just gone to the neighbor's for a New Year's drink? What if he'd been so upset he drank himself into a stupor and didn't hear the phone? She sat back and crossed her legs—criss-cross applesauce, they'd taught her to say instead of Indian-style when she first began teaching. In those days, she'd thought political correctness was a good thing. After wiping her eyes on the sleeve of Trevor's robe or whatever it was, she redialed, waited through the four rings for the message. At the beep she opened her mouth. She tried to say something, just "Hello" or "It's me," but the only sound she could make was the *uh uh uh* of her sob-bing, and so again, she pressed the OFF button.

Maybe some bourbon would calm her. She left the phone dangling on its overstretched cord and got to her feet. The bottle still glistened on the counter in the glow from the porch light outside. Where was Lannie, anyway? It had to be three in the morning. She poured a healthy shot into one of the used glasses and took it like medicine, then gasped for air when her throat constricted. Who was this woman she'd become? And what the hell was she wearing? She picked her arm up and looked down at what appeared to be the remains of an old stuffed animal, a huge one. It had the faint odor of paint and dirty-haired boy, but it was warm and soft.

Calmed by the whiskey, she walked back to the phone, bent down to retrieve it, and dialed her number. After one ring, Parker answered, sounding out of breath. "Hello?"

"Fuck!" Mira said and pressed the OFF button. She closed her eyes and sighed. She'd become a phone harasser.

Had he been running to get to the phone, or . . . god, he wouldn't. Would he? On the first night she was gone? Could she really not know her husband at all? Mira licked her dry lips, swal-lowed against a raw throat, and hung up the phone.

The sun had just started to poke through Trevor's Speed Racer curtains when Mira heard the rumble of Lannie's truck in the drive. She couldn't remember getting back into bed. Thank god she'd slept. She rubbed the throb in her forehead and rolled to her side, swung her feet to the floor. She had gotten far too old for this kind of drama.

At the sound of the door opening, Mira stood. Had she put away the bourbon, hung up the phone? At least she didn't have to justify having a man in her bed.

"Hi," Mira called out, walking down the hall toward the kitchen.

Lannie sat at the kitchen table, unzipping her knee-high boots. She looked up at Mira and laughed.

"Why on god's green earth are you wearing Trevor's beaver costume?"

"Ah," Mira said. "How appropriate." She wrapped it tighter around her waist and sat at the table across from Lannie. "I take it you had a good night." She tried to smile.

"Better than yours, I bet." Lannie reached across the table for Mira's hand. "What the hell is going on with you and Parker?"

"He wants out." Mira shrugged and clutched Lannie's cold fingers. "I don't know what happened. Everything seemed fine, then, boom. He says he's not happy anymore." That was all she could say. Anything else would make her go fetal.

"Hey," she said, turning over Lannie's hand. "Where'd all your nails go?"

"Here and there," Lannie said. "Mostly there. Let me fix you some bacon and eggs. I'm starving, how about you?" She stood and yawned, stretched her long arms toward the ceiling, nearly touching it. Her tube top pulled earthward and she tugged it up, then walked to the counter. "Since when do you drink whiskey?" she asked, picking up the bottle.

"Kenny Ballinger drinks whiskey. And he can't get it up."

"Mira!"

"At least he wanted me. Sort of." She winced at the blatant self-pity.

"Of course he wanted you. He had you lined up from the moment he saw you. I can't believe you fell for a creep like that."

"We didn't do anything, don't worry."

"Well, honey, we should probably talk about that." Lannie tossed the bottle from hand to hand, then set it back down. "Half the town thinks you did."

"What? Why?"

"I told you not to walk out with him. Your car sat at the hall

all night, you know. What would that mean to you? Remember when Missy Baker's car sat out all night in front of the Driftwood a couple years ago? What did we all talk about for the next three months?" Lannie sighed and turned to open the refrigerator, extracting a carton of eggs.

"But this is me, for god's sake. Mrs. Serafino, the science teacher. Church-attending, homeless-feeding, Girl Scout–leading me. Saint fucking Mira."

"Doesn't matter. And cursing does not become you, you know."

Mira dropped her head into her hands. Thea would hear about this. Big Al. Nonna. God, Parker. How would she explain this to everyone? How could she make sure they heard her story before the town began to buzz?

She stood. "I have to call Thea."

"Sweetie, it's seven a.m. New Year's Day. Don't you think she'd like to sleep in a little longer?"

"You're right. Can you take me to my car? I'll drive up so I'm there when she wakes up."

"After breakfast. You're not going anywhere without some food in you, not after the night you had. Little Miss Party Hearty."

"You're the one who made me that drink! What was it?"

"Sex on the Beach. And let me tell you, it worked like a charm." Lannie reached into her Lycra pants, then extracted her hand and poured a trickle of sand onto the kitchen floor.

Thirteen

———•———

THE OLD LOGGING ROAD TO WODEN WAS CALLED HELL WAY, AND it was hardly paved with good intentions, let alone asphalt or gravel. Boulders were more like it, Mira thought, dodging the larger stones that had been deposited by gully-washing rains, creating rivers wherever there weren't trees. Trevor's green sweat pants fit her almost perfectly, though they were a little snug in the rear, covered nicely by one of his fuzz-worn flannel shirts. His shoes were huge, however, as were Lannie's, so she'd tugged on some of Trevor's tube socks before donning Lannie's orange rubber flip-flops, the length of which made it hard to feel the gas and brake pedals beneath her feet. Even though she had perfectly good shoes in the suitcase in back, she didn't want to waste the time it would take to stop the car, dig them out, and put them on.

On a relatively smooth stretch of road, she pulled her cell phone from her purse. She'd checked it first thing, but Parker hadn't called. No one had, not that she was expecting anyone to—

she'd seen pretty much everyone she knew the night before—but it left her with a lonely feeling. No one wishing her a happy New Year, no home to go to, no pointless resolutions to make, like "sign up for yoga" or "read more nonfiction." Suddenly, she had no life to improve. How was that possible? She'd always had just a little too much life to get everything done, and now she had the feeling she was merely vapor.

She moaned and hit speed dial. "Happy New Year, Dad," she said with forced cheerfulness when Al answered. "I'm not waking you, am I?"

"No, honey, of course not. I've been up since five." He'd kept to his sheriff's hours after retirement, not quite relaxing into his golden years. "Is everything all right? I couldn't find you last night, and what, did your car break down or something? Something coulda jiggled loose from that accident you had, maybe. You never know with those little Jap mobiles; they're not made so well. Now, my Buick—that's a solid automobile."

"No, Dad, the car's fine. I just had a little too much to drink and had to catch a ride home. Everything's fine." She cringed as she said it; she thought she'd called to tell him about Parker. "I spent the night with Lannie. You know, kind of a girl's-night thing. Parker's got this terrible flu."

"Tell him that I use the Advanced Cold Care, that one in the green package, and I never have nothing more than a day or two. The stuff in the orange package, that's no good. That's for sissies."

Ahead on the road stood a deer, paralyzed at the sight of her car. Mira slowed, then came to a stop, looking into the deer's brown marble eyes. "I'm a little worried that people are going to be talking, you know. About my car sitting there overnight." The deer blinked.

"I won't let them, honey. I'll tell them to go to hell."

Fix it, Daddy, she used to say, and he always did.

"I left Parker," she said, swallowing.

"Oh, no. Ah, Jesus. What happened? You didn't find someone else, did you? Because you know, you'll never find a man as decent as that one."

He'd never, not in a million years, guess that it was Parker who'd found another. "No, Dad, no. It's not that. We've just . . ." She sighed, and let the car roll forward slightly. The deer looked nervous. "I don't know, really." She laughed and it turned into a sob. "I can't believe it."

"Don't make any big decisions right now, Mira. Time has a way of working things out. Look at your Aunt Lucia, leaving Joe for that whole year, and now they're happy as clams. Forty-five years of marriage with only one little blip." He blew his nose. Every year he grew more emotional, and Mira wondered if he was crying now. "You don't know until you've lost someone, honey, you just don't know . . ."

"I'm sorry, Daddy." God, now she'd made him think about her mother. "Don't worry. I'm sure we'll work it out." She inched the car forward. The deer spooked finally and leapt away, disappearing into the forest. "Please don't tell anyone. Not yet," she said, knowing he wouldn't. He'd find some other cover story to proclaim her innocence. She pressed Lannie's flip-flop to the gas. "I didn't get to meet your friend last night."

"I'm sorry I didn't tell you, honey. I didn't know what you'd think. She wanted to go to the party together, but I should have said no."

"And she is . . . ?"

"Dottie Santonopoulos, widow from Rockaway. We met at bingo, at St. Mary's."

"You met at bingo last night?"

"No, no, it was a couple . . . well, probably a few months ago now."

Mira winced. "Months?"

"I know, honey. I should've told you."

Yes, you should have, she thought. "I just want you to be happy," she said, but she was lying. She wanted him to be her father in her time of need, not this, this new thing, this dating-older-man thing. The thought of it made her shudder.

"Geez Louise, I'm an idiot. I shoulda known better, huh, honey? I'm sorry."

He'd protected her from anything upsetting since her mother died. She'd tried to protect him, too, even when she was so young she only did it by instinct, and they'd shared that benevolent refuge together, just the two of them. Now this too had cracked apart, creating the opportunity for other things to get in, get between them, to change them forever.

After more awkward pleasantries, they hung up. Mira thought of the deer's dark eyes, the way its ears had pointed toward her, like slender radar dishes, perfectly tuned to her every move. She wished she hadn't scared it away.

Woden's large timber-frame schoolhouse was built in the late 1800s as a multipurpose community hall and school for the children of the bustling logging camp, now long defunct. It was the only structure still standing among the ruins of cottages, a supply store, stables. The Serafinos had come here for picnics when Mira was young, Big Al and her uncles scouting for tinder while the aunts laid flowered tablecloths on the ground and unpacked hampers of peanut butter and jelly and grape juice for the kids, sausage heroes and Chianti for the grown-ups. There was generally a transistor radio playing Frank Sinatra or Glenn Miller, already oldies in the 1960s, but yet another Serafino was the DJ at KTIL in Tillamook and provided the sound track for most family affairs.

Mira parked in tall dewy grass next to a storage shed made of rusted car hoods and old tires. There'd been no residents here until the 1960s, when a small encampment of hippies took over and started growing marijuana in the open meadows left cleared by the loggers. The people of Woden had always found ways to sustain themselves, shut off as they were from even the closest town a good twelve miles due west on mud-slick roads. The hippie encampment became an artist colony in the 1980s and grew considerably around the time of the millennium. When the world didn't end at its arrival, the crowds thinned, and now it was really more of a place for social outcasts than anything, as far as Mira could tell. She had her doubts about how much art or music played a part in these unbathed people's lives. It seemed more about the release from responsibility, the acceptance of slovenliness, than anything spiritual or creative.

The place was eerily quiet considering it was nearly ten a.m., and considering how many people lived in the schoolhouse, let alone the ferals who camped in the surrounding woods. The slam of the Subaru door shot into the hazy morning air.

"Yo!" a voice replied, and it was only then Mira saw the Rasta-haired man squatting next to the large fire pit in front of the schoolhouse, poking at the smoldering remains of a fire.

"Oh, hello," she said, walking toward him. Her socks were immediately drenched with cool moisture from the grass, and her flip-flops sucked against the earth's muck. "I'm Thea's mom, Mira Serafino."

"Greetings," he said, standing, offering his hand. He was so slight he could have been fourteen, but his face was lined and worn. "I'm Clark." She'd expected a name more like Fireheart or Stoner, something less of-this-world. His hand felt callused and small inside hers, and she felt an urge to take him home and give him a bath, cut his hair, but then she remembered she had no home anymore and began to cry. Again.

He held onto her hand and cocked his head at her. "You want me to go find Thea?" The rough pad of his thumb made little circles on the back of her hand.

She nodded and sniffled, wiping her nose on Trevor's flannel shirt, realizing how much she looked like one of them in her hand-me-downs. "Sure," she said, and he led her to a hollowed-out stump that served as a fireside easy chair.

"Best seat in the house," he said, winking before he strolled off toward the schoolhouse. Mira thought he might be dancing as he walked, his gait rhythmic and rolling, but then she realized that one of his legs was shorter than the other.

Scattered about were remnants of the previous night's bacchanalia: beer bottles, Mardi Gras beads, orange and purple feathers ground into the soil. Many feet had trampled this area, she saw, remembering her fantasy of dancing around the fire. She closed her eyes and sank back into the smooth burl of oak, suddenly exhausted.

"Mom?"

Mira opened her eyes and Thea stood in front of her, eyes puffy the way they always had been in the morning, even before she began staying out till all hours of the night. She'd always had a hard time waking, a hard time getting to sleep the night before. Thea had never been on the rest of the world's schedule.

"What are you doing up here? Is everything okay?" She looked frightened, and Mira stood and held her arms out for a hug, realizing as she did that she'd set herself up to be rejected. She dropped them, but Thea shuffled over to her, let herself be embraced. Mira closed her eyes, felt her chin tremble. She clenched her jaw to stop it. If she cried now she'd mess up everything.

"Everything's okay, sweetie. Happy New Year. Did you have fun last night?"

Thea nodded against her shoulder. Mira let her face linger in her daughter's curls, breathing in woodsmoke and vanilla, until Thea pulled away.

"It was an amazing night. Everybody did shrooms, which I know you think is horrible, but they're not like drugs, Mom. They're organic, they're right from the earth, these woods right here, and the experience is just so fu—so freaking mellow." She paused, squinting. "It's just like you can see, all of a sudden, you know? Like the truth, the whole truth is right there in front of you but you could never really see it before. Everything is so beautiful, and perfect, even if it's not."

Thea looked at her wide-eyed, wanting her to understand, so Mira nodded and tried to smile. "What did you see, exactly?" she asked. *Could you see your father and another woman? Could you see me loving him more than he loves me?*

"Is that a trick question?" A half-scowl darkened her daughter's face.

"No, I just mean, what seemed different when you were . . . what, stoned, high?" Mira laughed nervously. This was not a conversation they'd ever had before. "I mean, what do you call it nowadays?"

"Tripping." Thea looked at her as if she was trying to figure out who she was.

"Oh! We had tripping, too. Of course! Psychedelics. Mushrooms." Mira was babbling now. "Although I never did it—tripped, that is." Did that sound like she'd done other drugs instead? "Or, you know. Anything."

Thea shrugged and scratched her arm. "We're having breakfast, buckwheat cakes and huckleberry jam. Want some?" Indeed, Mira noticed for the first time that the sweet vanilla smell was also floating in the air around them.

"That would be nice," she said. "I did, um, actually come here to talk to you about something." They walked toward the house.

"God, so mysterious! Nobody died or anything, right?" Thea stopped suddenly, turned. "Nonna's okay, isn't she?"

"Yes, sweetie, everybody's okay. Nobody died."

"Thank god," Thea said. "You know, you're kinda scaring me. Why are you dressed like that, for one thing?" She folded her arms across her chest. "And what's so important that you drove all the way up here so early on New Year's Day?"

"You don't bug me about my clothes, I won't bug you about yours." Mira surveyed Thea's seventies-era polyester dress with orange concentric circles, and the ragged purple bell-bottoms she wore underneath. "Let's get some food and find a private place to talk, okay?"

Thea sighed, but turned back toward the house. "I really hate secrets, you know that, right?" Her daughter had always expected to be filled in on even the most inappropriate news for a kid, and listened closely to all of her phone conversations, the talks she and Parker had when they thought she was otherwise absorbed in a book or video.

"Exactly why I'm here, honey," Mira said, and swallowed. She hoped these people knew how to cook, because suddenly, in spite of her earlier breakfast with Lannie, she was starving.

Fourteen

INSIDE, THE SCHOOLHOUSE WAS BUSTLING. MANY ROOMS HAD BEEN made from scrap materials in the original large classroom, and people were in various stages of cleaning up from the night before, chatting, laughing. A space had been left open for the cookstove and a long wooden table at which several other residents sat on equally long benches, drinking mugs of tea and eating. Three young men played guitars in one corner, and Mira couldn't help noticing that one of them, a small sickly-looking boy, played Thea's.

Thea followed Mira's gaze, and said, "Oh, that's Colby. It's okay. We're tight."

Whatever that meant. Mira wanted to ask but did not.

They picked up heavy earthen plates someone had probably made on-site, and not all that skillfully. A surly-looking woman, somewhat older than the rest and with a huge pile of dreadlocks on top of her head, forked thick, mealy-looking pancakes onto them.

"You know, honey, we have that extra set of dishes you could—"

"Mom." Thea looked embarrassed. To the woman, she said, "Zoe, this is my mom, Mira. Mom, this is my friend Zoe."

The woman stared at Mira. "Charmed," she said, sounding anything but.

Mira nodded and smiled, then felt her jaw drop at the realization that what she'd assumed to be large earrings were in fact the woman's earlobes, or what was left of them, stretched to just inches above her shoulders by rows of heavy hoops.

Thea nudged her along, a little more insistently than Mira thought necessary.

"Jam?" a saried young Indian woman asked, smiling in such an open friendly way that Mira hoped she and Thea were friends, too. Probably not. Thea went for the strays, the bedraggled down-on-their-luck types, the Zoes and Colbys of the world.

When Mira had first visited this place eight months before, she'd wondered how she could leave her daughter to survive there. It all seemed so primitive. Now, watching the orderliness of the activities, the way people interacted, courteous if a little out in zombie land, she realized this had become Thea's new family. Wasn't that what you were supposed to want for your grown children, a new family that was loving and supportive? She used to like a little wildness, a little uncertainty, too. But even as a young woman, would she have been able to live somewhere like this? Among people who were so different from the, well, the normal kind? She realized, suddenly, that she was a middle-aged woman who'd grown complacent and stodgy, and it hit her again that she had no idea where she was going to live, or with whom. For a fleeting moment, she thought, *Maybe Thea wouldn't mind . . .* Then she shook her head. *Get a grip,* she thought. Lannie or her father would always take her in.

"Let's go sit in the loft," Thea said. "No one else will be up there."

Mira nodded, slowly understanding that this meant she had to climb a ladder, in too-big flip-flops, carrying a plate of food.

Thea went first, nimble as she pulled herself up the rungs using one hand. Mira stood at the bottom and looked up at her. "How did you do that?" she asked, and Thea sighed, climbed back down and took her plate, then climbed up.

Mira's heart quickened halfway up the ladder, from the height or the impending conversation she didn't know, but she felt an uneasy sense of relief arriving at the shag-carpeted top. The space was tiny, barely room for the two of them to sit, but it had a wide skylight that looked out onto the green palette of forest. Thea had set their plates on the floor between two satin yoga pillows.

"Okay, spill it." Thea cut a wedge of pancake with the side of her fork and stuffed it into her mouth. She'd always loved to eat, nursing like a vampire, sucking Mira dry before relaxing her rosebud lips, unclenching her tiny cream-puff hands.

Mira settled onto the small pillow, trying to find her balance. She felt her rear end hanging off each side. "I guess I didn't have to come all the way up here, but I wanted you to hear it from me, so you'll know the real story." A brilliant streak of blue flew over the skylight and Mira looked up. "Oh, honey, a Steller's jay!"

"Mom. Focus. The real story." Thea's right army boot beat impatiently against the floor.

"Well, I went to the party at the hall last night and I drank a little too much. I stayed at Lannie's." She stopped, licked her dry lips, unsure how to proceed.

"And? Mom? What will I hear?"

"Well . . ." Mira breathed in, deep, out. "My car was in the parking lot overnight. You might hear that I left with a man, which I did, but it was only Kenny Ballinger from my high school days giving me a ride to Lannie's place. Period."

"God, Mom. You know better. Remember Missy Baker's car in front of—"

"Of course I do, honey, which is why I've already called your grandfather, who will tell Nonna and everyone else on the planet, and I've come up here to tell you, and that's all I can do, really. What else can I do?" She felt tears threatening.

Thea took another bite and leaned her head slightly to the left, chewing slowly, considering this. Through a mouthful of pancake, she said, "So, you went to the party alone?"

Mira sniffed, blinking too quickly.

"Oh god, you're getting a divorce." Thea stopped mid-chew, her fork hanging from her fingers, dripping jam.

"No!" Mira said too forcefully, then tried to subdue her voice. "No, honey, but we are having some . . . some problems."

Thea resumed chewing, her Parker-gray eyes wide. She swallowed. "What kind of problems?"

"Well, we've, um . . . God. We've separated."

"Who left?"

Mira bit her lower lip but said nothing.

"You."

Mira nodded.

"Why?"

Was it her imagination or did this sound like an accusation? Should she say, *Because your father wants it that way?* or do the thing she'd always counseled her divorced friends to do and place no blame, cast no aspersions on the lying, cheating, no-good spouse?

"It's not my choice." What else could she say? How else could she paint this picture that had always been so perfect, like some stupid Norman Rockwell painting that she had put every ounce of her faith into believing was real? But it was real, goddamn it, wasn't it? How could she be the only one who thought so? She heard the sound of sobbing and it took a moment for Mira to realize it was her, not Thea.

"I'm sorry, I wasn't going to cry." She wiped her face on Trevor's sleeve again. "He's just so . . . unhappy."

Thea shook her head. "You're probably just freaking out, Mom, like you always do. You're always overreacting. It's male midlife crisis, right? Sports cars, bad facial hair? Don't they get over that? Unless . . ." She looked down, a blue ringlet falling across her forehead. "Unless he's got someone else." She looked back up. "Is that it?" Her eyes had pooled and her chin puckered.

Mira shook her head no, hating herself for lying, but she would not do that to her daughter. Let her father break her heart.

Thea swiped at her eyes. "Then it will be fine. You'll see. We'll go talk to him."

Mira sniffled and sighed. Wouldn't that be perfect? The look on Parker's face when he saw what he'd done to her, to Thea—to their family. Their lovely, lovely family.

She shook her head. "It's between your dad and me. You shouldn't be in the middle. You don't understand wh—"

"Mom, I just got dumped by Alex like five weeks ago. Of course I understand."

So she hadn't dropped that multicolored perforated drug addict after all. Had she raised her daughter to be as complacent, as unaware and vulnerable as she was?

The pain in Thea's eyes washed over Mira like a fresh tidal wave, and she felt her face screwing up to match her daughter's. She reached over dirty shag carpet and the plates of uneaten pancakes, and the second miracle of the day occurred as Thea reached, too, and held her hands. If the circumstances hadn't been so awful, Mira would have been ecstatic at the way she and her daughter were finally connecting again, crying together over their broken hearts.

Mira looked at the four of their hands together between them: Thea's plump pink skin and chewed-to-the-quick fingernails and assorted rings of fake turquoise and colored glass. Her own smooth olive skin stretched tight over green veins, the simple gold band on her finger, the practical gold watch just above on her wrist. The watch Parker gave her in San Francisco, at some trendy little restaurant where they'd felt totally out of place. What had it been, their fifteenth anniversary? Sixteenth? He'd still loved her then. She could almost feel the inscription on the underside of the watch face: *Forever.*

Mira looked back up at Thea, blue mascara now streaking her daughter's flushed cheeks. "Honey, I just don't think I can see your father right now, but that doesn't mean you shouldn't go see him, and talk to him. It doesn't mean he doesn't love you or want you in his life."

"But you have to go talk to him, too."

"I can't."

Thea pulled her hands away. "Why not? You have to, Mom. It's Marriage 101. Duh."

Mira's voice trembled. "Because it won't do any good."

"So you just give up? Bullshit, Mom. What's the real reason? Because you'll have to leave the land of denial to have a real discussion? Depart the planet of happy happy?"

"Thea"—Mira's voice trembled—"I just can't."

"I don't believe that for one second. You won't. You won't because then you might find out you're not so perfect after all. You don't want to face the truth. You don't want to hear the bad stuff, or know what anyone else is feeling unless it's good, or, or . . . Fuck."

Thea wiped her face, smearing wet mascara into her hairline where it blended almost perfectly, blue on blue, on pink, on green. "This is why I hate you," she said, then shoved her plate aside and crawled across the carpet, disappearing down the ladder. Her boots clopped quickly across the floor below and faded.

Mira sat on the pillow for a long while, pancakes untouched. She watched through the skylight, hoping to see another blue bird fly past. After she was sure Thea wasn't coming back, she sighed and scooted herself to the ladder and looked over the edge. How could one floor down look so dangerously far away? If she fell, she'd break something, an ankle. God, a hip. She was losing estrogen, after all. Her bones were probably turning to powder. To dust.

"Help?" she said, weakly, hoping no one would hear.

"Yo," a voice said, and the little man from outside, Clark, appeared at the bottom of the ladder. "What's up?"

"Could you take these plates for me?"

Clark hauled himself easily up the rungs, even with his short leg, stopping when he was high enough for Mira to hand him the dishes.

"Thank you," she said.

"You look sad, Thea's mom. You need some weed? Maybe some shrooms?"

Mira smiled, shook her head, although she was tempted by the mushrooms. What she wouldn't give to have the feeling Thea had described, that everything was beautiful and perfect, even if it wasn't. God, it so wasn't.

"No, thanks, but maybe you could help me down, too, after you put the dishes away. I'm a little afraid of heights."

"You got it, Thea's mom," he said, smiling, and Mira saw his crooked teeth for the first time, his impish grin. She hated to even think it, but he looked a little like a baby goat. He was gone only a few moments before he returned and climbed back up to the halfway point and waited while she maneuvered herself around. As she turned to place a flip-flop on the ladder, she realized she should have thought this through. Her behind was now squarely in the face of this nice man, but he kindly ignored it as he coaxed her down each step. When she wobbled at one point, she felt his hand on her hip, steadying her.

"Thank you so much," she murmured, their little encounter so strange, but nice. Almost intimate.

Once on the ground, Mira followed Clark into the open living area.

"Anyone seen Thea?" Clark called out. Mira looked around and noticed Zoe was missing, too.

"She went for a walk," the Indian girl said. She sat at the big table now, eating breakfast. "Would you like to sit and wait, Mrs.

Serafino?" She patted the bench beside her, and Mira shuffled her flip-flops over to the table, exhausted suddenly, grateful for the invitation. Why couldn't she have a daughter this affable, this polite?

Mira was about to ask her about the blue jays when a boy with a pimply shaved head and jug-handle ears came through the front door, letting it bang shut behind him. "Holy shit—Mrs. Serafino? Remember me, Luke Pitt, class of '04?"

She forced a smile at him and nodded, although she didn't remember him, which was odd. She knew all of her former students. Out of habit she folded her hands on the table. "And how are you doing, Luke? Did you go on to college?" Probably not, if he was living here, but she felt she ought to ask.

"Yeah, but it sucked. Life's treating me pretty good right here." He slid into a seat at the table, drumming thick dirty fingers on the table. "I'm kinda surprised you'd come up here. My parents wouldn't be caught dead anywhere near this place." He laughed and looked around at the group. "They're gonna love this: old lady Serafino coming here and drinking shroom tea with the riffraff."

"She's my mother, Luke," Thea said, walking through the front door with Zoe. "She's not drinking tea and she's just here for a visit. And why are you still here, Mom? You have to go home now. Right? To deal with that little problem of yours?"

Thea stood with her hands on her hips like a tiny hippie Wonder Woman as Zoe skulked away.

"I was just waiting till you got back to say goodbye." Mira turned to the Indian girl. "Happy New Year," she said, then to Luke, "Please tell your parents hello for me."

He snorted and nodded his unshaven chin at her. "Yeah. They'll get a kick out of that."

She stood and climbed over the long wooden bench too slowly, it seemed, for Thea, who was tapping her army boot again, but Lannie's flip-flops were not the easiest things to climb over anything in.

Outside, they stepped into a cool silver mist that felt better than any facial she'd ever paid Missy Baker thirty-five dollars for. The tall trees glistened with dew. "Isn't it beautiful out here?" Mira said, trying to bring the conversation back into a reasonable place, wanting to leave on a brighter note.

"Mom," Thea said. "Luke's trouble. He just started hanging out up here and I've been trying to tell everyone he's bad news."

"I don't even remember him."

"Mom. The Pitts. The *Pacifica Tribune*."

"No, that's Margaret Adderly."

"Like fifty billion years ago. The Pitts took over the paper two years ago." Thea sounded exasperated, a tone Mira knew far too well from her daughter. *I'm the mommy,* she wanted to say, the way she had when Thea was little and bossed her around.

"Honey, he's just a former student, saying hello."

"Are you tripping? Oh god, you didn't actually drink tea, did you?"

"No, of course not. I just want everything to be"—she sighed—"to be okay between us. Why does it always have to be so hard?" She rolled her lips together between her teeth to keep from crying again, but her voice had wobbled as she spoke.

"Because you fucking act like everything's supposed to be perfect all the time, all *la-la-la*"—Thea snaked her head and wiggled her fingers, and Mira would have laughed if her daughter's voice didn't sound so cruel—"and it's not! Life isn't perfect, Mom. I'm not perfect. Dad's not perfect. Nobody's fucking perfect, especially not you! If you want to see the truth, the real truth, you better fucking open your eyes before it's too late."

"I'd appreciate it if you didn't speak to me this way, Thea, and I certainly don't think everything's perfect." Mira's voice wobbled again, this time in anger.

"Yes, you do! Your whole life is about denial!"

"No, it isn—"

"You're doing it right now! You're denying you live in denial. Do you hear yourself? God!"

Thea stood with her arms crossed, her eyes hurt and angry, face bright pink in the gray-silver light. She'd looked this way a thousand times over the years, as a two-year-old, a ten-year-old, a teenager.

"For god's sake, Thea, just calm—"

"No, I've calmed down too many times, and it never does me any good, only you. If you don't go talk to Dad right now, I'll never speak to you again. I mean it."

Mira's voice trembled, with anger or fear, or both. "Please don't threaten me, Thea."

"Or what, you'll disown me? Too late, 'cause I'm fucking disowning you." Thea turned and stomped away, climbing the steep hill behind the schoolhouse, and disappeared into the woods.

Fifteen

GOD! WHY DID PARENTALS HAVE TO BE SO FUCKED UP? EVEN AS she asked herself that question, watching from high on the hill as her mother's car jolted and bumped down the dirt road, Thea knew she didn't mean parents in general.

Clark walked up to stand beside her, took her hand in his own little rough one.

"I hate her," she said.

"How come? She's a nice lady."

"She only appears to be nice because that's what looks good." Thea kicked at a tree root and Clark squeezed her hand. She shifted her weight, rubbed her nose with her free hand, then turned to him. "Can you believe I'm related to her?"

He shrugged. "Like I said, she's a nice lady."

"No way. She's always trying to ruin my life."

"Your life seems okay."

"Only because I got the hell away from her. She doesn't want her daughter to be me, she wants the daughter she made up in her little fantasy world of what the perfect family looks like. It doesn't matter what I want."

"What do you want?"

"To be who I am. To be a musician, not some do-gooder Miss America college girl with straight As and honors and perfect behavior. Like her."

"So she didn't stop you, exactly."

"Fuck you, Clark." Thea tried to hold the frown on her face, but rolled her eyes and landed a soft punch on his arm. "You know what I mean. And now she's freaking out on my dad, too. He probably needs a break from her as much as I do."

"You look a little like her, you know? Around the mouth. Your hair."

She snorted. "Mine is far more interesting."

Thea knew she sounded childish, but she wasn't backing down on this one. If Mira really loved her, she'd go talk to Parker and work whatever their shit was out. If she didn't, well, like Thea had told her. She'd made her choice.

Clark chuckled. "You are you," he said. "That's for sure."

Thea leaned over and hugged him, smelling marijuana and the faint odor of goat. "Let's go get seconds on pancakes," she said, and they walked back down the hill, Thea feeling a new beat emerge from the roll-step-roll of his gait.

Later in the day, Thea carried her guitar up the steep deer trail to the dilapidated shed she and Colby and Damien used as a music studio. The schoolhouse was always noisy and chaotic, and she didn't know how anyone else got any writing done, let alone sleeping. Thea seemed to be the only one interested in getting any rest. The bunk rooms were decreed quiet areas, but noise always filtered in from other areas of the house where night owls sat tinkering on riffs or space jamming into the wee hours, or having deep philosophical discussions that sounded pretty lame to Thea.

Woden was not quite the utopia she'd tried to convince her parents it was, but where else was she going to go and have the time and space to work on her songs? Here she got fed and housed for free—profits from the weed sales took care of everyone. She didn't mind working, not like some of the other lazy weirdos taking up space in Woden, but there were no jobs in Pacifica, in Tillamook, anywhere, other than the kind she'd already tried: shoving greasy fried food at tourists, most of them fat and rude, or holding reversible STOP/SLOW traffic signs in the rain while trucks and heavy equipment belched diesel exhaust into her lungs. She'd been sick for months after that. It used to be that a person could get a job on a fishing boat and make good money working just a few days a week, but that was ancient history. In fact, Thea had only heard about it from other people. Nowadays her friends went to Anchorage for those kinds of jobs, or to work in the fish processing centers there, but she had no desire to be that cold. That far away.

She'd once imagined that she'd like to live as far as possible from Pacifica, but when she'd gone to school in Missoula, even Eugene, she'd missed the ocean, the town. And as much as she hated to admit it, her family. Her cousins, her great-aunts Rosa, Sofia, and Lucia. They were badass old ladies. Her grandfather. Nonna, too, but Nonna scared her. She was a little too up-in-everybody's-face all the time, trying to make sure they all followed some kind of code or something that Thea had no interest in understanding. Thea had missed her father while she was in school, but in an okay way, nothing desperate. What had freaked her shit out entirely was how much she'd missed Mira.

She pushed open the shed door, set her guitar case on the plank floor to light the oil heater in the corner. The place would get good and toasty fast. She clicked the case latches and opened the lid, gazing at the guitar for a long moment before lifting it carefully into her arms. As much as she could hate her mother, she knew this guitar had been entirely her idea, other than the make and model, and she fought against the ache she felt in her chest whenever she let herself remember that in spite of how pissed off she got at Mira, and no matter how hard on her she was, her mother always only loved her back.

Sixteen

THE SUBARU'S TIRES GRABBED AT PATCHES OF DIRT AND GRAVEL AS Mira veered around trees, boulders, steering with one hand and wiping her eyes with the other. Her head pulsed at the thought of what it would feel like to run headlong into a tree this time, instead of merely sideswiping one, so she took her foot off the gas, coasted along the ever-narrowing tracks, then braked when the road came to an end and she realized she was lost.

"Goddamn it, Thea," she said, turning to look over her shoulder as she backed along the tracks, trying to find where she'd deviated from the main road. What right did her daughter have saying those horrible things? All Mira had ever tried to do was build a happy family, and now she was being punished for it. What was so wrong about wanting things to be perfect? Wasn't that everyone's goal in life? To strive for the best?

"Life isn't perfect," Thea had said. "I'm not perfect. Dad's not perfect."

Well, of course no one was perfect. Was Thea insinuating

that Mira expected them to be? Is that how everyone saw her, as someone who demanded perfection? Was that why Parker wanted out?

God. Should she go talk to him? Even considering it made her want to throw up. Too much had happened between them already. He wasn't the same person anymore, the one she'd trusted would be her partner until they drew their last breaths. She began to cry anew and had to stop the car. The windows immediately fogged and she opened the door, stumbling out into the woods in her soggy socks and flip-flops.

"This is so stupid!" she yelled, then waited. "I hate this!" she yelled again. "Fucking motherfucker son of a bitch fucker . . ." Her voice trailed off, absorbed by the dense green growth surrounding her.

The woods were astoundingly beautiful in a way Mira hadn't noticed when she drove up. She sniffed, wiped her nose. She'd only seen the rutted roads, the tight twists and turns, the gray mist. Now she noticed the varying hues of green from tree to tree, the intricate design in the bark of the cedars and how they differed from those on the Doug firs, the hemlocks. She heard birdsong and the wind high in the treetops, though at ground level it was perfectly still.

If she wanted to see the truth, she had to open her eyes, Thea said. Before it was too late.

She walked to the rear of the car and opened the hatch, dug through her suitcase for her Nikes. She could easily change her clothes as well—no one was within miles—but she couldn't quite bring herself to get naked outdoors.

Mira perched on the back of the car to change her shoes. Maybe she should go talk to Parker, but first she needed a pep talk from her father.

The road home was so familiar Mira could have driven it with her eyes closed. She felt tired enough to. She hoped Big Al had coffee on. He hadn't answered when she'd tried calling again but no matter. She had a key.

As she turned into her childhood neighborhood, Mira felt an old sense of calm. She slowed as she pulled up to the house and parked beneath the huge weeping willow she'd played house under as a child. She could see Big Al sitting at the dining table through the front window. He was still in his robe, and it was nearly noon. It was a holiday, but still. And why hadn't he answered the phone? Something stirred behind him, then came into view. The redheaded woman, also in a robe, bringing him a plate of food.

Mira shoved the car back into gear and pressed on the gas. She wanted to duck, but her father would recognize her car, for god's sake. She turned to look over her shoulder as she passed the house, but he wouldn't have seen her if she was in a big red fire truck. He had something else, someone else, on his mind.

Mira ran the stop sign at the corner, trying to get away as quickly as possible. That woman had been there when Mira called this morning, and he'd never said a word. At the main road, Mira turned toward town.

Arriving at a neat brick building on a quiet street a block off Main, she parked and looked down at herself. Nonna would hate what she was wearing. She'd have to tell her she'd been deep cleaning, or painting. Why was she even doing this, going to see the most judgmental person she knew?

Because she will tell me what to do, she thought, and it was the most comforting thought she'd had all day.

The old woman pulled the door open and peered up at Mira as if she were a door-to-door salesman.

"Happy New Year, Nonna," Mira said, bending down to kiss her grandmother's powdery cheek. Nonna wore full makeup every day of the year, a dress, stockings.

"What are you wearing?" Nonna adjusted her glasses on her face, as if that would magically transform Trevor's clothes into appropriate daywear for a good middle-aged Catholic wife and mother. Not that she liked what Mira usually wore, which rarely included skirts.

"Just some cleaning clothes," Mira said. "I needed to pick up some groceries, so thought I'd drop by and say hi, see if you needed anything."

"Come in, come in." Nonna continued to look at her with the suspicious squint Mira had loathed as a child. They walked to the kitchen where the old woman poured Mira a cup of coffee with shaky hands, then refilled her own cup. Then she sat at the small table and motioned for Mira to do the same. "The stores are closed today, *cara*. What are you really doing here? Even your cleaning clothes are not this bad."

Yes, this was why she had come. Because she knew Nonna would know something was wrong, because she'd be forced to confess all. Nonna would outline the right course of action, and maybe even talk some sense into Big Al, and Parker, and Thea. How was it that Mira had become so distant from these three people—the most important people in her life—in such a short span of time?

Mira sat in the straight-back chair opposite her grandmother and began to cry, telling her everything: how Parker had been sneaking around, how he didn't want to be married to her anymore. How Thea had threatened to disown her if she didn't work it out. She even told her about Al and the redhead, feeling like she used to when she told on Fonso, knowing that it would only cause grief in the end, but needing to tell someone, someone who would do something about it and make her feel safe again.

Nonna listened with a flat expression, nodding impatiently once or twice when Mira digressed or cried so hard she couldn't speak.

When Mira finished, she surrendered her tired and achy body to the hard back of the chair and waited while Nonna stared at her, looking grim but thoughtful. This she remembered from childhood as well. Waiting for Nonna to pass judgment could kill you.

"This is not the time for such tears and overreacting," she finally said. "You are being a selfish girl."

Selfish! And why did everyone say she was overreacting? No one understood the situation; no one understood her at all. She'd spent her life trying to understand everyone else, trying to take care of their feelings, but no one seemed to care about hers anymore. Or had they ever?

"Nonna, my husband's cheating on me! Dad's lying to me, to you."

"How could you not know men are like this, hmm? Men are not like us, *cara mia*. They have needs we can't understand. Did you think your father was different?"

"But that doesn't excuse it. And he lied. They both lied."

"Ah, I forgot part two. Men have needs, and they lie to protect us. It's their nature."

Mira shook her head. "That doesn't matter, Nonna. They can control their impulses; they're not animals. Women have needs, too, but—"

"But we don't break up the family over them."

Mira looked at her hands, twisting her ring round and round her finger.

"When you were a little girl, Mira, you liked to play pretend. You're a grown woman now, and you're still pretending, but it's time to face things as they really are. You must go home and forgive Parker. Be a good wife, like your dear mother before you. Don't you want what's best for the family?"

The family. Her family. It was all Mira had ever wanted. Why didn't Parker still want it, still want her? Was she really that awful? She began to cry again. Nonna stood and tottered slowly to the tiny bathroom, then back with a box of tissue.

"Cry, then go home."

Mira took a tissue and blew her nose. Nonna scooped up her coffee cup in both hands to take a drink. When had she started doing that? Mira wondered. And when had she developed that tremor in her right hand?

"But what if Parker doesn't want me to come back?" Mira's chin trembled again.

"He's not stupid, that one. Go talk to him."

Somehow, Nonna still had the power to make her do things she wasn't at all sure she wanted to. Mira sighed. "God. Fine. I'll try."

"That's a good girl, *cara,*" Nonna said, reaching to touch Mira's cheek in benediction.

Half an hour later, Mira still sat in her car in the driveway at home, even though the drive from town was only five minutes. She was afraid to go inside, afraid to move. Afraid Parker might come out and find her sitting here, dressed in Trevor's clothes, looking like hell, looking like the frumpy old ugly wife when Jackie Anderson probably always looked young, and pretty. She was probably one of those women people described as "well put together," someone who coordinated accessories and put on makeup to go to the hardware store.

Mira sighed and leaned back in her seat, gazing at the elegantly weathered sea-tones of their 1918 beach house. She loved this house; she and Parker loved this house. They'd restored and renovated it from the ground up over the past twenty-some years. They'd had the sagging foundation jacked up and supported, rotting siding replaced along with water-damaged plaster, the roof, the wiring, the plumbing. They'd redone everything that could possibly need fixing. Then, last summer, after waiting until they were sure they'd put Thea through as much college as she'd go to, they finally built a new kitchen and great room off the back, filled with windows to let in the vastness of the Pacific. A dream kitchen with gleaming new appliances that actually worked, soothing ocean-colored tiles on the counters and floors, the cozy breakfast bar where you could sit and gaze out at nature and think of nothing at all. It was the coup de grace, the final puzzle piece. Their lives could really begin now. How had Parker lost sight of that?

A headache thudded deep in the middle of her skull. It had started on the bumpy drive away from Woden, each jolt exacerbating it, each thought of Thea threatening to disown her, of Parker abandoning her for someone else. Or maybe it was just a hangover. Who knew how much booze had been in that drink Lannie made. *Jesus,* she thought. *Sex on the Beach.*

She and Parker had attempted it only once, back when they first moved into the house, on a blanket and under cover of complete darkness, but they'd lost their nerve when a neighboring home suddenly illuminated like a lighthouse and voices came through the dark. They'd scrambled back into their clothes, trying to muffle their laughter, even though they had every right to be on their stretch of beach, laughing, talking, even messing around a little. "Maybe sometime when it's foggy," Parker had said as they shook out the blanket, but then Mira got pregnant, and life changed. They'd never tried again. Had that been her doing?

Maybe they needed more excitement in their lives now that it was back to just the two of them, a little something different now and then. That's why men strayed, right? Out of boredom? "Men have needs." Maybe it was as simple as that. Mira climbed out of the car and walked toward the house, heart thumping. Maybe this was just one of those big wake-up calls you always heard about. They hadn't been paying enough attention to their marriage, and boom. Just like when she hit the tree. Thank god Parker hadn't had a heart attack instead. She hadn't gotten breast cancer. They were alive and well and surely capable of making their marriage work after all these years together. She knew about Marriage 101. Hell, she'd written the curriculum.

The front door was locked. As Mira dug for her keys, she heard the excited scratching of dogs' toenails upon the wood floor inside—tap dancing, she and Parker called it—and their impatient moaning and woofing.

"Hi, my puppies." She opened the door and squatted to let the three of them bestow wriggling, wet greetings upon her. Dogs were all about love, she realized. How could she have left them behind?

Rising, she called, "Parker?"

There was no answer.

Why did it feel like she had a bird trapped in her chest, beating its wings against her ribs, stuffing her throat with feathers? Parker was her best friend, her life partner. They were supposed to be able to talk about things like this.

She drew a deep breath and walked down the hall, past the kitchen and into the mudroom. Nothing. She opened the garage door, and there sat Parker's old khaki Land Cruiser. Her heart thumped one extra beat, hard.

Maybe he was asleep, or . . . not. Upstairs. In the bedroom.

She tiptoed back into the hall. At the entryway, she looked up the stairs. "Parker?" she called again, then clumped loudly up the stairs with the gaggle of dogs at her heels to announce her arrival. She peeked into the bedroom before entering. The bed was empty and neatly made. No empty champagne glasses or high heels strewn about the room, no smell of sex in the air. Everything was in its place.

Mira walked toward the bed and ran her hand over the cream-colored velvet duvet she'd coveted at Meier & Frank in Portland, and that Parker had bought to surprise her just last year. He must have still loved her then. She yanked it down, searching the sheets for . . . what? Stains, errant hairs? They could be hers, hers and Parker's. She remade the bed, then went back downstairs to wait.

Outside, the sun was trying to break through the early afternoon clouds. Mira opened the sliding door and walked out onto the deck. Leaning on the rail, she closed her eyes and felt the ocean wind blow each strand of hair. *I can actually feel that,* she marveled, *and each drop of cool damp sea air upon my face.* That was why Serafino women looked so good, Nonna claimed. They all lived by the sea—lots of moisture, and in the Pacific Northwest, very little sun.

Mira opened her eyes and scanned the beach as she always did. She knew its dips and rises and dunes and gullies as well as she knew her husband's face. Children threw rocks into the surf to the south near the access road and an older couple dug for clams just beyond them. Scores of people were out walking, enjoying a mild New Year's Day. Parker had probably gone for a walk; that was it. She looked to the north and saw groups of people in the distance: family groups, some couples. No singles. Her heart thumped again in that disconcerting way. Perhaps Parker was in one of the groups, walking with the neighbors. Or at one of their homes. The Finns often had a New Year's brunch. That was it. That's where he was.

She went back inside and fed the dogs. She paced from kitchen to great room to look out the window, then to the living room to look out the front window. Where was he, really? She could call the Finns, but that would seem odd to them, her trying to track down her husband.

Why was she still dressed this way? What a way to win him back. She shook her head and went back up to the bedroom to remove Trevor's clothes, neatly folding and stacking them on her dresser to return to Lannie later, along with the flip-flops. After a quick shower, she opened her underwear drawer and extracted a pair of comfortably broken-in gray cotton underwear, then stopped.

That was the whole problem. Comfortable gray underwear.

Digging deeper she felt the whisper smoothness of silk and extracted a thin triangle of turquoise paisley encased in purple elastic. The thong her cousins had given her for her fortieth birthday. She'd never even tried it on. "Not with this luggage," she'd said that night at the Driftwood, slapping the sides of her thighs. Now she rubbed her thumb across the fabric in little circles, from the top elastic band down to the crotch, remembering Clark's rough thumb upon her hand.

"No," she said to the image already fully formed in her mind: a younger, less flabby Mira wearing only the thong, reclining on the oak burl log, spread-eagle, while crooked little Clark stared down at her, his thumb teasing her inner thigh.

Usually, when thoughts of someone other than Parker aroused her, Mira did mental math or tried to think about cutting up a chicken until it went away. Now, her hand snaked back into the drawer, weaving through fabric until her fingers wrapped around the hard plastic handle of El Wando. Replacing the image of Clark with her husband, she stepped into the thong. When Parker returned, by god, she'd be dressed in sexy lingerie and infused with the heat that had gone missing in their marriage. They'd had it once, and over the years it had glimmered through occasionally: on vacations, when Thea was at a sleepover. She couldn't believe it was gone entirely; they just hadn't summoned it in so long.

She could picture that old look on Parker's face: surprise, desire, a little embarrassment. She'd make him forget any other woman existed. It would be a new beginning, a happy New Year's Day after all, and she'd win back both her husband and her daughter.

Feeling a little silly but determined, she lay on the bed, arranging herself so that the flabby parts of her were as taut-looking as possible, vibrator at the ready. She'd let Parker watch her masturbate once after they'd gotten drunk on jug wine at the town's Labor Day barbecue. He'd loved it, but like sex on the beach, they hadn't tried it since.

What if he came home, and seeing her car, called out for her? She'd say, "Up here," and he'd climb the stairs, open the door, and . . .

Downstairs, the dogs began to bark, scrambling through the house as they ran to the back door. Mira jumped up and ran to the window. Down below, ten yards from the house, Parker and an unidentified figure in jeans and a hooded navy sweatshirt approached the back door.

Mira grabbed her yellow fleece bathrobe from the hook by

the door, knocking the pile of Trevor's clothes to the floor in a heap. At the sound of the back door opening, she froze, an aluminum taste in her mouth, every artery and vein and vessel pumping overtime. *Stop it!* she thought. *Don't panic.* Maybe it was Lester. He'd be lonely on this holiday. Once Parker knew she was home, and what she was dressed in, he'd shoo Lester out. After they made love—long, lingering love—they'd have a good cry together at the thought that they almost let each other go before they really got to know each other again.

Dear God, she prayed. *Please, please let it be Lester.* She felt like throwing up.

At the sound of voices in the mudroom, she pulled the robe tight around her and inched farther into the hall. A male voice, Parker's. She could barely breathe, waiting to hear who else was down in her beautifully tiled mudroom, with the perfect bench they'd found at an antique store in Coos Bay just three months ago, the large pastel portrait of Thea at age seven hanging over it so they could see her sweet little girl face whenever they came home.

And then, there it was. A woman's voice.

Fuck. She knew it. She knew it and she'd let Nonna's old-fashioned morals and Thea's childish threat influence her to do this stupid, stupid thing. He'd replaced her already and here she was, the idiot ex-wife, stalking her husband, pathetically trying to appeal to him sexually when clearly he preferred a younger, blonder model.

Mira sprinted barefoot down the stairs and grabbed her purse from the front hall table. Patsy Cline ran in, nipping and jumping, quacking her funny small-dog bark.

"Hello?" Parker's voice called out. It was curious, almost friendly.

Mira pushed the front door open and Patsy ran past her, spinning on the sidewalk with excitement. "Patsy, get back here," Mira whispered as loudly as she could. The dog ran to the car door, barking and pawing at the already scraped paint, begging Mira to let her inside.

"Mira?" Parker called, voice drawing closer. "Is that you?"

"Oh god," the woman said. She sounded as if she were just behind him.

Mira pulled the door closed and ran for her life, nearly tripping as she stubbed her toe on uneven concrete, heart pounding so hard she could feel it in her ears, fingers tingling, vision sharpening, adrenaline fueling her, pushing her away, away from danger and out into the vast unknown.

Seventeen

———————◆———————

AN HOUR EAST OF PACIFICA, MIRA HAD ASCENDED AND DESCENDED
the coast Range, hit Highway 26 and turned north toward Portland. Emotionally, she'd scaled even grander highs and lows, her
frenetic brain cells screaming at her to turn around and go back,
then minutes later to drive on: *away, away.* Which was it going to
be, fight or flight?

She pulled her bathrobe tighter across her chest beneath the
seat belt as a logging truck inched from its lane toward hers. The
driver had to think she was a total nutcase out on the open road,
not dressed, not really. She could feel the elastic band that separated one buttock from the other, the scratch of stiff lace. What the
hell was so sexy about that, anyway? And what the hell was she
doing? Where on earth was she going? All of this was so unlike
her. It made no sense at all, but here she was, driving naked and
north to no place in particular while her husband entertained a
special friend at their wonderful, perfect home.

Mira turned on the radio for mental distraction. Through

static, Peter, Paul, and Mary had packed their bags—they were ready to go—and Mira hit the SCAN button as quickly as she could. Next stop, Bonnie Raitt. *Good,* Mira thought, and sat back, humming along mindlessly until she realized what she was humming to. A lump the size of a baseball wedged into her throat as Bonnie realized that she, too, could not make someone love her. Determined now, Mira tapped the SCAN button, forwarding impatiently through static and talk radio. When she finally found another song, she knew she was cursed and clicked off the radio. There was no way she could to listen to Paul McCartney singing "Yesterday."

Patsy Cline slept in the passenger seat. The suitcase was still in back. Her purse was on the floor, El Wando jutting from it at a rakish angle. Mira hadn't even realized she had it in her hand during her hasty escape, but thank god she hadn't left it on the bed. *Oh shit,* she realized. Trevor's clothes were lying on the floor. *Good,* she thought. *Maybe he'll think I was with someone else, too.*

She desperately wanted to call someone, anyone—anything to make her cell phone stop buzzing with calls from Parker. So far she'd let them all go to voice mail, and she wondered how she could delete them without actually having to listen. What would she say if she answered? "Sorry to interrupt your little tête-à-tête, but I just had to come home and masturbate?"

Lannie still wasn't answering her home phone, and Mira had already left her eight messages. There was no one else she could call—not her father, not her grandmother, not her daughter. They'd all told her to go home and work it out and look what had happened. She'd tried to tell them and they wouldn't listen to her. She couldn't call her aunts, or her cousins, because they all came from the same old-world mold and would tell her the same things: *Be a good girl, Mira, a good wife,* but she couldn't be that anymore. Everything had changed.

She bit her lip and dialed Lannie's store, even though it would no doubt be closed for the holiday. Maybe she'd be doing end-of-year inventory or something.

"Hey there, you've reached Lannie's Yarn and Guitar but not Lannie. I'm probably doing something way more fun than answering the phone—you know how I am. Leave a message."

"Lannie, are you there?" Mira spoke loudly, in case her friend was in the back room. "I'm sorry I've left you so many messages at home but I think I just left Parker." She paused to wipe her nose on a tissue she'd rummaged from the glove box. Drawing a shaky breath, she continued. "You wouldn't believe everything that's happened. I caught Parker with, with her. He had her at our *house*, Lannie. Can you believe that? And Thea disowned me, and Nonna will, when she finds out I left. And my dad's sleeping with that freaking redhead. God. And I'm no better, not really. Sex, booze, drugs—what's next, murder?" Mira blew her nose and laughed, which turned into crying again. "Yeah, that's it. Maybe I'll just murder my husband and his little girlfriend. That'll show them." Mira sobbed.

"I know you'll want me to come stay with you, but I can't, I just can't. I have to get the hell away from this place. I'm sorry, but I left Trev's clothes at the house. I don't know how to get them back to you. I'm just driving north. I have no idea where. You'll probably get this tomorrow. God knows, I could be in Canada by then."

The gas tank was three-quarters full. If she didn't keep driving, she'd be humiliated in one way or another—if not by her husband's affair, then by her own very public actions of the past few days. She could just see the headlines in the *Pacifica Tribune*:

TEACHER ON WILD RAMPAGE OF DRINKING, SEX, AND DRUGS!

No, it would be worse than that. FORMER SHERIFF'S DAUGHTER FIRED BY TILLAMOOK COUNTY SCHOOL BOARD AFTER WILD RAMPAGE OF DRINKING, SEX, AND DRUGS!

Even that she could overcome, if her family was on her side, but they weren't. Not anymore. It would be LOCAL BUSINESSMAN REMARRIES AFTER FORMER WIFE'S WILD RAMPAGE OF DRINKING, SEX, AND DRUGS! and there was nothing she could do about it but start over somewhere far away. She was just now coming to the realization that her family didn't care about her, about her feelings. They only wanted someone who would cook the big family meals, act like the good wife and mother and daughter, always be there no matter what. Well, she wasn't going to be there anymore. She would remove herself from the family picture, leave a big gaping hole. Let them see if someone else, someone young and blond, could fill it as well as she had.

Afloat in a sea of flat farmland, Mira swallowed. If she wasn't part of something big, what was she? Right now she felt small as a guppy inside the car as truck after truck passed bearing not just logs, but construction equipment, unidentified freight, chemicals—an assortment of materials that would surely kill upon impact with a car as small as hers. She'd always hated the trucking traffic along Highway 26 and couldn't wait to get to Portland, where she could find her way onto a wider interstate going east, south, or north.

"I could be in Canada by then," she'd said to Lannie. Fonso lived in Canada. Fonso was an outcast, an outlaw, and now she was, too. Mira bit her lip to stave off any more crying. She could find her brother and have some kind of a life close to him. Could she get her teaching certification in Canada? Would they call her former employer? Who on earth could she use as references for anything now?

"Fuck!" Her voice woke Patsy Cline, who shivered. Mira realized she was getting used to that word. It felt right to dig her top teeth into her bottom lip on the F, release the guttural *fuh* with a sharp blast of breath, and end with a disgusted *kh*. "Fuck," she said again.

Mira pointed the heating vent at the scruffy little dog and turned the car stereo back on. She just had a feeling, and she was right. She cranked the volume so it filled the car, nearly drowning out Patsy's spirited yipping as she sang along with Chrissie Hynde and the Pretenders about being back on the chain gang.

Less than an hour into Washington, the landscape seemed different than Oregon's. Sure, there were the ubiquitous trees, the hills at the horizon, but it all seemed more stately, less chaotic. In a way, Mira realized, more comforting. She'd passed Washington's Vancouver, and Battle Ground, and was closing in on Olympia. Even the names sounded more serious, more sure of themselves than Pacifica, Rockaway, Tillamook.

Patsy Cline had grown impatient with the trip in Portland, trying to weasel her way into Mira's lap every few minutes. Now she pranced about on the passenger seat, whining and giving Mira worried looks from beneath her bangs.

"Yes, sweetie, I need to pee, too," Mira said, scratching the dog's bony cranium. "And look, there's a rest stop in just a few miles. Think you can hold on?"

Mira would change into real clothes, and when she got somewhere, buy new ones that fit her new life. Divorced middle-aged women who lived in large cities wore black, sleek lines, expensive shoes. Maybe she'd get a new haircut, something a bit more updated. Sophisticated. She'd kept her modest inheritance from her mother in a trust all these years for when Thea was mature enough for it. Mira realized that might be never, and she had no idea how quickly she'd be able to get a job, wherever she was going. She could save up again for Thea. Mira swallowed and tried to relax her shoulders. Just thinking this way made her feel better, like something had been decided.

Her cell phone buzzed again, home number on the display. *Let Jackie Anderson have him,* she decided. *Soon enough she'll be too old, too, and he'll go spreading his precious seed somewhere else.* Why hadn't she ever paid attention to all of the women this happened to?

She'd always said, "Not me. Not us," but the penile compass and its magnetic attraction to youthful depositories was all-powerful. She lowered her window, gasping at the cold wind it let in, and tossed the cell phone outside, watching in the rearview mirror as it bounced and broke apart on the pavement.

PART TWO

Eighteen

THE CHARRED SMELL OF YESTERDAY'S ESPRESSO ENTERED MIRA'S consciousness first, then the noisy rumble of traffic outside, then the insistent nudging of Patsy Cline's moist nose in her armpit. For such a small dog, she manufactured more urine than Mira would have thought possible. In the distance the clanging electronic bell of the Fremont Bridge announced its impending ascension and Mira imagined the small blue expanse rising in the misty morning like a backhanded salute to Seattle's crazed morning commuters. She yawned and scratched her head through the cropped tangle of hair she was still getting used to. At least her commute consisted only of a short walk down the rickety steps and inside through the purple back door marked NOW ENTERING THE COFFEE SHOP AT THE CENTER OF THE UNIVERSE.

The unwieldy name was a reflection of the neighborhood she now lived in, the Republic of Fremont, an urban mass of odd public art, old hippies, new hipsters, old fishing outfits on the canal, new dot-coms in refurbished old buildings. It was Seattle at its Seattle-est, the kind of place she never would have expected to end up in.

What if her alternator had gone out up in Everett, or even farther north in Bellingham? What if she'd made it all the way to British Columbia? But she hadn't, and even as she'd sat at the only open coffee shop near where she broke down three weeks earlier on New Year's Day, she'd had a feeling that maybe she'd landed in this Oz, like Dorothy, for a reason. The people were friendly, the coffee was strong, and there was a HELP WANTED sign in the window. She found an ad for a Subaru mechanic on the bulletin board. And when the nice young man at the counter encouraged her to bring Patsy Cline inside instead of leaving her tied to the bench in front of the window, Mira realized how much easier it would be to stop than to keep driving into the night and the unknown.

Just for three months, she told herself then, and still did, every day. She'd unpacked her suitcase and started a new life, just like that. When time had passed and she was stronger, she would find a more appropriate job and living quarters.

In exchange for insanely cheap rent in a city so expensive, Mira opened the coffee shop at six a.m. sharp. The sharp part was her idea, as she awoke every morning at what Lannie called "pee thirty" anyway. Perimenopausal women and small dogs had equally small bladders, it seemed. Patsy Cline was lucky; she always got back to sleep after scrambling down the steps to the small patch of weeds and back up. Mira would lie awake fighting the repetitious screening of her miserable life, over and over, until four thirty or five when she might slip into a comatose state, only to be roused by the alarm minutes later.

Gus, the coffee shop's largely absentee, goateed owner, would hardly have noticed if she slept in and opened late. He hired her as soon as she said her former husband (the words nauseating at first) owned a coffee shop, as though that made her somehow credentialed in operating an espresso machine or cash register, when in fact she'd never touched either. Mira knew her advanced age and teaching experience hadn't hurt, either, considering the youth and demeanor of the baristas she now managed. For almost three years she'd been witness to all that happened at the Buzz through Parker's nightly venting sessions: the good, the bad, the really bad. Still, working in a coffee shop didn't seem that hard compared to managing a classroom of twenty-eight kids every day.

Unfortunately, she had none of the clout or authority she'd wielded at Pacifica K–12. Sure, the occasional student would try to ignore her or talk back, but in her classroom, she was the boss. She made the decisions, she planned the lessons, she sat kids where she wanted to seat them, told them when they could and couldn't speak, when they could and couldn't go to the bathroom, and for the most part, they listened. As a last resort, she could always threaten them with the principal's office, detention, suspension.

Gus didn't seem to care much about things like punctuality, customer service, cleanliness, or professionalism, and his motley staff knew it. And he was no kid, even though he dressed and acted like one. He was savvy enough to know when he'd stumbled across a stand-in, important when your life calling involved surfboards and snowboards rather than ensuring Mommy's investment was well managed.

Driving north on New Year's Day, Mira had imagined reinventing herself as a sleek, sophisticated divorcée, an irony not lost on her now as she pulled on jeans and a tight black T-shirt imprinted with a coffee cup orbiting the sun. When she found a full-time teaching job, she'd get the new clothes. At least she'd managed the haircut, losing the shoulder-length tent of hair that marked her as a mom, a wife. Her new style was asymmetrical, a bit ragged, and she'd thought it might help her fit in at the Coffee Shop at the Center of the Universe, where most of the help thought "older" meant she was in her thirties. Apparently, even that was just too old to know anything.

Mira lotioned her Serafino skin and tried to count her

blessings—good bone structure, a roof over her head—but the face in the mirror sagged in the gloomy way of, say, a basset hound, or a paint-by-number clown. She placed her finger over the scar on her cheek, swallowed against the ache she fought back every day, every minute.

Fuck him, she thought, *fuck his stupid blond girlfriend.* She sighed. She couldn't chase away images of Thea quite so easily. She hadn't made it twenty-four hours before breaking down and trying to call her to explain, to no avail. Thea wouldn't talk to her. Whenever Mira called the schoolhouse, she was told—after awkward scrambling and whispering—that Thea was busy, or out.

Did Thea take Parker's calls? Of course she did. Was she as angry at him for creating this situation? Somehow, Mira doubted it.

She gripped the edge of the sink and tried to take a breath deep enough to sustain her through the feeling that her chest might cave in. She took another breath, then another, and opened the medicine chest. Maybe a little blush, a few swipes of mascara and lipstick would help her look less horrible.

Mira sighed and turned away from the mirror. Eight hours on her feet and countless servings of coffee in its myriad forms would dull the pain for the time being, and then she'd just have to figure out how to get through the night. Again.

On her way out the door, she pulled her arms through the pilled and baggy cardigan she'd always thought of as her teaching sweater, and turned to check that the lights were off, that everything was in its place.

"Be good," she said to Patsy, who remained curled in a ball on the bed next to Mira's pillow. Over the bed hung her favorite piece of art, the sensual blue woman she'd miraculously thought to pack New Year's Day. Mira stood for a moment, looking at it, waiting there like a promise. Then she pulled the door behind her and steeled herself for a busy day.

Nineteen

"COULDN'T YOU JUST SAY HELLO TO HER?" LALI COVERED THE phone's mouthpiece with her hand. "She sounds so . . . forlorn."

For someone who spoke English as a second language, the girl had an annoyingly precise grasp of it. Thea wished she'd quit bugging her every single time her mother called. No one else even asked anymore; they just made up excuses for her.

Across the room, Zoe rolled her eyes in solidarity with Thea, but her older friend was starting to piss her off, too. She didn't get that this was a big deal. Her mother had fucked up. On top of that, she'd lied.

"Serafinos don't lie," Mira always said, sounding way too much like Nonna. "We tell the truth and we deal with the consequences." Thea had believed her, a thought that made her want to spit now. She'd never lied, not even to her parents, not really. Sometimes she didn't tell the entire truth, like she might say she'd been out at a party until two, then gone to a friend's house because that friend was upset over breaking up with some dude, and that would be the truth. Those circumstances would be the reason she was just getting home at four a.m., which was the question they asked. They never asked her directly what she'd been doing at the party, or with her upset friend, so she never felt compelled to tell them. They didn't really want to know the details anyway. Mira's MO was denial: just act like everything's okay, no matter what. No matter if you're angry or hurt or scared to death of something, just smile and say everything's "fine," a word Thea detested above all others.

Had the parentals asked what she did at parties, she might have actually told them she had a few beers, or smoked some bud, or tried E but hated it. That she'd lost her virginity to that jerk Aaron Rossi (god, she hoped he wasn't a cousin), but that she'd had safe sex. She wasn't a stoner or a skank, and she wasn't a loser. She didn't steal, hurt people on purpose, and she didn't lie. It only struck her now that, in fact, Mira had been a liar all along. Denial was lying, plain and clear.

Mira had lied to her, stolen her trust, and she'd hurt everyone—Nonna, poor old Grandpa, and especially Parker. Thea had always thought of her dad as solid, like one of the haystack rocks dotting the coastline, her mother as water swirling around him. Now Mira seemed to have turned to stone, and Parker was as deep and dark and mysterious as the Pacific. No matter how hurt or upset he had to be, he hadn't said one bad word about Mira. Well, actually, he hadn't said anything.

Thea sighed, walking along the beach road toward home. She'd hitched a ride into town with Ryan in a van packed with Woden merchandise to sell, feeling a little nervous to be in a vehicle so loaded with weed. She should be rehearsing with Colby and Damien, but her dad was lonelier than Thea had ever seen him, even when Mira had gone away for two weeks with her cousins to Maui that one time, just "the girls." Thea felt her fingers dig the quotation marks into her palms.

"Whore," she said. It sounded ugly. She'd never called her

mother anything that awful before, but Mira had never acted like this before. Now she wanted to pull Thea into her drama but Thea wasn't going to play that game. Mira left messages like "Tell her I tried," "Tell her I'm sorry," but fuck her. She clearly hadn't tried hard enough, and then she'd just split without a word to anyone. If her mother loved her, she'd prove it by coming back and making it up first to her husband, then to her father. *She can't ever make it up to me,* Thea thought, shivering against the surge of ocean wind. The house sat just ahead. *Besides, I'm finally free of her, for good.* That was what she'd wanted for so long, right? Just to be left alone so she could be herself and not some genetically predispositioned appendage of her mother? Thea exhaled and nodded. *Right.*

She stopped at the end of the driveway and rubbed her nose, runny from the cold and the big viscous lump of emotion that threatened to break through whenever she thought too much, but no way was she going to let it. Should she tell her dad that Mira had been calling? How could she tell him that his wife would rather talk to her daughter than her husband? No. Hell no. And that pissed her off, because now her mother was forcing her to lie, too.

Anger was good. She liked anger. She no longer felt like crying.

"Selfish whore," Thea muttered again, but it didn't feel all that convincing. She'd get used to it in time. As she walked toward the door, Ralphie appeared in the window, then Twiggy, looking so damn happy to see her that Thea couldn't fight the bitter lump in her throat. It wasn't sadness making her cry. Hell no. It was knowing that her mother could leave her, her only fucking daughter, and take that stupid little dog with her instead.

Twenty

——————•——————

By seven, the coffee shop was filled with murky daylight and noisy regulars: the corner table full of salty-voiced out-of-work fishermen who now loaded commercial vessels for a living. A multinational assortment of Seattle Pacific University students scattered in ones and twos. The serious young woman with the bulging spiral-bound journal who reminded Mira of Thea.

Already Mira had memorized their orders like the periodic table of elements: double shots of espresso dunked in cups of black coffee for the ship workers; white chocolate mochas and caramel lattes for the students. It seemed this age group had become the Starbucks generation, ordering complicated combinations of milk, coffee, and the myriad syrups stocked on the counter. *Whatever happened to a plain old cappuccino,* Mira wondered, *or just a really great cup of coffee?* The young woman with the notebook cheered her, though, as she always ordered a large pot of extra strong Earl Grey and a small pitcher of milk.

The rush seemed over for now. "Jarrett," Mira said to the back of a Cloroxed shag haircut beside her at the counter.

The dead-pale barista turned from his comic book to look at her, his Asian American eyes outlined in blue eyeliner.

"Dishes," she said. "Piling up. In back."

He feigned interest for half a second, then contorted his impossibly thin body into a question mark as he went back to reading. She could hear him mouth breathing. So much for her years of influencing young minds to do something other than read comics. So much for her position as manager. She wondered if Gus had forgotten to mention it to the rest of the help.

"Fine," she said. "Then you watch the front while I do them." His head moved slightly, a nod she supposed, but she actually liked washing the dishes, puttering around and cleaning spaces long neglected. It kept more than just her hands occupied.

Mira filled the dish sink behind the half-wall that separated front from back and lowered cups, saucers, spoons, pastry plates, pitchers, and teapots into the steaming water. She'd bypassed Gus's usual assortment of loud angry CDs this morning and put on Celia Cruz from the collection she kept in her car, and now Celia was wailing a fiery salsa tune. Mira hoped Patsy Cline couldn't hear upstairs, or soon she'd be frightening the customers. A slice of sun streamed through the wide front windows for just a moment, making the umber walls and wood floor glow, and all heads turned to hail it before it disappeared back into the gray. The heads turned back to their *Seattle Weeklies,* or computers, or conversations, and Mira turned back to the dishes.

Seattle seemed darker than Pacifica, more days obscured by cloud cover, if not rain, and Mira tried not to remember sunlight bouncing off sand, reflecting from ripples and waves, warming her through the great room windows in the afternoons. A moment of panic closed her throat and she dropped a stainless steel milk pitcher against the metal sink with a painful clang. Heat radiated from her chest to her neck to her head like a blossoming

mushroom cloud. Her face tightened, eyes involuntarily squeezing shut, and her morning coffee threatened to revolt and find
its way back into the outside world. Mira took a deep breath and
held it. There would be sunlight in Seattle, eventually. *Of course
there will be,* she thought, her breath easing back out through the
tiny slot her throat allowed. *And my daughter will talk to me again
someday.*

If only she could find more to fill her time so she wouldn't
have to think. She'd nixed the idea of substituting when she realized the city was filled with other unemployed teachers vying for
each shift. There were no full-time openings in the Seattle public
school system this late in the year and a long list waiting for those
that might open up next year. The private schools were worse,
and paid less.

For someone whose life had always been too busy, Mira was
at a loss. She couldn't read anything but the magazines left behind
by customers. Books, anything other than the briefest of articles,
left too much potential space to let in other thoughts. The small
furnished studio had no television.

"Sex!" she imagined Lannie saying, and while it vaguely
appealed to Mira to exact revenge using the same method her
husband had used to destroy their marriage, their family, she
snorted out loud. She'd never been less interested in anything.
She couldn't even muster up enthusiasm for El Wando, not even
as a distraction from her dismal life.

Mira's shift ended every afternoon at two, but she generally
busied herself with tasks until well after, though she never wrote
the extra hours on her time card. Gus was getting his ten-dollars-
per-hour managerial pay out of her, that was for sure. He paid
everyone else minimum wage, which had a lot to do with the skill
level of workers the job attracted.

Sometimes—most of the time—she came back down to the
shop after eating a can of tuna or soup for dinner, poured a cup
of decaf and logged on to an idle computer to look for jobs, or

more often, Fonso. She had a feeling that he might still need her as much as she now felt the need to find him. So far, though, she'd run into only dead ends.

She checked in on the Pacifica K–12 Web site, and, indeed, no other science teacher had been hired yet. She hadn't shown up for the second semester and they'd simply removed her eight-year-old photo, her name, her credentials and honors and awards, as though she'd never been there. Ed Pedersen's horn-rimmed and serious expression suggested victory.

She checked in on Thea through blogbaby.com, where Thea had long kept a running journal of her every emotion, if not the reasons behind them. At the height of Thea's craziness, Parker had found the blog site with their browser's history function and pointed it out to Mira. She then spent hours sorting through the multifarious teen-angst blogs of girls who cut themselves, girls who kissed other girls to turn boys on, girls who claimed to have a new breed of eating disorder called "ano-mia" where they alternately starved themselves and binged until they puked. It was exhausting. When she finally came upon Thea's, she knew it immediately by the 1940s pinup art Thea had used instead of her own photo. Where other teen drama queens posted way-too-sexy photos and bled their lives on the page, Thea merely kept a list of her daily emotions. A normal school day might list "bored" several times, then "mildly interested," then a confusing list that had to have referenced after-school hours: intrepid, gleeful, jacked, cruising, bruised not bleeding, worthless, buried. She hadn't checked it in months, but there were sporadic entries from before Christmas, aching disconsolate words that must have had something to do with her breakup from Alex. She'd never said a word about it to Mira.

Every day Mira considered logging on to the Cyber Buzz site, but she worried Parker would somehow know. He would feel her lurking miserable presence. He would know how much she missed him. She'd picked up the store phone to call him twelve times in the past three weeks, and hadn't once mustered the courage to finish dialing. Over and over she imagined the worried "Hello?" of New Year's Eve, wondering if he'd still sound that way, but after this long, she doubted it. Maybe if she'd have talked to him that night, he would have changed his mind, told her he'd been acting like an idiot, asked her to come home. Unless of course he'd had an overnight guest. She'd never know now, and it made no sense to even think about it. Time was creating more distance between them than she'd ever imagined possible. The only way she could survive was to keep moving forward.

Mira wiped perspiration from her forehead and the back of her neck with the towel she kept tucked into her apron, then stacked the last cup in the drainer and pulled the plug, chasing coffee grounds and tea leaves down the drain with the sprayer. She rested her palms against the steel sink, soap bubbles dribbling down her fingers, sweat dribbling down her sides beneath her T-shirt. "Don't think, don't think, don't think," she murmured. It did no good.

She would call Lannie again today. She'd been passing along messages to Thea, Al, and Nonna through her: *Please don't worry. I'll call soon. I'm sorry.* Even though she was still mad at all of them, guilt reigned supreme. Lannie said that when she relayed her messages, Al cried, Nonna demanded that Lannie tell her to come home, and Thea expressed nothing. As kind as Lannie was, Mira worried she'd break down and give them the number of the shop, or tell where she was. What would they do? Would Big Al come get her? Would Thea tell Parker where she was? *Yes,* Mira decided. Thea's favorite movie as a little girl had been that horrid Disney remake of *The Parent Trap;* she'd have some misguided plan to get them back together. And because Parker loved Mira, at some level, he would call, or come to Seattle, and if he saw her now, doing a teenager's job, dressed in a teenager's clothes, living in an apartment smaller than theirs in college, he'd feel guilty, he'd apologize, he'd . . . Well, he'd sound sorry for her. And that was the last thing she could stand.

Celia moved into a down-and-dirty Latin-blues number, and Mira smiled at one of the foreign students sitting alone, a tall, thin African boy in a white oxford shirt, nodding his head in time. And then there it was, a dissonant *eeeooo-eeeooo* sound, growing louder and more frantic until everyone looked up at the ceiling. Mira sighed and grabbed her keys. Patsy Cline was singing the blues.

Later, the after-lunch crowd snaked in a loose line back to the entrance, waiting to procure caffeinated insurance against nodding off in cubicles and afternoon meetings. Mira pulled double shots as quickly as she could, steamed two percent and soy and half-and-half for the health-oblivious. Jarrett sleepwalked through his orders as if in a dream. A small, polite Nicaraguan student, Felix—the young man she'd met the first day—had clocked in after his last class and washed dishes, replaced empty milk cartons with full ones, mopped up puddles tracked in every time the bells on the front door jangled. He bussed tables littered with napkins and cups and water glasses, carried the gray bus tub back to the sink, washed dishes. He might have been the best employee Gus ever hired, Mira thought, watching how hard he worked, how often he smiled. He was the kind of kid she and her friends would have thought cute in her college days, but never dated.

Mira loved this time of day best. Even though mornings were busy, they did not have this intensity. While workdays seemed to start anywhere from seven to nine a.m. as far as she could figure, everyone needed to be back on the job by one thirty each afternoon, or so it would seem from their wrist-flicking and watch-watching, finger-drumming and urgent ordering.

"What's the quickest thing you've got?" A thirtyish woman wearing pinstripes and a hoodie gripped the mosaic-tiled counter with chewed fingernails.

Jarrett's long thin arms rose slowly, palms floating upward. "Well . . ." he mused, looking thoughtful.

"Coffee," Mira said, sliding a to-go cup toward her. "Pour it yourself over there. That's a dollar fifty."

"Right," Jarrett said, and his next customer quickly scooted to Mira's side of the cash register.

Down the line, a familiar face caught Mira's eye, and they smiled at each other between customers. *Not a flirty-type smile,* Mira thought, *just nice.* Martin was a regular, a playwright who wrote in a studio half a block down, and he came in twice daily to fuel up.

"The usual," he said when it was his turn. "If you would be so kind." He laced his fingers together on the counter and leaned in. She smelled cologne, or whatever he used to tame his poodle crop of dark hair. No gray. She had no idea how old he was, but he was of a generation after hers. *If it is flirtation,* she thought, turning to pack ground espresso into the filter, *it's meant only for amusement. Give an old lady a thrill.* Still, it lifted her spirits every time—one of the few things that did these days. She poured a single espresso into a tall to-go cup, added a squirt of hot water, and turned to set it before him.

Martin, she had learned, liked a little coffee in his cream, and she watched as he poured steamed half-and-half into his cup from the pitcher she offered. Any other customer would have had to walk to the condiment bar for the cold stuff, but she liked talking to him.

"Your family have any history of heart disease?" she asked.

"My family would jump up and down applauding if I were to have a heart attack," he said, finally satisfied with the creamy beige of his coffee.

"Don't say that." Mira shuddered. She wondered if her family might feel the same way.

She would have asked why—what could this nice young man have done to deserve such a thing, and did family include wife, significant other?—but the militant herbalista with gray hippie hair standing behind him was working hard to catch Mira's eye

with her own stern ones. Mira resolved to talk more with him
another time, when it wasn't so busy. She watched him walk
toward the door, coatless in a room full of rain gear, then turn
and twiddle his fingers at her in a funny wave. Maybe they could
have coffee together. Maybe . . . *Jesus,* she thought, dumping the
espresso she'd poured out of routine. The evil-eyed woman always
ordered green tea chai with rice milk. *Am I that desperate for a little
human contact?*

Yes, she realized. Yes, she was. She didn't know why exactly she
liked this funny young man so much, other than he seemed to
like her, but she had a feeling they'd be able to talk to each other.
Maybe if she acted like a person completely unlike herself, she
could find the courage some morning to suggest he drop by for
coffee later after her shift. Not likely, but maybe.

She needed to be able to talk to someone. It had been nearly a
month since she'd had any kind of meaningful conversation at all,
except for the few quick chats with Lannie during lulls at work.
She'd felt guilty about using the phone, but she was going to tell
Gus to dock her for the long distance.

As the rush died down at a quarter till two, the back door
banged open, a raccoon-tanned Gus breezing in with wet boxes
of pastries meant for that morning. "Looks kinda slow," he said,
glancing around at mostly empty tables. Then he looked up at the
stereo speakers, frowning. "What is this noise?"

"Um, just one of the greatest cellists of all time," Mira said.
"You've never heard of Yo-Yo Ma?"

"Uh, no no, Ma." He laughed at his joke. "It's kind of stuffy,
don't you think?"

"Fine, I'll put the very unstuffy Nine Inch Nails back on and
scare away all your customers over thirteen."

"Hey, Jeremy," he said to Jarrett, who looked up from his
comic book. "You like Nine Inch Nails, don't you? You're over
thirteen."

Jarrett's shoulders began the slow ascension toward a shrug.

"I just thought that—" Mira began.

"I didn't hire a pain in the ass, did I, Mira?" Gus squinted at her, then smiled. "Just giving you shit. Can you stay a little longer today? I need to get some P-Tex burned into a nasty scratch on my board, before the snow on Stevens Pass gets rained away." He tugged on his goatee, a nervous habit she noticed whenever he was trying to find a way out of working.

"I guess I could," she said, glad he was leaving. She might as well get paid for what she would have done anyway. She had big plans for reorganizing the production line so it was more efficient. She and Jarrett were always bumping into each other, and nothing at the Coffee Shop at the Center of the Universe was in its logical place. Especially not her.

On Thursday evening, Mira sat in front of the computer that she'd come to think of as hers. Customers seemed to acknowledge this as well. Somehow, everyone who entered the Coffee Shop at the Center of the Universe considered Mira the boss, except for the employees.

Trying a new search engine, Mira typed in her brother's name. No Fonso. No Al Junior. No fellow black sheep family member with whom to lick her wounds. She'd exhausted the entire freaking Internet. So much for worldwide anything. She'd have to figure out a different way to find him, because if she didn't, that was it. He was her last chance at family.

The bells on the front door jingled, and out of habit Mira looked up. Martin cocked his head at her and smiled, walking toward her instead of the counter. She'd never seen him in the shop at night.

He smiled his nice, easy smile. He had the perfect teeth of the orthodontic generation, that no-child-left-behind approach that occurred somewhere between her childhood and Thea's. Tonight he wore a brown wool coat—not unlike Thea's vintage prized possession—and a brightly knit Nepalese hat with earflaps that he quickly pulled off, trying to smooth his springy hair down in the process. "What, do you live here, too?"

"As a matter of fact, I do," Mira said, clicking the red X to close the screen she'd been looking at. "I like your hat."

He stuffed it in his pocket. "It keeps my ears warm." Indeed, they looked warm now, having turned pink along with his face.

Mira chewed her lip, wishing she'd changed out of her work clothes before coming back down. "So," she said, wondering if he could see the pulse tapping in her neck. "Why don't you have a cup of coffee with me? Keep me company." There, she'd done it.

"Oh, I'd love to, but—"

"No, that's okay. Really—" *Christ,* Mira thought. *Why couldn't I just have said hello?*

"No, I really would like to, but I'm just picking up a couple of hot chocolates to go. I have a friend out in the car, and, um, we're just on our way to a movie, over at the Egyptian." He cleared his throat. "That new one with Philip Seymour—"

"Oh, great, yeah, that's supposed to be really good." Mira nodded too hard. "You'd better hurry, then. I'm just working on this project and actually, I should probably—"

"Oh, sorry, I didn't mean to disturb you, I jus—"

"No! I mean, no, of course you didn't." Mira wondered how miserable she looked. *Please leave,* she thought. *Please.*

"Okay, well." He nodded toward the counter where blue-haired Sequoia thumb-wrestled with Felix instead of stocking the cups as she'd asked her to. "Guess I'll go . . ."

Mira smiled a tight fake smile.

"See you in the morning?" He backed away.

"Mm hmm!" Mira kept her lips tight, nodding, then pretended to busy herself on the keyboard, not looking back at him. When he'd gotten his drinks and gone, Mira shut down the computer and sighed.

Sequoia was now talking on her lime green cell phone behind the counter, examining her cuticles, while Felix wiped down tables.

Mira walked over and stood in front of her, the heavy scent of patchouli filling the space between them. She stood there until Sequoia frowned and said, "What?"

In her best patient-but-authoritative teacher tone, Mira said, "I need you to get off the phone and restock the cups. It has to be done tonight so we have cups in the morning."

Sequoia tilted her head, a smirk sliding across her lips as she handed Mira the phone. "Say hello," she said.

What kind of crap was she trying to pull? Mira took the phone and put it to her ear. She thought she had a pretty good bullshit detector but she hadn't run into a kid like Sequoia in a long time. "Hello?"

"Who's this?" a voice said. A familiar male voice.

"Oh, Gus. Hi." She could beat Sequoia at this game. "It's Mira. Listen, I was just trying to encourage Sequoia to restock the cups so we'd have some for the morning." She was impressed at how matter-of-factly she said it.

Sequoia snatched back the phone, rolling her eyes. "I was just about to. Shit, you'd think the place was going to fall apart or something. I mean, I've worked here like almost a year. I think I know when to restock the stupid cups, dude, right? You know?" She laughed and shot Mira a dagger of a look before turning away and lowering her voice so Mira could no longer hear. Apparently she and Gus were friends.

Lovely, Mira thought. She was tempted to restock the stupid cups herself, but she'd already worked a ten-hour day. She called good night to Felix and walked out into the dark, looked up the steps, trying to think of the small room at the top as home.

Twenty-one

THE FOLLOWING WEEK, WITH HER FIRST-OF-FEBRUARY PAYCHECK, Mira decided to purchase the cheapest cell phone available in the electronics department at the Fred Meyer store down the road in Ballard. With the pay-as-you-go plan, she could pay just ninety-nine cents on only those days she wanted to make calls. She stood at the glass display case, holding the charcoal oblong at arm's distance, trying to see the tiny print on the phone's face. "Can you read this?" she asked what looked to be a twelve-year-old salesclerk.

"Um, yeah," the girl said, hitching the side of her lowrider jeans up over a sizable midriff. "But a lot of, um, older people, like this model"—she pointed a sparkly blue fingernail at a more expensive phone in the case—"because it has the biggest numbers."

"This one will be fine," Mira snapped. She'd been wondering if she needed glasses, but she shouldn't take it out on this . . . this child, who was younger even than Thea. And if this girl could be considered a "wireless expert" as her ASK ME! badge proclaimed, why couldn't Thea do something normal, get a regular job like everyone else? *Like what,* she thought, *waiting on old cranky people at Fred Meyer, schlepping out coffee for minimum wage?* Mira sighed and shook her head, then realized the girl would think it was at her. She tried to smile. "Is it possible to get an unlisted number?"

"Um, I think so," she said. "I'd better go check with my manager, though."

She shuffled across the dirty linoleum toward the checkout desk and another young woman with impossibly low-waist pants, tattered and muddy at the bottom. They conferred until the "manager" shrugged (Mira wondered what her badge proclaimed), then picked up a phone and dialed. *Who now,* Mira thought, *Fred himself?*

Half an hour later, Mira had a brand-new cell phone, a Seattle phone number that both girls promised would display only as "private caller," cute red plastic reading glasses from the rack at the pharmacy, a new chew toy for Patsy, and a pair of low-rise jeans that had nearly skimmed the floor over her red clogs in the dressing room. They'd been on sale for fourteen dollars, and she was getting tired of wearing the same pair all the time. Besides, she was starting to see why Thea always called her pants "mommy jeans": the tight high waist, the peg legs, the light blue wash seemed horribly old-fashioned all of a sudden. Seeing as most of her bulges were well below hip level, she doubted she'd be pulling the new ones up constantly in front of customers, and they didn't look half bad on her. What would Parker think if he could see her in them? She grimaced and tried not to think about it.

As she passed through the wall of glass doors into drizzle and the fish smell of the empty trawlers along the canal, another thought surprised her: *I bet Martin will like them.*

That night, instead of returning to the coffee shop, Mira sat in her apartment, though "apartment" was too grand a word for the place. The kitchen appliances took up one wall, the bed the other. In between, a tiny bathroom was crammed next to a tinier closet. Beneath the window sat a small chintz love seat, and next to it a café table and chair from downstairs, which she sat at now, holding the cell phone. She'd already washed her dinner dishes—a bowl and a spoon—and recycled the soup can. She couldn't put it off much longer. Thank god her will to break through to her daughter was stronger than her aversion to rejection. Most of the time.

She'd call Lannie first, to warm up for Thea. She punched in Lannie's number, but couldn't make out which button to push next. "Fuck," she said, extracting the reading glasses from the plastic Fred Meyer bag on the table. After sliding them on, her peripheral vision glowed red. Perhaps the senior citizen wire rims would have been a more practical choice, she thought. The phone's buttons, however, came magically into view, slightly enlarged and disturbingly askew. Is this what it would be like from here on out? Seeing the world through lenses that distorted the way things really looked? She moaned and removed the glasses as the call began to ring through.

"Hey, stranger," Lannie said.

"You know who I am? Goddamn it!"

"Excuse me, is this the psycho I think it is? Honey, what the hell are you up to now?"

"Nothing, I just . . . Jesus motherfucker."

"Charming."

"God, I'm . . . I'm sorry. I just got this new phone, and . . ." She cleared her throat. "Lannie. Hello. How are you?"

"Worried sick. How do you think I am? How are you? Not too good by the sound of it."

"I will act normal if you just tell me exactly what you see on your caller ID."

"I see a lost and weary traveler who needs to get her sweet ass back home before she totally screws up her life, that's what I see."

"Humor me." Mira tried not to think about the words "lost" and "weary." "Besides, I already screwed up my life."

"Don't say that. Parker—"

"No," Mira said, sharply. "We don't talk about him. What's on your goddamn caller ID?"

"My goodness, we're testy."

Mira heard the hurt in Lannie's voice, but she'd had enough disastrous relationships of her own—she should know Parker was the last thing Mira needed to hear about right now.

"Okay, okay; let's see. It says: Serafino, M., 206-635—"

"Fuck!" Mira yelled, and Patsy Cline jumped to her feet from beneath the table and began to bark.

"What on earth?" Lannie said. "Is everything all right?"

"Shh, Patsy," Mira said, picking up the dog to sit in her lap. Patsy licked her face, the phone, her fingers, then settled. "I'm sorry, but those stupid teenagers promised me . . ." Mira hugged Patsy against her torso a little too tightly. "I just don't want anyone to know where I am. Not yet. Especially Thea. You know she'd tell Parker, and my dad."

"She's talking to you?"

"No, god no. I'm still evil incarnate. I just need to hear her voice, to hear if she really hates me."

"Oh, she loves you and you know it. And besides, who cares if anyone knows you're calling from Seattle? It's a big city. It's not like they're going to be able to track you down just because they know your number."

She was right. "Please don't tell anyone anything yet. Please, Lannie."

Lannie sighed loudly. "I haven't yet, have I? And let me tell you, they're not making it easy on me." She chuckled. "Your father is especially persuasive."

"I'll call him so he quits bugging you." Mira paused. "What's, you know . . . what's everybody saying?" She hadn't let herself ask this question before. She wasn't sure why she was asking it now.

Lannie was quiet for a moment. "You know how people are, especially in this town. You can't let it bother you."

"Lannie."

"There was a little mention in the *Trib*."

"The *Tribune!*" Mira squeezed her eyes shut. That goddamn Luke Pitt. "What exactly did they say?"

"Mostly just that you had left your teaching job rather abruptly. It hinted at a kind of, well, a breakdown of some sort. Erratic behavior witnessed by unnamed sources."

"How on earth can they print gossip?"

"Ever since the Pitts took over, it's more like the *Enquirer* every day. You know that."

"Apparently, I'm the only one who doesn't know that."

"People who know you know better, honey, that's the important part." She paused. "Actually, Missy Baker's been very vocal about not judging you until . . . Well, until people know more."

"Isn't anybody talking about Parker and his little friend?" Mira felt testy again, and she wished she could control this new venomous side of her. Hormones, shmormones. This was more like being poisoned.

"They just feel sorry for the guy, to tell you the truth. Parker's just being Parker, going to work, going to council meetings, eating alone at the Driftwood. Honey, he's always alone, except that he takes those two goddamn dogs everywhere with him. It's really pretty pathetic."

"Of course he isn't going to trot out the new girlfriend until an acceptable amount of time has passed." Still, she was touched he'd kept Ralph and Twiggy. She'd assumed he'd haul them right back to the shelter.

"Well, there does not appear to be a new girlfriend, and you should probably know that quite a few people heard the message you left on my store machine the day you left. You do remember I do a special stitch-and-bitch on New Year's Day, right? First of the month and all?" She cleared her throat. "I, uh, keep the volume up real loud on the machine, in case I'm too busy to answer, which I was that day. It was only the ferals that heard, but they can be a chatty bunch."

Mira froze. What had she said? Something about sex and drugs, and murder; god knew what else. She'd sounded crazy. Mira pressed the phone hard against her temple. She was tired of this conversation. "I have to go, Lannie. I need to gather my thoughts before I call Thea."

"Can I at least come see you?" Lannie asked, and Mira closed her eyes.

"Not yet," she said, "not until I've figured a few things out." Like a decent job, a decent living arrangement, hopefully in Vancouver with Fonso. "Besides, you can't leave the shop."

"Sure I can," Lannie said. "It's just a shop."

Mira sniffed. "You're the best friend I ever had, Lannie."

"Okay, now I gotta go. You're getting all gooey on me."

"Sorry I'm such a psycho."

"Ah, hell. I just figure it's your turn. You were always so damn sane."

When they'd hung up, Mira sat staring at the phone. Without glasses it was just a piece of plastic with indecipherable markings. It had no heft. It was too light in her palm to be anything other than just another thing in her purse, like a tin of mints, a hairbrush. She'd put far too much importance in it, Lannie was right. So she was in Seattle. If anyone came looking for her, they'd call the high schools, then the middle schools. They'd check respectable apartment buildings, rental units. They'd never guess she now spent her life making coffee at the Center of the Universe.

A call to Woden meant another rejection, and when Thea finally decided to talk to her, she could only imagine the hurt and anger in her voice.

But Mira had an ace in the hole: Big Al. Maybe if she talked to him, she could steel herself for another call to Thea. So what if he had a girlfriend? Even though he didn't appear to need her

anymore, she couldn't deny that she yearned for his big boom-
ing voice, his "I'll love you no matter what" assurances. Maybe
later she'd write Nonna a letter trying to explain why she'd had
to leave home, why she had to start over. How her whole world
had changed in a matter of two days and she could no longer be
the person she was in Pacifica. There was no way they'd ever be
able to have that or any kind of meaningful conversation on the
phone. Mira had suspected Nonna of lipreading for years.

Mira dialed the number she'd known ever since her dad made
her memorize it in kindergarten.

"Hello?" A woman's voice.

Fuck, Mira thought. What, was she living there already?

"Hello?" the woman said again. "Hello?"

"Hi, is my, um, is Al there?"

"May I tell him who's calling, please?"

Mira sighed. "His daughter."

"Oh my goodness!"

Mira heard the phone knock against something hard. It would
be the harvest gold linoleum counter beneath the old wall phone
Al had never exchanged for a new cordless model. More fumbling
sounds, and then her father, breathing heavily, as though he'd run
across the room, and Mira worried she'd give him a heart attack.

"Honey, honey, is that you? Where are you? Are you all
right?"

"Dad, I'm fine. I just—"

She could hear his gulping sounds; he was trying to stifle his
crying.

"I'm sorry, Daddy, really, I didn't mean to . . . to upset anyone,
I just . . ."

There were more fumbling sounds, and then the woman
again. "Hello? Your father just needs a moment. It's Mira, isn't it?
Like your mother?"

How much did this woman know about her, Mira wondered,
about her mother? "Yes. And you are?" She sounded churlish but

how could she be all warm and chatty with this woman she'd seen only once from across the room?

"Well, I'm sorry, that was rude of me, wasn't it? I'm Dottie. Your father has told me so much about you. He's had a pretty rough time of it. It's good you called."

"I'm not so sure. He sounds pretty upset."

"You can understand, can't you? You have a daughter yourself; in fact, I've met her and she's a delight."

Mira tried to picture this. When? Under what circumstances? She hadn't factored that life would go on without her in Pacifica. When she left, she'd somehow pictured everything there freezing in time until she was ready for it to come back to life, with or without her.

"Can I please talk to my father? I don't care if he's upset."

"Al? You okay? Okay, then, here he is," the woman said. "We all hope you come home soon."

Mira ignored the "we." After more fumbling sounds, a whisper, her father said, "Hello?" He sounded small, fragile.

"Daddy," Mira said, "I'm sorry I worried you so much." Of course he would have freaked out. Hadn't he been through enough with Fonso? God, with his wife dying? Mira squeezed her eyes shut. "I should have called you sooner. I'm sorry."

"Mirabella," he choked, then cleared his throat. "Honey, please come home. Whatever Parker's done, you have to forgive him. Guys are different than ladies. Sometimes they do stupid things, but it doesn't mean we don't love our wives, our families. We just make mistakes sometimes."

How did he know? Had Parker told him? Not likely. She didn't like his tone, the way he pleaded with her. *Jesus,* she thought, even as she tried to calm him down. *What is he trying to tell me?*

"Dad, I promise I'll call you every week." Her stomach had turned sour, but she did her best to convince him she was fine, everything would be fine. Thank god he and Dottie were late for bingo in Rockaway. Their conversation was short, and when Mira hung up, she knew she'd hurt him more than she'd thought she was capable of and chosen not to notice until now. The old Mira would never have done that—she took everyone's feelings into consideration before trimming her toenails, for god's sake.

But the father she used to know was the way she thought husbands should be: faithful, devoted, too starry-eyed in love with their wives, their families, to even notice anyone else. Had there been other Dotties before this, women he'd never told anyone about? God, while her mother was still alive? Was that why he was so good at deception—he'd had practice?

Mira closed her eyes at the familiar rawness in her throat, the pain in her chest, the hole between her ribs and stomach widening to incorporate this new awareness.

Next, she tried calling directory assistance in Vancouver, BC; they had no listings for Fonso. She could try different cities in British Columbia, work her way across Canada, even—but she had to face the fact he'd disappeared, and probably on purpose. She entirely understood.

The room had gone dark, and Patsy had fallen asleep after a few good romps around the apartment with her new toy. Mira's back was stiff from sitting in the straight-back chair. She stood and stretched, then walked to the window, looking down over the small graveled area they used as an employee parking lot. Rain pelted the cars, hers and Sequoia's old Barracuda, which was precisely the electric blue of her hair. Felix had no car; he walked to work. Light from the store's back windows reflected off the scraped bare metal of the Subaru's passenger side door. It would rust, and soon, Mira realized. She had to get it fixed but she hated to keep depleting Thea's trust fund. The alternator had cost six hundred and thirty-two dollars.

Cold blue-tinged headlights turned into the lot, followed by Gus's black SUV. Mira pulled back and behind the curtain, watching as Gus and two men got out of the car and entered the coffee shop. He often came by at closing time, or even later at night.

Almost always with other people. He was the owner, after all. He probably needed to check on things, maybe even to supervise Sequoia's reconciling of the till. Mira turned away, thinking, *No way.* Gus never supervised anything but his own good time.

She grabbed her good coat—the only one she still had possession of—and Patsy Cline's leash. The dog woke and sprang to all fours, dancing and yipping like her namesake.

"Come on, sweetie," Mira said, clipping the leash to her collar. "Let's take a little walk."

She picked Patsy up to descend the steps as quietly as possible. Even so, Patsy panted and squirmed in her arms. "Shh," Mira whispered. "We have to be very quiet."

She first took Patsy to the weed patch, waiting as light rain tapped her head, her shoulders. Patsy obliged by squatting, but Mira doubted she peed. She just knew she'd get a "good girl" out of Mira by doing so. "Come on," Mira whispered, tugging on the leash. Patsy resisted. "Okay, okay. Good girl, Patsy, good girl." The dog wagged her tail and allowed Mira to lead her under the awning at the back of the building.

Two windows framed the purple back door—one in the storeroom and one in the kitchen. Mira walked to the side of the kitchen window on the right, trying to get a decent view without standing in front of it. Her heart pounded, but she didn't know why. If someone saw her or came outside, she was just walking Patsy. Maybe she was coming in for her usual decaf.

From her vantage point she could see only Felix at the dish sink. Mira shook her head. That poor kid did all the work when he shared a shift with Sequoia. She craned her neck a bit and, sure enough, Sequoia sat at a table out front, talking to an older man and a younger one. They looked like father and son. The storeroom window to the left lit up, and Sequoia stood, as if summoned, and walked over. Felix had finished the dishes and was filling the mop bucket. Something had to be done about Sequoia, but Gus seemed a little too chummy with her to be able to act like a boss.

She tugged Patsy's leash again and sidled over to the storeroom window, the lower half mostly obscured by boxes of supplies on a shelving unit. She couldn't see anything but the gunmetal gray safe next to the freezer, and two pairs of old wooden skis Gus stored there.

The window scraped open and Mira jumped, then pulled Patsy back into the rain and toward the steps. What was she doing spying on people, on her co-workers? Her boss. Her landlord. As she sneaked up the first few stairs, voices filtered out into the damp cold air, then laughter, then the smell of marijuana smoke.

How unprofessional—an employer who smoked pot with his friends in front of his employees. She should have known, just looking at Gus. He was a party kind of guy.

Mira stopped and breathed in, remembering the burn in her throat, the taste on her tongue. What if she just ambled in and joined the party? One of the men downstairs was far older than she was. Maybe he was one of those old hippie guru guys that never went mainstream. *I don't think so,* Mira thought, *not in those Sansabelt slacks.* But it was Fremont, after all.

She thought about going back down and making an excuse to go in, but pushed that thought away as quickly as it came. Just because she was living among pot-smoking slackers didn't mean she had to become one.

Later, Mira lay in bed, listening to the rain against the roof and Patsy wheezing and snorting beside her. When she'd finally summoned the courage to call Woden, the boy who answered the phone said, after much hemming and hawing, that Thea wasn't at home. Do you know when she might be, she'd asked. Not really, he said. She could tell it wasn't Clark, and thank god not that Pitt boy. Can you give her a message, she asked. Well, okay, he said, a bit too noncommittal for comfort. He sounded stoned, but Mira said, as slowly as possible: "Do you have a pen? Write these exact words: 'Your mom needs to talk to you. Call her cell phone as soon as you can.'" She'd given him the number, made him repeat it back. It was the teacher in her; anything said aloud was more likely to stick. Who knew whether or not Thea would call, but it was all she could do.

Patsy's snoring reached fever pitch and Mira reached over and rolled her to her other side. How long could she live this way, inside this empty hole? Living in this noisy city wasn't helping. The only time she couldn't hear traffic through the thin walls was at three, four in the morning, like now. Even before dawn filtered in the window, cars would be coursing by, spinning their tires if it was raining, which it usually was; honking horns if traffic was congested, which it always was. She tried not to think about the cloud of carbon monoxide she must be living in, after always having lived in such a pristine, beautiful environment. Once light broke, the crows would start up their cawing and complaining and it would be time to get up and begin again.

Mira tried to find something else to think about, anything— how many pounds of decaf she needed to tell Gus to order, what color curtains she should get with her next paycheck—but her thoughts kept returning to the empty space Patsy couldn't fill on the other side of the bed. She hated sleeping alone. No warm body to turn toward her when she reached, nowhere to warm her feet, no hip to drape her arm over, no comforting sound of a beloved sleeping. She missed Parker's chest the most at times like these. She had nowhere to burrow her head, no place to breathe in the comfort of another. Vasopressin, she tried to remind herself. The pair-bonding chemical that males emitted—that's all it really was. Not the person himself who no longer loved her the way she loved him. She had to get used to the fact that even if she'd never left Pacifica, she'd have been just as abandoned.

Mira pushed herself into a sitting position and stared into the dark. She would never get to sleep now. It was the week of sweaty insomnia that preceded her period; she'd been away from home for an entire cycle.

She almost wished she were living in the house in Woden,

hanging out with so many people you could never get lonely. Dancing around fires, making music, taking mind-altering substances that helped you see the truth. As much as she hated to admit it, if someone offered her mushrooms right that moment, she would take them, gladly, to experience that feeling Thea had described on New Year's Day.

She pictured her daughter, sleepy-eyed and happy, letting Mira hug her, her voice so earnest as she tried to tell her this thing she knew her mother needed to hear: "It's just like you can see, all of a sudden ... Like everything is so beautiful, and perfect, even if it's not."

Twenty-two

DUNGIES DIPPED IN LEMON BUTTER. GRILLED STEAK WITH ONIONS. Spaghetti Bolognese, with real fucking meat sauce, not that soy stuff that tasted like hamster pellets. Thea missed real food. At Woden, there was no eating anything with a face. Not even mussels or clams, which she was pretty sure did not have faces, not even microscopic ones. Now there was talk of going all raw, but so far there were plenty of votes against it. Zoe was leading the charge in favor. She could smoke cigarettes, take tabs of E like they were candy, but she couldn't eat a cooked vegetable. Sometimes Thea wondered about her choice in friends. She always seemed to end up with the tips of the fringe. Like Alex.

Here at home she could eat anything she wanted to, although with Mira gone, she had to make it herself. She was beginning to suspect her dad was going a little over the edge. He ate out for most meals that Thea didn't prepare or that the neighbors or Grandpa and his new girlfriend didn't invite him for. His hair had grown scruffier than she'd ever seen it, and it didn't appear to have been washed lately. His clothes didn't exactly stink or anything, but they were rumpled. He'd always insisted on ironing everything, even jeans, something she teased him about mercilessly. And he'd started talking to the dogs the way Mira did, as if they were four-legged humans who actually understood full sentences, who might even answer a question like, "What's my good boy want for dinner, huh, Ralphie?"

"Dad," Thea called into the front room. "Dinner."

And since when did he hang out in the front room to read, or more often, stare into space? Ever since they'd finished the remodel, he'd loved his prized high-tech recliner in the new great room, but he didn't sit there anymore. Now he sat on the cats' chair in the front room, for some bizarre reason. The seat of his pants was perpetually covered in cat fur, something Thea was sure made the employees at Cyber Buzz nervous, along with all his other odd new behaviors: his quiet staring, finger tapping, his forgetfulness. Her cousin Joey's best friend Tim was one of Parker's techs, and he said they'd been paid twice the last pay period. Thea had to threaten cutting them all off from the Woden weed supply before he'd promise to tell Parker about the mistake.

Thea arranged their plates on the breakfast bar, the forks on the left with a napkin, the knives and spoons on the right. She'd always loved setting the table: the fork was the mom, the knife the dad, the spoon the child. The plate was the family's world—the mother and father partnering up on the tough parts, the child dipping into the sweetness of dessert at the end. Thea felt a rawness open at the back of her throat as she filled water glasses and set them to the right of the father and child. Why had she paired herself with her father? Wouldn't most kids, most daughters, have thought of the knife as the mother, so close by, and the father on the other side? Idiotic. She was just being a sentimental weirdo. Inside the fridge she found a six-pack of Rogue Ale, no doubt left over from the Christmas Eve party. She uncapped one bottle for each of them, then called out again: "Dad?"

He walked in carrying one of the cats in his arms like a baby. He'd always made a point of ignoring the cats as much as possible, saying, "Cats are outdoor animals. They're only good for one thing: mousing," like he still lived on the Kansas farm he'd been raised on. Now he palmed the cat's exposed belly, tickling her chest as she purred.

"I made Nonna's spaghetti," Thea said.

"Oh. Okay." He bent down to place the cat on the floor, then took his seat. He picked up his fork, set it on his plate, picked up his napkin and smoothed it over his right thigh, then squared his knife to the plate, touched his glass of water.

Thea resisted the urge to sigh.

"It's your favorite, right?"

"What?"

"Spaghetti. It's your favorite, isn't it?"

"Oh, yeah, honey. Thanks." He picked up his fork again and poked at the noodles, then twirled a few around the tines and placed them in his mouth. He looked as though he were chewing sand.

"Is it okay?" Thea tasted it herself—maybe she oversalted it, or forgot some crucial ingredient, but no, it was fine. Not quite like Mira made it, but not horrible.

"Yeah, it's good." Parker placed his fork on the plate, rearranged his napkin.

"Um, guess what? I got a gig." She'd been saving this news until they were seated. It was pretty much the best thing that had ever happened in her life. Lannie had been completely stoked.

"Hmm?" Parker looked at her.

"Gig, Dad. I got a job playing music. The Blue Cow. They're going to pay us and everything." Ten bucks a person wasn't much, but it was a start. Even Lannie had said so.

"That's great, honey. Really great." Parker nodded, then fell silent again.

Thea felt the sigh before she could stop it, sounding way too much like her mother. He hadn't even heard her. She took a swig of beer, then set the bottle down hard. "Dad. You're freaking me out, all right?"

He looked at her. "What do you mean?"

"You're not . . . you. You're acting weird." She hesitated, chewing her lip. She'd never spoken to him like this before, but nothing like this had ever happened before. "It's like aliens have stolen your brain and left your body behind, because you're not taking very good care of it, you're all wrinkly and you're not eating, and you're acting all *oooo-oooo*"—here Thea made ghostly movements with her hands in front of her face before covering her eyes and dropping her chin to her chest, shoulders heaving. Why the fuck was she crying? She was mad, mad at Mira, not him. Not sad, not the crying kind of sad. "I mean, I know this is really hard for you and all, but you never talk about it, or—"

She heard a snuffle and looked up to see his chin trembling, his eyes pooled.

"I'm sorry, honey, I'm so sorry. I've ruined everything."

"No—"

"I don't want to chase you away, too."

I'm the one who did the chasing, she thought, which made her cry harder.

"No, god, Dad, I didn't mean . . . I'm not going to go away or anything." She picked up her napkin and blew her nose. "I'm just saying . . . I don't know. Don't you want to talk about it, or . . . something? If not with me, then maybe with someone else?"

Who would that be? she wondered. It wasn't like there was a shrink in town, and if there were, no one would go because then everyone would talk. And what did he mean that he ruined everything? He was still here, wasn't he? He hadn't run away; he hadn't deserted anybody.

Parker shook his head. "This is just something I have to do alone, Thea. I made this mess. I have to deal with it."

What mess did you make? she wanted to ask. *What went wrong?*

Whose fault is this? There were so many things she wanted to know but she was afraid to hurt him any further, or to tell him about her fight with Mira. Maybe she shouldn't have been so mean to her that last day. Maybe she should have tried to be more understanding.

Fuck, she thought. Maybe Mira would be living at Grandpa's right now, or with Lannie or something. Maybe they could have worked it out. Goose bumps rose on her neck, her arms.

She had to talk to Lannie. She'd know what to do. Plus, once Thea told her how creepy Parker was being, she'd talk to him and get him back on track, too. Hell, knowing Lannie, she'd fix the whole thing.

Lannie had opened her front door to Thea so many times after an argument with her parents that it had become almost a joke between them.

"What, you again?" Lannie said that night when Thea was fifteen, mock exasperation in her voice, but when Thea didn't just start babbling as usual, she grew serious. "Come in here, come on. What's going on? Are you all right?"

Thea had felt herself on the edge of something hard, something irrevocable, but she had no words for it. "I just fucking hate her," she'd said, hearing the tears in her voice and hating that, too. "I have to leave. I have to get out of there."

Trevor sat in front of the TV playing Super Mario, wearing a too-big Nirvana T-shirt and Darth Vader boxers. He didn't look up until Lannie shooed him out of the room, saying, "Honey, Thea and I need some girl time. Go practice your arpeggios or something. And for god's sake, put some pants on. We have company."

"It's just Thea," he grumbled, but he gave her a little wave before shuffling his skinny legs and oversized feet back to his room.

"Now sit down and tell me what's going on." Lannie threw a pair of sweat pants and a tattered copy of *Rolling Stone* to the floor to make a place for Thea on the couch and sat next to her. "What happened?"

"I told her I thought Bill Clinton should be castrated." Thea smirked in spite of herself. That had been a good one.

"What on earth?" Lannie said. "Why would you torture your poor mother like that?"

"She's so full of shit. How can you even be her friend? I mean, she thinks it's so great that you're a musician and all, but I'm not allowed to even think about not going to college, about not being some perfect version of what she thinks a daughter should be. She wants to ruin my life before I even start it."

"Why are you thinking about college already? Hell, you haven't even gotten laid yet. Let's take life one step at a time."

Thea snorted. Good old Lannie. "I know, but she's got it all planned out. My whole life, practically. She thinks playing music is a good 'hobby.'" Thea made the quotation marks in the air with her fingers. "She says I have to focus more on studying, or joining stupid clubs or doing sports, and if I want to do music I have to play in the school band. I can't play in that stupid band. Mr. Thompson is the biggest loser on the planet and they do songs like 'Tequila Sunrise.'" She turned to face Lannie. "I'm good, right? You think I could be a real musician, don't you? Instead of wasting my life in school forever? How can I go to college? All my best years will be gone by the time I get out."

Lannie tried to hide her smile as she tucked a loose strand of Thea's hair behind her ear. "Your best years will extend far beyond twenty-two, my little drama queen. And I think you need to at least consider what your mother's saying. I would never ever tell you to do anything against her wishes, you know that, right?"

Thea nodded.

Lannie sighed. "But, yeah. I think you have the chops to be a musician, but you gotta know, it's a tough life. Not for the pansy-assed."

"I know." Thea rubbed her nose. "I don't care."

"Well, but you have to listen to your parents right now because you're still just a kid and they really do care about you. They may even know a thing or two, believe it or not."

Thea shrugged. She doubted it.

"Who knows what will happen in the next, what, three, four years? You're not going away to college tomorrow. Can we just agree that you will see how you feel about it when you get closer to it? You can keep practicing in the meantime, keep writing."

Thea nodded. She sighed and relaxed back into the sofa.

She loved Lannie's house. It was so messy and comfortable. She didn't mind if you put your feet on the couch or the coffee table, even with shoes on. She only did the dishes like every week or so, artfully piling stacks of plates and bowls on every surface in the kitchen until they were completely out of things to eat on. Even then they might use paper plates for a few days.

"Do you want a Coke?" Lannie stood, scratching one big long arm, then stretched them both overhead with a yawn, nearly touching the ceiling. "I could use a little sugar rush myself."

A Coke at eight p.m. Another thing Mira would never have allowed, even though Thea was more than old enough to make those kinds of decisions for herself.

"No, thanks," Thea said. "I just really don't want to go back there."

"I know." Lannie smiled at her, shook her head. "But you have to." As she walked away, she said, "You really said that about the president of the United States?"

Thea snorted. "Only to piss her off. She doesn't even get why I'm mad at her."

"Well, that's easy," Lannie called from the kitchen. "Tell her. Just, you know. So she gets it."

Thea closed her eyes and shook her head against the soft upholstery. Why should she have to tell her? She let out a long sigh, wishing she could lie down and sleep right there, and never have to go home again.

Twenty-three

MIRA WOKE LATE THE NEXT DAY, AT FIVE PAST SIX, TO THE SOUND of a seaplane droning overhead. It was just the beginning of the seaplane parade that took place every day in the Center of the Universe. They buzzed down the ship canal with the frequency of bees leaving a hive. Her T-shirt was damp front and back. She'd slept through the alarm. Even Patsy hadn't stirred.

With no time for a shower, Mira wiped her torso with the shirt before throwing it in the laundry pile, then pulled on the nearest clothes and quickly brushed her teeth. There'd be no time for mascara or blush. She tried to arrange her hair in a presentable shape, then gave up.

As she unlocked the back door to the shop, she saw the handful of early birds waiting outside the glass front door. Patsy Cline was doing her thing in the weed patch and Mira didn't know how she was going to let her back into the apartment, get the chairs off the tables, turn on all the machines to warm up, stock the condiment bar with fresh dairy, and start three separate coffees brewing while waiting on customers.

She clumped noisily to the front in her clogs, keys clanging, and unlocked and pulled the door open. "Sorry! Sorry! I
just woke up. Come on in." Heat threatened deep in her core;
the last thing she needed now was a freaking hot flash. "I'll have
everything ready in just a second. I'm so sorry. I don't know how
I overslept, I just . . ." She was babbling, she knew, but it seemed
impossible to stop.

Three of the usual four fishermen walked in, looked at each
other, then started pulling chairs off tables and setting them neatly
in place. The African student set his backpack on the floor by
the counter and draped his jacket over it, then started helping,
his long dark arms graceful, outreaching the fishermen's. The girl
who reminded Mira of Thea hugged her spiral notebook to her
navy pea coat and shrugged.

"I could do something," she said.

Finally silenced, Mira stood still, hand to her mouth. She
would not cry. She took a deep breath and said, "Okay, you guys,
today is on me. Whatever you want. Thank you so much." She
turned to the girl. "Could you take these keys and go get my
dog, Patsy, and put her back up in my apartment at the top of the
stairs? She's out back."

"Sure," she said, reaching to take the keys.

"This is the one to the apartment. Just lock it back up."

The girl nodded.

Mira caught a whiff of vanilla sweetness, girl smell. She didn't
look like Thea, exactly; her hair had a chopped quality and she was
decidedly less animated. It was more that she had that entirely-
too-wise-for-her-age demeanor.

"I'm Mira. What's your name?"

"Sidney. Like the actor, not the city." She smiled, shyly, and
curtsied just the way Thea always did with her dad.

"You remind me of my daughter," Mira said. Sidney's lips were
blue-tinged in the early gray light, and Mira wanted to button her
coat, put mittens on her small hands.

"Oh, does she live here too?" the girl asked.

Mira swallowed. "No, she lives in Oregon, near the coast."

"My mom lives in Fresno."

"Do you miss her? When's the last time you saw her?"

Sidney shook her head. "It's been a while. She doesn't really want to see me."

How on earth, Mira thought, biting her lip so she didn't make Sidney feel worse. Did Thea feel abandoned, too, even though she'd pushed Mira way? Had Mira actually done the pushing, by leaving instead of sticking around to work it out? *Duh,* a voice said.

"Well," Mira said, attempting a smile, "I hope your mother knows what a lovely daughter she has."

"And I bet you're a good mom." Sidney smiled and turned to go rescue Patsy Cline. Mira felt her sinuses fill as she turned the CLOSED sign to OPEN.

Just as the first paying customer walked through the door, the phone rang. It was Jarrett calling in sick. She was tempted to ask him for a note from his doctor. *That's fine,* she thought, *I can work the counter alone. How bad could it be?*

Bad, she realized, as the day began with an order for six mochas to go, each with its own distinct variation on pumps of chocolate and caffeine levels, even the amount of whipped cream to be placed on top. How could people be so picky about freaking coffee? she wondered as she tried to keep up. The line grew ever longer in front of her, the customers less patient. "I'm sorry for the wait," she said to each new customer. "I'm the only one here this morning." She'd left a message for Gus to get someone else in to help her, but by seven forty-five, it had yet to happen.

Ever since the night of the awkward encounter with Martin, Mira had been avoiding him by finding some task to do in back whenever he came in. As he walked through the door, Mira flushed. Today there was no escape. As he drew closer in line, Mira grew increasingly sweaty. *Lovely,* she thought, using her forearm to both wipe perspiration from her forehead and shove her bed-head hair from her unmade-up face.

"Triple vente nonfat latte with two Equals," said the skeletal waif who worked at the trendy clothing store in the next block. Like a little fat, a little sugar, would kill her.

Mira slammed two filter handles into the espresso machine, flicked the switches, then poured a fresh pitcher of nonfat to steam.

"Is that skim?" the girl asked.

Mira felt her face tighten and tried to relax it before turning her head. "Yes," she said, dropping the "of course" she wanted to add. Still, it came out terse, so she tried to smile, but she was pretty sure it looked more like the grimace she'd been fighting.

The girl's purple-shadowed eyes widened, looking past Mira, and a loud hiss of steam burned Mira's wrist. Jumping back, Mira dropped the pitcher to the floor, hot milk splashing across her new jeans and red clogs. One of the filter handles had come loose, spraying hot water and coffee grounds over everything within a three-foot radius. Including Mira. She cranked off the steam knob and flicked off both switches. The hissing stopped. The room went silent. She hadn't even found time yet to turn on the music.

Soaked in sweat, hot water, hot milk, and coffee grounds, Mira closed her eyes. She could walk out. Head up the stairs, pack her few measly things and grab Patsy and keep driving north, just as she'd originally intended. Fuck Gus, fuck Seattle and these over-caffeinated, rude city people.

"Are you okay?" a female voice said.

"Poor thing," someone murmured.

"I can't believe she doesn't have any help."

She heard footsteps and opened her eyes. Sidney and a customer she didn't know had grabbed handfuls of rags from beneath the counter and were mopping milk from the floor. "Thank you," Mira whispered, wanting to reach down and touch the top of Sidney's head.

The front door bell jangled, and Mira was sure most of the

customers were bolting, desperate to find another coffee shop on their way to work, but when she turned around, it was just another customer coming in. The faces in front of him all looked concerned, not angry. Not even impatient.

"Are you okay?" the skeletal woman asked again. "Did you get burned? Should we put some ice on your arm?" She made her way around the counter in four-inch heeled boots, asking Sidney, "Where do you think the ice is?"

Martin stepped up to the counter. "Is there someone I can call to come in and relieve you, or at least help out?" He'd pulled a cell phone from his brown corduroys. "I mean, I'd offer but I'm a total klutz."

Mira began to laugh. "A bigger klutz than this?"

He studied her soiled clothing, her crazy hair, the red welt rising on her wrist. "Well, no," he said.

Mira grabbed a tall stack of to-go cups and handed them to him. "Free coffee for everyone while I go take care of this mess. I'll call the owner on his dime, but thanks."

This time Mira didn't leave a message; she dialed over and over, hanging up when voice mail kicked in, waiting a moment, then dialing again.

A sleepy female voice finally answered. "Hello?"

So Gus had a girlfriend. Mira leaned against the counter in back, phone tucked to her shoulder while she held ice on her wrist. Out front there was a happy buzz as customers poured their own coffee and helped themselves to the pastries she'd pulled from the case as an afterthought.

"Is Gus there, please?"

"Mira?" said the voice.

"Sequoia?" God. He was sleeping with the help. The very young help. Mira felt any composure she might have retained fall away. "Put him on."

"He's"—Sequoia interrupted herself with a long yawn—"he's still asleep."

"Well then, I guess you'll have to wake him up."

Mira heard snide mumbling and murmuring, then Gus.

"Mira? What's up?"

"You or your girlfriend might want to get over here and help me out. I'm the only one here and I'm giving away all the coffee."

"Whoa, slow down. You're giving away what? What's going on? Where's that Q-tip kid, Jeremy-whatever?"

"Jarrett called in sick, and even when he's here, he's useless. There was no way for me to keep up with the morning rush all alone, so in a gesture of goodwill for your very important customer base, I gave away coffee. Oh, and all the day-old pastries. And now I'm going to go out and make everyone who wants one a free latte or mocha, until I get a warm body in here to help out." Mira hung up, then went out front to give everyone the good news.

By the time Gus arrived nearly an hour later only a few customers remained, relaxed at tables, well coffeed and immersed in newspapers or conversations. After giving away as much as she could, Mira had set to work. The day-old pastries were gone and the display cases sparkling clean and lined with clean butcher paper, awaiting fresh baked goods. The coffee grinders were stocked with oily black beans, the brewed coffee dispensers filled with hot fresh Italian Roast and Organic Free-Trade Fremont Blend and decaf Sumatran. The counters were clean, the floors swept, and the condiment bar neat and stocked. Mira stood at the back counter, humming along with Mavis Staples on the CD player, completing a list. All of this orderliness, this cleaning and stocking and taking stock, had improved her outlook considerably.

Gus hung his brown snowboard jacket on the hook by the back door and ambled over to Mira, scratching his chest. "So, like, what's the big problem?" Clearly he had other plans for the day.

"If you'd been here at any point up until half an hour ago,

you'd know. We need a better system around here. I've made a list of changes we need to make—"

Gus widened his eyes and pulled on his goatee.

"—and I think I've got most of them figured out."

"You do, huh? After a few short weeks you've got it all figured out?"

Mira nodded. "Mm-hmm, I think I do."

He jammed his hands into his pockets. "Huh."

"Do you want me to go over it with you," Mira asked, "or do you just want me to take care of it all for, say, another two dollars per hour?"

"Geez, Mira, I already pay you—"

"Poverty wages, frankly. I've taken into account that you can't pay me what I'm worth. I'm not asking for much, and I think you'll find that it actually frees up your time even more."

He cleared his throat. She had him. "Let's see your list."

Mira slid the pad in front of him. "Coffee? I'm getting a refill."

"Oh, uh, sure. I'll have a—"

"Grande quad shot in the dark with three Sweet'n Lows. I know." Mira smiled at him. He really wasn't a bad person, just in over his head.

Over coffee, Gus balked at a few of her ideas—especially the suggestion that he fire Sequoia—but he didn't turn down her proposal outright.

"Let me think on it," he said, and left again for the rest of the day.

That evening, Mira ate fruit salad for dinner. She'd splurged on half-price California strawberries, a ripe mango, and a tub of fresh pineapple rings at PCC, the natural food co-op a few blocks from the Coffee Shop at the Center of the Universe.

The walk there after work had been cold but sunny—a rare treat in February. Squawking seagulls careened overhead, and purple crocuses poked up from flower boxes at the windows and along the walkways of Fremont's patchwork of import shops and ethnic restaurants. Rambling forsythias exploded in thousands of tiny yellow blooms here and there, a particularly prolific one between a tiny ramshackle Thai restaurant and a used bookstore. Mira picked up a take-out menu from the mailbox of the restaurant's front porch, and peeked into the window of the bookstore. She might have to go in sometime and browse.

She passed Fremont's various claims to public art fame: the Cold War–era rocket attached to the side of a building, the statue of Lenin on the other side of busy Thirty-sixth Street. So invested were the town leaders in their "Keep Fremont Weird" rhetoric, they had proclaimed themselves the Center of the Universe in the 1990s. Mira now recognized those coffee shop customers that were tourists, there because of the name, presumably. They liked to have their pictures taken outside with the sign.

Mira had planned only to study the labels of herbal hot flash remedies, but once inside the store, the warm bright colors of the produce section won her over. It wasn't really spring, but it was close—close enough, Mira decided, to let this one day be happy.

It was on this tentative high that she'd also let herself add a tube of twenty-eight-dollar natural progesterone cream to her basket. Packaged in a pleasingly low-key way, it could almost have been a prettier pharmaceutical, with an olive and lavender logo of a leaf morphing into a woman's profile. "For problems associated with estrogen dominance," the small type explained. "Hot flashes, memory problems, mood swings, loss of libido, severe PMS." Well, that fit her to a T. Estrogen dominance, that was the problem. She opened the tube in the checkout line and rubbed a tiny dab of cream on the inside of her wrist, as the instructions said to. She tried not to calculate the two plus hours she'd have to work to pay for it.

After dinner, Mira rinsed her bowl and fork, the stained cutting board and cheap dull knife, and stacked them neatly in the drainer. Maybe it was the nice weather, or the cream already kicking in, but Mira was having a thought. She paced the floor, coming again and again to the window. The sky was painted in east-moving patches of indigo and violet and charcoal. The winds had kicked up; the paper had reported a strong storm on the horizon.

Finally, she picked up the phone once more and dialed.

The Indian girl answered, and Mira said, "Hello, this is Thea's mom. Look, I know she's avoiding me, but could you just tell her that I'm living in Seattle now, and I'd like her to come visit? I can send her a bus ticket, and—"

"She's not here, Mrs. Serafino."

Mira closed her eyes, sniffed.

"I know she is. You don't have to lie."

"No, she's actually out this time, but you're right. We do usually lie to you." She paused. "I'm sorry. It's not my choice."

Bless her heart. "What's your name?"

"Lali," said the girl. "We met when you visited."

"I remember," Mira said. "Please, Lali, can you just tell her that I know she's hurt and upset? Tell her I'm so, so sorry. And . . . you know. That I love her."

"I'll try," she said, but she sounded doubtful.

Somewhere in the middle of the darkest part of the night Mira woke up with a phrase running through her dreams: *the sins of the father revisited upon the son.* Or, in this case, the mother upon the daughter. How had she let this happen? How had she committed the one crime she'd never thought herself capable of?

Just as her mother had, she'd abandoned her child. It didn't matter that her child had pushed her away. She should have chased her up that damn hill. Mira sat up and sighed. She'd never get back to sleep now.

At home when she hadn't been able to sleep, Parker would always pull her against him, spooning, and whisper, "Shh," until he started to twitch, and then snore, and she'd roll him back over to his non-snoring side.

"Hey," she said aloud in the dark. Even though she'd destroyed her old cell phone, it might still be in service. Parker might be keeping her account active, paying the family plan bill, even though the family had disintegrated. Would he do that, for her? The old Parker would have, she knew. As for post–Jackie Anderson Parker, she had no idea.

"God," she said, climbing out of bed. Although it had been over a month since she'd thrown his messages away with the phone, not wanting to hear them, she suddenly needed to know exactly what he'd said before she could live one more moment. What if he'd been trying to tell her that the woman with him wasn't Jackie after all, just one of the neighbors, or an employee who needed advice? What if Nonna was right, and he'd wanted her to come home?

Trying not to wake Patsy, she tiptoed across the room to her purse on the table, fished out the phone and dialed.

One ring. She sat and crossed her legs, bouncing her foot, blowing rhythmic puffs of air in time to the bouncing. Two rings. God, it was the middle of the night. What if the number had been reassigned, and she woke up some poor stranger? Three rings, four, and then—there it was: "Hi, this is Mira. Well, it's my cell phone, anyway."

"Duh," Thea said in the background. They'd been in the car, sitting in the parking lot of the RadioShack in Tillamook, trying to figure out how to work the phone. Actually, Thea had been figuring out the phone, then handing it to Mira at the appropriate times to speak. Mira heard her own self-conscious giggle, then pictured Thea's eye-roll, but her reluctant smile, too.

"Fine, whatever," the former Mira's voice—her happy mom voice—said. "Leave a message."

Mira quit bouncing her foot. She clicked off the phone and closed her eyes. That was all she could handle, for now—just hearing her daughter's voice. Maybe she didn't want to know what Parker had said.

So what if he'd been asking her to come home? Nothing would have changed. Something old ached inside. *If I hadn't left, I'd still be that old me,* she realized, *the one that drove my husband and daughter away.*

Twenty-four

THE NEXT WEEK, MIRA PUSHED THE CART UP THE CLEANSER AISLE
at Costco and added a six-pack of Comet to the shrink-wrapped
36-count package of toilet paper. She'd talked Gus into letting
her do the Costco run this week, arranging for extra coverage
while she was gone so that he wouldn't have to do anything extra,
or even make an appearance. She just needed to get away from
the shop for a while.

She turned toward the back of the store, aiming for produce
to pick up some fruit for the dollar bowl they'd started at Felix's
suggestion. She was beginning to think that her mind might be
coming back. She could remember what items to buy once she
got to a store. She could remember where she'd parked her car.
Whether it was a miracle or the progesterone cream, she wasn't
complaining.

She'd almost reached the produce section when a large blue
ball rolled in front of her cart, chased by a young boy dressed in
a too-large black T-shirt and sporting a dirty blond mullet. He

picked it up and stared at her, and he looked so familiar she said, "Hi." But she couldn't possibly know him. She knew no one in Seattle other than the people she'd met at the Coffee Shop at the Center of the Universe, and from the look of this boy's mother and grimy younger siblings, coffee shops in Fremont were not high on their priority list of places to visit.

Mira smiled at the mother, a tired-looking woman of indeterminate age with the same dirty blond hair. The woman ignored her, wheeling in an arc away from her as though Mira might reach out and steal her children.

She knew this family from her years of teaching, the families who could only afford to live in trailers or basement apartments, the families who always seemed to have too many children, too many pets, and semioperable motor vehicles of one type or another. She tried not to judge them, but she always wondered why they kept adding mouths to feed, engines to repair or replace, when they had so little money. She wondered why they distrusted teachers and food bank volunteers, social workers and people who smiled at them in the middle of Costco, for Christ's sake, just to be friendly. And Mira wondered why it always hurt her feelings when they looked at her that way. She shook her head and pushed out into the wide aisle away from the woman and her dirty children. No matter how poor you were, you could always find something to wipe your babies' faces and hands with, even if it was the hem of your own shirt.

Later, in back of a train of overloaded carts waiting to check out, Mira saw the family again, one line over and two carts ahead. A chubby dark-haired baby stood in the cart chewing on the corner of a three-pack of Frosted Flakes boxes, and three other young children, including the boy who seemed to be the oldest, clung to the cart, rifling through the various shrink-wrapped multipackages of generic cookies, macaroni and cheese, diet cola, frozen pizzas. Mira started to fret about the nutritional value of such food and stopped herself.

The oldest boy spotted her and waved, and both parents turned to look at her. Determined, Mira smiled again at the mother who turned frontward. The father kept staring at her, though, the same dark eyes as the little boy, a face just like Big Al's, and before she could even think about it, Mira cried, "Fonso!" and rushed toward him, weaving through carts and bodies until she was hugging him and crying.

"Oh my god, Fonso!" she said again, pulling back to look at him. "I've been looking all over for you!"

He looked at her the same way the woman had, and she wondered if she'd made a mistake. This man did look older and thicker through the jowls than she remembered her brother.

"Al?" the woman said. "Do you know this lady?"

The children stood mute, eyes rounded in wonder at the strange woman hugging their father. Only the baby ignored her, chewing on shrink-wrap and cardboard to the extent that Mira worried she'd choke on it.

The man's expression softened and he said, "This is my sister, Mira. Mira, this is Terry."

"It's so nice to meet you," Mira said. "God, sorry I'm so emotional. It's just that we haven't seen each other in, what, Fonso? Nearly fifteen years?" He'd come back for her and Parker's tenth anniversary. It had been a disaster between the two Alfonsos, and Fonso had departed early, before the party even began. Mira wished she hadn't brought it up, and continued quickly: "I can't believe I'd run into you in a Costco in Seattle, of all places! Can you believe it?" She reached to shake the woman's hand.

The woman, Terry, looked at her a moment before offering a limp handshake. Her hand was small and rough, and she pulled it back to cross her arms over her thin chest. "I didn't know you had a sister," she said.

Fonso shrugged his shoulders, dressed similarly to his young son in jeans and a black T-shirt with a brightly colored logo on the front, dirty white athletic shoes. His hair was longish, not styled, and he was heavier than she'd ever seen him. Only his eyes were the same, and each of his children had them.

Mira waited for him to say something, but he didn't, so she searched her purse for a piece of paper to write her cell number on, then left the family to go back to her own cart. She tried not to let her gaze drift toward them, but the little boy kept playing hide-and-seek with her from behind the cereal boxes, and then from behind Fonso himself, but his father jerked sharply on his arm and he stopped, turning to face forward as his parents seemed so determined to do.

When Fonso, or Al as he now seemed to be called, ran away from home the first time, he was eleven years old. He'd grown from a rowdy misbehaving boy into a belligerent and unstable preteen. Big Al arranged to be home after school more often to relieve Nonna, who was finding it harder to handle her grandson. Not that Al could handle him. Fonso didn't like being handled, disciplined, cajoled, bribed, threatened, or punished—it didn't matter by whom. On this day, Al had decided to withhold Fonso's allowance for three months to patch a hole he'd punched in the bathroom wall during a rage.

"You can't do that!" Fonso screamed, rushing Al with his arms flailing. "That's not fair! I hate you!"

Fifteen-year-old Mira ran to her room. She'd always been able to calm Fonso, to talk to him steadily and quietly until he lost his fury, but more often now he was beyond it, and with Big Al more present in the equation, everything seemed more precarious.

When it went suddenly quiet in the living room, she poked her head out of her bedroom. "Dad?" she called.

He didn't answer. She walked down the hall and found him sitting on the couch with his face in his hands. Fonso was gone.

"I didn't hit him," her father said, "I swear to God almighty. I wanted to, but I didn't."

Leland Hansen, Pacifica's former high school quarterback and

Big Al's deputy, found the boy six hours later in a storm culvert at the edge of town, cold and wet and obstinate. Leland had to throw him over his big shoulder to get him into the patrol car, and nudge him from behind up the walk to the Serafino house. Big Al opened the door and said only, "Thank you, Leland. I'd appreciate it if you kept this to yourself."

Fonso marched past them to his room and wouldn't eat or talk for days.

The scene would be repeated many times until Fonso finally escaped for good five years later. Each time Leland or other patrol officers would drag him home, Fonso would be a little worse for wear, high on something, or drunk, or beat up. He spent much of his fourteenth year at the Boys' Farm reform school in Corvallis and lit the neighbor's garage on fire upon his return.

The year Mira went away to college in Portland, her father and brother's brittle relationship snapped without her presence as their buffer. "If you absolutely can't live there with Dad, come to Portland," she'd said on the phone when Fonso called her late one night in her sophomore year, drunk or stoned. She couldn't tell which, but he never called her unless he was high on something.

That night, however, he sounded calm. Reasonable, even. "I just have to go somewhere else and be by myself. I'm no good to anyone, anyway."

Mira sighed. She had a paper due in the morning.

"Why do you say that? That's not true. If you could just . . ." Mira rubbed her forehead and leaned forward, elbows on knees. "I don't know. Can't you just get your high school diploma, then move out and find a job? It's only two years away. You can put up with Dad that long, or go live with one of the aunts, or come here and we'll find a school for you, or . . ."

He laughed an unfamiliar, disaffected laugh, and it scared Mira. Who was her little brother becoming?

"I kill everyone I know, one way or another," he said.

"What are you talking about?" Mira sat straight in her chair, an electrical pulse pinging between her eyes. "You don't think—"

"Goodbye, Mimi," he said, his childhood name for her. "Goodbye, Mommy. Goodbye, goodbye."

The click of the line going dead reverberated against Mira's skull. An acidic wave washed through her and she swallowed a surge of bile. He thought he'd killed their mother. Why hadn't she helped him more when she was still at home? All she'd really ever done was smooth everything over when the two Alfonsos argued. Whenever they hurled verbal daggers at each other, she stood between them and let them sink into her instead.

Saint Mira, absorber of all family pain.

Twenty-five

Dear Mira,

Thank you for your letter. My eyesight is not so good but you have always had such beautiful penmanship, even in first grade, and I can read your letters with only my glasses. The newspaper I must read with my glasses and the magnifying glass your aunt Sofia gave me for Christmas. It takes so long to read the obituaries now I've almost given up. But I don't know so many people in this town as I used to. Just as well. I don't need to make as many lasagnas. People used to love getting my lasagna during their time of sorrow. I wouldn't go so far as to say they hastened their poor mother or father's deaths to get one, but . . . ha ha! You know I tease.

I tell you this for a reason. I am not just an old lady who babbles, you know, no matter what your aunts say. I make my lasagnas because I feel it is my duty to provide for others in their time of need. We have a duty to take care of each other, cara, in our towns and in our families. It is not the time to be finding yourself or whatever it is you're doing up there. Sometimes we have to put our own feelings aside. We will never understand men and what they feel they must do. A good wife learns to see a little less, to tune out gossip and rumors and take better care of her children, or her home and garden, or to take up a hobby. Why do you think I have such beautiful dahlias? Why do you think your aunts play so much pinochle? We each find our ways to forgive and forget.

When you were just a little girl and your beloved mother passed away, I told you that Serafinos don't give up. We go on. In the first Great War, the second, even when we lost my darling brothers, all three of them, we went on. During the Great Depression, and now that the fishing is all but gone, we go on. We lose those we love, or someone hurts our feelings. We go on. You used to know this when you were just a small girl and dealt so bravely with your mother's passing.

It is time you remembered. There is not a doubt in my mind that Parker will take you back, and you cannot listen to what anyone else says. Your family needs you, and you never know what will happen. Just like your father, men find new wives. Old people die. Come home before it is too late.

Con amore,
Nonna

Twenty-six

IT TOOK MIRA NEARLY TWO DAYS TO CALM DOWN ENOUGH TO CALL her father. Two days in which he did not contact her even though he should have been the one doing the calling.

"Hello?" he said, his mouth full of something.

She'd tried to wait until after dinnertime, but maybe the new wife liked to eat a little later than Al's early-bird five-thirty routine. Maybe he was snacking on leftover fucking wedding cake. He always was a sucker for sweets.

"Hi, Dad," Mira said, trying to keep her tone civil. "I hear you might have something to tell me."

"Oh, yeah, honey. I, uh . . ." He swallowed, cleared his throat, the sound of an old engine warming up. "I do have something to tell you."

"Mm-hmm." How could he have not told her, his daughter, for god's sake?

"Me and Dottie, well. We got hitched last week. We're married, honey."

In the background, a woman's voice: "Oh my god, without so much as a how do you do."

"So I heard." Last week? When was he going to tell her?

"I should've called you, I know. Dottie's telling me I'm about as sensitive as a Mack truck. We're happy, honey. Really happy."

Mira didn't know what to say. She'd always been his only girl. Now she was nobody's anything. Each tie to her old life was breaking, one by one.

She took a deep breath, trying to think of a pleasantry. "Well . . . congratulations. Did you have a service or anything?"

"It was just the two of us, honey, over at St. Mary's. We didn't want to make a fuss, you know. Well, with all the . . . with everything everyone's going through."

"What? What's wrong?" Was Nonna all right? The aunts, the uncles?

Her father was silent for a moment. Then he sighed. "Well, you know, honey. With you being gone. That's all I meant."

She flinched; guilt flushed through her. "So you didn't even have a reception?" This Mira couldn't imagine, not in her family.

"Well, the family wouldn't exactly let us get away without a party or something, so we had a little get-together at the Buzz over the weekend."

No one had called her. No one had invited her to her own father's wedding reception. At the fucking Buzz. Her family had divorced her—her own goddamn family, of which Parker still seemed to be a vital member. She couldn't let herself believe that he would bring her, Jackie Anderson. That would be too much to bear.

"Was Thea there?" Mira asked.

"Oh honey, you're crying," her father said. "Are you upset? It's been a long time, you know, since your dear mother departed."

"No, Daddy, I'm happy for you. I just wish I could have been there."

"Oh," he said. "Oh. Well. We didn't think you'd, you know. Want to drive all the way down here just for the day."

"I would have." She bit her bottom lip and gulped back tears. "Of course I would have."

"Ah, honey, I'm lying. I just thought it might be . . . god. Awkward or something. You know. For you. I should've called you, huh? God, I'm an idiot. I'm sorry, honey. I should've called you."

Yes, you should have, Mira thought, *I'm your only fucking daughter,* but she muddled through enough small talk to get off the phone.

When she'd hung up, Mira realized that she hadn't even told him about Fonso, but Fonso didn't appear to want to be found, and her father didn't appear to place quite as much importance on his offspring as she'd always thought he had.

God! Mira thought, not quite believing it. Maybe it wouldn't have been so bad had he not been the only real parent she'd ever had.

After Fonso's birth, Mira's mother remained bedridden for months. Looking back on it from adulthood, Mira wondered if there really had been a physical reason for her lethargy, as she'd assumed as a child, or if it was simply postpartum depression. Four-year-old Mira tried many things to either entice or force her mother from her bedroom, but her father's favorite story was always the one about the razor: "This little tiny girl with soap bubbles and blood all over her face, screaming and crying, and it took four big strapping orderlies to hold her down while Dr. Robertson stitched her up. Didn't give her a drop of Novocain." This said proudly, as though Mira was somehow strong and brave, not terrified and in obvious pain from a needle being threaded through her cheek.

Mira didn't remember the drive to the Tillamook hospital, or the emergency room, the same one she'd taken Thea to on more than one occasion. She didn't even remember getting the stitches, just the story about getting the stitches. And she wasn't sure if she remembered her mother dying, or just the story about her mother dying.

Everyone knew the elder Mira suffered from "female problems" incurred during the traumatic delivery when baby Fonso became stuck and, after thirty-six long hours, delivered by emergency Caesarean section. As a little girl, Mira had heard her mother and aunts talk about how such a thing could do horrible things to a woman's insides, and as an adult, as a biology teacher, she'd wondered how badly her mother's uterus had been damaged during the surgery; perhaps infection had set in.

Once her mother was able to get out of bed, she walked slowly, slightly stooped, gripping chair backs and tables to steady herself. She rarely dressed in anything other than a supply of housedresses Nonna purchased at the five and dime in Tillamook. She took pills in the morning and at lunchtime and before bed. All of this Mira remembered. It had been her one and only job to be quiet, to be good. She was vigilant but invisible.

The day of the botched hysterectomy was a blur. Mira's aunt Rosa came to school just before recess to take Mira home. The teacher and the school secretary kept saying "family emergency," and the excitement in her third grade classroom was palpable. Mira didn't remember much else. Her clearest memory of that day was her grandparents and the aunts and uncles pulling up to the house in a caravan of cars. They stood in bunches outside talking to Al, to each other, glancing nervously at the window where Mira peered out while Fonso banged on the coffee table with a yellow toy truck.

She did not remember if her father spoke to her that day. When they finally came inside, he sat hunched over the dinette table, chain-smoking, shaking but silent, one of the aunts or Nonna at his side comforting him. Later in the day, perhaps, or on another day, Mira remembered rocking in Nonna's arms, her grandmother telling her it was God's will that her mother had gone to live with the angels. When Mira asked if it was because she'd been bad, her grandmother only shushed her.

Mira didn't remember a funeral. She couldn't recall saying goodbye to her mother before she left for the hospital, or if she'd visited her there, or spoken with her on the phone. Nor could she remember what her mother had been like before Fonso was born, which was the worst thing of all. In the back of her mind, though, lay memories of a skirt brushing against her face, the perfume of powder, fresh flowers on the kitchen table. These had to be memories of her mother, she'd decided long ago, and kept them carefully tucked away, like the pearls in the jewelry box at the back of her closet.

The search engine box blinked bright white in the darkened room. Mira swallowed, then typed "Alfonso Serafino Seattle." He'd been here under her nose the whole time, but now she wasn't all that sure she wanted to know anything more about him. She hit ENTER, wondering if he still did drugs. Nothing. She tried every permutation of his name she could think of, but he was not a part of the computer age. Was he in hiding? Dodging warrants, drug deals gone bad? Mira sat back, rubbed her eyes.

She sat up and fished in her bag for her cell phone and dialed 411. "Duh," she could hear Thea saying. Yes, there was an Alfonso Serafino listed in the greater Seattle metro area. For no additional charge, she was being connected.

The phone rang five times. Mira was about to hang up when a child answered: "Hello?"

"Well, hi. Is your daddy there?" Mira said.

The sound of mouth breathing filled the earpiece.

"Hello? Are you still there?"

"Uh-huh," said the child, and Mira tried to picture which one it might be.

"I'm the lady you met at Costco, your daddy's sister. I'm your Aunt Mira."

"Hi."

"Hi yourself. Could I talk to your dad?"

"Okay," the child said. A loud television show played in the background.

"Hello?" Fonso's tone was guarded.

"Hi, it's me. Which one of your kids was that?"

"Gino. The oldest boy."

So he had stuck with some tradition after all.

"He's a really nice kid, I can tell." Mira knew from years of experience that the quickest way to a parent's heart was to praise his children. She didn't ask what he was doing up so late on a school night.

"Well, not always," Fonso said with a clipped laugh, and he began to sound a little more relaxed.

"So I actually have some big news for you," Mira said, glad to have a reason for calling. "Dad got married last week, to a woman named Dottie Santonopoulos. From Rockaway Beach."

"Oh. Okay."

Mira sighed.

After a pause, Fonso said, "You tell him about me?"

"Actually, no," Mira said. "I didn't know if you wanted me to. Do you?"

"I don't know. No. Whatever."

How could she have known that Fonso still cared what their father thought of him?

"Fonso? I mean . . . would you rather I called you Al?"

"No, Fonso's okay."

"I really have been looking for you these past few weeks. Parker and I split up, and I'm living up here now. I thought you might still be in Vancouver, but here you are, even closer. Maybe we could, I don't know. Reconnect."

"What happened? You two were good together." Fonso had always liked Parker, the few times he met him over the years.

"Yeah." Mira sighed. "I thought so, too. I mean, we had our problems—"

He laughed. "Not you. You don't have problems."

"Of course I do. I've never said I didn't have problems."

"Well, yeah, but your problems were things like getting a B instead of an A, or what color should you paint the living room, white or off-white."

"Oh, come on. That's not fair." Jesus, they'd been through so much together, and this was how he saw her?

"Saint Mira the good."

"Fonso—"

"Saver of all souls."

"Fonso. Cut it out."

"Did you call to save me?"

"No, of course not! I just wanted to . . . I don't know." *Know that you were okay,* she didn't say. God, he was right. "I'm not really a goody-goody, you know."

He snorted. "You're the queen of goody-goodies."

"Why are you being so mean?"

"It's just a fact."

"Stop it, Fonso, or . . ." What, she'd tell Nonna?

"You sound like you did when you were twelve."

She did. She sighed. "Why won't you ever come see me?"

"I can't."

"Because . . ."

"Because I'm finally doing good. Really good. I've got a family, a decent job. I've been clean for three years. I'm taking the meds. I'm doing good."

Mira swallowed. Clean? Meds? "That's so great, Fonso. I'm happy for you. I would love to get to know your wife and kids. Maybe we could get together for dinner or something. My place is pretty small, but—"

"I can't. I told you. Don't ask me to."

"What? Why? We're right here in the same city."

"I get all messed up again when I get around family."

"But it's me, Fonso, not family. It's not like I'm Dad, or Nonna or—"

"I can't."

"Do you think I blame you or something? Because I don't, Fonso. You had nothing to do with Mom, but that's what kids do, blame themselves. I did, too, at first. You were just a little kid, Fonso. You weren't to blame."

"Fuck you, Mira. I don't need saving. I'm fine. I've worked my ass off to get the hell over all that, and I would appreciate it if you just left me and my family alone."

The line clicked dead, and Mira turned off her phone, too. Just like that, she was entirely alone. No family. No friends, except Lannie, and they now lived five and a half hours apart from each other. Mira felt the phone trembling in her hand, but it wasn't in vibrate mode. It was her hands, shaking. She took a deep breath, blew it out. Well, now she could move even farther away—California, Colorado, the East Coast if she wanted to—but suddenly nowhere seemed far enough.

Maybe Fonso was right about her wanting a perfect life, but not about her. Mira had the same blood running through her veins that he did, and had fought her whole life to keep it contained. But now she could do anything she wanted to, be anyone she wanted to be.

She had no idea what that meant, but she was sure of one thing: Saint Mira was no more.

Twenty-seven

By the end of the week, Mira had sat Jarrett down and explained that the Coffee Shop at the Center of the Universe had to let him go.

"But, like, why?" he asked, looking so baffled that Mira thought he was joking at first.

"Maybe customer service–oriented jobs aren't your style," she told him, touching his shoulder to soften the blow. "I've seen the comics you draw. Maybe you should do something more art-related, or go to art school." He looked thoughtful at that, nodding his bleached head with more energy than she'd ever seen him do anything.

This is good, she thought. *Forward motion, moving forward. Just keep moving forward.* She hadn't exactly gotten Gus's blessing to take on the hiring and firing, but he wasn't doing anything himself, and he wasn't complaining.

She interviewed three candidates and hired two. She knew Gus wouldn't let her fire Sequoia, and Mira had to admit the girl made the best foam of anyone. Mira wrote a job description for her that included training the others and cleaning and mopping every other shift. Sequoia received the news the way Mira might have expected: with a roll of her eyes and most likely an immediate complaint to Gus.

Mira also arranged a daily delivery of pastries so that they needn't depend on his sporadic visits, and ordered sandwiches to try out at lunchtime. In the back of her mind she was thinking it might be fun to make a daily soup—she'd always loved making Nonna's savory Italian wedding soup with little meatballs, and fresh tomato soup with plenty of herbs and a large dash of cayenne.

She'd yet to dip into Thea's trust money, other than for the alternator. Life was beginning to smooth out a bit. The progesterone cream was producing all kinds of positive effects. She felt lighter, less fogged over. Instead of hanging around the coffee shop every night, she often watched movies on the cheap combo TV/VCR she'd picked up at Fred Meyer, and she made a special effort every night to watch the eleven o'clock news instead of ruminating about her own problems before trying to sleep. She told herself it was so that she'd get to know the city, but it didn't hurt that the weatherman possessed a deliciously square chin and large brown eyes. When he looked into the camera and said that he was sorry, folks, but the next day would be rainy again, it felt intimate, as though he were speaking directly to her, truly sorry for any inconvenience or hardship it might cause her. It was crazy to have a crush on the weatherman, but it comforted her, this little moment with him before going to bed. "Good night," he'd say. "Good night, Steve," she'd whisper. "Good night, Patsy."

Sure, the bad things were still there—a husband who'd stopped loving her, a daughter who wouldn't speak to her, a father who might miss her but didn't need her anymore, a brother who wanted nothing to do with her, and a grandmother who seemed to be threatening her own demise—but Mira resolved to forget about everything but Thea. Maybe when the two new employees, Yoshi and Amanda, were up to speed, she could take a day or two off and drive down to Woden to see her face-to-face.

On the night of Valentine's Day, Mira was prepared. She'd rented enough movies to keep her mind occupied throughout the night, even if she couldn't sleep. She'd eaten a large tub of macaroni and cheese from the PCC deli and a pint of chocolate chocolate chip ice cream. Now she sat tucked into the love seat with Patsy, watching a movie she hadn't seen since college: *Coming Home* with Jon Voight and Jane Fonda.

She'd forgotten how erotic their lovemaking was, or maybe it hadn't seemed as sexy back when she was doing the same thing all the time. Granted not with a paraplegic, but once there was a boy with a broken leg. They'd had trouble keeping his leg propped on the pillows as he lay flat on his back, Mira writhing enthusiastically on top. She couldn't even imagine that girl was her anymore. She'd never have the abandon to sit on a strange man now, completely naked and grinding like that, in daylight, no less. He'd see the science experiment that middle-aged women were, the cruelty of gravity pulling everything that was once taut into flabby folds. *Think what it would look like from underneath,* she thought, grimacing, absently reaching to pull the underneath of her chin up toward her jawline.

Why had she picked this movie, on a night when she felt more alone than ever?

A car door slammed in back and Mira rolled to her knees to peer out the window. Gus's shiny black SUV sat next to Sequoia's car. She paused the movie, grabbed her sweater, and said, "Come on, Patsy." Patsy Cline wagged her tail and Mira picked her up and tucked her under her arm like a handbag. Moist air soothed her face as she stepped into the darkness. She trotted down the steps, avoiding a newly loosened board. The last thing she needed was to be alone.

Inside, Gus and another man stood against the counter in back while Sequoia and Yoshi wiped tables and stacked chairs on them in preparation for mopping. Mira didn't know if Sequoia was doing it to put on a good show for Gus or not, but she didn't care. The girl was finally working.

"Hey," Gus said, nodding his goatee in Mira's direction. Then, to his friend—a shorter man, fortyish, who'd probably once been too pretty to be handsome—he said, "Dude, this is my new, uh, manager I was telling you about, Mira. Mira, this is—"

"Dude, if I'm not mistaken," Mira said, smiling at him, extending her dogless hand.

"It's Doug, actually. Gus here is just stuck in the nineties." His hand was hard, smooth. He was probably only a few inches taller than her, but he looked fit, muscular. He was trying a little too hard to look young with a Lance Armstrong yellow wristband and an army fatigue jacket, but then Mira remembered what jeans she was wearing.

She nodded. "Now that was an unfortunate decade for the English language," she said, and Doug laughed. Was it the thrill of meeting someone near her own age that made her so flirtatious? Someone so good-looking? The movie she'd just been watching? She felt a little like Jane Fonda when she stuck out like a nerdy sore thumb with the Vietnam vets, but kept going back to the VA hospital. "And this is Patsy Cline," she said, cuddling the dog in front of her.

"Hey, dude," Gus said. "You should hear this dog sing. It's awesome."

"Well, then, let's hear it." Doug reached to scratch behind Patsy's ears in a way that demonstrated he'd had other dogs in his life. Mira liked that he had dark hair, dark eyes, and that he wasn't tall. He was the exact opposite of Parker. He leaned back against the counter and dug into his jacket pocket, producing a joint and a green plastic lighter. "Smoke?"

"Whoa," Gus said, glancing at Mira. "Uh, I don't think—"

Mira smiled at Doug, then at her boss. "Gus, why don't you put on that Nine Inch Nails song Patsy loves so much? Doug and I will save you a"—what word did they use now?—"a hit," she decided. She could hear Jane saying that. Jane, the open-minded, courageous heroine who got to sleep with Jon Voight. Mira was feeling more open-minded and courageous all the time.

After Patsy's performance, Mira let her have the run of the place, knowing she'd behave. Gus produced bottles of Rocket Brew, a local Fremont ale, from behind the overstock at the bottom of the juice display, and the three of them stood and drank and chatted and smoked. Mira took a long pull from the joint every time Doug passed it to her. She was surprised that she didn't actually feel it as much as she thought she would. The night with Kenny Ballinger must have been more about leaving her husband and guzzling hard liquor than smoking pot.

While Gus had been nervous about smoking in front of her, he seemed to have no qualms about doing it in front of Yoshi, their new employee. Yoshi, for his part, smiled shyly at them as he clocked out and retrieved his bike from the storeroom. Mira knew she should worry about having any credibility with him as a manager, but she couldn't muster the concern. If Gus smoked in front of his employees, she decided, why shouldn't she? Maybe they'd think of her more as someone . . . cool. Someone like them. Maybe that's who she was becoming. Or maybe that's who she would have been if she hadn't take the mantle of sainthood at such an early age.

Sequoia finished counting the till and joined them, handing Gus the black zippered bag full of cash and checks. She stood as close to him as possible, taking the joint and inhaling dramatically. Her eyes scanned Mira, though she didn't acknowledge her. "We're still going out for Valentine's, aren't we?" she asked as she exhaled. "You promised."

"Yeah, baby," Gus said, wrapping his arm around her dragon-tattooed shoulder. "Just waiting on you." The downside of this new arrangement was that Mira wasn't so sure she really liked seeing her boss cuddle the help.

"Well, if I didn't have to do everything around this place," Sequoia said, exhaling smoke from her nostrils.

Mira laughed—out loud and all of a sudden.

"What's so funny?" Gus asked, taking the joint from Sequoia. "Damn, Dougie, this shit's pretty amped."

Mira tried to stop laughing but couldn't. Gus and Doug smiled at each other and Sequoia tried to ignore her as only a young woman can ignore a middle-aged one. When Mira looked at her and snorted, Sequoia crossed her ink-swirled arms across her chest.

"What the hell?" She looked at Gus. "Are you going to let her dis me like this?"

Gus shook his head. "Chill, baby. She's not dissing you, just feeling the love."

Sequoia backed away from him. "Oh, you're taking her side? You better watch yourself, dude, or you'll be without a girlfriend and the best damn barista you ever had."

Couldn't be soon enough, Mira thought.

"Now, now," Gus said. "Don't be all like that." He reached out and stroked the green dragon tail on Sequoia's forearm. "I thought you wanted to go out. Well, then, let's go."

Sequoia let him pull her to his chest, and when he leaned in to kiss her, she bit his bottom lip, pulling it with her teeth until he winced. "Just so you know who's really boss," she said, turning her back to Mira.

"Damn, baby," Gus said, rubbing his mouth. "You got a wicked set of fangs there."

Sequoia walked toward the door. "Let's get out of here. I'm bored."

"Doug, how about you?" Gus reached in his pocket for keys. "You wanna come, or you want me to drop you off at your place?"

"Nah, I'll let you two lovebirds go alone. Besides, I'm pretty beat." Doug stretched his arms overhead, shirt rising to reveal the bottom half of a muscular stomach beneath the jacket, a dark trail of hair leading from the top button of his lowriding jeans to beneath his shirt. Mira couldn't take her eyes away from it, and she was sorry when he lowered his arms. "I'll walk home," he said. "It's not that far."

"Dude, you're crazy. It's like—" Gus stopped and grinned.

Mira felt all eyes turn to her. "What?" she said, still giggling a little. She wondered, in a vague sort of way, where Patsy Cline had gotten to.

"Hang out as long as you want," Gus said. "There's a few brewskies left. Just lock up when you leave."

"Have you seen Patsy?" Mira asked, turning to look behind her. The dog was sitting against the back door, looking worried. She needed to pee. "I'm sorry, sweetie," Mira said. Outside, Gus and Sequoia climbed into the SUV as Mira walked to the weed patch where Patsy was already doing her business. The truck rumbled to life and swung its headlights around, then slipped into the steady stream of traffic on Thirty-sixth.

The air felt sultry on Mira's skin. Was that all marijuana did to you? Made you laugh and just not care? Why hadn't she been smoking it for the past thirty years? She opened her eyes and looked up at the sky. Directly above, the clouds had parted to reveal the Jewel Box, and the Seven Sisters inside.

"So," she heard a voice say, and turned. Doug was standing in silhouette between the light of the open back door and her. "You're not exactly Sequoia's best friend, huh?"

Mira laughed. "No. Not exactly."

"You want another beer?"

She thought about the trail of dark fuzz on his stomach and swallowed. "You ever see the movie *Coming Home*?"

Patsy finished peeing and trotted to the steps.

"Wow, like a million years ago." He laughed. "You live up there, huh?"

She nodded. "Wanna watch a movie with me and Patsy?"

"Sure." He shrugged.

"Grab some beer. I'll meet you up there," she said, calmly, easily, as if she had men up to her apartment all the time.

Once they'd settled in, Mira realized the small loveseat made for a tight sitting arrangement, which was fine by her. She took a swig of beer. Her head buzzed pleasantly, and she felt somehow altered, but not in a bad way. Floaty. It was the only word she could think of to describe it.

"I'd just watched a few minutes of it," she lied—she'd been well over halfway through the film—"so I'll rewind."

"Wow. Videotape. Cool." Doug shifted so his leg wasn't pressed against hers.

"Sorry, not much furniture in this place," she said. Did he not want to touch her? Should she sit on the chair?

"Hey, I don't mind if you don't mind." He shrugged and draped an arm over the back of the loveseat.

Mira started the tape again and they relaxed against each other bit by bit until Mira forgot to think about it. Patsy wiggled between them and ended up sprawled half on Mira, half on Doug's thigh. Doug absently scratched her ears and Mira patted her flank.

When Jon Voight went down on Jane Fonda, Mira drew a sudden breath and held it. She hoped it wasn't audible. She sneaked a look at Doug and guessed from his own breathing that he found it as erotic as she did. She was afraid to look down for fear she'd stare at his crotch.

A tickle developed in Mira's throat, along with the one that now pulsed in her groin. She coughed, cleared her throat, but she couldn't make it go away. "Sorry," she whispered, taking a drink of beer. Her throat and mouth were so dry she felt like she'd been licking a chalkboard, and she couldn't resist the urge to cough. She reached for the remote and hit PAUSE. Doug looked at her like she'd woken him from a trance.

He swallowed. "Are you okay?"

"I think I need a glass of water."

"Cottonmouth." He nodded.

She'd always heard that term. Now she understood it. "You want a glass, too?" She slid out from under Patsy and walked to the sink in the dark, wondering if her ass looked huge to Doug, who no doubt generally watched dirty movies with younger women. She felt him watching her in a different way than he had before, though, and knew it had everything to do with the glowing freeze-frame image of naked and nubile Jane Fonda splayed across the TV screen. She pulled two unmatched glasses from the cabinet and filled them with tap water, then walked back to the love seat.

"Here." She handed him a glass, then watched him drink as she chugged her own. Water had never tasted so fresh, so cool and velvety inside her mouth. She felt she could drink gallons of it. "More?" she asked, holding out her hand for his glass.

He smiled and shook his head, took her hand and pulled. She leaned down until his mouth was soft and open against hers, moist and cool from the water. She smelled skin, smoke, shaving lotion, and what had to be the sandalwood musk of male pheromones. Her own mouth opened and welcomed his so easily, so naturally, how could that be? How could she be kissing another man with no qualms about it, letting his beer-sweet tongue explore her mouth, exploring his with hers? She hadn't had her mouth on a man other than Parker in twenty-some years, yet it had happened so easily. Was she emitting her own pheromones? Of course she was. She'd probably been doing it the whole night. This seemed so much more intimate than the thought of fucking Kenny Ballinger had been. That had been only an ugly experiment in revenge. This felt the way drinking water had: smooth, velvety. Quenching in a way that made her want more. She and Parker hadn't kissed like this in years. If ever.

Doug took her glass and placed it on the floor with his, then pulled her on top of him, lying back against the length of the small sofa. Patsy scrambled to the floor. Mira heard her little toenails click to the bed and the small thud she made as she leapt onto it, then the rustling as she circled her body to resettle. The rain began to pat against the roof again; the paused TV hummed. Mira lay on top of Doug, one arm behind his neck, the other hand in his hair, kissing him and being kissed. They were similar enough in size that they fit together like a puzzle, part for part.

Mira shifted until his thigh was between her legs, then moved against him rhythmically, instinctively, the urge coming from a place so long buried that she'd almost forgotten ever feeling this way. Doug moaned into her mouth as he pulled her hips tight against him, shuddering.

Mira felt like weeping, even as her dry throat began to emit sounds she hadn't heard herself make in a very long time. *Thank you,* she wanted to whisper, *thank you, thank you,* but who was she thanking, and for what? Was she thanking this stranger just for wanting her, herself for giving in to it? At some hormone-suppressed level she knew this was wrong, but Mira felt like weeping for joy, and for all of the sadness beneath it.

Twenty-eight

A quarter to six the next morning, Mira slipped into the coffee shop, turning on lights with trepidation. She'd been so stoned and horny the night before she'd forgotten to lock the back door. Somewhere in the middle of the night, when Doug finally left after hours of their making out like inebriated teens who didn't know what to do next, she'd hoped that he'd think to lock it. She'd then fallen instantly to sleep.

Now she tiptoed into the storeroom, the bathroom, then back out into the shop. It was okay. The cash register was intact, and everything looked the way it always did. This was why people didn't smoke pot, she realized. It stole your brain, and just when you needed it most.

It also made you kiss people you didn't know and hump their leg. She was no more evolved than Patsy Cline. At least she hadn't slept with him. He'd started to unbutton her jeans, and she'd moaned, "No, I can't. I'm sorry," and they'd gone back to kissing. He'd felt her breasts through her sweater. She'd grabbed his ass, his incredibly muscular ass, and pressed herself back into him, knowing it was the worst thing she could do to him, just to feel him shudder again. Thinking about it now induced a dizzying sensation.

Mira closed her eyes at a clammy wave of heat in her chest, gripping the counter. Arousal or low progesterone? She'd forgotten to use her cream for two days in a row. The heat grew inside her, permeating her groin, her breasts where they'd rubbed against Doug's chest.

Doug would tell Gus, who'd tell Sequoia, who'd tell—*Stop it,* she reprimanded herself. *Nobody here cares who I make out with. This isn't freaking Pacifica.*

Technically, she was still married, but what if she and Parker had split up the way normal people do, the way he'd wanted to, and he'd moved to an apartment in town? It would be expected that they would each date again, eventually. It wasn't like Parker didn't have someone else. It wasn't like he died and she should wait a year before moving on. She was tired of being in mourning.

Who knew if she and Doug had anything in common—she doubted it. Anyone who claimed Gus as a friend was probably not someone Mira would have ever thought about this way, much less had an actual relationship with. Still, he kissed her the way she'd always wanted to be kissed, languidly yet somehow fervently at the same time, and she shivered just thinking about the way they so naturally fit together.

What would they do now? Date? Or would he even want to see her again? Mira had no idea how all of this was supposed to work.

As she removed chairs from tables, Mira saw Sidney leaning against the window outside, holding her notebook against her chest and shivering. Mira grabbed her keys from the counter and went to open the door.

"It's too cold for you to stand out there, come in."

Sidney turned, then cast her eyes downward.

"It's okay. I can wait until you're ready."

"I'm ready, I'm ready," Mira said, laughing. "Get in here before I drag you, okay?"

"Thanks." The girl shuffled past Mira to her usual spot.

"How about some tea, or some orange juice?" Mira followed her. "Do you need some breakfast? I've got a basket of day-olds here, but they're still delicious."

Sidney shrugged and sat down.

"God," Mira said. "I've gone completely psycho-mommy on you, haven't I?" A thickness rose in her throat. "I guess I just . . . I miss my daughter." She hadn't been thinking of Thea; she hadn't been thinking of anything sad—a happy aftereffect of the night before—but now it was all she could do to keep from bawling.

"It's okay," Sidney said with a shy smile. "I kinda like it when you're psycho-mommy."

Later that morning, Mira was beginning to think she'd made a mistake hiring Amanda. Although she was seventeen and had interviewed well, she acted like a giggly preteen whenever an attractive male entered the shop, tossing her hair, looking up from beneath long lashes as she took orders. Jutting out a hip as she pulled espresso shots and whizzed smoothies in the blender. She was proficient enough at the job, but Mira didn't know how long she'd be able to take the hormonal prancing. It was like watching a cat in heat roaming the neighborhood.

After the rush died down, Mira sent Amanda in back to wash dishes. She'd washed so many dishes herself lately that her hands were permanently chapped; she pumped lotion from the dispenser beneath the counter. Her mind kept returning to the events of the night before, shivers and twinges reverberating through her body at the memory of Doug's hand, or mouth, or body upon her. The front door opened just as she realized she'd pumped far too much lotion into her hands, and she looked up to see Martin's friendly smile.

"Good morning," he said. "You look . . . well, I would say 'on cloud nine,' but I'm not allowed to use clichés in my profession."

"It's okay. You're on a coffee break." She gestured helplessly with her white slathered hands. "You want some lotion?"

Oh my god, she thought. *Couldn't you just wipe your hands on a towel?* "I mean, Jesus, never mind." She laughed a hyena yelp, then stopped herself. She was insane.

"I'd love some," Martin said, reaching over the counter and taking her hands in his, then sliding his palms and fingers slowly down the length of hers before rubbing his own hands together. "Smells nice. What kind is it?"

Mira shifted at the sudden dampness in her underwear. "Nivea," she said, wondering what Martin looked like beneath his bulky sweater. Did he have body hair? He was thin, but that didn't mean he couldn't have a nice chest, a muscular stomach. Not like Doug's, but—

"So, could I get the usual? If you please." Martin smiled, leaning into the counter the way he always did, and it was all Mira could do to keep from jumping over and mounting him like a stallion. What on earth was wrong with her?

"Mm hmm," she mumbled, and forced herself to turn to the espresso machine. Did Martin think her ass was huge? Did he think she was ancient? Did he even think about her other than as a supplier of caffeine?

She turned to hand him his cup. "How old are you?" she asked.

"Thirty-two." His brow furrowed, but he smiled. "Why?"

"I don't know," she said, feeling her face color. "Just in case I come across someone to fix you up with."

He laughed. "Don't bother. I'm hopeless at blind dates."

"So you're single?" Why was she pressing him?

"I love that word," he said. "As though I could be double or triple."

Mira forced a smile and slid the pitcher of steamed half-and-half toward him.

He sighed. "Why are you so good to me, *bella* Mira?"

She held his gaze longer than was comfortable. What did she want from him? "My dad used to call me Mirabella," she finally said. Tears came to her eyes.

"Then I will, too." He reached for her hand, in a friendly way, she thought, until he brought it to his lips and kissed it. "Mm, Nivea," he said.

That night after a dinner of take-out sushi from PCC, Mira paced the floor. She'd tried calling Lannie to confess all about her startling new sex life, but got her machine. She knew better than to leave a message this time. Mira still wanted desperately to call Thea, every minute of every day, actually, but her new approach was to give her daughter some time. She would have to come around, eventually. Wouldn't she?

Then a terrifying thought hit her. What if she called Parker? What if he answered the phone, and she said hello like a normal person, asked how he was? Was that totally out of the question in a situation like this? How would he react? Would he cry with relief, as her father had? Would he soften at the sound of her voice? Would he be angry, or worse—aloof?

God. Did Parker really have a girlfriend? Lannie seemed to think not, but Lannie had turned into the most annoyingly optimistic person on the planet when it came to Parker. She'd even had the nerve to suggest that maybe Mira worked at the coffee shop as a way to feel closer to him.

"Right," Mira said, shaking her head, rolling her eyes. God, she hoped it wasn't true. What she did know was that she'd found a place to just be for a while, a place filled with kids not that different from the ones she'd been around every day for the past twenty years. It might not feel like home, but at least she no longer felt lonely.

Patsy watched from beneath her bangs as Mira sighed, sat down at the table, then the couch, then jumped back up. Maybe she should go down to the shop, be there when Gus arrived, hopefully with Doug in tow. Or would that be too obvious? Patsy followed her into the small bathroom, sat on the new fluffy bath mat as Mira applied a few strokes of blush, inspecting herself in the mirror. She'd never asked Doug how old he was. Maybe he wasn't in his forties; maybe he just didn't age well. Maybe, but there was no way he was as young as Martin. Mira tried not to think about the thirteen years she'd been alive while Martin wasn't. She was old enough to have been his babysitter, his much older sister. Technically, she supposed, his mother.

"Technically," she said to Patsy, who beat her tail against the floor. "Okay, then, let's go downstairs for a while."

Down in the coffee shop, what looked to be a high school girl sat at Mira's favorite computer, chewing on bright pink fingernails and drinking a raspberry smoothie as she did her homework. She reminded Mira too much of Thea at that age to give her the evil eye, so she settled in with a decaf at the temperamental PC near the front. Patsy lay at her feet, chin resting on the top of Mira's shoe.

Felix was on tonight with Yoshi, and Mira sensed something in the air as they stood together at the counter, trying not to smile at each other.

Ah, she thought. *Of course.* An ache formed in her throat. Love was so sweet. She smiled at Felix, who blushed and hurried into the back. Yoshi shrugged, and picked up a pencil, trying to twirl it in his fingers like a drumstick.

After checking the Seattle school system's job posting site, Mira went to blogbaby.com, but Thea's page was no longer available. Sighing, Mira closed her eyes and heard herself moan. Quickly, she sat up and looked around, but no one had noticed. "Shit," she said. She wished Doug would drop by. She wished something would happen. The term "wire in the blood" occurred to her, and that was exactly how she felt. Wired. Antsy. Uncomfortably aware of every nerve ending, like an exposed wound. She typed "progesterone side effects" into the search engine box. She squinted at the screen, then reached for the red glasses in her purse. Just before hitting GO she added "libido."

The first home improvement project Parker and Mira took on after they settled into the long-neglected beach house was just after Thea's first birthday. She had recently mastered the art of escaping from the crib Parker had built on the sneak in his buddy's barn when Mira was pregnant. Her Christmas gift. They'd set it up in a small anteroom off their upstairs bedroom, and Mira had nightmares about Thea falling down the slippery hardwood stairs in the middle of the night. They needed to relocate their own sleeping quarters to the main floor for the duration of her childhood, which meant combining two small bedrooms into one, and fix up the remaining bedroom for Thea. "She needs a little girl's room," Mira said, imagining the underwater mural she'd paint on the ceiling, the aquamarine glass floats she'd hang in the windows.

Enlisting help from cousins and a couple of Parker's co-workers from the water treatment plant, they'd sledgehammered through walls, torn up layer upon layer of old flooring, each surface exposing even uglier periods of home décor, until they arrived at the original fir planks. Mira's second cousin Enzo was a carpenter of sorts, and he took great care restoring the old home's floors and wood trim. He patched where one door had to be removed, and for years afterward, until they moved back upstairs to their old master bedroom, Mira would lie in bed and try to remember where it had been.

They finished their new bedroom first, and had plenty of space in it for Thea's crib, although most nights she climbed out and into their bed some time after Parker and Mira fell asleep. Progress on Thea's room slowed, their initial enthusiasm waning as funds ran dry. They gave up on the crib altogether when Thea took a tumble out of it one night, headfirst, raising an ugly purple red bump on her forehead.

In the post-baby throes of regaining her desire for sex, Mira took up a campaign to finish Thea's room. They needed an electrician to rewire the dead sockets. Parker had tried, joking that his degree might come in handy for something, finally—the job market in Tillamook County didn't provide much work for electrical engineers. Although he was a whiz at soldering circuit boards, he was no electrician, and gave up after exposing singed and rotting cloth-covered wires in the walls.

Big Al knew a guy in Rockaway whose wife's brother was a licensed electrician, and he offered to pay for the work as a second-anniversary gift for the couple. Mira knew Parker felt even worse about accepting the money than he did about failing at his attempts to do the work himself, but she also knew she needed to have sex again. She didn't know how Parker had been coping during their first year as parents, but she imagined he was taking care of himself during morning showers. She, on the other hand, never felt alone enough to try even that. Thea had discovered she loved taking showers with Mommy.

The electrician's small white truck parked in front of their house late on a Monday morning, just after Thea went down for a nap. Mira watched from the front window as a man thinner and younger than she'd expected walked toward the door. She'd pictured her uncle Tony, a portly plumber with the prototypical plumber's crack. This man was dressed neatly in denim shirt and chinos, belted high enough that there'd be no unfortunate exposures. Actually, Mira thought, it might not be such a bad thing on him.

She pulled open the front door before he rang the bell. He wasn't as handsome as Parker, but there was something in his ruddy complexion and nearly black eyes that she found mesmerizing.

He was quiet and took his job seriously, getting right to work and turning down all of Mira's offers of coffee, Coke, a piece of banana bread she'd just made. She found excuses to come into the room as he was working: measuring for curtains, holding up paint chips to the wall. She tried starting conversations, asking how long he'd been an electrician, where he was from. He replied in polite but short sentences.

"How long do you think this job will take?" she asked, positioning herself against the wall he was working on.

He stopped, finally, and looked at her. "A lot longer if you keep talking to me." He winked and leaned his shoulder into the wall. Mira didn't know whether she should run or keep standing there, but she knew her face had turned crimson.

Seeing her embarrassment, he laughed. "I'm sorry. I'm just kidding around. There's only about a day and a half of work to do here."

"Okay," she said, backing out of the door.

That night, in bed with Parker and Thea, she couldn't stop thinking about the electrician. He wore his hair longer in the back than Parker did, shorter on the sides, the way the musicians on the new music channel did. She'd started watching music videos during the day, fascinated by the posing and strutting, the clothing styles, the sense that everyone out there was having a lot more fun than she was at the age of twenty-four, stuck in her old hometown with a child who was Velcroed to her side.

As Thea poked her ribs with tiny feet and Parker snored, Mira imagined the electrician in a band, singing into the microphone the way that sinuous guy in that Australian band did. He practically had sex with the mike stand. She swallowed and blinked her eyes at the ceiling, then climbed carefully out of bed, tiptoeing to the bathroom down the hall.

She turned on the light and flinched against the glare, turning it back off. She locked the door, then knelt over the bathtub, turning the faucet a quarter of the way on. Who knew how long it would take to fill the tub that way, but at least the sound of blasting water wouldn't wake anyone. As for her, she'd have to be quiet, too, not moan or gasp too loudly. She tried to picture

Parker in her mind as she rubbed her hand between her legs, not the electrician, but every time she began to lose herself, she saw dark hair, those searching eyes.

Later, when she returned to bed still damp, Parker mumbled, "You okay?"

"Mm-hmm," she said, letting him drape his arm across her stomach until he began to snore again. Then she rolled away from him and fell asleep.

Mira lay in bed, unable to sleep and feeling like an idiot. So what if Doug hadn't called her, or come by? Why did she want to see him so badly after knowing him for such a brief, albeit intimate, few hours?

She shouldn't have made him stop.

"Oh, Jesus," she said, sitting up. That was it. She hadn't . . . well, she hadn't come. Not last night, and not in a long time.

Patsy rustled beside her, then rolled over on her back, waggling her legs in the air and exposing her pink freckled tummy. Mira groaned. She was more like Patsy than she realized. All she wanted was someone to rub her secret parts, to put her into a state of ecstasy.

Mira pushed herself from the bed.

Patsy leapt off the bed and ran to the door.

"No, we're not going outside." Mira walked to the closet, pushed behind her clothing and coat for the suitcase in the corner. She pulled it out and carried it to the bed, snapped open the latches and lifted the top, staring at the only item she'd left unpacked.

"Hello, stranger," she said. The cream-colored plastic of El Wando shone in the darkness, and felt comfortably substantial in Mira's hand. It wasn't love, it wasn't companionship, but if it could release the insistent thrumming in her body, in her mind, maybe that would be enough for now.

Mira put the suitcase back and resettled in bed, plumped the pillow behind her and drew the blanket up over her chest. Patsy had curled into a ball on the couch, for which Mira was grateful.

With a click of a button, the vibrator buzzed to life and Mira placed it against the inside of her thigh, then rolled it slowly inward. She closed her eyes and pictured the night before, felt her pelvis grinding into Doug's hard thigh, his hands grasping her hips and pulling her harder against him. She replayed his moaning, adding her name: "Mira, oh god, Mira." She'd always fantasized this, someone saying her name in his own passion, the way she always moaned, "Oh Parker, oh Jesus." It was involuntary, just as the sensation of fullness was in her abdomen, the way it rose to fill her chest when she neared orgasm, filling her with an effervescent tremor that exited through her throat in this chanting.

"Doug, oh Doug," she moaned, imagining his hands sliding under her sweater, then down the front of her pants. Her body tensed, and as she tried to conjure his face, she saw Martin's instead.

"Oh god," she whispered, eyes rolling back against closed lids. She convulsed, her spine pulling her upper body forward like a nautilus shell, folding in on itself, over and over, endlessly connected to something so vast she could only sense it in this otherworldly state of release.

Twenty-nine

"SMILE, PLEASE." YOSHI HELD A CAMERA INCHES FROM MIRA'S FACE as she stood at the counter in the yellow-gray light of a March afternoon.

"Um, don't you think that's a little close?" Mira cringed at the digital whirring of the tiny silver box.

"'Up close and personal with the staff.' That's the idea."

Yoshi, as it turned out, was a budding Web designer, and Gus was paying him practically nothing to put up a site for the Coffee Shop at the Center of the Universe.

"Yeah, well, most of the staff don't have wrinkles." Not to mention broken blood vessels and uneven pigment from pregnancy, she thought. The occasional whisker she could no longer see unless she remembered to wear her reading glasses when plucking. "Please, Yoshi, give me a break."

Yoshi sighed but backed up. "I'll just have to crop in," he said. "Now, smile, please."

Mira smiled, trying to think of something funny or happy so it didn't look forced. Her mind was blank.

"Let's try one with your glasses on," Yoshi said. Mira obliged. Maybe that would hide the crow's-feet.

"You want to see?" He turned the camera around to show her the postage stamp–size screen. Her image looked like a thumbprint wearing red glasses.

"Not particularly," Mira said. Who would go looking at their Web site anyway? Especially at a photo of her.

"Take mine next," Sequoia said. She'd changed her hair color from blue to an almost-normal burgundy, and Mira had to admit she was a pretty girl. Pretty full of herself, too, but still.

With the camera a foot in front of his face, Yoshi walked toward Sequoia, who mugged and hammed in a variety of poses. Girls these days were well practiced at posing in mirrors, a fact Mira knew from supervising girls' restrooms at dances and graduations. All of the female blog site photos she'd ever seen besides Thea's were posed like magazine covers, generally of the *Cosmo* and *Maxim* variety.

Mira watched Gus, wondering if he saw how much better everything was now that she'd taken over. She hadn't relieved him of his duties exactly—he was still officially the boss—but they never ran out of supplies now, they were consistent in the way they made their drinks, and the quality of their employees had to have been at an all-time high. Gus seemed surprised that they all showed up for photo day, but Mira wasn't. They liked working here.

Mira sighed, thinking of the many school photo days she'd participated in—thirty-two of them, counting her own years as a student. When she was a kid, she and her friends had hated it, or pretended to anyway, then dreaded seeing the prints weeks later. Perhaps this whole digital thing wasn't so bad. At least you could delete and try again.

Felix was shy in front of the camera, while Amanda smiled like a cheerleader. Gus wanted his to be serious, hand stroking his goatee, but Sequoia sneaked up and grabbed his waist, tickling him.

"How about Patsy Cline?" Felix asked. "We have to have her."

"Definitely," Amanda said, and Gus nodded

Mira trotted up the steps to the apartment and grabbed Patsy. She usually waited until nighttime to let the dog come visit, in case there were any persnickety customers, but Seattle, it turned out, was a dog town. Everyone took their pets everywhere and the health department turned a blind eye.

Back in the shop, Doug had arrived. It was the first time she'd seen him since the first time she'd seen him, nearly three weeks before.

"Oh," she said, "hi," trying not to look either miffed that he hadn't called or pleased that he was there now. He and Gus were no doubt going off to do something. Gus had been talking about how great the spring snow conditions were at Mount Baker.

"Hi," Doug said, walking over and squatting to scratch Patsy's ears. He looked up at Mira and smiled without looking at all sheepish or guilty. "How would you like to go with me to the Tractor Tavern next Friday night? My buddy Howard's band is playing. Maybe you've heard of them—the Screaming Hematomas."

Mira had seen ads for the Tractor in the *Seattle Weekly*. It seemed terribly hip and young. "I'd love to," she said, feeling hipper and younger all the time. So what if Doug hadn't called her? She didn't want a serious relationship any more than he did. This was the new Mira, the Mira who could have a casual relationship and just enjoy it. "What kind of music is it?"

"Old people's," Sequoia said.

"I like the music there," Felix said, and Mira wanted to kiss him.

Sequoia rolled her eyes and unwrapped a day-old chocolate croissant, unraveling the pastry down to the dark chocolate morsels and popping them into her mouth. "Whatever," she said, chasing the chocolate with a large hunk of croissant.

Doug shook his head and stood up. Winking at Mira, he said, "As far as I'm concerned, they play good old rock and roll. They're loud, and they're fun. And my buddy plays a mean guitar."

"Sounds good to me." Mira couldn't remember the last time she'd seen a band play live, or gone to a bar that wasn't the Driftwood. She also couldn't remember the last time she'd had sex, though it must have been the last Saturday in December, and the thought that she could very well be having it within a matter of days made her flush. El Wando was fine as a stand-in, but she craved another human in her bed. Maybe they'd smoke pot again and she'd feel carnal and shameless the way she had that night. Just thinking about it turned her breathing shallow.

"Hold Patsy up for her photo," Yoshi said, coming closer and closer with his camera.

"Smile, Patsy Cline," Felix said, and the dog reached her long pink tongue out to lick the camera lens.

Later, Mira and Gus were alone in the storeroom unloading boxes of supplies he'd brought in that day. As she suspected, he and Doug were on their way to Mount Baker. Doug had gone outside to load his things into the SUV.

"So," Gus said, taking a slurp from his Red Bull granita. "You and Dougie must have hit it off that night."

"All we did was watch a movie," she said, then heard how defensive she sounded. "He's a nice guy."

"He's a great guy," Gus said, and they heard the car door slam outside. "He's had his heart broken a few times, though, so be nice to him."

Mira laughed. "Why wouldn't I be nice to him? Besides, I think I win in the broken heart department. I ran away from home after twenty-four years of marriage because my husband was cheating on me." *Or about to,* she didn't say. Even she could hear how lame that sounded.

"Whoa," Gus said, eyes widening. "That I did not know."

"Well, it's not something you tell just, you know, anyone."

"Well, I'm glad you told me. I guess we haven't really gotten to know each other very well so far."

"No," Mira agreed.

"Listen," Gus said, "there's something I should probably tell you."

Oh, thought Mira, *how sweet. He's going to reveal something about himself, too.*

"We don't need everything so, so . . ." He paused, tugging his goatee. "So perfect around here. This place is a little more Zen. I like a little imperfection, you know? Perfectly imperfect."

Mira couldn't believe what she was hearing, even from Gus. "You like employees not showing up and running out of soy milk during a rush?" She tried to appear calm but she could feel her teeth clenching, her eyes narrowing. The expression Thea always called "teacher face."

"Look, all I'm saying is you might want to back off a little. I'm worried there's going to be a revolt, and if it comes down to losing longtime employees, I'd probably be forced to make a choice I really don't want to."

"But—"

The back door slammed open and Doug called, "Yo, Gus. Ready?"

Gus looked at her. "Are we good?"

Before she could reply, Doug walked in, saying, "We really need to hit the road, bro." And to Mira, "I'll pick you up Friday at seven. We can get a bite before the show."

She'd wanted to see him so badly, and now all she could do was force a shaky smile and try to act as if everything were normal.

As Doug and Gus headed for the door, Sequoia yelled, "Wait!" She ran over and whispered into Gus's ear.

He sighed and removed a key from his carabiner clip.

She grabbed the key from him and smiled. "Thanks, August."

"Please don't call me that."

"Oh, get over yourself." She reached up to tousle his hair.

"Jesus." Gus smoothed it back down. "Okay, we're out of here."

"Bye-bye, Auggie," Sequoia called in a singsong voice, pocketing the key.

Once Gus was gone, Mira relaxed as the festive atmosphere of photo day lasted into evening. All the employees stayed on at the Coffee Shop at the Center of the Universe, sitting at the large oval table in the window, laughing, joking, making drink concoctions for each other to try. Amanda made a round of Fluffer Nutter Mochas with dollops of the peanut butter and marshmallow fluff she kept in the fridge for lunch. Yoshi created something he called Grasshopper in a Blender, using crème de menthe syrup and sliced almonds, "for the crunchy parts," he said. He was the only one who seemed to enjoy the texture. Felix whizzed together caramel sauce, vanilla syrup, frozen yogurt, and whipped cream. The result was sweet and heavenly, "Like crème caramel," Mira said, and a new drink was written on the board: *Carmelito de Felix.*

See? Mira thought. *I can do Zen.* Gus was just trying to stay in his girlfriend's good graces. *Or her pants,* she thought, wondering what the two saw in each other. She'd be happy to back off a little now that everything was working so well.

Half an hour before closing time, a band of what Mira could only think of as thugs came through the door, tall and hulking, various parts of their heads shaved, studs and rings running amok in their flesh like so much metal salvage, clothed in leather and torn fabric and spikes. *And filth,* Mira thought, trying not to hold her breath.

"May I, uh . . ." She stood to walk to the counter to help them, then faltered when they gathered around Sequoia, who squealed and gave them each a hug.

"Oh, okay," Mira said, sitting back down. It figured. What other kind of friends would Sequoia have?

They dragged chairs from other tables and squeezed in. The conversation turned from silly and lighthearted to loud one-upmanship in a slang Mira could not comprehend but suspected had something to do with hip-hop, even though these whiter-than-white kids had probably only experienced black culture on MTV.

Felix fled quickly to the back to wash dishes. Yoshi slid his chair from the table in minute increments. Mira wanted to do the same thing, to scoot until she was away from this loud group altogether. Amanda tried flirting at first, then looked scared when one of them eyed her hungrily.

Mira stood. "Can I get anyone anything?" she asked. *At least they could buy something,* she thought, but they ignored her. Yoshi asked for a refill on his jasmine green tea, causing smirks all around. Amanda stood and walked over to him, sat in his lap and put her arms around his neck, causing thoughtful nodding and raised eyebrows to replace the smirks. *Good girl,* thought Mira.

As Mira squirted steaming water from the espresso machine into Yoshi's teapot, Sequoia breezed past her in a patchouli cloud and disappeared into the storeroom, pulling the door halfway closed behind her.

Mira sighed. She needed more green tea anyway. Taking a deep breath, she walked to the storeroom and pushed the door open.

Sequoia leaned over the safe, slamming it closed and turning at the sound of Mira's footsteps.

"Don't sneak up on me like that."

Mira held her arms to her sides so she wouldn't reach out and slap her. "I needed some tea," she said. "What are you doing in here?"

"None of your business." Sequoia had clearly stuffed something up her shirt. She started to walk out, but Mira held out her hand to stop her.

"Wait a minute. What's going on?"

"Keep your big nose out of it." Sequoia scowled and stormed past her.

Little bitch, thought Mira, touching her nose. No one had called it big in years. She sighed and hurried out to the front where Sequoia's gang had all gathered around her. She was doing something beneath the table. Rolling a joint, Mira suspected.

"Stop it, Sequoia," Mira said. "You can't do that here. The store's still open. Anyone who's walking by can see in."

"So?" the girl sneered. "I can do whatever the hell I want. Gus said. Just back off."

"You can't do anything illegal in here. I think Gus would back me up on that."

"You don't know a thing about what goes on around here. Besides, you toke up on the free bud just like everybody else, Little Miss Schoolteacher." She laughed. "Now that's a role model for you, huh?"

Amanda gasped and looked at Mira. She and Yoshi stood and faded back, out of the hot circle of light that the table and the thugs had become, Sequoia at one end and Mira at the other. It was like a Wild West showdown and Sequoia would fight dirty, but Mira didn't care.

"Gus isn't here, so what I say goes. I want everybody out of here. We're closing."

"Can she do that?" Amanda whispered.

Sequoia looked up and shook her head. "I'm not doing anything you say, teach, so just get over yourself." Her lips turned up in a viper smile, and with the new dark red hair, the tattoos, the Cleopatra eyeliner, she looked like a horror movie ingénue. "Why don't you just go back and help that wetback homo with the dishes, and when you come back out, your little world will be all perfect again."

Amanda gasped again, and Mira sensed her moving forward in her peripheral vision, her voice little-girl high but mighty: "You shouldn't talk like tha—"

"And what the fuck do you know? Do you realize Mira got the guy you replaced fired for no good reason? Gus didn't even say she could do it, she just did, so you better watch out who you take sides with. You might be next. She doesn't own this place even though she acts like it, changing everything all the time. Gus doesn't like change. When he hears about this, I don't know. I don't think he's going to be happy."

"Let's call him, shall we?" Mira's heart rocked against her chest wall, but she felt pretty sure he'd back her up. Sequoia was out of control, even by his standards.

Sequoia fished in her pocket for her lime green phone, flipped it open. She eyed Mira with disdain as she dialed. "Yo," she said into the phone. "It's just like I told you, a fucking mutiny's going down. You better call me back." She flipped it closed again. "There you go."

"I'll need to talk to him, too, Sequoia," Mira said, trying to keep her voice calm, her actions adult, but she wanted to strangle this spoiled and deranged girl, or run as fast as she could away from this place. She could so use a principal's office about now.

They glared at each other for a long moment. Even the hoods barely breathed. Then Sequoia shrugged and went back to whatever she'd been doing under the table, snickering and shaking her head.

Mira walked to the back of the store. Felix had to be rewashing dishes at this point, he'd been back there so long. "Hiding out, huh?" she asked, and he shrugged. "Good idea," she said, and picked up the phone to dial.

"Yo," Gus said.

"You need to hear my side." Mira's heart pounded in her head.

"What? Mira? What are you talking about?"

He hadn't gotten Sequoia's message; she'd probably completely faked the call to him.

"Sequoia's out of control, Gus. You need to talk to her."

"God, I'm not even gone a day. Can't you two just—"

"She took something from your safe and now she's sitting out in the front of the shop with a bunch of scary-looking punks, rolling a joint or something under the table, I can't tell. We're still open, Gus. I don't know what she's planning, but I don't think it's a tea party. I asked her to leave and she won't."

Gus blew a long breath. "Did you see what she took?"

"No. She stuffed it under her shirt."

"It's not what you think."

"Whatever it is, I told her she can't do anything illegal. I mean, I don't want to get into your personal business or anything, but you agree, don't you?"

"Put her on. Fuck."

Who knew if he was angry with her or Sequoia or both of them. She grabbed her purse from the hook by the back door, passing Yoshi and Amanda as they hurried to the back. She heard the rear door slam as they left.

"It's Gus," she said to Sequoia, handing her the phone.

The girl sneered up at her. "A little privacy?"

The thugs tittered. Mira smelled smoke. They were smoking cigarettes in the coffee shop, tipping ashes into Yoshi's abandoned teacup. Three joints lay on the table next to a book of matches. At least there were no customers.

Mira's fingers twitched at her sides. Words of outrage formed at the back of her mouth, but she swallowed them. "Fine," she said, and walked out the front door, flipping the OPEN sign to CLOSED as she went.

Mira walked east from the shop in the damp dark until she was at the main intersection of Thirty-sixth and Fremont. To her right sat the little blue bridge, usually packed with traffic but quiet now. She turned and walked toward it, past closed shops and low-lit restaurants, past the bus stop she'd heard about, where a group of sculpted passengers await the bus in perpetuity, dressed or adorned in whatever the neighborhood felt like dressing them in. Tonight they all wore pink tutus, even the dog, and held a banner wishing Caitlin a happy birthday.

Mira walked onto the pedestrian walkway of the bridge. She stopped in the middle. Looking up, she saw a neon Rapunzel in the two-story control tower, yellow tubes of blond hair cascading over her shoulder. "Huh," she said. She turned and looked down into the dark water below, breathed in her favorite smells—sea and woodsmoke. She looked up at the larger and more trafficked Aurora Bridge to the east, a huge expanse of cantilevered metal girders and concrete. Mira had read in the *Seattle Weekly* that the city installed crisis-line telephones on the bridge for jumpers, Seattle's lost and desperate souls who saw no other way out than to slam into the hard surface of the Ship Canal a hundred and eighty feet below before drowning. *I wonder if it's the darkness here that drives them to it,* she thought. *Or how lonely it can feel living in such a big city.* She shivered and turned back the way she'd come.

Was it karma? Was life throwing Parker's cosmic barista hell at her for running away? Or for her pathetic subconscious attempt to be closer to him, doing the work he did? *Fuck,* she thought. If only she could talk to him, get his advice, but he wasn't her partner, her confidant, her ally anymore. Of all the ways she felt lonely, sometimes that felt the worst of all.

Maybe she should leave after all. It was March now; her three months would soon be up. Maybe she wasn't meant to be in this city, in this life. She was a schoolteacher, a wife, a mother. She could still be one of those things. There were smaller towns all around the Northwest, friendlier places just fifty miles away, with struggling school districts that might need seasoned teachers. They'd have smaller paychecks than in Seattle, but lower rents, too.

Wending her way north through the intersection and uphill, Mira thought about the neon woman keeping watch over the canal. She wondered if her mother kept watch over her, the way Nonna always said she had.

At the cross street ahead, cars streamed downhill toward Fremont from beneath the northern end of the Aurora Bridge to her right, where something seemed to be happening. She'd lived in Seattle for months without exploring her surroundings beyond the routes to PCC in one direction and Fred Meyer in the other.

As she approached the corner, another car came down the hill, occupants inside all smiling, talking, laughing. At the crest of the hill, cars slowed at the interior angle of bridge and land, then drove on. She turned up the side street, moving toward whatever it was that was making everyone so damn happy. Maybe it would rub off on her.

An amorphous mountain of dirt beneath the bridge started to take form as she got closer. Large hands with fingers the size of tree branches materialized, a strong facial profile, a big nose—*even bigger than mine,* she thought. Stupid Sequoia. She walked faster up the hill and arrived out of breath at the top as a family of many small dark children crossed from the other side of the road. The children giggled, speaking to each other in a language Mira didn't recognize, then ran toward the blob, a huge concrete troll who seemed to be crawling from beneath the bridge, an actual Volkswagen bug crushed in one hand, a glittering hubcap for an eye.

He was ugly, disproportionate, and he made her laugh. This was her idea of perfectly imperfect—the gift of art in an unexpected place, something so surprising and oddly endearing that it could make a city full of busy, rain-soaked, overcaffeinated people stop what they were doing and smile.

The mother of the children stood with Mira as the older kids climbed the beast's hands and ropes of concrete hair to his huge nostrils, where they poked their heads inside. The younger ones stared up in awe. Mira laughed again and the woman looked at her and smiled, shrugging. So what if she had her children out late, Mira thought. It was Saturday night; everyone was in a festive mood. Cars passed behind them, honking sometimes, people laughing. "God, I love this city," someone said from a car window.

After a few moments, the mother called to her children. Like obedient little soldiers they ran to her side, then crossed the road and climbed back into the car. Mira stood a few minutes more, looking into the troll's one eye. It took a happy people to be this creative and strange. And to appreciate this creativity and strangeness. The Sequoias of the world were few, and Mira would be damned if the girl outlasted her. She'd give it another month. She had nowhere else to go, anyway.

Thirty

T HE NEXT MORNING, MIRA OPENED THE BACK DOOR TO THE SHOP, not knowing what to expect. She hadn't gone back in the night before; she was still too angry. The place looked clean, at least. Pulling chairs off tables, she sniffed the air. No residual pot odor left in the air, no ashes anywhere to be found.

As she unlocked the front door, the store phone rang. Mira ran to the back to grab the cordless from its cradle, hoping it wasn't anyone calling in sick. What if it had been a mutiny, not just a Sequoia moment? What if no one came to work that day?

"Yo," Gus said. "Mira."

"Hey, Gus," she said. "Kind of early, isn't it?"

"The slopes are calling, dude."

Somehow Mira didn't mind the unisex application of this term from Gus. When her students in Pacifica had tried it, she made them write her name one hundred times during detention.

"So, did you work it out with Sequoia last night?" she asked. "I tried to take care of it, but—"

"You just gotta know how to handle her, is all. She hates authority and rules and all that shit, but I told her not to be such a pain in the ass."

Mira rolled her eyes. Pain in the ass? No, Mira was a pain in the ass. Sequoia was a nightmare.

Gus sighed. "All I'm saying is just try to get along with her until I get back, okay? No more confrontations. It's only two more days."

Mira pressed her lips together, trying to think of the best way to reply and keep her job. The bell on the front door jangled. "I have to go. I'll do what I can, Gus, but I can't in good conscience let her get away with murder while I'm here. Even if you decide I'm the one who has to go when you get back."

She hung up, heart thumping, but she felt an uneasy sense of righteousness. She might be the only one willing to take a stand in the Center of the Universe, and it might get her fired, but maybe that was okay. Mira stood motionless for a moment, finger over the scar on her cheek, then walked out into the impending busyness of morning.

She didn't see Sequoia that day, leaving immediately at the end of her shift. Sequoia wasn't due for another two hours. Unless provoked, Mira would do what Gus asked of her: avoid confrontation. She had, however, given the other employees her cell number in case of "emergencies." Everyone seemed a bit dazed, too polite, and she couldn't tell if they were afraid of Sequoia or just keeping their distance from Mira. Were they mad she hadn't done more the night before? Did they think she'd overstepped her bounds, that she should have allowed the smoking of pot in the party atmosphere? It had been nearly closing time, after all.

At closing time, she stayed in her apartment, hoping Sequoia and Amanda would close the place properly, even though Amanda was inexperienced and Sequoia was lazy. The next day, though, Mira and Sequoia shared the midday shift. They went about their business separately, avoiding conversation and eye contact. It

worked only because Mira didn't try to make Sequoia do anything she wasn't inclined to. In one more day, one of them would
probably be gone. If not, it was only a matter of time.

At the height of the crazed rush for caffeination after lunch,
Sequoia disappeared into the storeroom, this time closing the door
completely behind her. Mira continued pulling shots, steaming milk,
making change, running credit cards, pleased at how well she could
handle everything single-handedly. She hoped Sequoia would bring
out some twelve-ounce cup lids, but other than that, she wasn't going
to worry about it. Let Gus deal with her when he got back.

The militant herbalista—whose name was Sharon and who
was actually quite nice once Mira got to know her—shook her
head as Mira steamed her rice milk. "Hard to get good help, isn't
it?" She ran the GLBT bookstore next to Starbucks on Fremont,
but always walked the extra few blocks to get her chai fix here.

"Well," Mira said, trying to be professional. "She's young."

"You were her age once." Sharon raised an eyebrow. "How did
you act then?"

"Pretty much the way I do now." Mira smiled, and gave Sharon her green tea chai with rice milk on the house.

Regulars came and went, including Martin, dapper in a shirt
and tie. "I'm selling my soul this afternoon," he said. "King Microsoft has decided to shower golden coins upon one lucky playwright for the season. If it's me, I will buy you champagne and a
mink coat and take you away from all this, my dear."

"No champagne or mink required," she said, handing him his
warm pitcher of cream, "but you can definitely take me."

His eyes widened, and she added, "Away. I mean away."

"What a shame." He smiled and walked toward the door,
turning once for his customary wave before leaving.

The rush slowed, then stopped. A few students sat at tables
doing homework; a mom with a sleeping baby in a stroller read
in the corner. It had been nearly half an hour, and still no Sequoia.
Mira didn't care anymore what she was doing in there but she

needed her at the counter so she could take Patsy out for her pee break while it was slow.

Mira walked to the storeroom door.

"Sequoia?" she said. "How long are you going to be? I need to take Patsy out back." *How very civil,* she thought.

There was no reply. She wasn't in the bathroom; the storeroom was the only place she could be.

"Sequoia?" Mira tried the door. There was no lock, but it wouldn't budge. God, what if the girl really was sensitive, and had gotten her feelings hurt? Was she hiding from Mira? Surely she wouldn't be doing anything, well, self-destructive. Would she?

"Come on, honey, open up." She tried pushing harder against the door.

Outside, a car engine coughed, choked, and roared to life. Mira hurried outside as the blue Barracuda screeched out into traffic, leaving a fat cloud of exhaust hanging in the air. She turned and the storeroom window gaped open, screen lying half on the sidewalk, half in the gravel. From inside, it would be no problem to climb on a chair to get out of the window. From outside, it was too high for Mira to climb over, but she could see the shelves across the room, against the door, the safe wide open. It looked like Sequoia had expected a SWAT team to interrupt her.

"Oh, the drama," Mira said. And here she'd thought Sequoia might have a tender heart beneath all that tattoo ink. She walked to the phone. Should she call Gus or the police? She sighed and dialed Gus.

"Yo," Gus answered, line crackling. Mira guessed he was on the side of some slope.

"It's me. Listen, Sequoia—"

"No -ay, no -ucking way. Wh-now?" His voice broke in and out of static, but his anger was loud and clear.

"She's gone, Gus. She ripped you off." Mira wondered if Sequoia had put the bank bag in the safe the night before. She should have gone down and gotten it from her.

Gus sputtered on the phone. "Wha- -ou -ay? She wha-?"

"She barricaded herself in the storeroom, then climbed out the window and drove off. Fast."

The line crackled in Gus's silence, and Mira could make out Doug asking what was wrong.

"So, are you going to come back? Do you want me to call the police? Gus?"

"No -on't call—police," he said. "Shit." More static. "—that -oddamn—can't belie- trusted tha- blue-haired freak—" The line went dead.

Mira hoped Patsy could stick it out a little longer. She'd have to double up people on shifts to cover for Sequoia. She had a feeling that was the last they'd see of her. Rather than making her jump for joy, though, Mira felt like a failure. She wished she could have broken through to her, somehow, but Sequoia's shell was the hardest Mira had ever encountered in a kid. Thea was a relative softy compared to her.

Thea. What was it she had said, surrounded by Woden's tall trees in the silver mist, her face pink and animated, her voice angry and on the verge of crying? "I'm not perfect. No one's perfect." At the time, all Mira had thought was, "I know, but it doesn't mean we shouldn't try to be."

"God," she said now. No, Thea wasn't perfect. She hadn't finished college; she'd yet to finish anything really, but she was young. Like Sequoia, she resisted authority, and she had a mouth and a temper. But she was also kind and generous. She was independent and strong, and luminous in her desire to be wholly herself. Thea had the soul and nature of an artist, and Mira had been afraid of that, because how would she live, how would she survive? Lannie's life hadn't been easy. *God,* Mira thought, *whose is?* And Thea loved her family so much she was willing to sacrifice love for it. Because Mira knew her daughter loved her and needed her and always had, no matter how many times she'd pushed her away.

★   ★   ★

An hour and a half later, Gus's SUV lurched into the parking lot, and he huffed and puffed obscenities as he boosted Doug through the storeroom window. "I cannot believe this," he said, rubbing his shoulder. "What is it with women?"

"It's not women," Mira said. "It's Sequoia."

"Yeah, I know," he said. "Crazy fucking Sequoia." He shook his head, then called through the window, "She get everything?"

"What'd you expect?" Doug said, voice muffled. "Why'd you give her the key?" Metal screeched against concrete as Doug pulled the shelving unit away from the door. Gus and Mira went back inside and into the storeroom.

"I'm gonna track her down and get it back," Gus said.

"Gus, man," Doug said, shaking his head.

"You could press charges," Mira offered, even though she knew he probably couldn't. "I'm pretty sure the bank bag was either in there or with her. I haven't seen it. Maybe you should let the police handle it."

"He can't," Doug said, and Gus shot him a look.

"Ah, come on, Gus. She knows what's going on here. She lives right upstairs."

Mira swallowed. "You're a dealer."

"No," Gus said, voice shaking. "I am not a dealer."

Doug ran his hand through his hair. "Don't you think you should tell her—"

"I'm not a dealer. There's nothing else to say." Gus kicked the safe door, the metallic clang echoing in Mira's ears as he stormed out, climbed into his SUV, and drove off.

Doug looked at her. "I can't tell you if he doesn't want me to."

She nodded.

"I gotta go after him. He's probably going to her apartment. I'll talk to you later, okay?"

Mira returned his quick peck on the lips. She was almost glad that he kept Gus's secret. Maybe she didn't want to know any more than she did. She could work in any coffee shop in the city now, she realized. Until she found a teaching job.

Then again, if she left, she'd probably never get to kiss Doug again.

The electrician came back the second day to finish wiring Thea's room. Beneath her jeans and T-shirt, Mira wore the sexiest underwear she owned, lace bikini underpants that now pulled tight against her childbirth-widened hips. She forewent the nursing bra for a matching stretchy number, and as she walked into the room where he worked, she could feel the heave and shift of her milk-laden breasts with each movement.

"Can I get you anything?" she asked, feeling her hair brush her face. Since Thea, she'd taken to tying it back so the little girl wouldn't pull it, but today it fell loose around her shoulders.

The electrician looked up from where he kneeled in front of an outlet. He looked at her differently today, as though they'd somehow gotten to know each other intimately overnight. Had he thought about her, too?

"What have you got?"

Mira laughed a sudden nervous "Ha!" then felt herself blush, and crossed her arms over her chest. "I mean coffee. Coke. Are you thirsty?"

He stood and wiped his hands on the legs of his chinos, then put his hands on his hips. "How'd you get that scar?" he asked.

Mira reached to her face, touched the bump on her cheek. "I was a bad girl once." As it came out she heard it the way he heard it, and she decided not to explain.

"Only once?" he asked, taking a step toward her. His smile was narrowing, honing in on her eyes, her mouth, her breasts, even though she kept her arms wrapped over them. She edged back on one foot and he stopped.

"So, think you'll wrap it up today?" she asked.

"It could take longer."

"Depending on?" Mira's throat had gone dry; her voice cracked.

"How much you distract me." He leaned his weight into one hip. His mouth smiled. His eyes stayed serious, penetrating her, it seemed, seeing through her. Knowing her, and too well for comfort.

"Mah!" Thea bleated from her playpen in the living room. "Mah!" Mira had put her down for a nap there, thinking she was asleep before coming back to talk to him. Thea was a creature of habit, though. She was used to napping in Parker and Mira's bed.

"Mah!" she yelled again, louder and more panicked this time.

The electrician looked toward the door, then back at Mira. "Shouldn't you . . .?" He still smiled that smile, as if he knew Mira had planned and schemed this whole thing, as if he didn't mind one way or another if it worked out.

"I was just wondering when you'd be done so I could plan my day," Mira said. She walked to the living room, pulled red-faced Thea from the playpen. Thea made sucking noises, like she wanted to nurse, and grabbed Mira's breast with her chubby hand.

"No!" Mira said, pushing Thea's hand away, and the little girl looked at her in shock, then started to scream. Mira carried the wailing child back into the room and said, "I'm going to try to get her to sleep in the bedroom, so if you finish, just knock on the door and I'll get you a check."

Behind her closed bedroom door, Mira began to cry, too, whispering, "Sorry, I'm so sorry," over and over. She put Thea on the bed and undressed, pushing the underwear and bra deep into her drawer and extracting cotton underpants and her nursing bra. Thea watched, tear-streaked and hiccuping, as Mira put her jeans and T-shirt back on, then crawled into bed with her. The baby sucked her three middle fingers as Mira cooed to her, making a nest of her body for Thea to curl up in. It seemed to be only a few minutes later when the electrician knocked on the door, finished, but when Mira looked at the clock, she realized she'd slept for nearly two hours.

"Can you just leave a bill on the kitchen table?" she called. "I promise I'll mail a check today."

She heard him shuffling; then he said, "Sure thing. Let me know if you have any problems or anything."

"Thank you," she said.

All she'd ever wanted was what she had: a wonderful husband, a darling child. Why couldn't she stop thinking about the stupid electrician? *Because I want to have sex with someone who sees me only as an object of desire,* she thought, wincing. As much as she loved Parker, he'd already relegated her to life partner, workmate, mother of his child, and she still had that painful empty space within her that only a lover's desire could relieve. She had no idea how to stop needing that.

After dinner, Mira dialed the number for the Woden house. She'd left Thea alone for three weeks, long enough.

Lali answered.

"I don't suppose Thea's there," Mira said.

"No, she's at her gig."

"Her gig?" Mira swallowed. "She's playing somewhere?"

"Yes, at the Blue Cow in Tillamook. You should go see her band—they're very good."

"Her band?" Her daughter had a band?

"Well, it's actually a trio with two of the guys here. Kind of loose, but they're talented. Thea's been writing a lot of new songs lately." The girl paused. "Shall I tell her you called, Mrs. Serafino?"

"Oh, I don't know." Mira bit her lip. "You decide."

"Then I will," the girl said.

"Tell her I'm proud of her, too, okay?"

"Of course," the girl said. "She's been very sad."

Mira's chest heaved. "Why won't she just talk to me?"

"I'm sure it's only temporary. Maybe she just needs to hate

you for a while before she can love you again. That's what happened to me with my father."

Mira had never hated her parents, not really. Not her father.
She didn't know how she felt about her mother—she'd left Mira
so long ago that she was just a filmy specter. Mira had always just,
well, worshipped her. She was the family saint, the one Nonna
held up as an example of all things good whenever she felt the
need to.

One thing was for certain: Thea didn't see Mira as an object
of worship. That position had always been Parker's. He'd probably seen their daughter many times over the past couple months,
had long talks, a chance to explain himself. They'd hugged, Mira
knew, and her own arms felt useless, slack and insubstantial. He'd
smelled her herbal shampoo hair, her curls had brushed his chin.
Thea no doubt felt safe in his embrace, breathing in the faded
coffee smell of his sweater, the soap and sea salt essence of his skin.
He was her rock.

She needs a rock right now, Mira thought, as painful as that felt,
and I can't be it. Not yet. She blew her nose forcefully enough that
Patsy yipped in her sleep.

"Wake up, Patsy Cline," Mira said. "Let's go see what's happening out in the world."

Thirty-one

————•————

SOMETHING STILL WASN'T RIGHT ABOUT THE BEAT DAMIEN WAS laying down for Colby's new song.

"You know those old-school twangy songs by, like, Hank Williams and guys like that?" Thea asked. Damien looked at her as though she were speaking Martian. She sang the first verse of "Your Cheating Heart," snapping her fingers on the downbeat. "Like that. Almost kind of swinging."

Damien nodded and slapped the rhythm out on the African drum between his knees, adjusting the mike to pick up the sound better. Colby perked up and nodded along.

"That's cool," he said.

Now that they were getting more gigs, Lannie was letting them rehearse in the back of the yarn and guitar shop after it closed at night. She'd even donated her old sound system for the cause—"Old being the operative word," she'd warned them, but it was a fucking sound system. Thea could not believe her luck.

Colby had written the new one on banjo, an instrument he'd

just taught himself to play after finding it in one of the outbuildings at Woden. Thea strummed along and added a pretty harmony to his morose lyrics, something about bridges leading to nowhere. Those were the kinds of songs Colby tended to write. Thea wrote some sad ones, too, but she never cut as close to the bone as Colby. *He's the real deal,* she thought, wondering if she'd ever feel that sure about her own talents.

They were a funny-looking little group, Thea realized, with Colby so small and fragile and Damien so tall, his woolly red hair like a helium balloon bobbing above his thin lanky frame. She was considering going back to her natural hair color for their next gig so they didn't scare away the locals, but she wasn't really even sure what it was anymore, other than a point somewhere on the scale between her dad's blond and her mother's dark brown. They were extreme opposites in every way.

She'd always imagined them in the audience at her performances, Mira cheering too loudly, embarrassing her, Parker quietly beaming, arm wrapped around Mira's shoulders, looking like he'd just won the damn lottery or something. Looking so corny, so goofy. He'd come to the Blue Cow but he'd just looked sad and lost all night, even though family and friends surrounded him.

Thea closed her eyes and inhaled deeply, swallowing the salty welling in her throat. It took so much effort these days just to stay out of the deep dark ravine she was pretty sure her dad had fallen into.

"Oops," she said, opening her eyes. She'd missed the change, and now Colby and Damien were cruising along together into the chorus, and she'd been left behind, thinking about the absence of bridges in her life.

After rehearsal Colby and Damien said they wanted to buy Thea a beer to celebrate, so they dropped by the Driftwood. Everybody knew Colby was underage but they served him anyway. That was something Thea loved about Pacifica. Hell, in Missoula, Eugene, Portland, all those bigger places, they'd card you before even letting you in the door. Here it was just friendly. Everybody knew Colby wouldn't get drunk or do anything stupid. The kid would nurse one PBR all night long, just to fit in.

"So, you hear about Zoe?" Damien looked sideways at Thea.

"What about her?" Zoe hadn't been talking to her much, but that was probably because Thea was spending more time away from the house, going to her dad's, rehearsing, hanging out with Lannie. "She get in trouble or something?" *She'd better not have talked everyone into eating raw food,* Thea thought, wondering how she could sneak in hamburgers without anyone smelling them.

"No, man, she's moving out, like tonight," Damien said. "Like, now."

"She didn't tell you?" Colby asked.

Thea shook her head.

"Not about anything?" he pressed.

"What?" she asked, looking from Colby to Damien. "What?" she said again.

"Damn," Colby said. "That's so messed up."

Damien nodded. "She should've told you."

"Hello. What, you guys? What should she have told me?"

"She's, well . . ." Colby paused. "She's moving in with Alex." He wrinkled his nose and looked at her with so much hurt for her in his eyes that she reached out to pat his shoulder. The sad sinking feeling loomed ever larger.

"I can't believe she didn't tell you." Damien shook his head. "That's more than messed up. That's just wrong."

"Is that why you guys are buying me a beer?" Thea asked. "How sweet." How could some people be so kind and thoughtful and others so totally fucked in the head? Jesus. Alex and Zoe— two druggie losers moving in together. She'd never been able to deter Alex from doing hard-core stuff, and she'd known better than to even try with Zoe. They'd both be dead or in jail before they got the chance to get old. And knowing that still didn't take the pain away.

Colby sipped from his can of beer, grimacing at the taste. "We just thought you should know before we got back tonight and everyone was talking about it. In case you didn't already know."

"Thank you," Thea said, swallowing a large pull from her own PBR, the only beer any of them could afford. "I definitely appreciate it."

Thea had already made up her mind, but this clinched it. She was getting out of there, too. Woden attracted more wannabes than true artists, and she was not going to end up thirty years old and stoned, sitting on some dirty old couch noodling on her guitar while a guy across the room played "Stairway to Heaven" for the eighty billionth time that day.

Besides, there was nothing worse than people talking about you behind your back when they thought you couldn't hear, then zipping it tight as soon as you entered a room. People were people. They couldn't help themselves. Normally it wouldn't bother her—her mother had instilled more self-confidence in her than probably anybody had a right to have—but it was all too weird, all these big things happening all at once. It was like God or Buddha or John Lennon or someone was trying to tell her to become the person she was really meant to be.

She could see that person she was becoming, as clear as she could see Missy Baker sitting across the bar drinking whiskey with some older dude with bad dentures and a fancy leather jacket. He looked like a car salesman or something, and he gave Thea the heebie-jeebies. *Missy should know better,* Thea thought at first; then she shook her head. That sucked. Missy should drink with who-ever she wanted to—hell, sleep with whoever she wanted to.

Thea had heard the rumors about her mother getting drunk and having a fling with some old boyfriend on New Year's Eve. She was pretty sure they were bullshit, but what if they were true? What if that was why she couldn't work it out with Parker? It made no sense, though. Her dad thought it was all his fault. Thea had never realized how much she didn't know her parents, how they revealed to her only the stuff they wanted her to know. She'd always thought she could control her world through knowing everything about them, about everything. She knew it was childish to go on thinking her parents had lived and breathed only for her, but it was a hard notion to give up, and it made her feel lonelier than she ever had as an only child, even now, sitting with her friends.

Thea sighed. The beer was having its way with her. Her anger at Mira had deserted her weeks ago, replaced by this stubborn loneliness. Was Mira sitting somewhere with people who were kind, enjoying this evening, or was she all alone up in Seattle? It was such a big city it made Thea shudder. Lannie said she worked in a coffee shop, which was so freaking weird Thea hated to even picture it. She wanted her mom where she was supposed to be: in their house, in her classroom, walking the beach with the dogs, doing mom stuff. But maybe she just couldn't be happy here anymore. She swallowed against the lump that had taken up permanent residence in her throat. Thea had wanted to be free, and now, she guessed, her mother did, too.

Thirty-two

———————•———————

THE OILY PATINA OF BALLARD AVENUE GLISTENED BENEATH A BELL–
shaped streetlamp. Mist passed through its spotlight, disappearing
like a ghost into the purple ether around it. It was Friday the
thirteenth, a chilly March night. Mira shivered, standing in line
outside of the Tractor Tavern in the old-town section of Ballard
with Doug, wishing she'd worn her one and only coat. Vanity
had gotten the better of her. There was no way she wanted him
seeing her dressed in something so conservative and old-ladyish.
New Mira was hip, young beyond her years. She hitched up her
jeans—even her wide hips didn't make them stay put—and tried
not to chatter her teeth.

"Cold?" Doug asked, looking warm in his army jacket and a
black knit cap.

"A little," she said. "But I'm fine."

"Here." Doug slipped off his coat and placed it on her shoulders. "We should get in soon. They always run a little late."

Mira blinked at the form-fitting long-sleeve T-shirt he wore, golden yellow with the number 86 on the front. She smiled and pulled the coat tight in front of her. It was warm. "So, eighty-six," she said. "Does that mean you're out of you?"

"What?"

He had no idea what she was talking about.

"That's just restaurant talk for, you know. When you're out of something. 'Eighty-six the tomato soup.'" Actually, Nonna's spicy Italian tomato soup had become quite a hit at the shop. They often ran out.

"Oh." Doug nodded and folded his arms across his chest. He was cold.

The small tree-lined avenue exuded old Seattle charm, brick storefronts a mishmash of bars, boutiques, the ubiquitous indie coffee shops. No Starbucks in sight. Around them, the crowd buzzed with the excitement Mira remembered from going out in her college days. Young women wore sleeveless tops, open-toed shoes, hugging themselves in the cold, laughing. Posing. And why not, Mira thought. They looked like the spring blossoms they were. She must have looked just as fresh and exuberant at their age, but she'd never thought of herself that way. She'd never felt beautiful, or confident, and now she probably looked like somebody's mom, no matter how low-cut her jeans were.

The line started to move and Mira sneaked a look at her watch. Nine thirty-five. The show wouldn't even start until well after ten. When would it be over? How was she going to stay awake long enough to have sex? Would she even want to by then? Not that she felt like it now, anyway. All she could think about was how she'd feel at six the next morning.

Finally at the front of the line, she presented her hand for the lumberjack look-alike doorman to stamp. Without her glasses she could barely make out the image, a black ink outline of Betty Boop. Or a Chinese symbol, maybe. She hoped it was one for energy, or double happiness. Or improved vision.

Inside the bar, Mira looked around for a place to sit. The

floor stretched from the entrance to the stage, not a stick of furniture in sight. "Where do we sit?" she asked as people streamed
around them.

"We don't," Doug said, shrugging. "Let's snag a spot close to the
stage. I want to be able to see Howard hammering on that guitar."
He led her through the crowd, already hovering close to the stage,
and stopped in front of a large stack of speakers. "This okay?"

"Mm." She nodded. "Sure." This was how they did it now. She
remembered seeing pictures of crowds of kids standing in front
of stages, in movies maybe, or on television. Maybe Thea had told
her about it. They were going to stand for the entire performance
and she was going to wake up deaf. Her legs already ached from
a long day standing at the shop. Now she understood why there
were very few other people her age in attendance.

Doug slung an arm across her shoulders. "If you get tired, you
can just sit on the edge of the stage. Howard won't mind. You're
with me." He leaned in and kissed her mouth in that soft and hard
way that made her crazy. She kissed him back.

"Or we could skip the show," he murmured into her hair.

She pulled back and studied him. "We could?"

"Unfortunately, I promised I'd show up." He massaged the
small of her back, pulling her hips toward him. "And I know
you're going to love them, but how about if we leave a little early?
I'm not as young as I used to be, and I'd like to be alone with you
before it gets too late and I turn into a pumpkin."

"A pumpkin, huh?" Mira pressed against him. "That's not
quite the vegetable that comes to mind." She hadn't even had
a drink yet, and here she was humping her date in public. The
crowd packed in tighter. No one noticed, or cared. Mira relaxed
and let new Mira, bad Mira, take over as she wrapped her arms
around his hips, letting one hand traverse that perfect ass. They
slow-danced to an old Dylan song coming through the speakers.
At the chorus, Doug sang into her ear, more than a little off-key:
"Mm, mm, you're a big girl now."

"Good evening," the doorman said from the stage, not long afterward, long beard hanging as he leaned down to speak into the microphone. He sounded bored. "Please welcome Seattle favorites, the Screaming Hematomas."

Five men emerged from a hallway to the right of the stage and took their places. Two were youngish, in their late twenties or so, dressed in low baggy pants and too-big T-shirts, but the other three were decidedly middle-aged. Vindicated, Mira applauded with the crowd, as best she could with a plastic cup of beer in her hand, shouting "Woo!" into the magenta and green stage lights. One of the three, an attractive man in jeans that fit and a trim beard, walked to the guitar, lifted it over his head and strapped it on, then turned and saw Doug in the audience.

He smiled and walked over to them, strumming a few test chords at full volume. "Douglas," he shouted over the crowd, who were ready to dance. "I see you finally decided to exercise good taste." He looked at Mira and smiled; she'd never seen a face so unabashedly open and friendly. She blushed at his compliment, imagining herself acting like one of the younger women at the front, throwing her shoulders back, tossing her hair, flashing a bleach-whitened smile, if only she had a bleach-whitened smile. It was frightening how much she wanted to sleep with every man who looked at her these days.

Doug reached to knock fists with Howard, who winked at Mira and gave Doug a thumbs-up before strolling back to adjust his amp.

Mira closed her eyes, sudden heat overwhelming her, the room closing in until she thought she might faint. Hot flash or panic attack? It was hard to keep her balance as bodies surged toward the stage, but it wasn't just that. It was as if gravity had become suspended and she was turning along with the earth, about to fall off. She drew a deep breath through her nose, let it out slowly, then took another. Oxygen, she needed oxygen.

This was not her life, not anything like her life. Nothing for the past two and a half months had been, and yet here she was, living it. Could a person really change so quickly? Was she losing her real self, or finding it?

The music started and she opened her eyes to see Doug watching her. He knew nothing about her or her history. He was a fresh start. These should be good things, she reasoned, but she couldn't see a future with him. She still couldn't draw a deep enough breath; he probably thought she was panting for him. They were as different as the beer they drank now and the wine she'd always shared with Parker. How could she regress this far, all the way back to her college days when she'd slept with the bad boys because they were so damn easy?

"You okay?" Doug mouthed, torn between concern for her and watching the band.

Mira nodded. *Let go,* said a voice inside her. *Just enjoy this.*

Doug leaned to shout into her ear. "I told Howard I was bringing someone special, so he was just giving me shit."

He liked her. Too much, she suspected. "I'll be back in a second," she said. "I should have peed before the place filled up."

He squeezed her hand, then turned his attention to the band, who were playing a raucous song with a strong beat and indecipherable lyrics that to Mira's ear sounded like, "We are all penguins, happy!"

In the rickety stall in the women's restroom, Mira sat on the toilet to pee and tried to breathe deeply, but the smell of cleaning chemicals and mildew and entrenched bathroom odor changed her mind. Mouth breathing, she studied the farm implement–yellow poster taped to the inside of the stall door to calm herself instead.

COMING SOON TO THE TRACTOR, it read, with a list of strange-sounding bands: FERAL PECCARY, THE TWANG GODS, DOG FUCKER.

Really, Mira thought. *Dog Fucker.* Bands had such demented names these days. Whatever happened to names that made sense, like, well . . . like what? Led Zeppelin? The Beatles? At least they were clever. The Twang Gods was kind of good, she thought. It sounded vaguely familiar. She reached for the toilet paper, struggling to find the end inside the dispenser, then sat up with a start. The Twang Gods. That was Trevor's band. She looked at the poster again. March 28. They were playing in just a couple of weeks. Should she tell Lannie? Would she come to Seattle to see them? Maybe they were playing in Portland, too, or Eugene, somewhere closer to Pacifica. Mira hoped not. The thought of seeing her old friend again, of reaching up to give her a hug she'd squirm in, and talking, talking like she hadn't in months, with someone who got her and loved her and just plain knew her, well . . . That felt like more than she deserved, but she needed it, suddenly, so badly she couldn't stand it.

And there was something else she needed. Doug's body, his hands, his mouth. His desire for her. Had she ever wanted sex just for sex's sake before? Did she now? In college, it had always been mired in quelling emptiness, feeling accepted and loved. Never could she remember having sex for the pure pleasure of someone's skin against hers, exploration, sensation, the losing of one's self in another, the discovery of it. Not even with Parker. At first it had been about making him love her, and then it became all about keeping that love. And it hadn't worked.

In this new life, she could start again, rediscover that part of her she'd felt ashamed of, and tamped down for so long she'd nearly lost it. She didn't want a boyfriend. She didn't need a life-match, a soul mate, a compatible sire. Those days were over. Her biological needs had changed. She wanted one of those "friends with benefits" kids always talked about—someone to be naked with, to wrangle and rock and sweat with. It had nothing to do with love, not any kind she'd ever known, anyway. A "fuck buddy," Sequoia would have said, but then Sequoia probably liked the band Dog Fucker. Doug was a big boy, she decided. He'd have to take care of himself.

Back out in the melee, Mira shoved through writing bodies and spilling beer until she was pressed against Doug's side. She caught him unaware—he turned and, seeing her expression, smiled a slow questioning smile.

She leaned in until her mouth was moist against his ear. "I think we should go home and take all of our clothes off," she said over the music, stopping to suck his earlobe before continuing. "Then I think we should just go fucking crazy."

She felt her words jar him, the rock of body weight forward as his neurons received this information and registered it.

"Uh, okay," he said.

Mira stepped in front of him and pulled his face to hers, kissing him long and deep. They stood so close together she didn't have to look down to see what effect she was having on him.

Once in her apartment, they stripped off each other's clothes without turning on the lights, then stood inches apart, breathing in ragged gasps. Mira's hands tingled; dots swam before her eyes in the dark. Patsy pranced and bounced around them, and Mira thought both she and the dog would hyperventilate if they didn't do something soon. "Patsy, calm down," she said, but there was too much excitement in the small space.

She took Doug's hand and led him to the bathroom, closed the door, reached inside the shower to twist the faucet on.

"Do you want the light?" Doug's voice had gone husky.

"No." She held her hand under the spray until it was warm. "Come here." She backed into the small enclosure, pulling him with her under the warm water, feeling his mouth upon hers, his hands traveling her wet skin, hers on his, muscles and soft spots and smoothness and body hair, wet and slippery against her hands, her belly and chest.

"Oh god, god, god," she moaned, not wanting to utter any names, just to chant and plunder this sweet body in the warm wet darkness, to make it shudder and arch and react to her voice, her touch, her movements. She pushed him against the tile wall, pressed hard into him, then wrapped a leg over his hip.

"Oh, Mira," he groaned, pulling her closer, entering her, pushing her back now against the shower door. Their voices rose in unison, primordial grunts and cries escalating until Doug began to laugh, gasping for air.

"What?" Mira pulled back, dazed.

"Listen."

And there it was: a high lonesome whine from the next room.

"Somebody wants company," Doug said.

"Too bad." Mira pulled him back in, the need for him as cleansing as the hot water coursing over her shoulders and falling to the shower floor.

It wasn't until Mira swung her legs over the side of the bed the next morning and stood, naked, that she remembered. There was someone in her bed besides Patsy. She dropped on her haunches and reached up under her pillow for her nightgown. She felt naked, too naked somehow, in spite of the baring of body and soul that occurred the night before. Doug was still asleep, curled around Patsy, who opened her eyes and began to thump her tail on the bed.

"Shh," Mira whispered, pulling the tight cotton jersey over her head. She'd picked up a size small by mistake at Fred Meyer and gotten too lazy to return it, thinking it might eventually stretch to fit her. She had to stand to wiggle the gown down over her hips, and when she looked back at the bed, Doug was watching. She felt the flush working its way up from her abdomen to her chest and neck and face.

"Hi," he said, pushing himself up on one arm and smiling. "I like that picture up there. Kinda looks like you."

Mira followed his gaze to the wall above the bed. The blue woman with the curves and the dips and the triangles. The tight-fitting dress over round hips, the wavy hair framing her face. "Really?" she said. She'd have asked, *What parts exactly?* had she been the woman she was the night before. She'd have done any-thing the night before, and in fact she'd done quite a lot of things she'd never expected to do again, and in some cases, ever. She smiled down at Doug. *And wouldn't that have been a shame,* she thought, *to miss all that?*

He threw back the covers for her to join him back in bed and she gulped at his physique. She'd felt it beneath her hands, her mouth, her body in the dark, but she hadn't seen him in all his testosterone-laden glory. "Wow," she said, wishing neither of them had to get up. "If only I didn't have to go to work. Do you have to?"

"Nah," he said. "Microsoft was good to me in the nineties." He pulled her onto him and fondled her rear end, kissed her neck. She made a noise so libidinous it embarrassed her. How could she be so horny, still, after the hours they'd been at it the night before? It had to be dopamine, the miracle drug of lust and attraction. And it was a drug so potent and addictive that she didn't want anything else, just another fix, right then, right there.

She would be late for work, and she didn't care.

Thirty-three

───────── • ─────────

W<small>HEN</small> L<small>ANNIE</small> <small>FIRST</small> <small>SETTLED</small> <small>IN</small> P<small>ACIFICA</small>, <small>THE</small> <small>TOWN</small> <small>BUZZED</small> with a mixture of curiosity and gossip mongering. Nonna scolded Mira for her instant friendship with this strange tall rock goddess with the uncertain marital relationship and certain out-of-wedlock child. Lannie's boyfriend was at least half black, and Trevor was as towheaded as they come. It didn't help that they lived on a secluded strip of beach in their bus for the first few months, until the boyfriend drove it away one day when Lannie and Trevor were inside the IGA Market, grocery shopping.

"I'm sorry. I didn't know who else to call," Lannie said from the pay phone outside. Mira could hear Trevor crying, but Lannie never wept.

Without even thinking, she said, "I'll come get you. You'll stay with us."

When Parker arrived home that evening to a fuller house than he'd left, Mira took him aside and apologized for her rash behavior. "But they have nowhere to go."

"Kind of like that cat you've been feeding on the porch," he said, but he made Lannie feel welcome. They had the unused bedroom upstairs, after all, and it was only temporary. Thea loved baby Trevor. Lannie had already found work at the local fabric and yarn shop, where the proprietress, old Mrs. Andersdatter, was legally blind and hard of hearing. If any customers complained about Lannie in the beginning, she either didn't hear them or didn't care. Lannie found a little beach cottage and rented it within two months of being dumped at the IGA. Eventually, she became a part of Pacifica's social fabric, taking over the shop when the old woman died. No one talked badly about Lannie anymore; they hadn't in years.

As Mira dialed Lannie from the shop later that day, she wondered how long it would take them to get over talking about her. After Mira invited her to come stay with her in Seattle for Trevor's gig, Lannie cried so hard that Mira felt her own eyes fill. "Oh, Lannie, please don't cry."

"I thought you didn't want to see me, or I would have, I would have already . . ." Lannie's voice bent into another sob.

Mira closed her eyes and pinched the bridge of her nose. She would never have guessed that Lannie would be emotional or she wouldn't have called from work. The woman did not cry. Not when dumped, not when Trevor left home at seventeen to go on the road with his band, and not when any of her subsequent romances soured. That she had this kind of impact on her friend astounded her.

"I'm so sorry," Mira whispered, her voice failing. She cleared her throat and said again, louder, "Lannie, I'm sorry I've put you through this. I've been so selfish."

"No kidding," Lannie said, blowing her nose. "Anyway, I might bring a friend."

"Chet Moser? Oh my god, are you still seeing him?" Why had she never asked? She'd been immersed in self-pity, that's why.

"I'm not saying in case it doesn't work out," Lannie said. "I don't want to jinx it."

"Um, I don't really have room to invite you *and* a friend to stay," Mira said. And she wanted time alone with her friend, time that would be hard enough to get with her wayfaring son also in town.

"We'll work it out. The important thing is I'm coming, and I get to see you and Trevor, and I don't know what could be better than that."

"I can't wait," Mira said, signaling to an impatient Amanda and the line behind her that she'd help out in a moment. "I'm sorry, I have to go. We just got hit with the after-lunch rush. We'll talk more when you get here. I even have something exciting to tell you! One hint"—she turned her back and lowered her voice— "it's a man." That ought to cheer Lannie up, she thought.

"Oh, Mira, no. No. You can't."

"I can't?"

Amanda cleared her throat, pointedly, and when Mira turned, she was wearing that exasperated teenage-girl look Mira remembered so well from Thea. Was it her imagination or had Amanda been curt since the night of the showdown with Sequoia? Had she lost respect for Mira when she heard that she smoked dope, or when she saw how ineffectual she was as a manager?

Lannie seemed desperate on the other end of the line. "No, you can't have another man. Not now. It's too soon."

"It's not like I wanted my marriage to be over. Parker dumped me, remember?" Mira whispered.

"Just give it a little more ti—"

"For god's sake, Lannie, he told me he didn't want to be with me anymore. How much more clear could he have been?"

Amanda held her finger up to the next customer, then spun on her wedgie flip-flop and stalked over to Mira. "I need help, now!" she said, jutting out a naked hip where either the top of her pants or the bottom of her shirt should have been. Mira wanted to strangle her, but she admired her pluck.

"I have to go. I'll call you later," she said, clicking off the phone as Lannie sobbed anew.

"Happy?" she said to Amanda. "I just made my best friend cry." Tears came to her own eyes as she strode to the counter. "May I help you?" she said to the next body in line, trying not to meet his eyes until she had herself under control.

"Are you okay?"

She looked up.

Martin leaned into the counter. "You don't look so good, Mirabella."

Mira bit her lip. "I'm okay. Just a horrible person."

"Impossible," he said. He was so sweet. And so handsome today in his olive V-neck sweater, which fit a little tighter than his usual clothing.

He cleared his throat and Mira jumped. "Oh, sorry. The usual?"

"Actually, I'm also picking up something for a friend, a"— he fished a bright orange sticky note from his pants pocket and read—"a double grande white chocolate mocha no whip."

"You got it," Mira said, turning to make the drinks. She'd never made a white chocolate mocha for anyone male or over twenty-five. This was probably the same "friend" he'd picked up hot chocolate for before the movie. Why did this bother her so much? She had a man to share her bed with. Why did she want this one, too?

"Here you go," she said. "That's five even."

Martin slid a five at her, stuffing a single in the tip jar, then looked at her. The people in line behind him were fidgety and on the edge of revolt.

"Something else?" Mira said, flashing a tight-lipped smile at a burly guy wearing a Utilikilt, next in line. Was Martin trying to tease her, to invite her ardor? Was he reading her mind?

"Cream?" He shrugged.

"Oh, god, sorry." Mira turned to give the half-and-half pitcher a quick steam. "And what for you, sir?" she called over her shoulder, but Amanda had already taken care of the kilted man, and from the look on his face, he was a little too happy about it.

*   *   *

"Dear Parker," Mira typed on her favorite computer after her shift, then hit ERASE and took a sip of decaf. She'd opened a free email account, wondering at first if she should disguise her name, then scoffing at herself. Why should she be in hiding? Miraserafino@ freemail.net was allowed to exist, wasn't she? Why not remind Parker that she was still a living, breathing human, this wife he was so ready to discard?

"Hey fuck-face," she typed, relishing the sound of it a moment before deleting. Closing her eyes, she let herself think about her husband's face, feeling the lump rise, swallowing it back.

"Hey," she typed. "Remember me?"

This is nuts, she thought. *Why am I torturing myself?* She sniffed and continued, eyes still closed.

I'm the girl who couldn't take her eyes off you all those years ago in the rain. Did I ever tell you how hard it was for me not to make the first move? You were all shy and slow, a good Midwestern boy, respectful and so, so handsome. You were unlike any other boy I had ever met. Still are, actually. To this day.

Damn. She needed a tissue. Blinking hard, she rummaged through her pockets and, finding none, used a napkin to wipe her nose. Felix walked over with a freshly brewed pot of coffee.

"Warmer upper?" he asked. He loved that phrase; she'd said it to a customer on her first day and he'd laughed at this strange American-English colloquialism, pulling out his little notebook to jot it down.

"What else do you have written in there?" she'd asked, craning her neck to see, and read aloud: " 'Cher sugar'? What's that?"

"Equal."

Mira shook her head.

"Artificial sweetener."

"Oh." She laughed. "Right. What's this one: 'harmless'?"

"Decaf." Felix shrugged. "You like your coffee harmless, no?"

"Is it harmless?" she asked him now, trying to perk up her face as he poured her coffee.

"For you, of course," he said. "You look so sad over here."

"Do I?" She sniffed. "I was just writing a letter to someone."

"You are missing your family?"

She nodded. Sometimes she could go entire days without missing anyone, but then it would hit her when she least expected it. She missed her family, and, much to her chagrin and in spite of Doug, her husband.

He nodded. "I miss my family in Nicaragua, too."

"How long since you've seen them?"

"This is my second year at university," he said, and Mira winced.

"Didn't you go home for Christmas, or the summer?"

Felix shook his head and set the pot on the table. "I had to work. I need the money. How long since you've seen yours?"

"God, not very long at all compared to you. Not quite three months."

He nodded, a sad look on his face. "That is the hardest time. Before you've forgotten enough there and found enough here."

"How long does that take?"

Felix shrugged. "I don't know yet. I'm still waiting."

Mira sighed, shaking her head. There was no way she still wanted to be feeling this way in two years.

"But this is like our family, too, yes? Everyone here loves you."

Mira squinted at him. "No. How so?"

He picked the coffeepot up. "You are our hero, our fearless leader. Everyone is so happy that Sequoia is gone. Even the customers."

"Really? But I didn't do anything. She just left."

"You stood up to her, that's why. No one ever did that before.

Gus"—Mira loved that he pronounced it "Goosz"—"is a good man, but he lets his heart rule his head. You . . ." Felix paused. "You have both a heart and a head."

Mira laughed. "We all have hearts and heads."

"You know what I mean." He rolled his eyes and walked away, twitching his backside until he heard Mira laugh again. He turned his head and smiled.

Mira had thought the truth would be the best thing for their marriage. She was wrong.

After the electrician drove away, Mira left Thea sleeping in her bed and walked into the new bedroom. The light fixture was in place. The switch worked perfectly. The outlet covers were neatly installed. Just a coat of paint, some decorating and furniture, and their little girl would have her first real bedroom. Mira started to cry again and sank to the floor, her hand over her mouth. She would never be able to come into this room without feeling like the worst mother—the worst wife—in the world.

She had to tell Parker so they wouldn't have this festering secret between them. He loved her. He would understand. She wanted so badly to be a good wife and mother, he had to see that and appreciate her honesty. And nothing had happened. Not a thing. Mira tried not to think about the night before and the fantasies she'd had in the bathtub. None of them had included her husband.

That evening she steamed fresh mussels she and Thea had harvested earlier in the day. She melted butter, tossed a salad, made a blueberry cobbler for dessert. When Parker arrived home she avoided him at first, feeling odd about hugging him or kissing him, as if she didn't deserve to.

"You okay?" he asked, swinging a manic and giggling Thea up onto his shoulders. "Did the electrician finish?" He leaned over and kissed Mira's forehead, and Thea grabbed handfuls of her hair.

"Yes," Mira said, untangling Thea's fingers, then kissing her hands before Parker straightened back up. "To both. Dinner's almost ready. Want to eat on the beach?"

"Beat!" Thea yelled.

"I'll go get the blanket," Parker said. "Do we have any beer?"

"We have at least one," she said, hoping they had two.

Settled just outside their property line on a small grassy dune, Parker played itsy-bitsy spider with Thea while Mira set out the food. From the bowl of mussels, she selected a few to cool in a bowl for Thea, then handed her a sippy cup of apple juice.

"And a beer for Daddy," she said, producing a bottle of Anchor Steam, "and a beer for Mommy."

"Be foh Mommy." Thea grabbed her cup by both handles and threw her head back for a long swig. She was their comedian, their happy-go-lucky diversion from anything too serious, and Mira wondered if she should just enjoy this picture postcard moment, if she should let herself exchange that look of parental pride and astonishment with Parker—"This is our child, our mingled blood and love"—but she felt the tears running down her face before she could stop them.

"Honey, what's wrong?" Parker reached over the salad bowl for her hand, but she pulled it away to wipe her eyes.

"I don't know," she said. "Hormones, maybe." But they both knew she was well beyond the possibility of any postpartum blues.

"Mommy cry?" Thea dropped her cup, juice dripping onto the blanket from the four tiny drinking holes. She turned to Parker, eyes round. "Mommy cry?"

"It's okay, honey," he said. "Mommy's okay."

Thea shook her head sharply. "No, Daddy. Mommy cry. Mommy cry nap." Her eyes filled, and she looked back at Mira, chin puckering.

"Baby, it's okay," Mira said, voice catching. "Don't cry." Jesus. What if she'd actually fooled around with the electrician, with

Thea right in the house? She wasn't a mute little bundle anymore. She'd always been watchful of Mira, seeming to sense her every mood, absorb her every action and word like a sponge.

Thea crawled into her lap, clutching her bra strap through her shirt and sucking her two middle fingers, hiccuping. "Mommy crying," she said through a mouthful of fingers. "Baby crying."

"You should eat," Mira said to Parker, "before it gets too cold. The butter will harden." She let herself look at him finally.

"What happened today?" He made no move to eat or drink.

"I'll tell you later," she said, nodding her chin at Thea. "Could you open my beer? And please, Parker, eat. I'll eat in a minute."

After dinner, Parker walked Thea up and down the beach, picking up clumps of seaweed and broken sand dollars, empty crab bodies. Mira leaned back on her hands and watched. She was evil. She was detestable. But she never would be again.

The moment she told him, of course, she knew she shouldn't have. His face became granite in the gloaming light, Thea asleep and dreaming on the blanket beside him.

"Do you still want to, to be with . . ." He couldn't finish. He looked so hurt she could barely stand it.

"No, Parker, no," she said, reaching for his hand. This time he was the one to pull away. "That's why I'm telling you. I don't want to be with anyone but you. I think it was just my hormones or something, all out of whack. It was like something took a hold of me and I wasn't myself. I was just . . . I don't know. Possessed or something." She was glad she hadn't told him about the underwear, evidence of premeditation. "But I didn't do it."

"It isn't that you did or didn't," Parker said. "It's that you wanted to."

"I don't think he even knew." This lie meant to protect Parker, but it backfired.

"Oh, he knew."

Which meant anyone from Rockaway to Tillamook might know, given enough beers at the Driftwood or time spent in the dentist chair. Mira could hear it: "That Serafino girl turned out wild, didn't she? And with a little baby and all, and that nice young husband of hers all the way from Kansas. Poor guy."

"Honey, I promise you. I will never want to be with anyone else again. Even just thinking about it makes me feel like throwing up. I just wanted you to know so . . . I don't know."

"So you couldn't do it?"

She paused, tilted her head at him. The pink light was turning gray, and she could no longer see the expression in his eyes. "Maybe, but I don't think I could have gone through with it, no matter what."

They were silent then, listening to the waves roll in, wash out, the gulls fighting over a fish carcass down the beach. With the retreat of the sun it had gotten chilly, and Mira shivered. "Is Thea warm enough?"

Parker put his hand on the baby's back. "She's a radiator," he said, as he always did, and Mira thought maybe everything would be fine.

"Want to go in?"

He shook his head. "I think I'll stay out here for a while. You take Thea, I'll get everything else."

Mira sighed. It wouldn't be fine, not for a while. Maybe not ever. Over the next few weeks she lost Parker bit by bit as he worked longer hours, took longer walks with Thea when he got home. He was quiet more often than not, and the early sparkle of their marriage was gone. They still acted the way they had—a kiss hello, dinner out every other weekend—but their sex life became sporadic and mechanical, Parker going through the motions, she could tell, even when she tried her best to be tender with him, to break through his hurt.

Mira became almost saintly in her words and deeds, volunteering wherever she was needed, devoting herself to her family and her friends with a renewed fervor, and in the process, discarded the unsavory bits and pieces of her true nature. She learned

to turn off thoughts of sex until Saturday mornings. On Sundays
they would dress for church, going only to appease Nonna and
the Serafino clan, but when Mira kneeled to pray in the sanctu-
ary of St. Mary's by the Sea, she always prayed that God and her
husband would be able to forgive her for her seemingly uncon-
trollable lust.

Four months after they finished Thea's bedroom, Mira's grandfather died suddenly. No one took it harder than Mira, who finally found an outlet to grieve for so many things lost along the way.
She cried before, during, and after the funeral, and continued to
for weeks. One night she woke crying, heaving sobs from somewhere so deep she was sure it wasn't for the deaf old man who'd
turned mean long before he had grandchildren. She turned away
from Parker to bury her face in the pillow, trying to be as quiet as
possible, but she felt him roll toward her, scoot so that each point
of his body was in contact with hers.

"I'm sorry," she whispered.

"It's okay," he said, and kissed her shoulder. She rolled toward
him and kissed his mouth, running her hands down his back, her
excitement growing from the same deep place her sadness had
just been. Parker hesitated, then kissed her more passionately than
he had since their college days. Within moments he was pushing
between her legs, and Mira thought she might explode at this
sudden excitement between them, this novel act of lust-driven
sex in the middle of the night. Even though they were in their
twenties, they had already gotten so old, so stultified by obligation
and routine. Most of their friends were still single, out partying,
sleeping around, and that she and Parker were right now engaged
in such a ribald encounter made Mira want to cry again with
happiness.

The next day when Parker called her in the middle of the
morning just to see how she was doing, she knew her penance
had been paid.

*   *   *

At two a.m., Mira sat up in bed, her T-shirt soaked, her hair damp at the roots. The hot flash was over and she was cold now. Trying not to disturb Patsy, she slipped out of bed and grabbed her teaching sweater from its hook next to the door, wrapping it around her shoulders. Then she dug deep into her purse and pulled out the little oblong of plastic, punched in numbers, and sat in the dark at the table to listen: "Hi, this is Mira. Well, it's my cell phone, anyway."

She closed her eyes and shivered at Thea's voice, then punched in her message retrieval code.

"Your mailbox is full. Unheard messages will be deleted after twenty-eight days. To receive new messages, please delete those messages you do not wish to save."

"What?" Mira said aloud, and Patsy hopped from the bed to the floor, clicking her toenails over to lean against Mira's leg. Mira leaned down to scratch her ears as she listened to the first message, left twenty-eight days previously:

"Sad," Thea's voice said. "Mad. Scared. Pissed. But mostly sad."

At the click, Mira closed her eyes, then opened them and hit SAVE.

And then came the second message: "Really fucking mad. Lonely. Motherless." Thea laughed, but not happily. "Oh poor fucking pity-party me. God."

Mira listened to all twenty-eight days, taking Thea's words like blows, flinching, but taking them. Then she slipped her feet into shoes and went downstairs.

"Dear Parker," Mira typed once again, sitting alone in the closed coffee shop in the middle of the dark night. She'd never finished or sent the first email.

I know it must be very strange to be getting an email from me, after all this time. You may or may not have noticed that I no longer use my cell phone. Tonight I finally tried to listen to any messages you might have left for me when I ran away, but it was too late. If you did leave a message, I never got it.

I'm sorry I didn't answer your calls that day. I just couldn't. I was so upset, so mortified at everything I'd done, and yes, that you'd done. Do you know how hard it is to be the one who gets dumped?

She stopped to dry her eyes. She'd brought tissue this time.

Nevertheless, I went a little crazy, I'll admit that. But I had to leave, I had to go away if I was going to be able to survive and figure out how the hell I'd gotten to that point. I didn't know who I was anymore. I'm still figuring it out. I know it was selfish to just run away, I know I let my family down. God, Thea won't even talk to me, Parker, do you believe that?

If someone had been walking down the street at a quarter after three that morning, past the darkened Coffee Shop at the Center of the Universe, they'd have seen a woman's face lit by a computer screen, then watched it disappear as she doubled over into the dark, sobbing.

There weren't enough tissues in the world for this, Mira realized. When she'd finished crying, when her eyes had swelled half shut and her lungs and throat felt raw, she straightened back up and continued:

Maybe I first broke the spell between us way back when, when we'd been married such a short time and I—

Here she paused, wiping her nose. What had she done, exactly?

When I made the mistake of thinking someone else could come between us. He could never have, Parker, but I was so frightened by my feelings. And now, after months of looking back, I realize that, of course, you're human, too, with the same kinds of feelings. But I wish you could have told me about it, before it got so late that you didn't want to be married to me anymore.

Yeah, right. How would old Mira, Saint Mira, have handled that? *Not very well,* she thought. She was doing the same thing she'd always done: sugarcoating, whitewashing. Making herself look good. It would have sucked no matter what, and she would have handled it abysmally.

Mira erased the last sentence, closed her eyes, and made herself type the truth:

I know I can be controlling and holier-than-thou and hard to love. I know that. I know our perfect marriage wasn't really perfect at all, and I was hanging on to some idealized version of a marriage. I know now that was too much pressure for you. For me. For us.

She paused and wiped her nose.

It may not matter anymore, but I think I've changed since I've been gone. All my life I thought that if I was just good enough, everything would be okay. But, duh, the world isn't that way. Real people aren't that way. I have faults and desires and secrets and all kind of things that I could never admit to you before. I only wanted you to see me as perfect, so you wouldn't leave me.

She laughed, and it turned into a sob.

But it didn't work. It was stupid, so stupid. I love you, Parker, and I wish now I had just been myself. Maybe you would have loved me anyway.

Mira stopped and read what she'd written. It scared her, the honesty of it, like blood on the page. She typed, "If at some point you ever want to know the real me, I'd love to get to know the real you, too. Again. Maybe we could just start over from scratch."

He'd either think she was ridiculous, or he'd think she was human. She had no idea, but she hit SEND, and went back upstairs to bed.

Thirty-four

It took another week for Gus to admit that Sequoia was never coming back and a replacement needed to be hired. Mira rummaged among boxes of raw sugar packets and stir sticks on the storeroom shelves, trying to remember where she'd put the Help Wanted sign. Every time she came into this room, she wondered what it was that Sequoia had gotten away with, what Gus was up to if not selling drugs. The safe was again closed and locked. Was it still empty?

When Mira let her logical side, her "good" self—the former Saint Mira—think about what had happened, she knew she should leave the Coffee Shop at the Center of the Universe, but Felix was right—it was almost like a family. And it was so easy to wake up every day and just walk down the stairs, pull her shift, chat with the customers. How was she ever going to move on? These days, even the thought of writing a lesson plan was daunting. Making a triple tall half-caf soy latte extra hot, however, was a piece of cake—Nonna's Italian cream cake, to be exact, which sold out in minutes whenever Mira baked one the night before and brought it down to the shop.

She finally found the sign beneath a stack of newspapers to be recycled, and held it up in the pearl gray light from the window. Red stripes top and bottom on plastic laminate—it was generic and of the hardware store variety. "We can do better than this," she mumbled, carrying the sign back out into the shop, where Amanda filled a teapot with water for Sidney's morning Earl Grey.

"Hey Amanda, you have artistic ability." Mira held up the sign, knowing the girl loved to doodle and draw. "We need something a little more, well, seductive."

Sidney shifted her book bag from one shoulder to the other. "You're hiring?"

"Yup." Mira picked through the day-old pastry basket and extracted a spinach and feta croissant. She unwrapped it, put it on a plate, and slid it toward Sidney. "On me," she told Amanda, who was ringing up the tea.

Sidney smiled, pleasantly embarrassed as she usually was when Mira gave her something to eat, but Mira had a feeling she was living on next to nothing. And then, as she usually did when she fed the girl, Mira found herself wondering if Thea was getting enough to eat in Woden.

Sidney shrugged. "How about if I worked here?"

"Really?" Amanda and Mira spoke in unison.

Jinx! Thea would have said.

Sidney nodded.

"Well, have you ever worked in a coffee shop before?" Mira asked, hoping she'd say yes, but she shook her head.

"It's not like it's trigonometry or anything," Amanda said. "Please, Mira. It would be so awesome to have Sid work here. I could teach her, easy."

Mira swallowed, cleared her throat. Kids had the power to undo her at the strangest moments. She'd think she had one pegged as a prima donna, or as a bad seed, then they'd go and do something sweet and selfless. She missed her students, her nieces and nephews, and Thea, god, Thea, so much she wasn't sure she could speak.

"That would be great," Sidney said. "If it's okay with you, Mira, or that guy, or whatever." Shrugging like it wasn't a big deal.

"I'll run it by Gus," Mira said, clearing her throat. "And you need to fill out an application. But I'm almost certain he'll say yes. Amanda, thank you." She reached to hug Amanda, who giggled nervously.

"Geez, let's not get all emotional about it," she said, but she patted Mira on the back and allowed her a few extra seconds in her stiff teenage-girl embrace.

At closing time, Mira mopped beneath the counter. Brackish gray water puddled out from the string mop onto the dull oak floor. "This can't be sanitary," she mumbled.

"Hm?" Gus stopped counting singles and fives on the other side of the counter and looked at her. "Did you say something?"

"Have you ever considered getting cleaning equipment from this century?" She smiled to soften it. That she and Gus were closing the shop so Yoshi and Felix could have their first date was probably enough for him at the moment. He wasn't really a bad guy. He wasn't even that lazy. He just didn't think sometimes. And although she'd been watching closely, she'd seen no further evidence of illegal activity. Gus had brought no one by at closing time. There'd been no smell of marijuana in the air.

"Well, just go buy what you want, Mira."

"Oh. Okay." She heaved the mop back into the rolling metal bucket, squeezed it through the wringer, then slopped it back to the floor.

"You do the Costco run tomorrow," he said, not looking up. "I'll cover for you. I need you to take on a little more responsibility around here, anyway. I'm planning a three-week trip to Yosemite in June. Gonna climb me a big-ass rock."

"Okay," Mira said, swallowing. June. Would she still be here in

June? "We need, um, toilet paper, right? And whole milk and a case of sparkling water."

"And lemons."

Lemons. Gus knew they needed lemons. Maybe old surfers could learn new tricks. Maybe people really could change for the better.

The next day, as Gus helped Mira unload her trunk when she returned from Costco, he chattered away about improvements he wanted to make to the shop: Did she think they should remodel the back to install a small kitchen area? Was it time to get rid of the computers in front, seeing as everyone had laptops these days, anyway? She'd never seen him so excited about his own business before.

"Do you think you could come up with a lunch menu?" Gus asked, throwing the multipack of toilet paper over one shoulder, balancing a box on his hip, and slamming the trunk lid closed. "You're so good with the soup. Or maybe we should hire a part-time cook."

"It's definitely worth thinking about," Mira said, new mop in hand, trying to imagine herself making sandwiches for the rest of her life.

Out front, Sidney and Amanda seemed to have the place under control. They didn't even need her, really. Sidney, as it turned out, was a bit of a neatnik, and cleaned constantly. Mira watched the two girls laugh and talk together as they poured decaf, steamed chai, and ladled bowls of soup for a group of foreign students, including the tall African boy. He smiled at Amanda, who smiled back from under carefully mascaraed lashes. Mira winced at how sweet infatuation could be. Where was the sweetness in her life? All she wanted from Doug was the surge of endorphins, the satisfaction of being physically desired, and the million tiny explosions in each orgasm. Indeed, she did want something sweet and pure with Martin, but she doubted he wanted anything other

than a café breve and idle conversation with the friendly, matron-
ly barista.

Mira just *wanted*. Fuck, she wanted so much, and she always
had. She wanted her daughter to forgive her. She wanted someone in her life she could talk to, remember with, someone who
understood her at the cellular level, who knew her as well as she
knew herself. There was only one person on earth who knew her
that well, and she flinched at how thinking about him—wondering
how he was, what he was doing, who he was doing it with—
could still rip her insides into a bloody mess.

All this wanting got her nowhere. It never had.

By the age of three, Thea was precocious enough that Mira knew
she had to provide the little girl with more than her everyday life
at home offered, so she enrolled her in Sea Sprites Preschool at
Bethany Lutheran Church in town. Nonna grumbled that the
venue was not Catholic, but Mira convinced her the preschool
was secular and only held its sessions in the church because it was
the cheapest rent in town, keeping enrollment fees low enough
for Mira and Parker to afford.

Mira knew it wasn't only for Thea's benefit that she signed
her up for both the morning preschool and the afternoon day
care. Mira needed more, too. Her degree was doing her less good
than Parker's, and she had the itch to go out into the world and
do something. She never let herself think the word "mistake"
when it came to marrying and producing offspring so early, but
at home she felt too much like her mother, sleeping late and napping because she didn't have a reason not to, complaining about
small discomforts—a pulled back muscle from scooping Thea off
the playground slide, a headache that lingered too long. Her conversations with Parker in the evenings had become repetitive and
lackluster. She knew she wouldn't have another baby, although
she left the reason unspecified. Two had been too much for the

first Mira, and Mira the second didn't want to find out if the same
would apply to her.

Her former teachers were delighted to welcome her into
the fold at Pacifica K–12. Her first year teaching flew by as
she navigated the learning curve, coming up to speed quickly.
Constance Davies, her high school English teacher, became a
caring mentor, and Ed Pedersen tolerated her early stumbles as a
science teacher—the time she left the juniors unsupervised with
the Bunsen burners and Neal Lundstrom lit Allison Applewhite's
hairspray-lacquered frizz on fire, and the quarter she spent teaching anatomy to freshmen before she realized it was meant for
juniors and seniors only.

By her second year, Mira knew she'd found what she was
meant to do. It didn't matter what she taught; the subject was of
no relevance to her. She just loved going into her classroom every
day and seeing a roomful of faces that counted on her to tell them
something interesting, something new, something of value. Their
rawness and boldness invigorated her; she admired their haphaz-
ard and safety-pinned fashion statements, the pogo-stick way they
danced to their ugly new music, the world-weary attitude they
assumed to disguise their innocence. She lived to break through
to a tough case, to empower a nerd. She loved having so much to
think about every day and night that nothing extra could fit in.

One day in early February, Mira's fifth period chemistry class
was busy testing a variety of household liquids for acidity. Fifteen-
year-old Gavin Antonelli, a second cousin by marriage, loved to
test her in front of the other students, and had surreptitiously
drunk all of the coffee she'd brought from the teacher's lounge
for the experiment.

She knew better than to call him on it in front of the others.
"Hmm," she said, nonplussed. "We must have run out. I'll go get
more." She'd have sent a kid, but students weren't allowed in the
teachers' lounge.

Gavin elbowed his lab partner in the ribs. Mira ignored him.

"Continue on with the Coke and the Windex, but stop before you get to milk. I'll be right back."

She stepped out into the hallway, sighing. He'd probably drink all the Coke next. She'd have to hurry. Pulling the door closed behind her, she turned and stopped. Two doors down the hall, she saw him. The electrician who'd worked on Thea's bedroom. He stood sideways to her, wearing his tool belt and a hard hat, his dark curls poking out in back. Arms across his chest, he stood speaking with Buck Headley, the superintendent, and Julie Schuler, the new school principal they'd just hired away from Portland. All three cocked their heads at the ceiling, concerned expressions on their faces.

Mira wanted to turn and run back into her room, but she had a feeling she'd be seeing more of her old crush around the place. The board had voted to install a computer in each classroom and convert one of the home ec rooms into a computer lab. She hadn't thought about the technological requirements of such a thing, but suddenly she pictured miles of cable running through the ceilings, down the walls in empty spaces between joists, coming up through the old wood flooring. It was enough to employ a team of electricians for weeks, months maybe.

Watching the scuffed toes of her shoes, Mira concentrated on moving forward, stepping lightly, noiselessly. Invisibly, she hoped. She'd just pass the group while they were engrossed in the ceiling and continue on her way to the teachers' lounge, where she would hide until they were gone. She'd have some explaining to do to her students, but chances were they wouldn't even miss her. Somehow, she made it past unnoticed and she poked her head out of the lounge door every minute or so until the coast was once again clear.

In bed that night she couldn't stop thinking about the electrician. She rolled from side to side, plumped her pillow, kicked off the covers, then scrambled to drag them back over herself minutes later when she was freezing. The clock hands moved at cartoon-quick speed, and soon Mira heard birds chirping. It was nearly morning. She sighed and sat up, amazed that Parker had slept through it all. It had been as though a train roared through their bedroom all night.

That night, Yoshi cleaned the floors at closing time with the super-duper new industrial mop. "Wow," he kept saying, as patches of clean wood appeared before him. "I never knew what color this floor was before."

Mira loaded his messenger bag with day-old pastries, then waved goodbye as he pedaled away down Thirty-sixth, disappearing into red taillights and the night's thick mist. She pulled the door closed and turned the OPEN sign to CLOSED, turned out all the lights except for one in back to light her way out when she was ready to leave.

Sipping a tall decaf, she settled in at the computer and slipped on her reading glasses. Her fingers were restless on the keys, her mind swimming from just having pulled a double shift in anticipation of Lannie's arrival at the end of the week. How had it come up so quickly? She'd worked out deals with everyone to make sure she could take off all of Friday and Saturday, so that she and Lannie could spend as much time together as possible. Mira secretly hoped Chet Moser couldn't make it.

Even though things were going so well in her new life, an old loneliness kept pushing its fingers into Mira's rib cage, hollowing out a place inside her that felt dank. Familiar. She'd known this loneliness her whole life, but she'd tried never to be alone enough to acknowledge it. Now she blinked into the dark, as alone as she'd ever been.

Mira reached into her purse, pulled out her phone, scrolled through previous calls and hit SEND.

"Hello?" Fonso sounded half asleep.

"You know, I've been through a lot of shit, too, and I never abandoned you. Think about *that* for a while." She pushed the OFF button. She'd never been mean to Fonso before, always thinking it might make him break, or push him off some edge he danced too close to, but he'd survived far worse things. He'd survive one pissy phone call from his sister.

Mira closed her eyes. She should just go to bed. Gus and Doug were on their way to La Push to surf the last of the winter's huge waves. They'd talked about it as if they were going to Mecca, or a Pearl Jam concert. They talked about it as if it were better than love, life, family. Even sex. Mira was almost jealous, but she knew that when they got home, she and Doug would have sex again. Once—well, officially twice, counting the morning after—was definitely not enough. It felt like addiction. Lately she turned to El Wando again and again, longing for someone in her bed to release her from herself just long enough to surrender all emotions. To forget herself, to become someone else. To glimpse the divine.

The gaping hole widened and she checked to see if Parker had answered her email. She hit the REFRESH button several times to make sure it wasn't stuck somewhere in cyberspace. Nothing, and he'd had it for nearly a week. She turned off the computer, gathered her things and headed for the back, clicking out the last light, locking the back door, and ascending the steps through the mist to her tiny retreat above the Coffee Shop at the Center of the Universe and the unconditional love of Patsy Cline.

Thirty-five

BEFORE LANNIE GAVE THEA HER OWN COPY OF THE KEY TO THE yarn and guitar store, she gave Thea a funny look. "I'll trade you," she said, folding her arms and leaning against the yarn display case.

"What for?" Thea knew something was up. Lannie had been looking up hotels on the Internet when Thea, Colby, and Damien arrived to rehearse for their next gig, this one in Eugene. Maybe Lannie was going on a trip and wanted her to watch the store or something while she was gone. That would be sweet. Maybe it would turn into a job, even. Maybe she'd pay her enough to move out of Woden. There was a cheap little studio apartment for rent over in Wheeler, with a view of Tillamook Bay.

"I want you to come with me to Seattle this weekend to see your mother."

"Well, that bites." Thea tried to keep her cool demeanor, but she could not keep her foot from tapping, her fingers from digging into her palms. Why did this scare her so much? "If I don't, we can't rehearse here anymore?"

Lannie sighed and gave her the key. "Of course not, drama queen. It's just something I want. Something I'd like you to do for me."

Thea swallowed and pocketed the key. "Why?"

"Because I'm a mother and I know how I'd feel if Trev wouldn't even talk to me, even if I had done something really hurtful. It doesn't matter sometimes if someone's hurt you, when you love them and they love you. You gotta move on, forgive 'em and get on with it."

Thea was embarrassed that the guys were witness to all this. She'd done such a good job at the house of acting like she just didn't give a shit, and here she was, trembling and sounding like a hurt little kid, and wanting Lannie to hug her and stroke her hair and tell her everything would be all right. "Why should I forgive her?" she said, quiet now, quiet as a tiny mouse. Any louder and her voice would crack. What she really wanted to ask was, "Why should she forgive me?"

"There's no sane, rational answer, honey. But you could trust me. I'm like twice your size and age, and one of those ought to be good for something."

Thea took a deep breath, her hand upon the key in her pocket.

"Have I ever steered you wrong before?" Lannie reached out and tucked a strand of hair behind her ear.

"Don't expect me to act all happy to see her or anything."

"Oh, I won't," Lannie said, then pulled Thea toward her, and Thea didn't care what the guys thought, it felt so good to be hugged.

Fifteen-year-old Thea leaned into the mirror in her bedroom, twisting the new stud that entered her skin just below her left eyebrow and reemerged just above it. It hurt like hell, even though the scary-looking biker guy in the Portland tattoo parlor said it shouldn't. The skin around the piercing looked red and puffy. Thea needed to find some rubbing alcohol.

She listened for the sound of Mira or Parker in the vicinity before opening her door, walking quickly to the bathroom, and pulling the door closed. They usually spent Sunday mornings reading the paper upstairs in their bedroom, for hours upon hours, one of them coming down the steps occasionally to refill their coffee cups. Yes, they would have to see it eventually but Thea was still trying to decide herself why she'd done it. She wasn't ready to try to explain it to them.

Somehow, it had seemed so awesome the night before when everyone decided it would be a grand adventure to leave Becca's boring party and drive to Portland to get piercings, all together, en masse. A tribal bonding ritual for the small band of outcast kids Thea hung out with, and a way to showcase their individuality and superior coolness to the dorkier population at Pacifica K–12. Somehow, they hadn't factored parents into the equation until much, much later, when the beer wore off and half of them had holes and the others had decided not to go through with it after all.

Thea dabbed at the raw little wounds with a cotton ball soaked in alcohol, expecting it to sting. "Fuck!" she exclaimed at the searing pain she felt instead. She pushed the cotton ball harder against her skin and a drop of alcohol dribbled into her left eye. "Goddamn it!" she hissed through clenched teeth, both eyes watering, her left eye burning worse than the piercing.

"Honey," Mira said from the other side of the door. "Are you all right?"

"Yes," she said, but there was pain in her voice; even she could hear it.

"Are you sure? Can I come in?"

"No, Mom, I'm, like, in the bathroom! Can't I get any privacy?" Her eye felt like it might burn right out of her head. What were you supposed to do when you got alcohol in your eye? Should you go to the emergency room? Was it going to cause permanent damage? Would she go blind?

She unlocked the door, hand and cotton ball covering the piercing, her left eye squeezed shut. She knew her mother was still outside the door, and she knew her reaction was not going to be good. She pushed it open and saw Mira's expression change from annoyance to panic.

"What's wrong, honey? What happened?" Mira pushed into the bathroom, reached for Thea's hand, but Thea twisted away.

"Wait, wait. There's something I have to tell you first."

"Just let me see—"

"No, Mom! Stop it! I got my fucking eyebrow pierced, okay? Then I tried to clean it and some alcohol got in my eye. Am I going to go blind? I don't know what I should do." Thea dropped her hand, looking at Mira through one good eye, even though it too was blurred by tears. "It really, really hurts, Mom."

"Yeah," Mira said, studying it. "I bet it does." She reached to touch the puffy skin, gently, her fingers cool. "And no, you're not going to go blind but you need to wash your eye out." She reached and turned on the faucet. "Bend over the sink and cup your hand under your eye. You need to get as much water in it as you can, okay? Until it stops stinging."

Thea complied, but only because her eye hurt like hell. The cool water did feel good, and she blinked and splashed until her eye began to feel normal. She stood up and took the towel Mira handed her, steeling herself for the lecture.

"Honey, why don't we just take it out?" Mira's voice was surprisingly calm. "Maybe it won't scar as bad if it never gets a chance to heal with that thing in." Her face looked funny, pained somehow, and it scared Thea worse than if she'd just yelled at her.

"Mom. I paid, like, thirty bucks for it, out of my own money."

"Can't you just wait until you're eighteen? Then you can do whatever you want to your body." Mira's eyes welled. "Oh, Thea. Your beautiful face . . ."

"God! It's not hideous or criminal to have a piercing, even though you think it is. It's just the way things are now. Everybody has them. It's not like I got a big tat on my face or anything. It's just a couple of little holes." *Painful holes,* she didn't say. "Dad won't care."

Mira gave her a look, then stepped outside into the hall. "Parker?" she called. "Could you please come down here?"

The two of them listened to Parker clump noisily down the stairs and waited for him to round the corner.

"Whoa," he said when he saw Thea. "What's that all about?"

"Well, I'm glad someone finally asked me about it, instead of trying to make me take it out before even giving me a chance." The pain this caused Mira was evident in her face, but Thea couldn't let it go. It was like there was something inside her making her madder than she wanted to be, uglier, meaner. "Mom just wants me to be some goody-goody like she was at my age and I'm just not. I'm never going to be, either!" Somewhere in her mind this made sense, this simmering angry nastiness, even though it didn't at a logical level, but her mother was always doing this, always trying to make her someone she wasn't meant to be. Someone she wasn't going to be, ever. Ever. And as she continued her rant, she knew the exact moment she made Mira crumble. "I hate you," she screamed, wondering why her voice was so loud. The victory was not sweet, but it couldn't be avoided. It felt predestined, like it had already happened even as it was happening.

Mira looked at Parker, chin trembling. "You handle this," she said. "I'm too horrible of a mother to even talk to my child." And she went back upstairs.

Now, Thea sat alone in Lannie's shop, on the chair by the cash register, her guitar in her lap. Colby and Damien had split a half hour ago, but she'd just wanted some quiet time to herself.

She'd removed the piercing after wearing it for a couple of weeks, just long enough that it wasn't Mira's idea. She didn't really like it, and it never felt quite right to have something sticking out of her skin there. She'd roll over on it in her sleep and jolt awake for fear that she was going to get it caught in the sheets and rip it out. Now that would be a nasty scar. As it was, she only had tiny bumps at the entrance and exit points, tiny bumps she fingered now, remembering.

Maybe she'd go stay with her dad tonight instead of catching a ride back up to Woden. Maybe she'd ask him if she'd really been that nasty as a teenager, and he'd cut her a break and say no. *Fat chance,* she thought, and laughed, but a sad laugh. She'd definitely tell him about her trip to Seattle, though, so he could tell her how happy her mother would be to see her.

Thirty-six

THE NEXT MORNING, AFTER AN EXCEPTIONALLY HEAVY SURGE OF morning commuters in need of a jolt, Mira sat out back, watching Patsy sniff the now-towering green mass of weeds. As she sipped her coffee, she realized she had Gus's store keys. All of them.

"Okay, Patsy. Hurry up. I have to get back," she called, but the dog ignored her, finding a new patch of little white budding flowers in the corner of the lot to smell. Mira felt a surge of adrenaline, thinking about whether or not she should check the safe. Gus was becoming more of a friend than a boss, and she hated the thought of spying on him. Lately he'd been rifling through her CDs, playing Neil Young and even Etta James, and he brought her fish tacos from the joint down the street whenever he ate there. Still, he'd never confided in her what exactly Sequoia had gotten away with, what made him so upset. It had to be pot, but what if there was something worse? Meth, crack? Could such a good person do something so bad?

"Patsy!" she yelled. The dog sensed her impatience and finally squatted. "Good girl," Mira said, trotting up the steps to let her back into the apartment.

Felix stood at the counter, flipping through a *Seattle Weekly*. A few regulars sat at tables near the windows, all basking in the fickle sun, knowing it wouldn't last. The group of fishermen had grown larger of late. *No wonder,* Mira thought. She'd been seeing news reports of a bad salmon year, and couldn't help remembering the long slow death of the fishing industry in Pacifica. Her uncles had given up after the corporate fleets had made it impossible to make a living. None of her cousins had carried on the tradition.

Mira grabbed the empty day-old pastry basket and loaded it up with fresh Danish from the case. She walked out front and set the basket on the fishermen's table. "Here you go, guys. On the house."

"You know, Mira, you don't have to bribe us to keep us out of Starbucks," one of the older guys said.

"Yeah," said another, "we'd come here even if you didn't give us free food," and the group laughed.

Mira shook her head and walked back toward the counter, winking at Felix, who smiled and returned to the article he was reading: "Is Tea the New Coffee?"

Mira sincerely hoped not. "It's kind of slow out here," she said. "I'm going to clean up in back. It's a mess."

Felix nodded and flipped the page.

Mira walked into the storeroom and pulled the door closed behind her. Heart thunking, she examined the keys on Gus's ring. The front and back door keys, the outdoor fuse box key, another large key and two small ones. They could be for his house, his bike lock. Who knew? Mira took a breath and walked to the safe. She swallowed, rocked back on one heel, then squatted in front of the gray metal box.

The first of the two small keys slid right in and turned as smoothly as a spoon in yogurt. Mira turned to check the door

behind her, then pulled the safe open. Very little filled the space:
no stacks of cash, no large plastic bags of drugs. What she did
find, however, were two large white plastic bottles. They looked
almost medicinal. She picked one up and shook it; it sounded like
a maraca. Pills? Her heart pounded. Twisting off the lid she peered
in to find the bottle nearly full of small round seeds. She picked
up the other bottle and shook it. It didn't sound quite as full as
the first one.

"Huh," she said, putting the bottles back, closing and locking
the safe. She stood, pushing the glasses back on top of her head.

Gus grew pot. Why go through all that hassle, she wondered,
when it seemed so easily available already harvested?

"Weird," she said, going back out front. Very weird, but then,
it was Gus after all.

Late that afternoon, when Sidney had replaced Felix, business
came to a standstill. Mira stood at the counter watching Sidney
write.

The girl sat at a table, hunched over her notebook, writing
in quick bursts, then staring out the window for long moments
before writing furiously again. She wrote every morning while
drinking her pot of tea, and when the tea was done, she'd close
her book, a satisfied look on her face. Lately, as now, she'd take
breaks at work to write when business was slow.

Mira sighed, thinking of Thea. She'd never watched her daughter write, never been afforded the luxury. Thea was private when it
came to such things, spending long hours in her room playing her
guitar, or, Mira supposed, writing songs. She'd never really asked
her much about it, and now she wondered why. Maybe because she
was so busy corralling her into doing her homework, or going for
extra credit, or taking on some extracurricular activity that would
one day be good for her. Mira grimaced. Had she ever let her
daughter just have fun doing what came naturally to her?

She filled her coffee cup and carried it and two cookies over
to Sidney's table.

"Would you mind if I just sat with you for a while?" she asked, feeling shy but wanting the company. "I don't want to interrupt you or anything."

"That would be nice."

Mira grabbed a newspaper from the neighboring table.

Sidney unwrapped her cookie and took a bite. "Mm. I love snickerdoodles."

Mira smiled, taking a bite of her own. She opened the *Seattle Weekly* to the movie section and pulled her glasses from the top of her head. She hadn't been out to see a movie in ages. Maybe she would ask Martin if he wanted to go see something with her. This thought made her heart flip over like a fish, and she tried to imagine what they would do during the movie. Stare straight ahead? Share a bucket of popcorn, occasionally bumping buttery knuckles? Would they whisper clever things back and forth? What would it feel like to have Martin whispering against the side of her face? She imagined him pulling her hair out of the way, whispering directly into her ear, softly, his lips bumping into her skin.

"God," she said, shivering, and Sidney looked up.

"Cold?"

"No! No, I mean, sorry. I was just reading something, and, um ... I didn't mean to interrupt. I'll just keep ..." She nodded for Sidney to go back to her writing, then snapped the paper straight, turned past the movies. Classes. Maybe she should find a class to take.

When Sidney closed her notebook, Mira closed her paper. "So," she said, "do you want to be a writer? I mean, for a living, or is it just something you like to do? I imagine it would be a hard profession to get started in."

Sidney twisted her lips to one side, thinking, her hazel eyes serious. "Well, I am a writer. I mean, if I write, doesn't that mean I am one?"

"Of course! I just meant, do you want to do it for a living or do you do it more for yourself? I mean, you know, have a regular job and do it more for fun. My daughter wants to be a musician, so I was just, you know . . ." Mira fumbled with the ball of plastic wrap from her cookie.

"It's just who I am. If I didn't write . . ." Sidney shrugged. "I figure if I do what I feel I should be doing, which is writing, and I'm good at it, which my teachers say I am, then somehow it will all work out." Her eyes shifted and she smiled. "Actually, I got a short story published online. Wanna see?"

"Absolutely," Mira said, and they scraped back their chairs, walked to Mira's favorite computer.

Sidney leaned over and typed in the URL, waiting a moment while the page loaded, then stepped back. "It's kind of long," she said. "I'll watch the front while you read it."

Mira slid into the chair and began to read. When she was finished, she looked up. Sidney busied herself wiping down the cash register, pretending not to notice.

"Oh, Sid. It's really good," Mira said. "You're a wonderful writer."

Sidney looked up and nodded. "Thanks," she said, her voice cracking, then she giggled. "God, I get so nervous when people read my stuff."

Mira stood and walked over to hug her. "Could you watch the front for just another minute or two? I need to use the restroom. Too much decaf."

Once inside with the door locked, Mira let herself cry, standing in the middle of the room, arms around her torso. Sidney's story was achingly sad and beautiful, about a mother who was too busy prostituting herself to notice her daughter had gone mute.

"Fuck," Mira said, wiping her eyes. Thea probably had equally sad and beautiful things to say in her songs. Even if they were about her, which the worst probably were, it didn't matter. Her daughter needed to sing them.

That's what she would tell Lali to tell Thea tonight when she called.

★ ★ ★

After Sidney left, Mira stayed, brewing a press pot of decaf. She was so tired from two days of double shifts she could barely think.

She had to call Lannie, who'd left her a message asking about hotels, meaning, she supposed, Chet Moser was definitely coming with her. This was nothing more than a weekend getaway for Lannie, a romantic rendezvous and a rare chance to see her son. She was going to show him off to her new boyfriend and revel in the night at the Tractor Tavern, dancing, drinking. It would be fun, actually, but Mira couldn't imagine herself being in any shape to stay awake, much less drink and be sociable. Her back hurt, her feet hurt. She was cranky. Maybe the double shifts hadn't been such a good idea. Why had she thought Lannie would want to spend all of her free time with her?

She dialed Lannie's number and got her machine. "Hi, it's me," Mira said. "Just returning your call. I can't wait to see you, and I'm sorry, I don't know anything about hotels up here. I haven't really seen any in this neighborhood, but I'm sure there are tons of them downtown."

She paused, unsure what to say. Should she tell her she'd emailed Parker and he hadn't bothered to reply? No. It would only encourage Lannie to make excuses for him. "So, anyway, I guess I'll just see you here Friday sometime, right? I can't believe that's the day after tomorrow already. I really am looking forward to seeing you again, sweetie. Let me know what time you think you'll be here."

Mira rubbed her thumb over the keypad. She'd memorized Fonso's number. Should she call to apologize? But what should she apologize for, telling the truth? Having feelings? God, maybe she should just leave him alone.

"Right," she said. Like that possibility existed in her Italian DNA.

She punched in the numbers.

"Look," she said when he answered. "I'm sorry for the call the other night. I'm sorry I make you feel bad. But what about me, Fonso? I need you. Why can't you just be my brother?"

At the other end of the line, she heard a Serafino sigh. "You gonna let me talk this time?"

"Yes," she said.

"I'm sorry about all that stuff I said about you not having problems. I know that's bullshit. Sometimes I'm just a mean old bastard, but at least I come by it honestly."

Mira winced. He was right. Al Senior had been so hard on Fonso. "You're not mean," she said. "Our family is just so . . ." She stopped. "I don't know."

"Fucked up?"

"Are we that bad? Really? What makes us so terrible?"

He expelled a hard laugh. "That. That right there."

"What?"

" '*What?*' " he mimicked her. "The denial is un-fucking-believable. The way our mother died, for one thing. The way we all had to just push on and pretend it never happened, and never act like anything was wrong, and take everybody's weird silence—"

"Fonso, no one blames you." Mira couldn't believe they were finally talking about this, this horrible thing he'd carried his entire life, the thing that made him feel worthless and guilty and like he couldn't be part of the family.

He laughed, ugly. "You think I don't know that? I didn't jam that bottle of Seconal down her throat."

"What? Fonso!"

"Okay, Mira. You go on telling yourself she died from some stupid operation. You keep toeing the family line."

She'd thought he was fine, but maybe he wasn't. Maybe he was high or drunk, or just fried from the years of drug abuse. "Why do you say that? You were right there. She went to the hospital—"

"For a good old stomach pumping. Don't play so innocent with me, Mira. You never heard the whispers, the adults talking in the other room at night? That's when they'd tell the real story, after we were supposed to be in bed."

"But I remember . . ." Her voice trailed off.

"You remember what they wanted you to, what they told you. It was all just a fucking fairy tale they invented so they wouldn't have to deal with an imperfect family member in the great Sera-fino *famiglia*. Your poor sacred dear departed blessed goddamn mother. Nonna probably drove her to it. First her, then me. They couldn't wait to get rid of me. And you, always trying to save me. You're no better than the rest of them. Now, for god's sake, please, *please* just leave me the fuck alone."

The line went dead and Mira clicked her phone off, then placed it in her purse. She stood and pulled her purse strap to her shoulder, reached for the keys still on the table. Her knees buckled, and she searched beneath her for the seat, letting the purse drop to the floor. She couldn't breathe. She couldn't think.

Nothing, *nothing* in her entire world was the way she'd always thought it was. No one, not even her mother, was good. She wanted to scream, but she worried someone would hear, even though the shop was closed. *Keep your voice down,* she could hear Nonna say.

At home in bed she tried beating on her pillow, but she just felt stupid, especially when Patsy got excited and started jumping up and down, and then Mira worried she'd tear the pillow open and feathers would fly and she'd be the one who had to clean it up. She thought maybe she'd just go crazy and run naked and insane into the night, but she just lay there feeling like a squished-out tube of toothpaste.

Goddamn Fonso. She didn't want this in her life. Sitting up in the dark, she felt sick. "Oh god," she said, and placed her hands over her eyes. This was too real; it felt too familiar. Nonna comforting her father as he hunched over the dining table, saying, "Don't blame yourself, *cara*." Everyone watching her and Al and Fonso too closely, saying nothing, just watching them with those horrible expressions on their faces. Whispering, huddling together behind doors, around corners, going silent when Mira approached. That's not what would have happened if her mother had died any other way—the family would have rushed in with their overwrought sympathy and ethnic zeal for comforting. She'd watched it happen at every death in the family, in the community. Mira craved that kind of comfort right now, sitting alone in the dark, letting this information trickle slowly from her brain into her bloodstream, into her heart, her abdomen and lungs, her arms and legs and toes and fingers. This was real.

This had been her first denial, but many more had followed.

Thirty-seven

———•———

THE MORNING AFTER MIRA HAD SEEN THE ELECTRICIAN AT SCHOOL, she felt rushed getting ready, even though she'd been up since before daylight.

"Wow, you look nice today," Parker said from behind his Cheerios bowl as she packed Thea's snacks and toys for the day. Thea perched on her Garanimaled knees on a chair beside him, engrossed in a picture she was drawing. Her cereal was untouched.

"I've worn this before," Mira snapped, but she did feel a little obvious wearing the red-and-black-striped miniskirt to school. She'd paired it with a simple white blouse and flats, but still. She'd have to change. She'd throw on the black slacks she wore the day before. "Thea, eat."

"I'm just saying you look great," Parker said. "You look like you're about eighteen." He stood and walked over, leaned down and kissed her. "You're going to drive all those poor schoolboys wild."

"Which is why I'm going to go change," she said, spilling Goldfish crackers across the countertop. "Shit."

"Mommy!" Thea looked up from her drawing. "You said shit!"

"That doesn't mean you can, Miss Polliwog," Parker tried to say sternly, but he winked at Mira. "Now, quit coloring and finish your cereal. You and Mommy have to leave in five minutes."

The next three days at school were an agonizing mixture of hoping not to see the electrician and desperately wanting to. The teachers on the third floor began to chatter about where their computers would be placed, what Jim the electrician had said about how long all this might take. He was working his way from the top to the bottom. Mira's classroom was on the ground floor. How she hadn't at least run into him again, she didn't know.

On Friday at five past noon, as Mira got ready to leave her empty room for the cafeteria, the door swung open. She knew before looking up who it would be. He carried his hard hat at his side like a football, tucked inside his arm, and the sight of his dark hair curling down his neck, the look in his eyes at seeing her, sparked a nervous dance of neurons firing, hormones surging.

"Hi," she said, crossing her arms over her chest.

"Hey, hi. It's you. I thought I saw you the other day, down by the office." He stopped just inside the door, then scanned the room, the ceiling. Was he thinking about wiring? Or was he just nervous, like she was, avoiding eye contact?

"So, you're finally here to . . ." She stopped and giggled. She'd been about to say, *to do me.* "I mean, is it my turn now?" She laughed again, rolled her eyes. "For a computer, I mean."

He turned his eyes to her and smiled. He really did have a nice smile. She'd forgotten that. At the ripe old age of twenty-four she'd forgotten what it was like to flirt, to have a man look at her this way.

"Yes, Mrs. Serafino, it's your turn. Where would you like it?"

Mira snorted, shook her head. If he wasn't flirting, it was a damn good imitation. "Mira. Remember? My name is Mira."

"Mira," he said, then walked over and set his hard hat on a nearby lab table. "Jim."

"I remember," she said, looking around the room. "Where do you suggest?"

"Wherever you want," he said, and his voice softened. "Where would be the most private?"

She looked back at him, heart clutching, breath deserting her. It was the same look in his eyes that had made her run the first time. She looked toward the door. She could lock it as if she'd gone to lunch. The narrow strip of window would reveal very little to anyone looking in.

He stepped closer to her. Could he read her thoughts? Maybe she should just tell him to put the computer wherever he wanted to and get out of there as quickly as possible. She reached for her purse on the desk. "Maybe in the back corner," she suggested, deciding to ignore his double entendres. "Over there."

"Show me," he said. She couldn't tell what he was thinking.

"Just somewhere in this corner," Mira said, walking back through high tables and chairs. She nodded at a folding table stacked with used petri dishes and boxes of smeared slides, and shouldered her purse to say, *I'm leaving now*. "I could store this stuff somewhere else, move some of the tables around a little, and—"

"God, you're sexy," he said from behind her, then slid his hand around her hip to her belly, pulling her back against him.

She pushed at his hand and twisted away, laughing, but it sounded scared. "Hey. I thought you were here to talk about my computer." Her throat went dry. She tried to swallow; she tried to draw a breath, but her body was rebelling, shutting down her systems.

"You're a tease, you know that?" He grabbed at her hand, catching her wrist, and pulled her toward him. Her purse dropped to the floor, contents clattering across the linoleum.

"I'm sorry," she said, trying to wrench away. "I shouldn't have—"

"Oh, come on." He laughed and gripped her arm tighter, then wrapped his other arm around her back and jerked her to him. "Is this what you wanted me to do back then? Just make you do it so you couldn't resist?"

Mira struggled, heart thudding wildly now, breath coming in gasps.

"See? You're breathing hard. You like it." He put his mouth to her neck, wet, sticky, his hard tongue pushing on her pulse, threatening to stop it. One hand still held her wrist too tight, the other slid down the middle of her behind, fingers thrusting through the flimsy gabardine of her pants.

"No," she said, dropping her knees to put distance between his creeping fingers and the parts of her she didn't want touched, not now, not this way. Again she tried to twist from his grip. "Please," she said, "let me go." She tried to sound adamant, but she could hear that her voice had a whimpering sound, a sound he would interpret as sexual.

"It's okay, just relax," he said, bringing his mouth to hers, his eyes wide open and too close to her face.

He had to see the refusal in hers, she thought, the near-terror she was now feeling, and yet he was kissing her anyway, thrusting his tongue into her mouth like a sour-tasting gag. His tongue was like a penis, hard and forceful, and she couldn't pull her head away, and she couldn't breathe, he was so close. Biting down as hard as she could, she felt his head pull back, his long hard tongue scrape through her teeth, his hand release her wrist, his body reel. She tasted salt in her mouth and wondered if it was blood.

"Goddamn it," he said, grimacing, spitting, bringing his hand to his mouth. "What the fuck is wrong with you?"

Mira backed up, arms wrapped tightly around her middle, until she was leaning against something solid, the folding table maybe. She wanted to run, but her legs could barely hold her weight. "I'm sorry," she said, wondering why she was apologizing, but something inside told her it was safer than screaming, than beating his chest with her fists, than hurling a chair at his stupid black curly-haired head. She tried to breathe. "I never meant to—"

"Of course you meant to." His eyes narrowed, and she wondered if he would hit her, if anyone in the noisy cafeteria would hear if she tried to scream.

He shook his head, still wiping his mouth. "Fuck it, you know? And fuck you, too. If you want a goddamn computer in this room, you're going to have to go home sick or something. I'll be back in an hour and I don't want you here."

He strode to the front of the room, grabbed his hard hat from the lab table and left.

Trembling, Mira brought her hand to her mouth, felt her lips. There was blood there, but was it his? Was it hers? Running her tongue around the inside of her mouth she felt where she had bitten herself on the inside of the cheek as she bit him. Her wrist was bright red and ached. Her body felt raped, though he hadn't done anything but grope her and try to kiss her.

If you could call that a kiss, she thought, feeling squeamish. Why had she wanted this man to make love to her, for all this time? Why had she almost let him ruin her marriage? Even though she'd tried to be good, somehow he'd seen through her.

Ice. She had to get ice for her wrist, without anyone seeing her, and maybe it would help inside her mouth, which was already swelling against her molars. She had to remove all evidence of this . . . this encounter. *This assault,* she decided, though even when framing it that way she knew something vital: She was as much to blame for it as the electrician, and she would never tell anyone it had happened. Not anyone at school, of course, and she wondered what everyone would think when she did indeed go home sick for the afternoon. She could easily throw up right now, in fact.

But worse, so much worse, was this: She could never, ever tell Parker. She'd lose him for sure.

The trembling gave way to shaking, and Mira felt more alone than she ever had.

At home that evening, Parker knew something was wrong the minute he walked in the door, even though she wore long sleeves, even though she had figured out how to speak without lisping too badly.

"I had a little run-in with a student," she said, hoisting Thea up to kiss him hello. Thea grabbed her wrist and she flinched.

"God, honey," Parker said, dropping his coat to the floor, taking Thea in one arm and embracing her in the other. "What the hell happened? Does Buck know about this? Are they going to expel the kid?"

She pressed her face into his shoulder and squeezed her eyes shut, shaking. Clutching his sweater with both hands, she started to cry. Every bit of her wanted to tell him the truth, to just let the words and the feelings and the ugliness pour out, so they couldn't poison her anymore.

"Mira, Mira, come here, come sit down," he said, so softly, so lovingly, and Thea reached to pat her head, thumb in her mouth, worried eyes watching her. She let him lead her to the couch and curled up next to him, Thea on the other side. Mira hid her face in his chest, cooing to Thea, "It's okay, baby. We're okay."

To Parker, she finally said, "It's being dealt with, don't worry. Just some stupid kid with too much testosterone. He didn't mean to hurt me, I don't think." She sniffed and sat up, wiping her eyes. "I don't really want to talk about it right now, okay? Maybe later." He'd understand that, and in the meantime she'd come up with a better story. Anything to keep him holding her, not pulling away again. Not giving up on her.

Mira woke to the sound of car doors slamming out back. Patsy sprang up and ran to the door. "God, Patsy, it's only, what is it? It's only four forty-five. Come back to bed." Mira rolled over and stuck her head under a pillow. Every second of sleep felt imperative to her survival. Just one more double shift to get through and then she would have a little quality time with the one person she still considered family.

The next sounds she heard were beneath her, in the shop. Either someone was robbing the place or Gus was back. She heard water running and guessed the latter. Criminals didn't usually feel the need to make coffee or wash their hands.

Patsy whined nervously at the door. Someone was climbing the steps.

"No," Mira said. On any other day, this might have seemed romantic, but an unannounced early morning visit from a lover was the last thing she needed right now. She didn't want to have to think about the bags beneath her eyes from crying, the fact that she'd put off showering until the morning. If this weren't happening, she could still eke out another half hour of sleep.

At the knock on the door, Patsy Cline began to yip. From the other side of the door, Doug whispered, "Shh, Patsy, it's just me. It's okay, girl."

Mira rolled her legs off the side of the bed, then pulled herself up. She dragged her feet across the floor, opened the door, and turned around to head back to bed.

"I'm exhausted," she said. "I have one more double shift to pull today and I need more sleep." Mira crawled into bed.

"That's okay," Doug whispered, already shedding his clothes. "I just wanted to sleep next to you. I missed you so much."

"Yes, sleep. Good. Thank you."

He slid into bed next to her, turning on his side to spoon with her. "Sweet dreams, babe," he said.

Babe? she thought. They weren't supposed to have terms of endearment for one another. They'd only had sex twice, been on one date. This was supposed to be friends with benefits, not *I miss yous* and *babes*. She sighed and punched her pillow. *Sleep now,* she intoned. *Sleep.*

As she settled and drifted toward unconsciousness, Doug's hand crept over her left breast. *No,* she thought. *He isn't.*

"Doug, please," she said, lying as still as possible.

"Sorry, sorry." He kissed her shoulder, massaging her breast now. "You just make me so crazy."

Mira sighed. "Well, maybe you should go, then."

His hand retreated and he rolled onto his back. "Okay, I'll be good. Let's get some sleep and maybe we can sneak in a little quickie when we wake up." Within thirty seconds he was asleep.

She opened her eyes. Now she'd be awake until the alarm went off, thinking four-in-the-morning thoughts, the kind she had way too many of lately. They collided and sparked off each other, igniting new self-reprisals, uncovering old pain. Mira sighed. She wanted the joy back in her life, the sweetness.

She rolled toward Doug and studied his sleeping profile, his high forehead and small straight nose. He liked her. He liked her wide hips and small breasts and frizzy hair. It was so simple and clean.

She touched Doug's lips. He released a contented sigh, and his eyes eased open as he turned toward her, smiling. He looked so happy just to be lying next to her, anticipating whatever came next.

"Hi," she said, smiling back, and leaned closer to kiss him. "I'm sorry. What was I thinking? I can sleep any time."

"Oh, Mira," he moaned, taking her hips in his hands and pulling her against him. "I want you, god, so much."

She closed her eyes and smiled as his lips traveled down her neck, luxuriating in his words almost as much as his touch. All she'd ever desired, and rarely got, was this—just for someone to look at her, to see her as she really was, and want her.

Thirty-eight

DRESSED IN SWEATS AND SLIPPERS, WITH PATSY CLINE ON HER heels, Mira stood on tiptoe to see inside the storeroom window. Doug had fallen back to sleep upstairs after they made love, but Mira was wide awake. She decided to catch a peek at what Gus was up to down there.

The light was on, and she could see him from the back, but only the top of his head as he kneeled in front of the safe. She looked around for something to stand on and stepped off the sidewalk, feeling a small soft presence beneath her slipper. Patsy yelped with the volume of a Sonic Youth song in the hollow emptiness of the dark morning.

Mira saw Gus turn his head before she leaned down to scoop Patsy into her arms. "I'm sorry, sweetie," she whispered, rubbing each paw to check for broken bones, but Patsy was over the trauma already.

"Hello?" Gus stuck his head out the back door.

"Hey, it's just me, walking Patsy," Mira said, heart thumping. "I stepped on her foot, poor thing."

"God, you freaked me out," Gus said, hand over his heart. "What are you doing down here? I drove all night to bring you your boyfriend for some quality time. Dude, that is one lovesick puppy you got there, and I'm not talking about Patsy Cline."

"Yeah, well, he's already snoring. You guys must have had a good time."

Gus leaned against the doorframe, looking dreamy, like someone in love. "Yeah, it was awesome. Thing is, Dougie's a pretty good rider, but he's getting a little older. He gets winded faster now, can't go for as many runs as I can. I tuckered him out yesterday and we just decided the hell with it. Let's go home before these freaking waves kill us."

"Wow," Mira said. Patsy struggled to get down, then ran to the weed patch. "You know, the weeds are getting pretty high out here," Mira said. "Shouldn't we pull them out? Won't the city give you a citation?"

Even as she was saying it, Mira realized what she should have all along.

"I'm gonna pull them later today." Gus stood straighter and jammed his hands in his pockets, nodding at the ground.

"Do you know what kind of plants they are?"

He looked up at her. "Do you?"

"Marijuana?" she guessed.

"Not the kind you think."

"I didn't realize there was more than one kind." She knew she sounded judgmental, but Mira felt duped, stupid, old. "You should have told me," she said. "If you get arrested, it affects me, too. This is my whole life now, this place, this job. This." She gestured around at the gravel parking lot, the dilapidated stairs, the power lines overhead. She'd even been planning on how she'd fix the place up while Gus was gone in June, to surprise him when he got back.

"Come inside," he said, his brow wrinkling down. "I want to talk to you about it, but not out here."

Mira sighed. "Come on, Patsy." The sky was turning from purple to pink, and clearly, the tall budding plants were indeed marijuana. How had she not seen it before?

Inside, Gus asked, "You want a decaf?" So he had noticed something about her, her preference for decaf, just not that she drank the fully loaded stuff in the morning.

"Regular," she said.

"With cream." He pulled two cups from the rack.

Mira took the chairs down from a table in front and sat. Patsy settled under her chair and licked Mira's heel.

Gus walked over and set the coffee cups on the table, then swung his leg over the back of the chair and sat down. "You ever hear of medical marijuana?"

"Sure," Mira said. "But it's dispensed by a pharmacy or something, isn't it?"

"No. People have to grow it. It's kinda tough for a sick eighty-five-year-old to manage, though, so I try to help where I can."

"So, what . . . they pay more than regular pot smokers?" Why was she being so sanctimonious? She'd stood right against that counter in back and smoked a joint herself, right in front of God and Yoshi and everybody, and had wanted to again.

"They pay less," Gus said. "I grow medical-grade marijuana, which is like half the potency of what's out on the street these days. If your typical cancer patient or some old lady with glaucoma smoked the street stuff, they'd be too stoned to even function."

"Huh," Mira said. "What did we smoke that night?" She had certainly felt too stoned to function, other than sexually.

"Oh, that was Dougie's shit. He always gets the best."

Mira sipped her coffee. "There aren't that many plants out there. That can't be profitable, and it seems pretty risky."

"Yeah. I need to get rid of them." Gus pulled on his goatee.

"They're just some experimental varieties I'm working on, trying to see what people can grow themselves outside in colder temperatures. My stuff's all grown over in a warehouse, hydroponically, grow lights and stuff."

"This is what I don't understand," Mira said. "You have the coffee shop. You could put your whole business in jeopardy." She set the cup down. "Unless . . ."

"No, it's not a front. I barely make anything. I just like to do it. I started when my mom had breast cancer. She was so sick from the chemo that she just kept getting skinnier and skinnier. I was scared, so I started looking into it. And it just kind of blossomed."

"Bad pun," Mira said, but Gus didn't get it.

"You aren't going to leave, are you?" He looked down at his cup.

"How's your mom now?" Mira noticed for the first time how long Gus's eyelashes were, how dark and thick. *His mother must love that about him,* she thought, *and always will, no matter how old he gets.*

"She died three years ago."

"Oh! God, I'm sorry, Gus. When you told me your mother bought this place, I just thought you meant she was still . . ."

"I think she bought it because she knew I'd need something to do with my life, after . . . you know . . . and she didn't want to just will me the money. She knew I'd piss it away." He laughed.

"Do you think you keep growing it for her sake?"

He tilted his head, considering. "I guess. I never really thought about it that way."

"How much did Sequoia get away with?"

"Too much, but that wasn't what pissed me off. It was just that she'd do that, when it's something I try to do to help people. That girl has some serious issues."

Mira laughed. "No kidding. You miss her?"

Gus sighed. "Yeah. Isn't that the craziest thing?"

"No." Mira reached down to pet Patsy, then brought her onto her lap. "There's nothing crazy about that."

"So, Mira Serafino." Gus took a long drink of coffee, then sat back with his hands clasped behind his head. "What's your story? I told you mine. Fair's fair."

"I told you. I ran away from my husband because he had a girlfriend. I made the decision rather quickly." She shook her head. "Maybe a little too quickly, I don't know."

"Well, your old man's pumping some other broad, you do what you gotta do, right?"

Mira flinched. "It wasn't exactly like that. It was just the real-ization that he didn't want to be with me anymore. It was such a . . . a shock. It had never occurred to me that I might not be the perfect wife, or have the kind of marriage I thought I did. I made the whole thing up."

"So you left him before he could leave you?"

"Maybe. Or so I wouldn't have to know the truth. I don't know what I was doing, exactly. I was just . . . crazy. I wasn't myself, and then I couldn't change it all back, and time kept pass-ing, and now, well, here I am." She gestured grandly, trying to make the moment funny, but Gus stayed serious, and her hands fell to her sides.

"Why don't you just go home?"

"It's too late. And every day it gets later and later."

He nodded and they went silent as they sipped their coffee. Light began to ease in through the windows and Mira wished they could just sit there for hours, be customers enjoying their morning brew, the sun on the floor, the company of someone you could be totally comfortable with in slippers and bed-head hair.

Gus cleared his throat. "So, you still miss him?"

"Every single moment of every single day."

Gus laughed. "That is so messed up. What the hell is wrong with us?"

"We're hopeless." Mira shook her head.

"Hopeless romantics."

Wasn't that what Thea had said about Parker on Christmas Day? Mira cleared her throat, looked away, tears forming.

Gus sighed and reached for her hand across the table. "Maybe it wasn't about you. God knows I've dumped some fine women in my lifetime because I thought I wanted someone else, someone a little more exciting, then a little less exciting, someone prettier, then someone not so vain. Then I kicked myself later. You know?"

Mira nodded, wiping her eyes with her napkin. "Those who study such things say that a man's biological imperative is to impregnate as many women as possible, to make sure his progeny continue to populate the earth."

"I'd buy that. What's a woman's biological imperative?"

"To survive being dumped, and still take care of the progeny."

Gus squeezed her hand.

Mira squeezed back, feeling his callused palm beneath her fingers. "No, that's bullshit," she said, then patted his hand and stood up. "We're here to make as many babies as we can and help them turn into baby-makers one day themselves. Love has very little to do with it."

Gus yawned, stretching. "Well, you've got someone who loves you now, and Doug is no cheater. He's one faithful son-of-a-bitch."

"Mm." Mira nodded. It was time to get dressed for the day. Maybe, if she was lucky, she could do it without waking up Doug. If he woke, he'd look at her that way again and she'd never get to work.

Thirty-nine

Across the street, the goliath plum tree was in pink flower, its brilliance mesmerizing, and the almost-warm breeze pulled its scent toward Mira through the open door. Gus and Doug had gone home hours ago. Felix called in with a miserable cold, and Amanda wasn't due to come in until two.

Mira closed her eyes for a brief moment, felt herself sway. Only one more shift to go before she could fall into bed, pull the blanket over her head, and sleep. Then, tomorrow—

"Mirabella," a voice said.

"Daddy?" She opened her eyes.

"I love it when you call me that." Martin stood smiling in front of her.

She yawned, covering her mouth. "God, excuse me. I think I fell asleep standing up. Good thing it was you."

He laughed, and Mira was glad no other customers were in the shop.

"Hey," she said, "you look . . . different." His poodle hair had been clipped close to his head and his forehead was bright red from the previous weekend's spate of sun. It seemed most customers had a similar patch of red somewhere on their pallid Seattle skin.

"I've been shorn," Martin said, rubbing his head. "Like it?"

Mira nodded. "It looks soft. Can I touch it?" She blushed but reached across the counter anyway. Lord knew why she said these things to this entirely-too-kind young man, but he never seemed to mind. There was something so sweet about that. He bent forward, letting Mira caress the top of his head. She sighed and let her hand drift down the back of his head, to his warm, smooth neck, and around to the hollow in his throat before she drew a deep breath and pulled away.

"Wow," Martin said, straightening. His cheeks now matched his forehead.

"Sorry," Mira said. She was consumed with wanting to touch him more, wanting her face next to his, his skin upon hers. She'd just had sex with a perfectly fine—no, wonderful—lover, and here she was, lusting after another. Did she have no control at all anymore?

"No need to apologize," Martin said, looking at her in a new way. "You have a very, um, sensual touch."

Mira closed her eyes again. She was in a weakened state, that was all. Martin was not interested in her, not in that way.

"Are you okay?"

She opened her eyes and Martin was still looking at her with an intensity she didn't know how to read.

"No," she said. "To be honest, I have a hard time around you." *What are you doing?* a voice screamed inside. *Stop! Stop now.* But she knew what she was doing. She was poisoning the well. If she admitted this, out loud, it would expose her foolishness, her pointless romantic notions. He would look embarrassed but he'd be kind about it. He'd say, *I like you, too, Mira, but not in that way,* and she would be safe again. "Actually, Martin, I'm just really . . ."

She blew out a long breath and shrugged. "This is going to sound so stupid. I'm attracted to you."

"You are?" He cleared his throat, then reached across the counter and took her hand.

God, he's nice, Mira thought, *trying to make me feel better.* She clasped his hand, returning his friendly gesture, marveling at how very kind people in Seattle were, but then he lifted it to his mouth and caressed her knuckles with moist lips.

She inhaled suddenly. "You probably shouldn't do that."

"You know," he said, ignoring her, "I would say I have a hard time around you, too, but the pun would just be embarrassing."

Mira watched as he pulled his bottom lip beneath his teeth— his perfect pretty teeth—then watched it emerge, plump and glistening. He still had her hand, and she lifted it to the soft spot between his collarbones again, then pulled her fingers down until they rested against his sternum, where she felt a rhythmic thudding. She had fallen asleep, that was it. She drew a deep breath through her nose, opened her eyes as wide as possible, but still, here she stayed, standing at the counter in the Coffee Shop at the Center of the Universe feeling the heartbeat of the younger man she'd been fantasizing about for months.

"How old are you again?" Her breathing had gone shallow and she didn't know where to put her other hand, so she clutched the tile counter between their bodies, feeling every tiny speck of grout against her fingertips.

"A hundred and five." He stroked her hand, pressing it into his chest. Mira shivered and Martin smiled, his eyes soft in a new way. "Way too old for you."

She didn't dare shut her eyes—if she did, she would wake up without getting to see this dream through to its natural conclusion.

Mira had always fantasized that she and Martin would have great long talks, sitting together at the coffee shop at first, then taking their deepening friendship elsewhere. To a quaint little restaurant nearby for dinner, or a glass of wine on the waterfront, or a martini in Belltown. To an arty film at one of the theaters in Capitol Hill, maybe. Walking around the crown of Queen Anne Hill on a Sunday morning. That was after they'd spent the night together, she imagined. The nights she dreamed of were sketchy, vague in a way that was more romantic than sexual: hand-holding, kissing, blooming love declared, and then, only then, the two of them lying side by side, staring deeply into each other's eyes. She couldn't even picture him below the neck, naked—only his face, full of love and desire for her.

Instead, they were staring at each other over the counter, her hand in his, both of them breathing hard. She marveled that she could choose to make love to this young man who so intrigued her and he would reciprocate, right now maybe, say in the storeroom, or upstairs during a break after Amanda arrived, or later that night. *He would do it,* she realized, astounded, aroused. *And maybe he would love me, forever and ever and . . .*

Oh god, she thought. *This is crazy. He can't love me enough to make me feel better. Nobody can. There is not enough love in the world to change the fact that my mother left me when I was eight years old.*

Martin cocked his head at her. "What? What are you thinking?"

She shook her head, closed her eyes. If she remained very still, didn't try to explain, maybe she wouldn't cry. After a moment, she swallowed and opened her eyes to look at him. She was certain he could see that her eyes were moist. "Am I crazy, or do you have a girlfriend?"

"Well, not really a girlfriend." His smile began to wither.

"Someone you like, a lot?"

"Well, there is someone, yes, but she's concentrating on getting her master's. It's not the right time to get serious."

"Yes, it is, Martin. It's absolutely the right time. Love doesn't always last forever, even when you think it will."

"No?"

"No."

He sighed and squeezed her hand, kissing it one more time before letting go. "This is so not how I thought this was going to play out."

"Not because I don't—"

"I know, I know." He shook his head, his cheeks and forehead coloring. "Let's pretend this never happened."

"Must I?" Mira pressed her hand over her heart. "I want to remember this day for the rest of my life."

"I think I'd like to forget it," he said. "I'm sorry I misinterpreted—"

"You didn't." Mira shook her head. "God, you so didn't. This is really hard."

He laughed. "That's what I've been trying to tell you."

She snorted. "You're a bad boy, Martin."

"You're a good . . . person, Mira."

She sighed. "No, not really. But in this case, I'm going to try to be."

"You're sure about that?" He looked at her sideways, smiling.

Oh handsome boy, you don't know the half of it, she thought. "Yes. No. God, yes, I'm sure." She sighed. "I am."

They nodded at each other, smiling, embarrassed, until she said, "Would you like to go for a walk sometime? Or, I don't know. What do people who like each other this much do, if they don't have sex?"

He laughed. "They have coffee."

Mira smiled. "I would so love that."

"There's no one here."

"Right now?"

"Why not?" He leaned in closer than he ever had before. "I'll have the usual," he said, kissing her cheek. "If you would be so kind."

Forty

MIRA AND AMANDA WORKED A LONG, SLOW AFTERNOON. THE DAY seemed to have no end. With the weather nicer and the days longer, Seattleites were all outdoors somewhere, on the water if they were lucky, or sitting on the beach at Golden Gardens, or walking the trail along the canal. Mira propped open the front door to let in the warm air and the sound of boat horns honking at the Fremont Bridge, then the inevitable bell clanging as it rose, over and over, every fifteen minutes or so, with so much boat traffic.

She wondered if she and Martin would really become friends. Clearly, some fantasies were meant to be just that; she was relieved she hadn't slept with him. She was glad she'd slept with Doug—it was probably the best sex of her life—even though she knew it had to end before he got too attached to her. She was never going to love him the way he should be loved.

She'd run away from the only person she loved that way. She wished she could have let him see who she really was, that she'd tried to see who he was becoming, because he'd probably been changing for quite some time and she'd ignored it. Even if they hadn't stayed together, they each might have had a cleaner new start.

The spring sky had changed, the white puffy clouds now a mottled, bruised color, violet and indigo mixed with perfect pale baby blue when the sun broke through. Dark and light; bruised and hopeful. Like her life, which was exhausting, and Mira felt worn out. The next day she really wanted to be up for the arrival of Lannie, her one true friend through everything.

"Hey, Amanda?" she said.

Her young co-worker sat at a table along the wall, studying for a trig test the next day. "Huh?" She looked up, her face soft and open like Thea's when Mira would interrupt her from reading.

"Do you mind if I run upstairs and take a quick nap? I'm just so tired I can barely keep my eyes open, and I've had so much coffee I'm afraid I'll rot a kidney if I have any more."

Amanda waved a sparkly pink-nailed hand at her. "Sure. If it gets busy, I'll bang on the ceiling with the mop."

Mira smiled. She could just see her doing that. She'd grown fond of Amanda, in spite of herself. Young women weren't the enemy. They weren't the rivals of older women. Surely not every man preferred youth over experience. She'd encountered two already who seemed to like her despite her sagging neck folds and green-veined hands. Maybe someday she'd find one who was actually right for her.

Mira climbed the stairs, each one feeling steeper than the last. Inside, Patsy bounded around the room with excitement until Mira flopped on the bed. "It's naptime, Patsy Cline," Mira said, closing her eyes, and then the world was blank.

She dreamed of being in her parents' house, only it wasn't really her parents' house, it was some dilapidated old structure, more like Woden. Her mother was there, young and vibrant, and her father, and he was singing along with the radio, "Blame It on the

Bossa Nova," and taking her mother into his arms and dancing. A group of kids walked in, kids from a class she'd had years before, a particularly misbehaved bunch, and turned the radio station from her father's to their own, and a loud thumping music poured from the speaker.

Thump, thump, thump. Thump, thump, thump. It was maddening. Mira shook her head, slowly waking to realize it was coming from beneath her. Amanda. The store. Mira sighed. And she'd been sleeping so well.

She pulled herself up, dizzy and confused. *Thump, thump, thump.* Amanda must really need help now, she decided, and put Patsy on her leash. "Come on," she said. "You can hang out with us if you're very, very good."

As Mira walked in through the purple door, Amanda stood near the sink, still ramming the mop handle into the ceiling. There was no line of customers; in fact, there were no customers. It felt surreal. Was she still dreaming?

"What's going on?" Mira asked, taking a deep breath and shaking her head to clear it.

The girl pointed the mop toward the front. "They asked for you."

Mira walked Patsy to the front counter and saw a group of people standing outside on the sidewalk. Now she knew she was dreaming. There stood an older man with gray wavy hair and a tweed jacket, a striking redhead at his side. A curly brown–haired voluptuous girl holding the hand of a frail elderly woman. A large rock-and-roll goddess, with no Chet Moser in sight. And a tall, nice-looking man with receding blond hair, holding two leashes, at the end of which were a shaggy English sheepdog mix and an aging greyhound.

When she looked across the shop and through the window into this man's eyes, she remembered the principles of chemistry, how matter and energy collide, bonding, becoming an equation not found in the physical world, and not easily discounted or disputed.

She closed her eyes and hoped this dream would never end.

PART THREE

Forty-one

Mira came to when she heard Lannie yell through the open door: "We can see you, you know."

Her eyes flew open, and Patsy pulled her around the counter and across the wood floor, out onto the sidewalk. The air was warm, the sun low in the sky and casting pink light. Mira felt acutely aware of her disheveled appearance, her droopy eyes. Had mascara smudged beneath them in her sleep?

"You're a day early," she said to Lannie. God, she was wearing her coffee cup T-shirt, her low-rise jeans. She could feel everyone's eyes on her as they took in her strange new appearance.

"Surprise!" Lannie threw her hands into the air, a pleased look on her face.

"Surprise!" redheaded Dottie chimed in, but the rest of the group was quiet.

"Come here and give me a hug, damn it," Lannie said and Mira walked over and let herself be consumed in her embrace.

"I don't know whether to slug you or kiss you," Mira murmured.

"You can kiss my fat ass, honey, but I'm here to take you home."

Mira shook her head and planted a noisy kiss on Lannie's cheek.

Thea avoided eye contact with her, but allowed Mira's emotional embrace. It felt so good to feel Thea in her arms, to smell her hair and feel it against her face. She let go as soon as she could stand to. Thea watched closely, though, as Mira turned to Parker, stooping to let the dogs waggle and press their bodies against each other and her, tongues lapping at her face as she stroked and patted them. Patsy was ecstatic. Mira didn't know what she was. She looked up to see Parker watching her, too, and said simply, "Hey."

His lips tightened and he nodded. Had he come because of her email? God, what if she and Martin had been doing it when they arrived? What if he was just inside, having come down the stairs with her, straightening out his clothing, looking as mussed from bed as she did? She sighed. Just seeing Parker, seeing the face imprinted in her brain as husband, friend, co-parent, made her want to protect him from anything that might cause pain. She smiled at him and stood, then turned to her father and Dottie.

"Daddy, Daddy, I'm sorry," she said as he grabbed her in a tight hug. She meant about everything he'd been through, the loss of his entire family, one by one. Everyone had deserted him at some point, too, and willingly. Mira's eyes welled at the thought of him losing the other Mira in the way he did. She knew he would forgive her, his daughter, for her own leave-taking, but it would be a while before she could forgive herself. He looked ten years older than when Mira had seen him last.

Dottie patted her back, saying, "It's okay, honey." Mira had no idea if she was talking to her or to Big Al, but it felt good.

When her father let her go, Nonna took her by both arms,

looked her up and down, and said, "What kind of haircut is this? You should go to a professional. And you're too thin, *cara*. What are you eating? You look like all these homeless people we keep seeing."

"Nonna, enough," her father said, shaking his head.

"Well, you look beautiful." Mira folded herself carefully around the old woman like tissue paper, kissing her powder-soft cheek.

"Thank you for the letters, but you've been away long enough now," Nonna said. "I'm not going to live forever."

Mira *tsk*ed, but it was true. Nonna was almost eighty-five; her father was sixty-six. *At what point do you put aside your own needs to take care of those you love?* she wondered. She looked at Thea, meeting her eyes for a half second before Thea looked away. *For that matter,* Mira thought, *at what point do you stop?*

Maybe never. She'd lost her family once and now they'd come to her, unbidden. She'd been selfish in leaving, self-centered, self-righteous. But if she'd never left, she'd never have known that.

She sneaked another look at Parker as he talked with Lannie, backpack slung over one shoulder and his other arm around Thea. He had a fresh haircut, a shaving nick, and he'd lost weight. Still, he had that shadowy look she knew too well. He'd been depressed, not off gallivanting with a new girlfriend. She watched as he and Lannie laughed about something, and she smiled. They'd become friends.

Good, Mira thought. *He's probably needed a friend through all of this, and Lannie is the best.*

Inside the shop, Mira and Amanda bustled about, getting everyone drinks. "Look, Nonna," Mira said, bringing her a bowl of Italian wedding soup. "Your soups are famous here."

"Did you use the fresh oregano?" the old woman asked, bringing a spoonful of broth to her crinkled lips.

"Of course," Mira said.

Nonna swished the soup in her mouth and swallowed, nodding. "It's not too bad," she said. "Maybe just a pinch more salt.

Bring Parker a bowl, and some bread. He's gotten too skinny, I keep telling him."

"He runs on the beach every morning now with Ralph and Twiggy," Thea said reverently, as if no one else had ever exercised the dogs. Mira wanted to roll her eyes but just smiled. She was glad she had when she saw Parker looking at her.

"Do you want soup?" she asked. "A muffin or something?"

"No, thanks, but"—he bent to rifle through his backpack—"I did bring you something—"

Mira's pulse quickened.

He extracted a sheaf of papers. "Our taxes. All done and ready for you to sign."

Mira nodded. That's why he'd come. Her eyes stung as she thanked him for taking care of it. She could imagine the coercion it had taken Lannie and/or Thea to get him to deliver the paperwork himself. The dogs were a nice touch, though; she wondered whose idea that had been. As the afternoon wore on, they didn't speak much, other than about the tax return, but Mira did notice he still wore his wedding ring, as she did, which struck her now as odd. She'd never even considered taking it off.

That evening was even more surreal, eating fried clam strips and french fries at Ivar's Acre of Clams on the waterfront in the company of a daughter who resented her, a husband who looked uncomfortable to be there, a father who teared up anytime she looked at him, his seemingly pleasant wife, and a grandmother who ignored it all and dug into the clams with religious fervor. Lannie had eschewed bivalves in favor of spending the evening at Trevor's rehearsal.

Now Mira lay in bed unable to sleep. She kept replaying a sudden smile that had slipped onto Thea's face at one point in the conversation, then disappeared when she realized she'd lost control of herself. And a moment when Nonna brushed salt grains from Parker's chin. There were so many small moments to treasure, to horde, because she knew she wouldn't be going back with them when they left on Sunday. She had a shift to work, and as much as she loved them, she still had nothing to go home to. What would she do, find a crummy apartment somewhere in town, be the pariah of Pacifica for the rest of her life? Parker obviously had not come to convince her their marriage could be saved. Lannie or Thea had talked him into it, or maybe it had been both of them.

On the bed beside her, Patsy sighed with a contentment larger than herself, snuggling her wiry body into Ralph's ample one. Twiggy wheezed and dream-raced on the floor beside the bed, as she did at home. Mira wished she could keep them all, even though it would be impossible in the small apartment, but she could see the bond that had formed between the two big dogs and Parker. They were not Mira's rescue mutts anymore; they were his companions. He'd paused before agreeing to let her have them overnight. That Parker was even still in Seattle surprised her, but the pull to make Thea happy was a strong one; she certainly knew enough about that.

What surprised her most was that she didn't hate him. He'd just fallen out of the right kind of love with her. When she looked into his eyes, which she didn't let herself do fully more than two or three times, she could see that he'd suffered as much as she had, and he was a genuinely good, kind man. Even though the male of the species finishes his familial job when he helps raise his young to toddlerhood, a survivable age, Parker had stuck around for another twenty years. *Not bad,* Mira thought. So he'd kissed Jackie Anderson, once that he'd admitted to. She'd never known him to lie before, and his actions since certainly indicated nothing else.

At this point, she'd done far worse things for a woman still legally married, still wearing her ring. Did she love him less? Not at all, which was almost disappointing, considering he seemed to have moved on.

When I move on, she let herself think, *I want more.* More kissing, more talking, more, well . . . more sex. A lot more, but only from someone who was going to know the real her, and she the real him. Sex was so much better now than it had been even in college. Then, all she'd wanted was that one moment when a boy would look at her with grateful eyes and think somewhere in his testosterone-addled brain: *Me want.* She'd always mistranslated that to "I love you." Now she wanted sex with real love, mutual love, love that aged and deepened rather than fading or being pushed aside for other things. She wanted the connection she felt at moments that intimate—the connection to her lover, to herself, to something higher and deeper and more profound than anything that existed in the physical world.

Mira pulled the blanket higher around her shoulders. She needed to get some sleep. The entire clan, including Lannie, was ensconced at a Holiday Inn just a few minutes' drive from Fremont. In the morning, Mira would go have free breakfast with them in the lobby, and then they would go sightseeing: the Space Needle, the Public Market. All of the things she'd yet to do in her new hometown. And then there would be Trevor's show that night with Lannie, and everyone would leave the next day and she'd be alone again.

Mira rolled over, scratched Ralph's muzzle, and catalogued the rose geranium scent of Nonna's face powder, the scratch of tweed jacket against her arms when she hugged her father. Patsy snored and twitched, chasing god knows what in her dreams. Mira smiled. The tickle of Thea's hair against her face, the soft give of her body in her arms. The way her father and Dottie linked arms whenever they walked together.

The clear gray eyes of a boy who once held an umbrella over her head in the rain.

Forty-two

— • —

THEA LAY AWAKE IN THE HOTEL BED NEXT TO NONNA, UNABLE TO sleep. The old woman and Lannie, in the other bed, both snored heartily. Happily, it seemed. Thea sighed. She could not believe she'd let Lannie talk her into this . . . this cluster-fuck of a family reunion, no one wanting to be there except Lannie and Grandpa. Well, maybe Nonna, but who knew? She was getting so old she was probably just glad to be anywhere.

Her mother hadn't looked any happier when they first arrived, standing inside what actually looked like a pretty cool place, her eyes closed so she couldn't see them. She'd tried so hard to get away, after all. Why would she want to be found?

"Hey," Lannie had called to Mira. "We can see you, you know."

Her mother's eyes had opened and that little dog had pulled her outside, yapping beside her, all happy to see Ralph and Twiggy again.

When Thea had pictured this moment, she'd imagined Mira

running to her and smothering her with a big emotional hug, too many kisses, crying, blubbering all over the place. She'd thought she'd even hug her back, maybe say she was sorry. But her mother didn't run to her. She went straight to Lannie. Her mother didn't even try to call her anymore. No one ever told her she did, anyway. And she'd been asking.

The week before, when Thea had gone to see her dad, there was something different about him. He hugged her when she walked in, for one thing, and he noticed her new hair color. "I like it, Polliwog," he said, palming the crown of her head the way he had when she was little. "Reminds me of your mother's."

His eyes hadn't gone teary at the mention of Mira.

And he'd ironed his shirt.

When she told him about the trip to Seattle he'd nodded. "I know," he said.

"Do you really think I should go?" she asked, and he nodded again.

"I do."

"But there's something you don't know," she told him. "I'm the one who made her leave." She started to cry and he hugged her.

"No, honey, you didn't."

"I did, I really did, Dad. I told her if she didn't come work it out with you that day that I'd never speak to her again. And I haven't. She called me all the time for a while and I never talked to her. I just let her think . . . And now she doesn't . . ."

Thea couldn't speak, just sobbed against her father's pressed shirt.

"She did come home that day, honey. That's why she left." Parker pushed Thea out to arm's length. "I did something really stupid, something private between your mother and me. I'm the reason your mother left. Not you. She loves you. All you have to do is let her love you again."

And Thea had believed him. But her mother had changed, somehow. It wasn't just that she looked different, she . . . well, she acted different. From the inside out, somehow. She didn't seem so worried about everything. She was just kinda going with the flow of whatever was happening, not making anybody do anything, not overplanning and stressing out, not making Thea feel guilty about anything. It wasn't that Thea wouldn't like this person if, say, she'd just met her, but it was so fucking weird. This was her mother, and her mother was supposed to worry about her and hug her a little too much, ask her too many questions.

Thea had thought it would be easy to tell Mira she was sorry for being so awful, because she'd thought her mother would apologize first for leaving. But Mira didn't appear to have apologies in mind, and Thea hadn't been able to tell her she was sorry, either. It was almost like they were strangers now, two separate people who'd never been connected by blood, by an umbilical cord. By that thing Thea now missed more than she'd ever thought she would, even though she'd been fighting so long to dampen it.

She'd always thought all those drippy sentiments about mother's love were full of shit, all the stuff that old dead poets and greeting card manufacturers churned out, but now . . . Well. Now she wanted it back.

Forty-three

———·———

TREVOR LANGSTON STEPPED ON STAGE, HIS GUITAR STRAPPED TO
his rangy body like an underdeveloped conjoined twin. His left
hand held the neck, angular thumb hooked over the side, long
fingers itching to press frets and bend strings. His right hand lifted
in salute to the full house of two hundred or so fans, who were
already on their feet, this being the Tractor Tavern, stamping and
applauding, whistling and sending out siren whoops and calling,
"We love you, Trevor!"

Mira shouted, "Woo hoo!" and waved at Trevor like the long-
lost auntie she was. If she looked at Lannie on one side of her, she
would cry. If she looked at Thea on the other, she would, too, so she
looked straight ahead at this beautiful long-haired boy, the apple
of his mother's eye and every other girl's in the room. Mira had
never realized he'd become so popular while out on the road—
she'd figured Lannie's bragging had been optimistically delusional
in the way of all mothers.

When Trevor finally let his hand crash across the strings, the band simultaneously erupted in the opening chords of a twanged-up version of "Yesterday." One final cheer from the crowd and then they quieted, feet tapping, hands slapping thighs, heads all nodding in unison.

When Trevor got to the part about why she had to go, the crowd joined in, and Mira felt her eyes well. What a song for him to play. Did Lannie tell him to? She let herself glance over at her friend, whose face was glistening. Mira guessed it was Trevor Lannie was thinking about, not her. She hoped so, anyway.

The crowd packed tighter and Mira felt Thea's shoulder come into contact with hers. Mira waited for her to stiffen or pull away, but she didn't. Tears spilled over Mira's bottom lids and she reached quickly to wipe them.

"Isn't he awesome?" Thea turned to yell into her ear, and Mira nodded, smiling. She wouldn't turn to look at her; that would be too much. She'd allowed herself the overwrought embrace when she first saw her, and now she had to sit back and wait. This was Thea's first step back to her, and eventually she'd take another.

Outside the bar during the band's break, Mira watched in wonder as a line of women, young and not so young, thin and curvaceous, beautiful and plain, waited patiently for their time with Trevor. She stood to the side of him with Lannie and Thea, grabbing bits of conversation with him as they could.

"Yeah, so we got a two-record deal on Pigsty Records out of Austin," Trevor said before turning to the young pink-haired woman in front of him. "Sign your CD, darlin'?" He flipped back his hair and affected a twang so genuine and charming that even his mother smiled. He turned back to them. "And they're really promoting this one. We even have T-shirts."

Thea seemed under his spell. "God, Trev, you're doing so great. It's so awesome." She placed a hand on her jutted hip, pointing a sequined flip-flop at him, and Mira widened her eyes at Lannie. Who'd have thought their children, practically siblings, would have ever flirted with each other?

"Well, you're mighty kind to say so, Miss Thea,"Trevor said in an Elvis drawl.

"Why, thank you." Thea performed her customary curtsy.

Mira's heart ached for Parker. She wished he were here to see this, but he'd used the dogs and the old folks as an excuse not to come.

"Hey, Mira!"

She turned toward a voice coming from down the street, beneath the streetlamp. Wearing his yellow 86 shirt and long cargo shorts, Doug strode toward them, waving. "Hi!" he called, and as he got closer, "I can't believe I found you."

"That him?" Lannie asked.

"Who?" Thea squinted her eyes at him, then at Mira. "Who is that?"

"Just a—" She'd been about to say *friend,* and realized what that would sound like. "Customer. Hi, Doug. What are you doing here?" *Please don't hug me,* she thought. *Not in front of my daughter. Please, please, please.*

Doug walked through the small crowd and grabbed her in his arms. She embraced him loosely, quickly, then pulled back, dodging his kiss. "So, Doug, I want to introduce you to my daughter, Thea. And this is Lannie, my best friend from Pacifica, her son Trevor." With each introduction she enunciated the relationship, hoping he'd catch on. Lannie elbowed her in the ribs. "Stop it," Mira hissed as Thea shook his hand, looking confused.

"So you know my mom how?" Thea's hands winged back to her hips.

"I met her at the coffee shop," he said. "Guy who owns it's a buddy." He smiled at Mira, the look in his eyes that she loved now telecasting too much. "Gus told me you were going to a show, and I took a guess it was here. Pretty lucky, huh?"

"Mm." If the smile on her face looked as tight as it felt, she must appear to be a deranged mummy. How to change the subject? "Trevor here is going to be famous, Doug. He's the leader of the Twang Gods, and they're incredible, aren't they, Thea?"

"He is famous, Mom. He's on the college stations, like, all the time."

"Well, good to meet you, Travis," Doug said. "I've got a buddy in a band. Helluva guitar player. You ever hear of the Screaming Hematomas?"

"Can't say I have, but I'm sure they're bitchin'." Trevor clamped a big hand on Doug's shoulder, towering over him. Then he turned back to the next girl in line, who'd pulled her shirt up over her see-through bra.

"Whoa," Doug said.

"Sign my heart?" She said it so sweetly it was hard to believe she was baring her breasts to anyone who was interested in seeing them, like Doug, and anyone who wasn't, like Mira.

"Of course, sugar," Trevor said. "Believe I'll use my new name, Travis."

Thea snickered.

The doorman poked his head out of the door and said, "Dude, you're on in five."

Lannie hooked an arm through Mira's, then Thea's. "Ladies, let's get back in there and reclaim our spot."

"I don't have a ticket yet. I'll meet you inside in a minute," Doug said.

Mira's heart lifted. "Oh. They're sold out. I'm so sorry."

"Hey, no problem," Trevor said. "He's with the band."

"Lovely," Mira murmured.

Back inside, the crowd resisted their attempts to get any closer than midway.

"I'm Trevor's mother," Lannie kept saying to polite but unresponsive faces.

One young man with a Herman's Hermits haircut shrugged. "We all want to be closer," he said. "But this is where we are."

"At least you're tall," Thea said to Lannie. "Some of us can't see anything but the back of people's shoulders."

A dig at Doug, Mira guessed, who remained firmly attached to her side. Mira found a spot where she could see between two heads, then pulled Thea's arm. "Come stand in front of me, honey. Look, you can see Trevor's head and half of the drummer."

Just then, Mira felt a hand slide down the back of her jeans and give an affectionate squeeze. The band kicked into a hard-rocking number and Mira reached behind her and yanked Doug's hand out of her pants.

"What's the matter, babe?" he said into her ear. On stage, Trevor was writhing in a hypnotic snake dance, and the girls who'd edged them out of their spots stretched their hands toward him. Like a snake charmer, he remained inches out of reach.

Mira leaned back to talk as loudly as she dared in Doug's ear: "Please, not in front of my daughter."

"What?"

Thea turned and looked at them and Mira focused her eyes on the band, nodding her head in time to the music until Thea looked forward again. If Doug would just back off a little, Thea would never need to know. As soon as the family left Seattle, they could jump right back into it, into the sack, or the shower, or any number of places she had imagined having sex with him. She could have that feeling whenever she needed it, that hit of endorphins that passed for love. Tears came to her eyes. She wanted to touch Thea's shiny new brown hair so much she could barely stand it.

Mira turned and laid her hand on his arm. "I'm sorry," she whispered into his ear. "I'm so sorry. I can't do this. You had to have noticed I'm married. Separated, but definitely married." She waved her left hand in front of his face.

A shiny-bald man next to them looked Mira up and down, then smiled.

Doug reached a hand around her waist. "But I don't care—"

She pulled back. "You should."

"Mira—"

She grimaced and shook her head. "Please," she mouthed, nodding at Thea. "I'm sorry."

Doug frowned, then turned away, disappearing into the crowd.

The next morning, Mira woke early with a headache. She had no men and only one small dog in her bed. She rolled over and stretched. *I'm back to square one,* she thought, wishing she hadn't drunk a third beer, wishing she'd kissed Doug at least one more time before coming to her senses.

Her fuck buddy experiment had failed along with her fantasies of falling in love with a younger man, and she'd been the one to put the kibosh on both. *Go figure,* she thought, scratching Patsy's ears. She would talk with Doug sometime to try to explain, but maybe she'd have to go off the progesterone cream first. If she didn't, the only thing she'd end up saying would be, "Doug, oh god, Doug." Mira shook her head and smiled. It had been so amazing, but not quite real. She wanted real.

Today her family and her best friend would leave and she'd still be here. First they were coming to the coffee shop for a final get-together before hitting the road for Pacifica.

"It's back to you and me, sweetie," Mira said to Patsy, who rolled onto her back to have her soft tummy rubbed.

Midrub, Patsy cocked her head toward the door, then jerked away and to her feet. Mira listened; sure enough, she heard steps.

"Oh, Doug," she moaned. "Just give it up."

Patsy leapt over her and to the floor, barking with such a crazed fury that Mira thought she'd lost her mind. "Patsy, quiet!" she commanded, but the dog had gone into instinctual overdrive.

Mira stood at the knock on the door. "Coming," she called, shuffling across the floor, scratching her arm. How could this poor guy humiliate himself like this, after what she'd said last night? Luckily, the last thing she felt was seductive or sexy. She let out a long sigh and pulled open the door, looking down at herself a little too late—her nipples were sticking straight through her too-tight gown from the cold. Why hadn't she put on a robe?

A cyclone of cold air and wet fur whirled through the door in the form of Ralph and Twiggy, tumbling with Patsy across the floor and onto the unmade bed, where they stood wagging their tails at each other before colliding in a new frenzy of gnawing and brawling.

"Sorry, did we, uh, wake you?" Parker stood in the doorway, hands in his blue Gore-Tex pockets, as if a five a.m. visit from her estranged husband was nothing out of the ordinary. "I wanted to get here before you went to work."

"It's okay, I was up," she lied, crossing her arms over her chest and backing into the room. "Come on in. I'd make coffee, but I don't have a pot. I just, you know . . . wait. Until I get downstairs."

Parker nodded and ducked through the doorway. "I came to ask you a favor."

"Hang on a sec," she said, and moved to grab her yellow fleece robe from the back of the chair. A favor? At five in the morning? Mira had a feeling this didn't have anything to do with taxes. "It's chilly this morning, isn't it?"

He didn't answer, and she turned to look at him. His pale cheeks caved in beneath his cheekbones and his lips were dry, his eyes unreadable. This was not the same boy beneath the red Kansas City Chiefs blanket, or the husband he had become. It wasn't that awful look he'd had the day she left, but it was . . . different. He had changed while she'd been gone.

"Are you okay?" she asked. A few months ago, she'd have walked up to him, laid her hand on his cheek, stood on tiptoe to give him a kiss. Led him to the couch to sit with him and talk. Held his hand. But she was different now, too. "Parker?"

He shook his head, looked around. Mira imagined the apartment through his eyes: the sparse furnishings, their shabbiness. Did he see the blue woman, at least?

"I can't believe this is what you, what you . . ." He stopped and closed his eyes, then opened them. "What you want."

"What I *want*?" Mucus rose in her throat.

The dogs stopped rumbling on the bed and stared at them. Patsy pressed into Ralph, emitting a nervous whine.

"Who started all this, Parker?" She was suddenly loud, angry. The adrenal current that she'd felt when she first confronted him on New Year's Eve careened crazily in her head, her chest cavity. Her limbs buzzed and ached to lash out at him, to strike and kick him, and that longing made her want to cry. Or throw up. Or both.

"I didn't run away," he said quietly.

"But you found someone else."

He flinched. "She was just a friend."

"That you kissed."

"I was an idiot." He looked at the floor, arms folded tight against his ribs.

"Are you still?"

He didn't lift his head. "Why ask now? You haven't bothered to ask me that question one time in three months. You didn't return any of my calls." His voice shook.

Mira flushed at the thought of her cell phone breaking as it hit asphalt. "You didn't answer my email," she said.

"What email?" Parker looked up at her.

"I sent you an email two weeks ago trying to explain . . . god, whatever. It doesn't matter now."

"I swear I didn't get it, Mira. We've got this crazy new spam filter . . ."

"I didn't hear your phone messages, either," she said. "What did you tell me?"

He shook his head, but his face had softened.

"I need to know, Parker, if only so I can move on."

Sighing, he said, "That was Jackie that day at the house. I called her to see if she'd come take a walk so I could tell her face-to-face that I couldn't be her friend anymore."

"Oh." Mira swallowed against the bile rising in her throat. "Then why were you leaving me?"

He sighed. "That's not exactly how it went. I told you I didn't know what I wanted, if I wanted to leave or stay."

Well, that was technically what he'd said.

"But to be honest, I was starting to think it might be easier to just start over. We'd gotten so far away from what we'd started out to be, somehow. You had to have felt it, too, but you seemed content with the way everything was. I didn't know what to do."

Mira nodded, sucked her bottom lip. After a deep breath she said, "I wasn't content. I was afraid."

"Afraid? What? Why?"

"I never told you something that I should have a long time ago." She swallowed. "Remember that electrician, the one I had a crush on?"

He nodded slowly, bracing, it seemed, for a blow.

"We didn't have sex, Parker. No. Remember when we were getting the computers installed at the school for the first time? Remember when I told you that I was attacked by that kid?"

He nodded again, frowning.

"I couldn't tell you, but it was him, the electrician. He was the one doing the wiring, and when he came into my room, he attacked me."

She'd never said that aloud to anyone. It brought tears to her eyes.

"What? Why didn't you—"

"It was because we'd had that flirtation, I guess, but he . . ." She paused, trying to swallow. "He didn't get far; I bit him when he tried to kiss me. I think he thought I wanted it, but I didn't,

Parker. That's not what it was about for me. I just wanted to be . . .
I don't know. Young and sexy and desirable. Desired."

"You *were* young and sexy. You were all those things."

You could have said something, she wanted to say. She wanted to
be angry with him, but she wasn't.

"Anyway, I couldn't tell you, because—"

"Because what?" His voice shook.

"I was afraid you'd leave me. I was afraid you'd think I
deserved it."

"Jesus, I wouldn't have," he said, face going white. "That's horrible."

"Yeah," she said. "I guess it is." Maybe he would have, or maybe he wouldn't. She suspected now, though, that she'd been the
one who thought she deserved it.

"Mira, god. I wish you could have told me."

She nodded. They both wished a lot of things.

Parker cleared his throat. "So, this is really where you want to
be, huh? It just doesn't seem, I don't know. Like you."

She sighed, feeling exasperated, exhausted. "I don't know if
I belong here, Parker. I'm just here, is all. I don't know where I
belong anymore." Her eyes and sinuses began to flow, and there
was nothing she could do to stop her body from curling in on itself
until she was sitting on the floor, knees to chest, arms wrapped
around them, shoulders hunched and shaking.

You could say, "With me," she thought.

You could say, "With your family." But he didn't.

After a protracted silence, Parker said, "Jesus. Mira, I'm sorry. I
didn't mean to upset you, to get into all of this. I just came to ask
if you could watch the dogs while I take care of a few things."

She nodded, avoiding his eyes. She wished she had a tissue.

"Thanks," he said. "I'll explain when I get back. I've got a
bunch of stuff to look into, and I don't know the city very well,
so, you know, it could take a while."

It was something work related—a new espresso machine, new

computers. It was Seattle after all. Hell, maybe he'd open a Cyber Buzz up here and she could run it. She tried not to sigh. "Whatever, I'll watch them."

He waited, all awkward posture and fumbling hands, putting one in his pocket, then on his hip. Finally he walked over and offered to pull her up.

"No, thanks," Mira said, trying not to cry until he was gone. "I'm just going to sit here for a while."

Forty-four

It was the kind of Seattle morning that Mira knew she would grow to love best: the soft blanket of early marine layer just beginning to burn off, leaving tufts of cloud behind as the sun made crystals of the dew on tree leaves and grass. The weed patch had returned to dirt and gravel, a few dandelions struggling mightily to survive Gus's big dig. Mira sat on the back steps with her first cup of coffee, watching the three dogs nap together on the sidewalk in the shade of the building. On Sunday mornings, all was still, even in Fremont. No traffic hurtled by, no seaplanes buzzed overhead. The occasional seagull squalled from above, gliding down the canal to Elliott Bay and fresh fish. The gulls here were huge, almost regal, a different breed altogether from the smallish ones back . . . She'd almost thought *home,* but inserted *in Pacifica* instead. She'd cried herself dry after Parker left that morning and now all she felt was empty.

Sidney poked her head out the back door. Even her wan cheeks had a hint of peach now that the sun was making more frequent appearances. "I can't find any hazelnut syrup," she said, looking worried. "Do you think we're out?"

"I'll find it." Mira drained her cup with one last swallow and stood. "Come on, puppies. Time to go upstairs."

"Thanks." Sidney started to pull the door closed.

"So, Sid," Mira said. "Do you like it here? I mean, at the shop?"

The girl nodded and came out onto the sidewalk, letting the door swing shut behind her. She smiled up at the sun and closed her eyes, then sighed and looked at Mira. "It's weird. It feels . . . comfortable. Like I'm supposed to be here."

Mira smiled. *Child of my heart.* And she knew Sid felt the same way about her, unlike Thea. Sidney appreciated Mira's mothering. They were a good match. *I guess that's what we all want,* she thought. *To be with people who appreciate us for who we naturally are, whether or not those people are our blood.* She swallowed. *Or our mate.* Doug appreciated her. Jackie had no doubt appreciated Parker.

She turned her face to the sun for one last bask before heading up the stairs. The dogs were already waiting on the top landing like polite schoolchildren.

The clouds had burned off completely by the time Lannie and the Serafinos arrived, later than planned, and, as Mira feared, at just the hour churchgoing folk dropped by for post-sermon recaffeination. She'd dressed in her old clothes today, her teacher khakis and a light sweater. They felt odd on her, too loose. Too . . . someone else. She'd carefully applied makeup and tamed her hair a bit more than she'd become accustomed to. It was Sunday, after all, and she knew Nonna, at least, would appreciate her efforts.

"Did you find a mass to go to today?" Mira asked as she led her grandmother by the arm to the big table in front of the window.

"Nah, I slept in." The old woman waved her burled-wood hand as if batting at a gnat. "Church is just a good excuse to see your friends, your family, and I have mine right here." She latched on to the table edge to lower herself into the chair Mira offered.

"Now, what do you have to eat? The free breakfast is no good. I'm starving."

"Mama, I offered to take you to a real restaurant," said Big Al, pulling out a chair for Dottie across the table, then one for Thea.

Lannie had run off to the restroom as soon as they arrived, saying, "Coming through! I have to pee like a racehorse."

"This is a real restaurant, Alfonso," Nonna said. "She makes soup, surely she has a little something for an old lady to eat that doesn't come out of a plastic wrapper."

"As far as I know, bread always comes out of a plastic bag," Dottie said cheerily, patting Al's hand.

Mira and Thea exchanged wide-eyed smirks until Thea realized what she was doing and looked away.

"Not when you bake it." Nonna folded her hands on the table, declaring victory. Mira admired Dottie's nerve when it came to taking on her new mother-in-law. She had no idea what she was in for.

"I have a big basket of fresh pear cardamom muffins and cranberry scones I was going to bring over," Mira said. "What would everyone like to drink?"

"You're not going to, like, wait on us, are you?" Thea's face had flattened again.

"No, I'm going to feed you, like I always have." Mira forced a smile. *And two steps back,* she thought, writing down their orders. Thea asked for tap water, and Mira wrote on her pad "grande white chocolate mocha with extra whip." Thea could get the damn water from the pitcher on the condiment bar, like everybody else.

Behind the counter, Gus and Mira worked side by side, pulling shots, squirting syrup, filling teapots.

"Thank you for coming in to help this morning," Mira said. "I really do appreciate it."

"No worries," he said, spraying Thea's mocha with a tower of whipped cream. "You gonna introduce me?"

"Of course!" Mira was surprised he asked. "It's just so busy."

"No hubby today?"

"Not once he dumped the dogs on me. He's got big important things to do, apparently."

"Fucker," Gus said good-naturedly. "I heard about you and Doug, by the way. He's a little on the needy side, I guess."

Mira smiled, loading the glasses and cups onto a tray. "You've been very good to me, even after I ran off your girlfriend." She turned and looked at him. "Why is that?"

"I don't know," he said, face and neck reddening beneath his tan. "I knew she had to go—I was just pussy-whipped, I guess." He smiled when Mira frowned at his language. "You're good for this place. For me."

"Okay, stop." Mira picked up the tray. "I'm emotional enough today as it is."

He chuckled, wiping his hands on a towel. "All righty then. Let's go meet the whole fam-damily. Your daughter's freaking hot."

"Lovely," she said, realizing there could be far worse things than having Gus as a son-in-law, but when they arrived at the table, it seemed Thea had her sights set on Trevor from the way she was now talking with Lannie, breathless and animated—precisely the way she no longer spoke to Mira.

"And he said he'd pass my CD on to the A and R guy at Pigsty," she said, returning Lannie's high five. "And someday maybe I could go out on tour with him, be his opening act!"

"Wow," Mira said, passing out drinks. "You have a CD? Can I have one?"

"It's just a demo," Thea said, staring at the cup Mira placed in front of her. "Um, I didn't order this."

"I know, but I thought you might like it anyway," Mira said. "And I don't care if it's just a demo. I've saved every scribble on every scrap of paper since you were born."

Thea dipped her pinkie in the whipped cream, tasted it. "I only have one left."

Lannie took Thea's chin in her hand and gently pulled her face until she was staring into her wide eyes. "Give her the CD, okay?"

"How about if I burn a copy for your mom?" Gus stared at Thea as if he'd never seen a girl before.

"And you would be?"

How on earth did I raise such a brat? Mira wondered. "Forget it. She doesn't want me to have it."

"I'm your mother's employer. My name is Gus." He walked over to her and offered his hand. "And besides being the rude daughter of my manager, you are?"

"Thea," she said, shaking his hand, sizing him up. "Here."

"Thank you," he said, taking the CD. "I'll pop it into the player first, so we can all hear it." As he walked away, he said, "Cool name. *The Seven Sisters.* I like that."

As Thea's guitar, then voice, shimmered from the speakers, they all went quiet. Another guitar started playing, and a drum. The music grew louder, the singing more confident, and Mira recognized its throatiness from every nursery rhyme, TV jingle, high school solo, and radio pop song Thea had ever sung.

Thea fidgeted, chipping nail polish from her fingers. "I messed up this next part," she said.

"Shh," Nonna said, cupping her good ear to hear over the other patrons.

As the first song ended, Lannie reached to one-arm-hug Thea. "That turned out great, honey." Big Al and Dottie applauded, everyone joining in, even patrons at other tables.

Gus walked over and gave her a high five. "Dude, that's awesome," he said, and Mira didn't think he was just flirting with her. She was good. Another song had started, this one with a clear tenor male voice that sounded so sad Mira knew it was the slight boy she'd seen at Woden.

The Jewel Box, the Seven Sisters inside. Her daughter had absorbed at least one thing she'd tried to impart to her. She glanced at Thea, who was too nervous to look at anyone. "Fuck it," Mira said under her breath, and walked around the table to gather her daughter into her arms. She tried not to cry, not to do anything that might cause Thea to withdraw, but when she tried to pull away after their hug, Thea clung to her.

"Mom," she whispered, her tone nasal and upset. "Can we go to the bathroom or something, and talk?"

"Sure, honey. Let's go up to my apartment." To everyone else she said, "I'm going to show Thea my place. We'll be back in a little while."

Inside the apartment, Thea looked around, appraising much the way Parker had earlier, but she said, "Cool. I'd like to have an apartment like this someday."

Mira sat on the love seat, patted the cushion beside her. Thea's eyes filled again; her chin quivered and puckered the way it had always had when she was about to cry. "I'm sorry I made you leave," she blurted, still standing in the middle of the room. Mira got up and walked to her, took her hand. It was so cold.

"Honey, you didn't make me leave. I did it all by myself. And even though it's been the hardest thing I've ever done, I think it was probably good."

"But I was so mean, not even taking your—" Thea broke down, and Mira hugged her.

"Well, yeah, it hurt, but you were mad and you had a right to be. The thing is, I've had a chance to figure some stuff out, and I'm still figuring it out. Your dad seems to be doing better, too. Lannie said he was pretty down."

Thea nodded and rubbed her eyes. "Yeah, he's been kind of a mess. You should have seen him, Mom, it was pathetic. He didn't even iron his clothes for the longest time."

"Hard to imagine," Mira said, trying to stay bright for her daughter, but she'd suspected he'd been depressed, and knowing that he'd probably been that way before she left didn't completely erase the guilt. "How are you doing now, with all of this? Have you had someone to talk to?"

Thea bit her lip, nodding. "Dad, and Lannie. You know."

"That's good," Mira said, wanting to bawl, swallowing it back. "That's great."

"Mom," Thea started, then stopped. She sighed. "You're not getting back together, are you? I mean, whatever. You know."

"I don't know, honey. It doesn't seem that way." She wouldn't soften it; she wouldn't say maybe. She wouldn't sugarcoat or try to make Thea happy with false words.

Thea nodded, seeming to accept this, then cocked her head at Mira. "Did you already know about my band?"

"Only a little. Tell me everything. You sound great on the CD. What a beautiful song; did you write it?" Mira hadn't let herself listen to the lyrics, not yet, only Thea's voice. When she was alone, she'd let the words in.

Thea told Mira about Colby and Damien, about practicing at Lannie's Yarn and Guitar, and their performances, and her plans for moving into her own place, and Mira didn't once ask how she was going to support herself or whether or not she'd considered getting a "real" job. She just nodded and smiled, said supportive things, and it wasn't that hard. Thea mentioned maybe getting a gig in Seattle sometime, but Mira knew she'd be driving to wherever her next performance was, whether it was Eugene or Tillamook or Timbuktu.

Later, when it was time for them to return to Pacifica, they all walked down the sidewalk toward Big Al's Buick. Lannie sidled up to Mira and whispered, "So where's Parker?"

"I was going to ask you," Mira whispered back. "I thought maybe it was part of your big plan. He showed up at five this morning and left the dogs to go do 'research' on something. He's probably checking out new espresso machines or the latest in computers. Or else it was a euphemism for skipping town."

"Oh, honey," Lannie said. "Give the poor guy a chance."

Mira shook her head. "I just don't get why he even came. He didn't like the old me, and I'm pretty sure he doesn't like the new one, either."

"Well, I don't see much difference, other than the wacky haircut." Lannie ruffled her hand through Mira's hair.

"You don't like it?"

"Actually, I do. It's very . . . current. Very hip, mama."

"I like it, too," Thea said from behind. "It's cute on you."

Mira smiled, closed her eyes for a moment. "Thanks, honey," she said, casually, and kept on walking.

Later that night, after her shift ended, Mira sat on her too-small love seat in her tiny apartment with Patsy in her lap and the big dogs on the bed. She wept with both happiness and grief.

Thea had sat right here beside her, just hours before, and they'd talked in a way that was new for them, almost like two adults instead of parent and child. They'd been tentative about it, but it felt better than anything between them had for years, like rusty gears interlocking and remembering how to turn.

It felt so good to see Lannie again that Mira resolved to spend more time with her. Maybe she'd meet her at Thea's next gig. Or, who knew? Maybe Mira would spend a little time in Pacifica every once in a while.

Dottie had grown on her, and her father really did seem happy with her. Dottie fussed over him the way he liked being fussed over, even though he acted like he didn't. Mira had caught a smile that passed between them when her father was pulling back his new wife's chair at the coffee shop, a smile so intimate and downright lascivious that Mira had looked away immediately. *Way too much information,* she thought, but it made her happy for him, and happy to know that kind of love was possible at any age.

There were things that felt undone, unfinished, and thinking about them now brought on a new round of weeping. Why hadn't she spent her time alone with Parker letting him know how much he'd meant to her? How much she would always love him? She'd gotten angry instead of telling him she was sorry she'd deserted him at his worst moment, when he'd been depressed, unhappy, searching for something. It had scared her. He was supposed to be the strong one, and when he wasn't, she'd panicked instead of trying to be strong for him.

Maybe if she'd realized he wasn't returning, and she'd never have another chance, she would have told him these things. Maybe not. She'd felt almost paralyzed in his presence, waiting for him to make some big move, and when he didn't, she couldn't. She might be the new Mira, but she could still feel as scared as the old one. She'd kept her hope up that he'd be back until it turned dark outside, but he'd only come to rid himself of their—her—dogs. He'd been kind not to take them to the pound, but he shouldn't have said he was coming back.

And she'd wanted to ask Nonna about her mother's death every time the old woman looked at her, but she couldn't, not with everyone else around. She had a feeling her grandmother held the key to this secret, and now she'd taken it back home with her. Who knew when Mira would see her again, would see any of them. Who knew who might be missing the next time she tried.

Mira closed her eyes and leaned back, exhausted.

On the day her abortion was scheduled, Mira woke in a panic. She was suffocating. Her roommate lay in her own bed, buried by pillows and blankets. The early light bounced off the full-length mirror on the back of the door and glittered around the dorm room like broken glass. Mira sat up and tried to draw a breath but couldn't. She was dying.

Heart pounding, she scrambled from her bed and hurried toward the door, gasping. Not only couldn't she breathe, it felt as though a knife had been stuck into her lower abdomen and twisted.

"What's the matter?" her roommate mumbled from somewhere deep inside her cocoon.

"Nothing," Mira said, surprised that she sounded so normal.
"Just going to the bathroom." Indeed, it felt as if she were already
relieving herself, warm liquid pooling in her underpants, dribbling down her left thigh.

In the bathroom she grabbed handfuls of paper towels from the
dispenser and rushed to the stall farthest from the door. She locked
herself in, pulled off her bloody underwear, and sat with them in
her hand as a wave of nausea and searing pain gripped her.

"No," she cried as quietly as she could, rocking back and forth
on the toilet, but jagged gasps ripped through her words: "No,
no, no."

When it was over, she wrapped her underwear in paper towels
and stuffed them into the box meant for used sanitary napkins.
She wiped the blood from between her legs with toilet paper, all
the way down to her ankles. Fumbling behind her, she flushed
the toilet. She couldn't look. Too weak to stand, she leaned with
forearms on knees and let her face fall into her hands, the smell of
blood there and everywhere around her.

Later, when her roommate came into the bathroom looking
for her, Mira asked her to bring a towel, a pair of underwear, and
her sweats.

"Are you okay?" the girl asked from the other side of the door.
"What's going on?"

"I'm just having a really heavy period," Mira said. "I feel kind
of sick."

"Bummer," the girl said and trundled off, returning with the
items Mira requested.

Mira opened the stall door to take them.

"God, you really don't look good," the girl said. "Maybe you
should go to a doctor."

"I have an appointment later this morning," Mira said, trying
to smile. "I'm just going to take a shower and get cleaned up."

"Okay, but if you need anything, just come and get me. I have second period free, okay? If you need a ride, or something."

"Thank you, I'll be fine," Mira said, trying to convince the girl to close the door and go away so she could lean back over and try not to be sick. Rather than feeling relieved that she hadn't had to make this choice, it felt as if she had chosen something even worse, for it to be this awful and painful and sordid and completely of her own doing. Uninvited but expected images swam before her: her mother lying in a hospital bed, bloody like she was, down there. Could a person die from this, too? She wasn't sure, but she felt she could, at any moment, and if she didn't, well. Maybe she should.

Mira woke in the dark, Patsy still asleep in her lap. Her mouth tasted bitter. Her sweater was damp. "God," she said, trying to shake the long-forgotten images and sensations: blood, pain, grief. Would it have been better or worse back then to know the truth about her mother? The outcome was the same. She'd been abandoned either way, but maybe it had been easier to think it wasn't her mother's choice. Maybe it had been easier for Mira to abandon her own family thinking she had no choice. But she knew now that she had, and she'd left anyway. The sins of the mother.

Blood, pain, grief. The electrician and his tongue in her mouth, his blood on her lips. "Asshole," she said out loud, and it felt good to say it, finally, to realize he was no danger to her, not now. How could she have been attracted to someone who could do that? She'd always thought it was her fault, that he'd just been picking up on signals. After all, attraction was biology, hers as well as his.

"No," she said, out loud again. Biology didn't excuse behavior. If a young woman told her this story now, she'd tell her to call the police, press charges for assault. People didn't have to act on their impulses, no matter how strong. They chose to. She'd chosen to with Doug, Doug and his incredible stomach, and chest, and behind. Mira suspected it was also his soft heart that got to her. He would have loved her if she let him.

Who knew why he was attracted to her. God, why Martin was for that matter. She doubted she had any viable eggs left, but still, maybe her body knew its chances of fulfilling her biological destiny one last time were dwindling. Maybe it was still sending out the old messages and that's what made her sex drive all the stronger now, not the progesterone cream. Or maybe she had just woken up after being asleep for so long.

What good is all of this? she wondered. *Why do we go through all this pain for romance and marriage and sex and lust and babies? None of it's permanent. It all goes away in the end.*

Blood, pain, grief. Thea pushing her way out of the womb, then out of her life for so many years. Mira shivered, waking Patsy Cline, who looked up at her with big dark eyes. *Eyes of love,* Mira thought, remembering Thea's when she nursed.

It was all about love, as fleeting as it was.

Mira stood and walked to the bathroom for more tissue, turning on lights to scare away ghosts. If she could just talk to her mother and ask why she did it, why she stopped loving her after Fonso was born, how she could abandon her children when they needed her so much, then maybe she could begin to understand why she too had left behind those she loved.

She shook her head, then laughed, a *huh* sound without humor. The answer was clear. She'd been so afraid of being left alone again that she'd fled, running blind and ending up . . . alone.

As good as she had always tried to be, as bad as she'd always felt, there was no way to atone for her sins, or for the sins of her mother, because neither of them had done anything wrong. She was human. Her mother was human. Parker was human. And that was all.

Forty-five

AT TWENTY TO TEN THAT EVENING, MIRA COULDN'T STAND BEING cooped up in the apartment one moment longer. She walked into the bathroom and wiped away any vestiges of makeup, mostly worn or cried off now, and splashed her face, studying it in the mirror as she toweled it dry. She looked sad, drawn. No wonder Nonna said those things. She changed back into her Fred Meyer jeans and a clean T-shirt and grabbed her teaching sweater from its hook, wondering how long she'd continue to call it her teaching sweater.

After clipping each dog to its respective leash, Mira braced herself for the wild bolt down the stairs, but they were subdued, as if they'd caught her mood. She walked them over to the weed patch. Because of Gus, someone very ill felt a little better right now, which in turn made Mira feel a little better. She tried not to think of all the urine Patsy had contributed to the process.

Leaving the dogs tied loosely to the stair handrail, she let herself inside the shop. It was busy for this late on a Sunday night.

Even though Yoshi and Felix had the place under control, Mira wanted to make her own drink. She pulled a shot of decaf espresso, set a pitcher of milk to steam, then pumped white chocolate syrup into a tall cup.

"Mm, you're making my favorite." Felix opened the fridge, pulling out a fresh carton of soy milk. "Want some whipped cream while I'm in here?"

"Sure," Mira said. "I might as well go all the way, right?"

Yoshi walked up to the counter with a tub of cups and saucers. "Don't tell me you've become one of us."

"It's just an experiment," Mira said. "I'll let you know."

Before sitting, Mira poked her head out the back door to check on the dogs. Ralph and Patsy were asleep, but Twiggy sat and looked at her, wagging her whip-skinny tail.

"I missed you, sweetie," Mira said. The greyhound lowered herself to the sidewalk, placed her chin on her paws, still watching Mira. "Be good, okay? I'll be back in a little while."

Inside, Mira chose a table along the wall rather than her usual computer, and picked up sections of the Sunday *Times* to browse. She settled in, looking around at the familiar surroundings, the faces she knew, those she didn't. The umber walls would need a fresh coat of paint soon, and she and Gus had been talking about setting up an area with a couch and chairs, some floor lamps. She looked up to see Yoshi watching her, to see her reaction to the drink, so she took a sip. She made a thoughtful face, a "so-so" motion with her hand, then smiled. "I'm just kidding," she called to him. "It's delicious."

By closing time, Mira had worked her way through the main section of the paper, the regional news, arts and entertainment. She considered searching through the classified ads. *For what?* she wondered. An apartment, a job? They didn't seem important anymore. What did she need?

The bell on the door jangled, and Mira turned to look.

The man who entered was tall, fair haired, and middle-aged

handsome. Comfortable and real. The kind of man any sane woman would go down fighting for.

"Hi," Parker said. "Sorry I'm so late. I would have called, but I didn't know your number. By the time I remembered I could call information, my cell phone battery was dead. Duh."

Mira smiled. "That's okay." Electrical fizz skittered across her skin. She fought the urge to do anything other than breathe. "How are you?"

"Good, I think." He ran his hand over his head, something he seemed to do a lot lately. Or had he always?

"Would you like to sit?" Her control astounded her.

"Thanks," he said, taking the seat opposite her.

"Something to drink?"

"Sure, okay. How about a decaf?"

She studied him. He'd just shaved, she thought, and he had on a fresh shirt.

"You're in Seattle now—a regular decaf won't do. How about, oh, I don't know, maybe an iced double decaf mint mocha, with an extra shot of chocolate?"

"Wow," he said. "That sounds good. Should I . . ." He looked at the counter, but Yoshi and Felix were in back doing dishes.

"I'll get it." Mira stood and walked behind the counter.

"I didn't mean to put you to work," Parker called across the room, now empty and quiet except for the Dido song coming from the speakers.

"It's okay." Mira pumped one shot of mint syrup and three chocolate into a cup. *Of all songs,* she thought. Was it always this way in life, that your every emotion and secret were being revealed in song in real time and you only sometimes realized it? Mira swallowed, trying not to listen to the words floating around them. She tried to concentrate on the singer's fluid, easy voice, but she couldn't ignore the chorus; she wouldn't go down with the ship, either, damn it, or surrender love even though she would give up on the relationship to make Parker's life easier, if that was what he wanted. She couldn't tell what he wanted, though, or why he was here.

She carried his cup to the table and set it in front of him.

"I really am sorry about leaving you with the dogs all day," he said. "Everything took longer than I thought it would. This city is nuts to try to get around in." He picked up his cup, took a sip. "Mm. That is good. Thanks."

"I didn't think you were coming back." Mira wiped at an imaginary spot on the table with her napkin. "I mean, I hoped you would. I really appreciate that you brought the dogs, and that you're taking care of the taxes and all, but I know how persuasive Lannie and Thea can—"

"Mira." Parker set down his cup. "I'm here because I want to be."

"Oh," she said. Her legs trembled; she sat in her chair. "Okay." The electrical current worked its way from her brain to sacrum and back, filtering into her arms and hands and fingers and feet and toes.

"I spent the day looking at about a million dumpy rental houses. Geez, the prices are astronomical here. I finally signed a lease about a half hour ago after I tracked down the landlord—who speaks no English, by the way—for a great little cottage about a twenty-minute drive north of here. It's cute, about the same vintage as the house, and it has a fenced yard for the dogs."

Mira took a deep breath, let it out. Synapses snapped in her head like firecrackers. "And who's . . . you know. Who's going to live there and take care of them?"

Parker took another drink. "Well, at the very least me. Of course, I'd prefer it if you lived there, too. But that's up to you."

"Oh." Her hands wouldn't stop shaking. She hid them beneath the table, then sat on them for good measure. "What about the Buzz?"

"I put it up for sale. I think Lester's going to turn it into a convenience store, which will probably do a lot better than a coffee shop. Besides, I didn't know how long I'd, we'd, be gone. It could be fun living in the big city for a while." He licked whipped cream from the side of the cup. He was nervous, she could tell, but he was enjoying this moment. Parker and his secret projects. How long had he been planning it? How on earth had Lannie kept this to herself?

Mira swallowed against a throat that had gone desert dry. "Do you, um, want some water?"

"Sure."

"I'm just suddenly really thirsty."

"Me, too."

"I think it's these sugary coffee drinks, actually, all that sweet syrup."

"I don't know. I like this one. Maybe that's why I couldn't make any money. We were way too old-fashioned. We just had lattes and cappuccinos. I thought that's what coffee shops did."

"Not in the age of Starbucks," Mira said. "Every single beverage is a limitless combination of preferences and possibilities."

She walked to the water pitcher in a convincingly casual manner, she thought, and tried not to spill as she lurched water into the plastic cups, carried them back.

"You know, I like your hair this way," he said, looking up at her as she handed him a glass. "It shows more of your face."

She snorted, suddenly more self-conscious than she'd ever been in front of him. "And that's a good thing?"

"Well, yeah." Parker took a drink of water. "Of course that's a good thing."

Mira blushed. "I was thinking maybe I should let it grow out. Maybe it's too, I don't know. Too young or—"

"No, it's not. You look . . . you know." He cleared his throat. "Sexy." This was hard for him. He cleared his throat again. "I've missed you, Mira."

She felt her lips purse, her brow furrow. *What are you doing?* a voice screamed inside her. *Do not fuck this up!* She ignored it and sat down.

"Why exactly?"

He nodded his head, thinking, then crossed his legs. Mira remembered asking him why he liked her all those years ago in his little college apartment—he had the same determined look on his face now. He cleared his throat again and she felt a stab of tenderness for him.

"Because, well, because the house is just this big empty shell without you in it. And the dogs are lousy conversationalists. And, well, because I need you. To . . . I don't know. Just to be with me."

He paused, then uncrossed his legs and leaned forward, hands on the table. "Mira, when you left . . . god." Parker blinked, and his voice began to cave in. "You took that smell you have, that great lotiony smell of your skin, and your laugh, and your warm body under the covers at night, and your cold feet. Your cooking. Thea's been trying, but . . . god. I fucked up, Mira. I know it. I—"

"Stop," Mira said, closing her eyes. "Don't say any more."

"I'm sorry."

She heard rustling, and when she opened her eyes, he stood, fishing in his pockets as if for keys.

"Don't go," she said. "Please."

He sat back down.

She took a long slow breath, looking at him, feeling his pain from her throat to her solar plexus. He had been through as much or more than she had, but she could no longer protect him from who she really was. And she couldn't hide in the dream that everything would be okay if she was just good enough, if she just didn't need too much. Saint Mira was long gone, along with bad Mira. She was just Mira, real Mira, and no matter how scary this was, she had to tell him.

"I want to start over."

Parker's face colored, spots of pink high in his cheeks, and his eyes glistened as she continued.

"I can't go back to what was, Parker. I need more. I've lived my life trying to ignore my feelings and desires, and I won't do that anymore, I can't. I don't think I could stand to keep sleep-walking through life the way I did before.

"I want that feeling we used to have, that deep connection to each other, emotionally, physically. Remember those three days we spent in bed when we first met? I want that again—not just the sex, but yes, okay, the sex. That kind of passion, and deep conversation, and honesty, all that stuff relationships start out with that gets put aside when life gets in the way. I want to start over, fresh, and I don't want that part to go away this time."

His voice quavered. "I . . . I understand, Mira, and I won't stand in—"

"Dude, I mean with you."

"With—?"

"Of course, Parker, I mean with you. But you have to want it, too. You have to want me, the way I am. I don't know if you even really know me." Her heart knocked hard against her chest wall as she said it, then quit beating, it seemed, waiting for his answer. She watched his face change from apprehensive to . . . to what? She couldn't tell. She couldn't breathe.

"I want to know you," he said, and she reached across the table and took his hands, his big sweet hands, remembering them instantly, intimately, and leaned over to kiss his knuckles. All these years, and she'd never known that he liked the way she smelled.

Parker sniffed loudly. "Did you call me dude?"

"God. I did." She looked up and saw the boy with the gray eyes, crying and laughing at the same time. "Here." She handed him her napkin.

Her fight or flight hormones receded; her hands quit trembling. Her body relaxed against the hard wood chair bit by bit and her jaw loosened. It was like having a phantom limb reattached, the pain of its absence beginning to recede.

When Felix and Yoshi came out to stack chairs and mop, Mira said, "Let's skip the mopping for tonight."

They looked at her in astonishment, first at that and then when she introduced them to her husband. After pleasantries Felix tugged Yoshi by the hem of his shirt, and they left through the back.

She took a long cool sip of water, rolled it around in her mouth before swallowing. She should probably go rescue the dogs, but she didn't want to let in the real world. Not yet. She wondered if she'd tell him about Doug. She was pretty sure she wouldn't tell him about Martin. Would she ask any more about Jackie? No, she decided, not unless he wanted to tell her. Truth was great in concept, but what was true didn't always have everything to do with reality. Maybe sometimes, some things—good as well as bad—were better kept to one's self, even between husband and wife.

Instead, Mira told Parker about the white chocolate mocha she'd tried that night, how the sweet syrup mingled with the sharp espresso, the whipped cream softening and cooling the liquid. She told him about the double-pump-this and triple-shot-that people always ordered, the requests for extra heat or less, filled to the top or room for cream, sweetener, real or artificial—all the potential variations of something as simple and perfect as a cup of coffee.

Epilogue

Dear Mira,

   Thank you for writing such a nice long letter to your grandmother. I'm feeling fine, thank you, aside from the sciatica and the constipation. They say to drink Metamucil but it does no good. They say don't drink coffee, but coffee, it does some good. See what you have to look forward to? Start eating your fiber now, cara. When I wake up in the morning I still think I'm thirty-four years old, with a husband to feed and children to get to school. It's only when I try to get out of bed that I realize I've become one of the old people who move like snails and fall asleep in their oatmeal.

   Your questions are difficult to answer. We didn't tell you because who knows the truth? Who knows if your mother, may she rest in peace, even meant to take those pills? She hadn't been herself for some time, even before your brother was born. She was unhappy, but not with you. Don't even think it. She loved you and baby Fonso, and she loved your father. She just lost her way. Maybe you can understand her a little *better now that you have wandered yourself, cara mia. We all suffer, from time to time. You will suffer even more, you'll see. But you're not like her, or your father. He's so sensitive for a man! No, you're more like me. You'll be fine.*

I've never told anyone about the day I ran away. I was twenty-six years old. I left behind five babies under the age of seven—you probably don't remember your dear departed Uncle Maurizio who died from fever at age two—and I wore my best dress and I took the bus all the way up to Astoria. After I walked around for a while, I realized it was just more fishermen and canneries, so I rode the bus back down to Seaside, to the arcade on the Promenade. I ate pink cotton candy and flirted with the young man who cheated people out of nickels at the ring toss. I never felt so alive, cara. It was like I'd died and been reborn as a single woman. But I hadn't. I still had five hungry children back home and a husband who would be very angry with me. You only knew him as a mean old son-of-a-bitch because he got the diabetes right before you were born, but when we were young, he could be very sweet. I still like to think about that day sometimes, all those people on that bus going somewhere else, and me, one of them, all dressed up. I looked good enough that the young man never even asked if I had children. That's something when you've stretched your stomach to bursting five times, nursed five hungry mouths, sometimes two at a time.

Enough of that. I don't understand why you and Parker must live so far away, but Thea is taking good care of the house. Did she tell you she went to that shelter and got herself a dog? I don't know what she wants with this dog, to tell you the truth. It's nervous and ugly, one of those dogs with the flat face, you know the ones I mean? They breathe like they're about to expire. She says he has problems because he was left on the side of the road. I say, maybe they should have left him there, but I'm just an old lady, and I've written too long now and my hand has cramped into a claw.

It would be easier to tell you these things in person, but you're stubborn, like me. If I should expire of the constipation or the sciatica before you come back, know this: Your mother loved you more than life itself.

Some mothers, they take the children with them. Your mother left you to live a happier life than she did. Not such a bad parting gift, is it, cara? I expect you to use it wisely.

Con amore,
Nonna

LOVE AND BIOLOGY

at

the Center of the Universe

JENNIE SHORTRIDGE

This Conversation Guide is intended to enrich the
individual reading experience, as well as encourage us
to explore these topics together—because books,
and life, are meant for sharing.

A CONVERSATION
WITH JENNIE SHORTRIDGE

Q. *With your first two novels,* Riding with the Queen *and* Eating Heaven, *you created fictional stories using your own life experiences. Have you mined your own life again for* Love and Biology at the Center of the Universe?

A. Geographically, yes. I'm in love with the coast of Oregon, and wrote some of this book while at a writer's retreat there. And now I live in Seattle on a hill that overlooks Fremont, and I hear that little bridge rising every so often, and see the seaplanes buzzing down the canal from my home office window. But personally speaking, not quite as much. I've never had children, or been a biology teacher, or lived in a small town, or gone through a separation from my husband, but I do know the pain of feeling abandoned, which I think is at the heart of this story.

I'm also in the midst of my own perimenopausal craziness and brain fog, and the bewilderment over what it all means about who I am and who I am becoming. Am I still a sexual being, a biological woman? Obviously I'd like to think I always will be, but we get such weird messages from society about it. And I think I've always struggled with the whole "good girl/bad girl" construct, wanting only to be seen as "good." I am a people-pleaser, a middle child, a Libra, and, of course, female, so I have it in spades. But I'm getting better.

Q. Right. Mira begins the story as the "perfect" wife and mother, but we quickly see that façade crumble as the story progresses. Is she inherently a good person with naughty tendencies, or a bad girl who just wants to be good? Is there a difference?

A. Well, that's the thing. She's both. I think that probably most of us have some duality in our personalities, our natures, and we can have a hard time reconciling the two, as Mira does at first. The more important thing is to be true to yourself, and that's Mira's challenge in the story: to discover what that means for her.

Q. Your characters' names are often evocative of their inner states or personalities. Tell us about some of the names you chose for the characters in this book.

A. The main character, Mira Serafino, is named for her saintly mother. Mira means "light of the world," and Serafino means "angel." She's almost obligated by her name to try to attain sainthood, which is, of course, impossible.

Mira's husband's name is Parker, and there is a point in the story at which she sees him as parked, unmoving. Their daughter, Thea, is a bit theatrical, but also kind of wise, and this old Greek name seemed appropriate. Nonna is simply the Italian word for grandmother; Alfonso a name I just like. It feels big and friendly to me. I wanted Gus and Doug to be fairly simple, fun-loving guys, so I gave them guttural one-syllable names. Kind of like, "Dude!"

What I really had fun with were the band names ... and here's a little secret: The Twang Gods first appeared in *Riding with the Queen*. I brought them back because I loved their name so much. I wanted them to have their proper due.

Q. You tackle big life issues in your novels—including mental illness, homelessness, addiction, and death and dying in your previous books. In Love and Biology ... , *we have a woman facing menopause, empty-nest syndrome, and the breakup of her marriage. Do you specifically set out to chronicle certain issues, and why?*

A. I think I did at first, and probably pretty obviously to deal with some things I'd been through in my own life: having a mentally ill mother, never making it as a musician, being with someone I cared about who was dying. In this book, the issues I care deeply about have to do with how we view women at midlife, and how we feel about ourselves. I think one of the most invisible populations on this planet is midlife women! People no longer seem to see you, or place value in you. I don't know if it has a biological underpinning—we're no longer viable baby-makers so we have less biological importance—but I think we actually have so much more social relevance. We're wise, we're caring. We're strong—we've been through so much and survived it. And we're funny, and sexy, damn it!

Q. Yes, it's refreshing to have midlife women portrayed as sexual beings, and your protagonists certainly show that aspect. Does that just flow as a natural part of your character development, or do you make a conscious effort to include sexuality? And do you ever surprise yourself at what you've written?

A. Well, I always aim to write fully human characters, and sexuality is part of that. Even if you're asexual or nonsexual, that would be relevant to who you are. In this story, Mira's sexuality is at the core of her journey. She's been denying it for so long, trying to tamp it down, but that doesn't actually make it go away. By becoming a more sexual being, she becomes more herself. And yes, I do surprise myself with the sex scenes. I don't know where they come from. Matt, my husband, likes to tell people they don't come from real life—he thinks that's funny. All I can say is I write fiction. I like making up stuff.

Q. In the story, Mira and her grown daughter, Thea, have had a difficult relationship, especially as Thea tries to gain independence from her mother. You don't have children, yet you seem to know this dynamic intimately. Did you and your mother have a hard time separating as you became an adult?

A. Oh, yes. I don't think my mom knew who she was if she was no longer a mother. She had a hard time when I moved out, and I was the third out of four to leave. Mira tries to exert control and Thea pulls away more. I remember that feeling very well. It was difficult, and I was angry with my mom for a while. My sisters have children who are coming of age now, and I feel close to all of them, so I still feel the pull, in both directions. I can look at it from both sides now, to misquote Joni Mitchell.

CONVERSATION GUIDE

Q. Your readers often write to you, thanking you for sharing stories so personal that they feel they could be written about themselves. What do you hope your readers will take away from this book?

A. My readers are wonderful. They do write and share their stories, and it really touches me. And the book groups are great fun to talk with on the phone; we always have great conversations. With this book I just hope to break apart some of the myths and rules around being a middle-aged woman, to say it's okay if you still don't know what the heck it all means, or what you want out of life, or how to be a good wife and mother and daughter and sister and friend. As long as we're trying our best, and growing, and as long as we're being true to ourselves, I think we're on the right track.

Q. What's next? Do you have a new book in the works?

A. I'm really excited about the next book, which is inspired by a true story that happened a few years ago in Portland. A father and daughter were found living deep in a forest that abuts the city, and when the police investigated, they determined that the girl was safe and healthy, and in fact, well advanced from her homeschool education. Good-hearted people found them a place to live, a job for the dad, but the two disappeared again when they felt they were being hounded by the media. The last thing I would ever want is to make them feel exploited all over again, so I am creating a fictional story of my own imagination that examines what makes a family a family, a home a home.

Does it matter if you have a big house, money, if you can give your kids all the "stuff" other kids have, or does love and dedication trump all that? These are the kinds of questions that drew me to this story, and that excite me.

QUESTIONS
FOR DISCUSSION

1. Main character Mira Serafino enjoys being part of her big Italian *famiglia*. In what ways does her extended family help and support her, and in what ways do they perhaps keep her from becoming her true self?

2. Mira struggles with the duality of her nature. On one hand, she seems driven to be the perfect woman: a good wife, mother, daughter, and career woman. On the other hand, she wrestles with secret desires and unsettling feelings. Do most women in our society face this dilemma?

3. How does Mira's family history and the early loss of her mother affect who she becomes as an adult and her relationships with her family members, husband, and daughter?

4. Four generations of women are depicted in this story. How does each—the grandmother, the mother, Mira, and her daughter, Thea—impact and influence the other? What does Nonna pass down through the generations, and how do each of the younger generations either accept or refuse it?

5. Why does Mira run away from home? Do you think she's justified, or are her actions irrational and irresponsible? Do you

think she should have stayed and tried to work it out with her husband, Parker?

6. Mira makes a new life in Seattle at the Coffee Shop at the Center of the Universe. Why do you think she chooses this? Is it really only because it's where her car breaks down, or is it because, as she says, "she landed in this Oz, like Dorothy, for a reason"?

7. Why is Thea angry with Mira? Is it simple mother-daughter separation, or are there deeper reasons behind it?

8. Betrayal and abandonment are central issues in this story. How many characters feel they are betrayed or abandoned, and in what ways?

9. The story starts in a small town on the idyllic coast of Oregon and ends up in the noisy hubbub of an urban neighborhood in Seattle. How does this relate to Mira's personal journey as well as physical?

10. What does Mira learn from her male relationships at the coffee shop? From Gus? Doug? Martin? Others?

11. How has Mira changed by the end of the story? Why does she make the final decision she does?

To invite Jennie Shortridge to participate in your book group meeting, contact her through her Web site: www.jennieshort-ridge.com.

PHOTO BY DAVID HILLER

JENNIE SHORTRIDGE lives in Seattle, Washington, with her husband, and juggles her time between writing novels and working in the community to foster literacy. Visit her Web site at www.jennie shortridge.com.